Almost a year after the murder that shook Lobell College to its core, the start of a new academic year brings familiar faces back to the scene of the crime. Daniel Rosenbaum starts his first year as dean of the English department and takes a hands-on role in advising students. Lily Peterson and Gianna d'Angelo return to continue their undergrad studies after the death of the professor they were both in love with.

Meanwhile, on the other side of the Hudson, Tony d'Angelo is working hard. With his sister back in college, it's all hands on deck to keep his dad's auto shop running and take care of his infant niece. He still finds time to spend most nights with his boyfriend, Daniel, although he can't seem to find the words to talk to his family about his relationship. Tony's life is exactly what he's always wanted it to be—so why does he feel like he's struggling to be himself?

When a Lobell professor is once again found murdered, the idyll of the last months is turned on its head. Can Tony and Daniel stay out of harm's way this time? Or will the fragile new peace they've found together be shattered?

SECOND CHANCE

A Hudson Valley Murder Mystery,

Book Two

S.B. Barnes

A NineStar Press Publication
www.ninestarpress.com

Second Chance

© 2025 S.B. Barnes

Cover Art © 2025 Melody Pond

Edited by Elizabetta McKay

First Edition, February 2025

ISBN:

Also available in eBook, ISBN:

CONTENT WARNING:

This book contains sexually explicit content, which may only be suitable for mature readers. Discussion of a university student's attempted suicide (off page, in the past), knife and gun violence (on page), murder, kidnapping, drug use (off page), mental issues.

For J., who was with me for the whole book

Prologue

With a groan, Amelia Lawrence pushes away from her desk. The sun is setting outside, and since it's late August, that means it's about eight. The semester hasn't even started yet.

It serves her right for taking this long to finish the syllabus; she should have gotten the jump on planning last weekend or maybe sometime in July. It just didn't work out. For some reason, trying to make herself work on classes in the summers feels like stuffing a square peg in a round hole, with her brain being the square peg.

That's the burnout talking, Amy, the analytical goblin living in the back of her mind tells her.

She ignores it.

She's getting really good at that.

Amelia vaguely recalls a phase when she was better at this. She got more things done in the same amount of time. She planned her lessons, wrote her syllabi, and there was somehow still time left over to do her own research.

The sun sets over the trees at Wordstone Mansion, down by the river. Amelia can barely see it from the science building, but she can feel in an unsettled way how beautiful it would be to be there. There and not in her office, slaving away at things she should have been done with ages ago.

Her husband sent a text. It's a video of their daughter, Francie, waving goodnight.

Guilt swamps Amelia. Her husband didn't mean to make her feel this way, she's sure. He gets it. He got a doctorate, too, before leaving academia for the calmer and more lucrative waters of IT consultancy. She still feels guilty.

They talk about it in oblique references sometimes, she and her husband. The burnout. The thing looming on the edges of her psyche she can barely put a name to because it means failure. The reason she's already exhausted at the thought of teaching on Monday.

It's not fair.

Amelia has always loved teaching.

She was one of the few PhD students in her cohort who did.

But here she is, thirty-five years old and not even a tenure-track position to show for it. Instead, she has to hope every year she'll be somehow, magically, gifted something more permanent than a "good work this year, let's talk about contract renewal." Amelia barely dares to ask for a raise in those talks, only an inflation adjustment, because what does she have to offer? Her own research is stagnating, like so many zebrafish she has her students perform experiments on.

Psychology is so glamorous.

Amelia needs to learn to draw proper boundaries. Say no and mean no. Go to class with last year's slides and no other preparation. Not be available to everyone and anyone. Take time for her own stupid zebrafish experiments. Do some writing, catch up on journals, stop living day to day.

Take her daughter to the Catskills when autumn hits the hillsides in the Hudson Valley and turns it into a glorious riot of color.

Amelia takes a deep breath.

"Just finish up tonight, Amy," she tells herself. "Get it done and then be happier."

She sits down at her computer again, willing herself to work through the end of the syllabus.

Immediately, an email notification distracts her. An unread message from Lily Peterson. A vague memory surfaces in Amelia's brain, something to do with the mess last year after Professor Lombardi died so tragically. Lily was involved. Amy has a dim memory of an all-faculty email about it. She'd been seeing him, and when he died, she vanished from class suddenly and completely. Lily was on the roster of one of Amelia's classes, a two hundred–level lecture course about...something. Neuroscience, probably. That's the one everyone drops out of.

Amelia clicks on the email.

Apparently, Lily returned to Lobell, and she wants to know if she can still get credit for the class by retaking the final.

For a heartbeat, Amelia thinks about it. She'd have to dig into the mess of the file structure on her computer and figure out where she left the final exam. Then she'd have to schedule a time, remember how she graded the neuroscience final last fall, oversee one student taking the exam, figure out how to get the extremely late grade through the Registrar's office, and—

No, her burnout gremlin tells her very firmly. Boundaries. Amelia's setting boundaries this year. She won't let it stay this bad.

Dear Lily, she writes. *I'm sorry.*

Chapter One

The back of Daniel's neck is warm when Tony's nose collides with it.

"Good morning," Daniel laughs. He's in the middle of making tea, ladling out two scoops of his expensive, possibly pretentious chai vanilla looseleaf into the tea egg. The teakettle is about to boil.

"Mm." Tony buries his face into Daniel's shoulder, wrapping his arms around his middle. "Why are you like this?"

"Awake?" Daniel twists in Tony's grip until he's leaning against the counter, arms around Tony's shoulders.

His skin is still sleep-warm, and he hasn't shaved yet. It rasps a little when Tony kisses him, which is kind of thrilling.

"Hi," Daniel says when they pull apart.

It's one of those things he does that should be insufferably reminiscent of one of the Netflix Hallmark knockoffs Gianna mainlines in December. But because it's Daniel, because his eyes crinkle in the corners when he says it, because his thumb is stroking gently down the side of Tony's neck, it's adorable.

"Hi." Tony says, Daniel's lips soft against his.

The water boils; the switch on the electric kettle flips.

Tony keeps right on kissing Daniel, forcing him to ignore it.

"You in a hurry?" Tony asks when they pull apart.

"I'm doing extra office hours at nine thirty. Lily Peterson—"

"Great." Tony pulls Daniel toward the bathroom by the hips. It's only seven thirty. plenty of time.

"Hey!" Daniel sounds indignant, but he's laughing.

Tony walks backward as he kisses Daniel some more. They have to sidestep the low, wobbly bookshelf in the hallway between the kitchen and the bathroom. Tony's spent enough time here that he can do it blind, and Daniel seems happy to let him.

The bathroom ceiling slants under the roof of the building, barely leaving space for the cupboard Daniel keeps his five Target-bought towels in. It has a window, which Daniel tells Tony is prime real estate in terms of apartment hunting. Tony wouldn't know as he's never gotten quite that far.

They step out of their boxers, leaving them on the floor. Tony pulls his hair out of its ponytail and leaves the hair tie next to the sink as he climbs into the tub.

Two groups of fish in different shades of blue cover the shower curtain, swimming in different directions. It's one of the few things in the apartment Tony's sure Daniel picked solely because he liked it, along with the couch taking up half the living room and the table with a stand in the shape of bird's leg. A lot of the other stuff in the apartment is functional and plain, such as the bookshelves groaning under the weight of Daniel's collection. The shower curtain is functional and fun.

With two grown men trying to crowd into the shower, it's also a pain in the neck. In the small tub, the curtain always sticks to someone's legs.

Daniel grimaces as he disentangles himself from the cold, clinging material. "This is not how I pictured this."

"Bet I can make it worth your while anyway," Tony offers.

"I know you can."

The showerhead sprays to life above them, and Tony leans against the cold tiles, pulling Daniel against him. He shivers at the sharp contrast of the tiles at his back and Daniel's warm body against his front.

With one hand cradling the base of Daniel's head, Tony angles his head to kiss Daniel deep and slow.

Under Tony's fingers, Daniel's light brown hair goes dark and sleek, plastered to his head. The air around them becomes humid. Daniel lets his mouth slide past Tony's to his jaw and then his neck.

Tony's skin breaks out in goosebumps. "Not fair," he breathes. "I was seducing *you*."

Daniel hums against his skin. "Seduce me more later." His mouth is as hot as the water sluicing around them.

Between their bodies, Tony's cock twitches. He woke up kind of horny anyway, and Daniel's mouth on his neck, Daniel's body against his—*Daniel* is enough to get him there. Tony juts his hips up, rubbing himself on Daniel's thigh.

Daniel's hand wanders down, stroking across Tony's sensitive side. He wraps Tony's cock in a firm grip and strokes him slowly, root to tip.

Tony lets himself relax, lets the wall hold him up. "Feels good." His voice comes out low with the water pounding around them.

Daniel hears anyway. "Yeah?"

Tony cups a hand loosely over Daniel's ass. "Yeah. You always feel good, baby."

He can feel the curve of Daniel's lips as he smiles against Tony's neck.

Tony breathes in thick steam. "So perfect for me. Getting me off just how I like it first thing in the morning as if you have nothing better to do—"

Daniel's mouth cuts him off, his fist speeding up on Tony's cock.

"I don't," Daniel says.

Tony would understand, he's sure, but Daniel sweeps his thumb across the head perfectly, and Tony's so close, and Daniel's got this look like he's ready to eat Tony alive. All he can manage in response is, "Huh?"

"I don't." Daniel's lips curve in a smile, too soft to be sexy, too private to be anything else. "There's nothing better to do than this; there's nothing more important than making you feel good."

Tony's breath hitches in his chest. Daniel's hand tightens around him a fraction, and Tony comes, spurting up and over Daniel's fist and dripping to the shower floor. The water washes it away instantly.

It takes Tony a moment to catch his breath. Daniel's hands are steady at his waist.

When he can think again, he pushes away from the wall and slides to his knees.

"Tony," Daniel gasps above him.

Tony doesn't wait. He opens his mouth around the head of Daniel's cock and takes it in. There's barely enough space for him to kneel at Daniel's feet, and the porcelain isn't easy on the knees. But under Tony's hands, Daniel's thighs tremble. Daniel's broad shoulders stop the spray of water from hitting Tony, leaving him to concentrate fully on sucking Daniel's cock as sloppy and wet as he knows how.

"Oh, shit." Daniel moans as Tony speeds up.

Tony's learned after a few months that Daniel likes it messy. He'd never admit it. It sounds too crass for his delicate sensibilities. But he flushes all the way up his chest and neck when Tony lets spit drip out of his mouth and over his fist as he pumps the base slowly.

Daniel lets out a breathy, "Ah!"

It's Tony's sign to speed up his fist and to stop sucking, just holding the head in his mouth and tracing patterns on the underside with his tongue. A minute, maybe two, and Daniel groans low in his throat and almost doubles over as he comes. It draws him out of Tony's mouth, and the come runs across Tony's lips, shooting over his cheeks.

"Sorry." Daniel's out of breath when he realizes, which is gratifying.

Tony blinks up at him through eyelashes gone sticky.

They both burst into laughter.

"C'mon, help me up," Tony demands through chuckles.

Daniel helps him to his feet and graciously cedes his spot under the spray so Tony can get his face clean.

"Ugh." Tony groans as the hot water makes Daniel's come turn from sticky and wet to oddly flaky. "Why does that always happen?"

"It's protein," Daniel explains absently, uncapping his three-in-one shampoo, conditioner, and shower gel. "Heat makes it break up."

Tony squints at him through the water. "Like when you skim the white gook off of chicken stock?"

Daniel pauses in lathering up his hair. "Okay, one, thanks for comparing those two things. Two, what kind of chicken stock are you making?"

"You know, when you put the bones in a pot and—"

"You use *bones*?"

Tony sighs. "You're lucky you're so pretty. And smart."

Daniel rolls his eyes as he does every time Tony implies he might think Daniel is attractive—as if he can't believe the man dating him might legitimately think he's hot. He hands Tony his shampoo. He must have started buying it sometime a few weeks ago when Tony wouldn't stop complaining about Daniel's.

Showering together is nice.

In a very practical sense, it's awful. Their elbows and knees are always in the way, and sidling past each other to get under the water is fraught with the risk of slipping. The shower curtain keeps clinging to Tony's calves. But when they pass each other, Daniel's body brushes up against Tony's. When he needs to rinse out the shampoo, Daniel helps, running his hands through Tony's hair. When they get out, Daniel hands Tony the second towel he keeps out all the time for Tony these days.

"I could get used to starting the day like this." Tony's head is hidden under the towel as he rubs his hair dry, which is the only reason he says it. It would be too direct otherwise.

Daniel probably thinks he's being smooth, grinning into the mirror and not straight at Tony. "Me too."

It's enough to keep them both smiling as they run through their morning routine. Daniel brushes his teeth and shaves once the mirror defogs enough while Tony blow-dries his hair. While Tony's brushing his teeth, Daniel wanders back to the kitchen to finish up his tea.

"Hey, have you seen my hair tie?" Tony asks when he's put on fresh boxers and the T-shirt he accidentally left at Daniel's two weeks ago. Daniel must have washed it; it smells of his detergent.

Daniel sets his phone and his teacup down, looking over at Tony.

His eyebrows shoot up. "You know, I don't think I've seen you with your hair down."

Tony strikes a pose. His hair is pretty much covering his eyes. "How do I look?"

"You remind me of something..."

"A supermodel," Tony suggests. "One of those pictures of Saint Sebastian you were showing me the other week. An international soccer star who regularly gets his ass fondled by other dudes on the pitch but exclusively fucks women."

"No..." Daniel shakes his head. "Have you ever seen those Highland cows? With the fringe?"

"Asshole," Tony grumbles. "Seriously though, have you seen my hair tie? I left it by the sink. It's my last one."

"Sorry. Maybe it fell?"

They wander through the hallway and the bathroom, examining the floor.

Behind the cracked bedroom door, an ominous noise alerts Tony, and he pushes the door farther open.

On the floor in front of the bed is the cat, purring his heart out and pushing the hair tie back and forth between his paws.

"Worf," Tony admonishes, torn between amusement and frustration. This fucking cat. "You have toys." He snatches up the hair tie and sets about finger-combing his hair into a ponytail.

Daniel shakes his head sadly. "Those were legally acquired. Nowhere near as exciting as contraband. You want coffee?"

"Not yours." Tony kisses his cheek placatingly before he can get upset about it. Daniel is not a coffee drinker, and his coffee supplies show it. "We need to go?"

Tony opens the fridge and pulls out his sandwich, neatly arranged in one of Daniel's extensive collection of plastic boxes with click-lids that, despite being different sizes, are all exactly the wrong size for a large slice of bread. It's an excuse to slice a sandwich diagonally, which secretly thrills Tony by virtue of being nostalgic. Figuring out which is his and which is Daniel's distracts him—Daniel prefers two slices of bread with cheese and nothing else between them, the weirdo—and it takes him a moment to notice Daniel hasn't answered.

"Sweetheart?"

"Huh? Oh, sorry." Daniel looks up from his phone. "Just checking what I'm meeting Lily Peterson about."

Tony makes a noncommittal humming sound, passing Daniel his sandwich.

"I forget how young students are sometimes." A rueful little smile plays around Daniel's lips as he turns his phone screen so Tony can read.

...want to make sure I'm starting this semester on track. I'm doing really well. I found a great therapist in Hudson, and my boyfriend said he'd drive me. He's the same age as me. I promise! The boyfriend, not the therapist.

"Cute."

"Yeah."

Tony hesitates a second. "You think she's ready for all that?"

"All what?"

"School, therapy. Dating."

"Oh." A frown line tightens on Daniel's forehead. "I guess it's up to her. After what happened to Mario...I don't know. I mean, she was never with him, so she might be able to bounce back faster."

Tony swallows his instant reaction, which is to ask *faster than who*? Gianna, Mario's only other victim, as far as they know, is aggressively fine about the death of her daughter's father. Tony would risk a family fight if he so much as breathed the word "therapy" in her direction. And neither Daniel nor Colette, who were arguably closer to Mario before his murder, have tried to find a therapist or even talked about how they feel about his death. Then again, unlike Lily, they didn't attempt suicide in reaction to Mario's death. "She's young."

"Yeah. I guess I'll see how she's doing in..." Daniel checks his phone. "Fuck. Soon."

"Which brings me back to my original question. Do we need to go?"

"You're the one who keeps to business hours," Daniel says.

"Eh." Tony grins. "The boss has a soft spot for me."

"Well, I'd like him not to start hating me, so you should probably put on some pants."

Tony sighs. "What a cruel world."

Daniel squeezes his ass through the thin boxers. "I'd keep you this way all day if I could. Unfortunately, we are slaves to capitalism."

As Daniel finishes his tea, Tony fishes his second-best pair of jeans out of Daniel's dresser. He pulls them on then grabs his sandwich off the kitchen counter.

On the way downstairs, they stop at Colette's door.

She takes a few moments to answer.

"Colette?" Daniel calls through the door. "My office hours start in—"

"I'm coming." Her voice is loud, bare inches away.

The door flies open, and Tony jerks away.

Colette stands before him in her trademark black slacks with a blouse in a bright shade of aquamarine. Her long gold necklace has a pendant that reminds Tony of a wire whisk.

Her hair frames her face in a loose, hazy Afro.

"Nice," Tony says.

She smiles tightly. "You think?"

"Oh, yeah." Tony's not about to start telling people new and drastically different haircuts aren't working for them. He's not an idiot, but he's also not lying this time. The looseness of the hairstyle highlights Colette's high cheekbones and lends her professional outfit a softness he only sees in her at the end of particularly long nights otherwise.

"What brought this on?" Daniel's voice is weirdly high and tight.

Tony elbows him.

"I mean, uh, it looks great, Colette," Daniel adds hurriedly.

She shrugs, resettling the strap of her bag on her shoulder. "I was due for a change." She starts to walk down the stairs, reminding Tony they do actually need to get going.

"It does look wonderful," Daniel repeats. "Um, this isn't a post-traumatic hairstyle change or anything, is it?"

Colette glares at him over her shoulder as she pushes open the door and steps out into the early September sunshine. "Mario died ten months ago. My cosmetic decision-making is wholly unconnected."

"Just checking. Any other big life changes I should worry about? Are you getting a pet? Or a new girlfriend?"

In the time he's known her, Tony has never known Colette to express an interest in either.

She sighs, exasperated. "No, Daniel, and if I were, it wouldn't be cause for concern. I just thought... I don't know. I didn't quite feel myself anymore. Anyway, there isn't much to do around here these days; it seemed like an adventure."

"That's not true. You singlehandedly started a whole new advisee program this summer."

The look Colette gives Daniel could kill a less oblivious man. "What an adventure. Offering *more* office hours in my free time to students who couldn't pass their classes last year."

"I thought it was a cool thing to do."

"Yes, well. It was brought to my attention last year that perhaps my engagement with the students has been...too academically oriented."

It's Colette's way of saying she still feels guilty she didn't realize her friend was preying on his students. Daniel grimaces and says nothing.

"I agree," Tony says to break the awkward silence. "Cool idea. Definitely not an adventure."

"And a *haircut* is?"

"Would you like the reading list about Black culture and hair in MLA or Chicago?"

"MLA, please, Chicago is so ugly."

Colette shakes her head, affronted. "Your poor taste and your lack of awareness about other cultures have been noted. Is there anything else we need to cover, or can we get to work?"

Daniel presses the unlock button on his car key. "I really do think the advisee program for summer school was a great idea, and I'm glad you're doing it."

Tony can tell he's feeling guilty. He's been making noises for a while now about how he wonders whether Colette is coping as well as she claims to be.

True to form, Colette is not one to accept vulnerability or praise easily. "Yes, well. There isn't much to do around here."

"I heard the movie theater closed."

"The AMC?" Tony asks, alarmed. He knows small town America is dying and all, but he assumed the massive chains were safe for another year or two.

"No, the independent theater in Germantown," Colette corrects. "I used to go with...well, you know."

"Right."

There's a weird moment where they're standing in the parking lot between Daniel's Honda and Tony's Toyota, and no one knows where to go from the mention of Mario.

Eventually, Colette says, "This is ridiculous. I did my hair differently; it's not a crisis."

"And it still looks great." Tony's probably repeated it enough to be weird, but he's grateful for the out. "I gotta get to work. See you later, babe?"

"Yeah." Daniel gives him a weak smile. His big brain is still thinking. Tony can tell. "Hey, wait," he adds as Tony turns to leave.

"Hm?" Tony jiggles his car key in the lock. It needs its biweekly oil treatment.

"Forgetting something?"

He turns to Daniel, who has his arms crossed across his chest and an eyebrow raised like there's about to be some sort of naughty student/professor roleplay happening in broad daylight.

Tony blinks.

Probably not.

Daniel's eyebrow inches up a fraction higher, and Tony remembers.

"Have a good day." He presses a kiss to Daniel's lips.

"You too."

It does something for Tony's ego to make Daniel look so pleased with such a little interaction.

"Yes, yes, see you later. You're both insufferable," Colette mutters as she slides into the passenger seat.

"Don't get involved in any murder investigations," Tony calls to both of them and gets into the car. The radio's on the fritz again when he turns on the ignition. It's been getting more and more annoying now he drives between Kingston and Rhinebeck almost daily. The drive isn't that long, but the car is that old.

He gets to the shop ten minutes before opening. The AC is already on full blast against the oppressively hot and muggy Hudson Valley late summer. By eleven, it will be miserable in the garage if they don't cool it down in time.

His pa is on his back, under Mrs. Cooper's car.

"I'm not late," Tony announces to the garage.

Pa rolls out from under the car. "Well, I couldn't have known you'd be on time."

"Weird, given I've never been late."

There's a stack of coveralls in the closet by the entrance. Tony doesn't enjoy wearing them, but he has plans after work today and no time to go home and shower and change in between, so he pulls one out.

"You never know, do you." Pa shrugs. "I mean, kids these days, so much going on in your lives—"

"Pa," Tony says. "Stop doing undercarriage work."

"But—"

"You pay me to do it, so let me do the work you can't."

Joe d'Angelo is many things: a great dad, a lenient boss, and a doting grandfather. He isn't what Tony would call great at admitting his own weaknesses though. He grunts a noncommittal sound, definitely not an agreement, and heads to the storefront to unlock the doors.

Tony shakes his head at Pa's retreating back and gets to work on Mrs. Cooper's car. It's not a big job. She just has an inspection coming up and wants to make sure everything is in order. If it were a job of more than five minutes, they'd have put the car on a hoist yesterday.

Still, it's the principle of the thing. Since Pa's slipped disc three years ago, Tony has tried to take on more of the physically strenuous workload, especially the parts involving scrambling around on the floor or bending at weird angles. Pa has not been gracious about it.

"Mornin'," Kyle calls as he comes in. Kyle is also on time, and Pa could easily have left the check on Mrs. Cooper's undercarriage for him if he didn't want to give it to Tony.

"Hey, Kyle." Tony finishes up what he's doing and rolls out from under the car. "How's Susan doing?"

Kyle shrugs. His wife has been struggling with Lyme disease all summer, and it's taken a toll, not that he would say so in so many words. "She's getting there." He's said the same thing every day this week. He sets about putting on his coveralls and then makes a beeline for the coffee machine.

"Pour me one too?" Tony gets the clipboard his dad left on the roof of the car and fills out the checks for the undercarriage.

"Here ya go." Kyle sets Tony's cup on the table. "Your pa around?"

"I'm right here," Pa calls from the front office. "Still my shop."

Christ. He already sounds ornery. It'll be a long day.

Around eleven, a tow truck brings in a carload of Lobell students with a flat and a dented front fender. Apparently, the driver swerved to avoid a deer and hit the guardrail head-on. This doesn't explain the flat, but the kid looks shaken out of his mind as it is, and his two passengers lingering by the door to the garage aren't helping.

Kid.

Being a Lobell student means he's probably Gianna's age or maybe a little younger since she's older than most college seniors after taking a leave of absence last year. He has a handlebar mustache Tony's willing to bet is ironic, which doesn't make him seem particularly mature, but he's not a kid; he's only six or seven years younger than Tony. Of course, Pa disagrees because they're all kids to him, which Tony guesses is fair.

This guy's behavior doesn't make a case for being an adult, anyway. He's shaking all over, and sweat beads on his forehead as he tells them what happened. The tow truck guy, Carl, scratches his head as the student narrates, which supports Tony's impression that the story isn't quite adding up. Carl, who happens to be Tony's mom's cousin, often brings them easy fixes knowing that Pa squeezes in all the customers he can manage, keeping the wait times lower than other places. This saves Carl the trouble of putting a bunch of cars in his tow lot, which can barely fit five.

Pa takes the story at face value. "Never try to avoid the deer," he says. "Hit the brakes and stay on the road."

"Uh-huh." The student nods frantically. "Um, do you know what it's gonna be?"

Even someone with Pa's experience can't answer the question until they've inspected the damage. The car, an '07 Toyota Camry, isn't a luxury model in the first place, but up close, Tony can see they have more to fix than the fender. It looks bad, sure, but a little heat and elbow grease can work wonders. The light above it on the other hand was smashed to bits in the accident. Adding to which, '07 Camrys are absolute shit, and Tony's willing to bet there are some other issues hiding under the hood.

Pa shrugs. "I'll let you know." He heads into the front office. Tony knows he's probably looking for parts, but the student doesn't and looks like he got slapped in the face in addition to being in a car accident.

"We don't know yet," he tells the student. "We have to take a look at the damage before we can give you an estimate. I'm Tony, by the way. What's your name?"

"Sean." The guy works up a weak smile, which mostly makes his mustache look especially dumb. "Sean McAllister."

"Okay, Sean." It's not every day they get an accident in, but Tony's learned to keep his voice calm when they do. When it comes to breaking news to customers about unexpected and potentially expensive damage, half the battle is being kind, especially when they've just been through something scary. "You had a pretty rough morning, huh?"

Sean's shoulders slump. "Oh my god, yes. I have to call my parents. This is almost as bad as when I told them I wanted to be a film major."

Tony tries not to laugh. "How 'bout you have a seat in the office with your friends, and we'll get you all some water, and when we know what's going on, I'll let you know?"

"Thanks, man." Sweat still beads on Sean's forehead, far more than the cool air in the shop should allow, but at least he doesn't look like he's about to throw up anymore.

It's literally Tony's job to help, but he doesn't say so. He's well aware not all mechanics view themselves as being in customer service. He ushers Sean and his two friends, a girl with blue highlights who's worn red marks into her palms with her fingernails from worrying and a tall, gangly Black guy in a jean jacket with about seventeen patches for bands Tony's never heard of, into the office.

"Hey, you're Gianna's brother, right?" the girl asks.

"Yeah." Tony looks at her again. Her face seems familiar. "Oh hey, we've met before, haven't we?"

"I'm Lily. Lily Peterson? We met in January when—"

"Right." Tony did meet her in January, standing in front of her dorm room with her parents on New Year's Day after she tried to commit suicide because the professor who got Tony's sister pregnant and dumped her had died. Daniel gave Gianna her email address. And since then, Tony's gotten a consistent barrage of updates all summer on Lily's personal life and return to studies, courtesy of Daniel advising her through Colette's new program. Trying to act as if he doesn't know more about her than he probably should, Tony overcompensates. "Hey, you're back. That's great."

She nods, smiling a little shyly. She'd look sweet if Tony didn't know so much about her. "Thanks. It was great of you to get me in touch with Gigi. We signed up for some of the same classes this year."

"I'm glad," Tony says, a little wrong-footed. He had no idea Gianna got in touch with Lily or even wanted to talk to anyone about the professor she was having an affair with. She certainly doesn't talk to him. Still, it's good Gigi has friends who get what she's been through. She'll need them. Getting through her senior year of college with a baby won't be easy, and it's only the first week.

He gets the students set up with a bottle of water and some glasses and heads to the garage again. Carl leans up against the pickup with the rusted bumper Tony was working on before he showed up, shooting the shit with Kyle though they can't stand each other.

Carl looks up when Tony approaches. "Hey kiddo. They say anything about who's gonna pay for the tow truck?"

Tony sighs. "You didn't ask them?"

Carl shrugs. "The one with the dumbass mustache had a Triple A card, but with someone else's name on it."

"I don't work for Triple A," Tony reminds him. "You do."

"What was I gonna do, leave those kids at the side of the road? It'll work out, always does."

It does, Tony thinks bitterly as he retraces his steps into the storefront because he, unlike everyone else in this business, developed some semblance of people skills. It only takes him five minutes of awkward conversation with Sean, Lily, and their friend to work out that Sean's mother left her Triple A card in the glove compartment when she gave Sean the car for college and never told him whether or not he's covered by it. Sean doesn't want to call until he has an estimate, and it takes another five minutes of carefully hinting the bill for the tow truck will be significant if Sean can't work out how he's insured. Especially given Carl's still sitting around, losing working hours while he waits, talking to Kyle about how he wants to close up shop early on Friday and head for Tivoli Bays while the fishing's still good. All of this time will be on the insurance bill, and Sean doesn't seem to know what company he's with.

Tony leaves it to Sean to make the unpleasant phone call home and returns to the shop.

"You gotta stop towing people until you get their insurance details," he tells Carl.

Carl scratches his head. "I don't really do the paperwork side of things. That's all Cindy."

Tony takes a deep breath, considering how to explain that Cindy, Carl's wife, is the world's worst bleeding heart. She keeps sending him out to pick up cars without getting their insurance or Triple A numbers, a clear destination, or, in some particularly memorable cases, a name and address from the drivers. While this leads to great business for

Angel Automotive, it'll get Carl in trouble with Triple A sooner or later and, by proxy, Pa. *Someone* has to pay him for the repairs they do in the shop.

"Carl, god love you both, but someone's gotta run your business, and it ain't Cindy," Pa says, ambling into the garage.

Carl's chest puffs up, and he seems like he's about to answer something they'll all regret, but Pa steamrollers right on.

"Got a new headlight sourced, and I think we can get the fender straightened out as is. Tony, get her up on the lift and see about that tire. I'll write up an estimate for college boy in there."

College boy. Tony shakes his head. As if Gianna weren't attending the same school and wasn't friends with at least one of the kids in the front office. Kids. Again, Tony reminds himself he's not much older; he might spend a lot of time with Pa and Kyle, but he isn't their age.

"See," Carl says righteously. "Kid going to Lobell can afford the tow, insurance or no."

"Not with school bankrupting him he can't." Kyle is right, of course, but not helpful. Lobell is one of the most expensive schools in the country, and Gianna's going on a combination of grants and loans that make Tony's head hurt to think about. If Sean has the money to pay for it out of pocket, Tony doubts he still will after graduation. Carl, whose kids went to community college in the early aughts, is convinced taking out a loan for school is a matter of a few thousand, easily paid back with a cushy office job. Kyle has a stepdaughter who finished high school in June, and Tony's heard this argument about five times in the last four months.

"Carl, could you get the car on the lift for me?" Tony asks before the workday turns into a discussion on rising tuition costs and whether or not a good part-time job should cover them.

He situates himself in the driver's seat as Carl maneuvers the tow truck so Tony can reverse the car gently onto the lift, flat tire squelching uncomfortably as he does.

With the car set up, he and Kyle crank the lift up until the dented fender is at eye level. Of course, Tony can't find the spare tire anywhere in the trunk or under the car, but thankfully, they have the right replacement in stock. Switching it is the easy part. After twenty minutes, the busted tire is in the trash bin in the corner of the shop. The rubber boasts a long, narrow cut. There must have been broken glass on the shoulder where the car hit the guard rail. Tony can't think of any other way to explain it.

Either way, the flat tire is not the problem. Pa's estimation they can even out the bent fender without replacing anything, generous to say the least, remains the issue.

Around one, Tony gets called into the office to go over the estimate with Sean and his friends. By now, they've all got their phones out. Sean animatedly describes the accident to Lily, who's filming him as he speaks. It's become a herd of deer Sean only narrowly avoided, saving their lives in the process. Valiantly, Tony tries not to judge them. Sean's hands are still shaking, and Lily looks about ready to fall asleep in her seat. Their friend stares out the window, totally silent. Tony wonders idly which of the two guys might be Lily's boyfriend, the one who was supposed to take her to therapy this morning.

Maybe making dumb videos is a good alternative to therapy. Everyone processes stressful shit differently. Tony hopes they're not posting this online. Gianna's shown him a few TikToks. He thought they were funny. Car accidents are not funny in Tony's book, but how they process the event is up to them.

When they see him approach, they put their phones away hurriedly, which is both funny and sad. Tony's really, really not that old.

He gives Sean the estimate. It makes him wince but not panic, so he'll probably be fine. Tony takes down Sean's parents' insurance, which they thankfully put him on when he got his license, but he never asked about, and passes it on to Carl. This means Carl can leave, Kyle can relax, and they can all get some work done.

Lunch gets shifted to 3:00 p.m., when Tony's finally done with the pickup he was working on before the invasion of the college students. Said students haven't left the storefront and, instead, are now watching loud videos on their phones. Tony doesn't particularly want to end up going viral for the way he eats a ham and cheese, so he has lunch in the shop, leaning against the table with the coffee machine while Pa and Kyle work.

"Your ma packed you an egg salad sandwich." Pa eyes Tony's clearly-not-egg-salad when he gets off his welding mask.

"Sorry," Tony says with his mouth full. "Should have told her I wouldn't be home." It slipped his mind last night when the evening got late enough that the drive home to Kingston sounded less appealing than sleeping in Daniel's warm, comfortable bed. Anyway, Tony doesn't like egg salad much.

Pa shrugs. "More for me. You getting your sandwiches made for you over in Rhinebeck now?"

Kyle pulls off his welding mask and looks between them. The question is writ large on his face, but he doesn't ask it, bless him.

Tony takes another bite. "I can put some ham and cheese between bread myself, thanks." Asking Daniel to make him lunch would be—bizarre. They did make their lunches together last night, standing side by side in the kitchen, handing each other condiments and plastic packaging while Daniel complained about its effect on the environment. It makes Tony ache somewhere in his gut, but that's also not something he's about to express to his father.

"I didn't mean..." Pa starts, and then he sighs and shakes his head. "Whatever. So long as you're not hungry."

"Nope. All good." Tony keeps his tone light, but it niggles at him even more when he has to go out and handle the transaction with Sean, Lily, and their friend (his name's Frank, "like Frank Ocean," which doesn't mean anything to Tony). With college starting up again, Gianna only works two shifts a week so she can attend classes, and when she is at the shop, she's always got Lia with her. As a result, Tony picks up extra shifts so someone can cover the front desk, and for some reason, "someone" is always him.

It's those darn people skills. Pa gets grumpy if he has to talk to too many customers, and Kyle straight up doesn't talk.

All told, Tony only gets around to giving his own car the oil treatment it's been after at five, and it's six thirty before he manages to finish up all the paperwork for the day. Kyle's long gone, and the temperature in the lot has gotten less oppressive. The AC still hums away, blasting cold air through reception and the garage.

Tony struggles out of the coveralls he hates wearing and dumps them in the hamper. It's getting full; it's a good thing tomorrow is one of Ma's workdays, or Tony would have to ferry the laundry home too.

"Pa?" he calls into the garage. "You good to close up?"

"Yeah." Pa's voice is distant and muffled.

He's under Mrs. Cooper's goddamn car.

Tony closes his eyes. "I checked the undercarriage. Put it on the clipboard and everything."

"I know." Pa rolls out from under the car and struggles to his feet. "Dropped a screw; it rolled under. Don't give me that look, Tony."

"No look," Tony lies.

Pa shakes his head.

Irritation claws up Tony's throat sharply. He spent all day caught between customers and the shop. He's hungry and tired and late for his evening plans, and he's doing it all so Pa can run the shop without hurting himself, so Kyle can work without being fussed at, so Carl can keep towing every idiot in the state, and so Gianna can finish her degree in peace. All he gets for it are veiled comments about his personal life and Pa ignoring the one request Tony actually makes of him.

Pa claps a heavy hand on Tony's shoulder. "Good work today. Couldn't do it without you."

"Thanks." From somewhere, Tony manages to conjure up a smile. He lets his shoulders relax, tries to swallow down the frustration. He's not entirely successful.

"You coming home tonight?" Pa doesn't deal in heavy-handed hints or subtext. He sounds like he just wants to know. It still grates at Tony's nerves.

"Probably not," he says.

Chapter Two

Mike's isn't too crowded when Tony finally gets there. It figures, given school is in session again and the tourists have all gone home. Weeknights in Kingston are not hopping.

"Sorry I'm late," he says as he slides into the booth beside Blake. He wishes they were sitting outside while the weather's nice as it'll get rainy and cold soon enough. Blake has weirdly strong opinions about eating outdoors, though, and Tony doesn't want to get into it today. "Nice piercing. That new?"

"Yeah." Blake grins, flicking the eyebrow ring back and forth. "My boss had a conniption about it. Worth it."

Tony wrinkles his nose. "Why?"

Blake shrugs. "Professional workplace attire or something. It's 2019 though. People should be able to wear whatever they want to work."

"Hear, hear!" Lisa says from the other side of the table. She lifts her beer glass and takes a big sip. "One of my kids got sent home for wearing spaghetti straps the other day."

"Ah, the great American education system." Blake raises his glass in a mock-serious toast.

Tony's never been entirely clear on what separates spaghetti straps from other straps, but they don't sound like something worth sending someone home for, let alone a middle schooler who wouldn't know better if they *were* a problem. Tony had a phase in seventh grade where he only wore T-shirts for bands he had never listened to. No one sent him home about it, though they probably should have. He doesn't know how Lisa does it, even if he were earning twice his current salary, he doubts he could handle taking thirty prepubescent nightmares and teaching them to become real people.

"There you are." Daniel comes up from the bar. He settles into the seat next to Lisa and slides a beer and a burger across the table to Tony.

Tony closes his eyes in thankfulness. "You are my savior. Thank you."

He's about halfway through demolishing the burger when he manages to look up and realizes all three of his friends are watching him. He swallows a big bite. "What?"

"Rough day?" Lisa asks.

Tony shrugs. It was pretty par for the course, all things considered. Gianna's maternity leave segued seamlessly into her return to college, and while they technically could afford to hire someone else at the garage, it would put them in a tight spot if any unexpected costs come their way this year. They crunched the numbers in January when Gianna's due date was looming, and it was much cheaper for Tony, Pa, and Kyle to take on an extra shift here and there than it would be to have a new receptionist. After all, Ma comes in two days a week, and Gianna still does Friday afternoons and Saturdays. She has Lia with her, squalling away, but that might be good for business given how customers coo over her. Covering for Gianna's absence means more shifts with all three of them, him, Pa, and Kyle, clambering all over one another to get the jobs finished and the customers seen to. Adjusting to the new normal has been difficult, but Tony will get there.

At least, Tony thinks guiltily, he isn't sleeping in the same house as a screaming infant most nights. Pa is.

"Didn't pack enough for lunch." He's self-aware enough to know he's not telling the whole truth but not willing to get into any more detail all the same.

"I knew we should have gotten some bananas yesterday," Daniel says.

Tony shrugs. "We didn't know I was staying over when we went shopping."

He usually decides to stay over casually, depending on how late it gets and how comfortable it is on Daniel's couch, in Daniel's bed, or on one occasion, with Daniel wrapping his arms and legs around Tony because he didn't want him to go.

Tony just happens to be in Rhinebeck late frequently, and Daniel has a very comfy couch.

Again, Tony becomes uncomfortably aware of Lisa and Blake's eyes on him.

He takes a long sip of his beer to ignore it and then nearly spits it out. "Jesus. What is this?"

"Oh no." Blake gives Daniel an accusatory look. "Did you get the new one on tap?"

"Yeah. I thought—this is Blake's new beer, right? I mean, other Blake?"

Blake rolls his eyes. "Call him Blake G. That's what our English teacher did."

Lisa's eyes slide over to Tony, willing him to get in on the joke. "Fair's fair. Then you have to call this one Blake W."

Tony takes another sip to hide the laugh and nearly chokes on the weird, yeasty cinnamon taste.

Not for the first time, Blake huffs, irritated. "I was the original Blake. It's not fair. And Blake W sounds so dumb."

He's not annoyed. During the month that Blake G wore the same kind of flannel shirts and ripped jeans as him in sophomore year of high school and told everyone to call him Blake G, Blake W was briefly irritated, but only while Blake G pretended to do it on a dare. As soon as Blake G told him that the whole thing wasn't a bit, that he was much happier as Blake G than he ever had been before he transitioned, Blake

W was entirely on board and spent the rest of high school complaining loudly about how he should be known as the original Blake. This led to a lot of discussion about how Blake wasn't Blake W's real name anyway, but he'd gotten tired of people misspelling Baalkrishan and sweet-talked the school secretary into changing it on his forms though it wasn't technically legal. The ensuing discussion usually derailed the conversation so thoroughly no one thought to complain about anything else to do with Blake G.

By now, the whole thing is mostly nostalgic.

Daniel looks between them, mildly confused but willing to go with it, just like he goes with Tony deciding to stay over all the time. He even started buying Tony's favorite brand of prepackaged ham, though he thinks it's bad for the environment. Daniel joined Thursday night drinks at Mike's at some point in April when Tony wanted both to get mildly drunk and stay over at his place and, therefore, needed a designated driver. Tony's friends apparently like him enough that it's become a standing invitation.

Tony tries not to read too much into the way their lives have become so seamlessly tangled. He fails most of the time.

He still hasn't told his friends in so many words what Daniel is to him. He doesn't need to; he's aware he's not subtle about it. But still.

The ease with which Daniel took to it and his friends' acceptance in return makes something big and tender swell up in Tony, and he has to take another drink to will it down.

"For fuck's sake." He sets the beer glass down and pushes it away.

"Oh, right." Blake thankfully awakens himself from high school reminiscing to explain what is wrong with the drinks tonight. "Blake G made a cinnamon bun flavored beer, and Mike's put it on tap this week to crowd test it for him."

Tony wrinkles his nose. "Oh, that's what that is. Huh."

"Yeah," Blake agrees. "I think he and Charlie scheduled their vacation for this week on purpose so he wouldn't have to take questions about it."

Daniel's eyebrows crawl up. "Can I try a sip?"

Tony gestures for him to go ahead.

Daniel takes a sip and then another. "I like it."

"You would," Tony mutters. Daniel is not exactly a beer connoisseur.

"What was that?"

"Oh, nothing." Tony smiles guilelessly. "You wanna drink it?"

"Are you driving, then?"

Tony shrugs. "It's one beer, but yeah, I can if you'd rather." Now he's eaten something, he's less annoyed. He'd rather stay sober and sleep at Daniel's than spend time at home. It will keep his irritation levels lower.

"Sounds good." Daniel takes another long drink. "Hey, Lisa, how's... uh..." He trails off, obviously trying to remember the name of the guy Lisa brought to New Year's and a few other things in the last few months. He tries to catch Tony's eye for help, but Tony can only shrug.

"There's your answer," Lisa says darkly. "He's deeply boring, and we broke up two weeks ago."

Blake and Daniel debate whether this merits cheers or commiserations while Tony finishes his dinner. He leans back against the booth with a satisfied sigh when he's done.

Blake and Lisa compare notes on the perils of app-based dating, which Tony never got around to trying in as much depth as they have, and Daniel makes listening sounds Tony associates with how he gets when he's doing research.

Tony looks out the window at the sun longingly. This would be perfect weather for a picnic. Or a hike, or a long walk, or—

"Okay, but is there such a thing as a welcome dick pic?" Lisa asks skeptically.

Tony's attention is drawn forcibly indoors.

"I mean," Blake hedges.

Tony leans forward, resting his chin on his hands.

"Okay, you shut up." Blake points at him. "You've never even downloaded Grindr, you luddite."

"No, no, I'm interested to see how this plays out. Tell me more about this modern technology you speak of."

"Oh, shut up." Blake puts his head in his hands. "Sometimes dating apps are for NC-17 dating, okay?"

"Sure." Tony keeps his tone as light and pleasant as he can without cracking up. "I can see that. What are your favorite angles for taking dick pics, Blake? Do you go for the upright soldier? The banana comparison? Hey, are you circumcised? You could do the pig in a blanket—"

"Shut up. Shut up, shut up, shut up."

Tony gives it a moment longer, and then he lets himself look over at Daniel and laugh.

"I don't know why I talk to you people." Blake sits back in his chair, arms folded in wounded dignity. He doesn't mean it. Tony's known him for over a decade, and he can count on one hand the number of times Blake has been honestly upset about being teased.

"Anyway," Tony says. "We should go hiking."

"Hiking?" Daniel sounds alarmed. He should. For someone who's lived in the northeast for upward of five years, he has an alarming lack of decent shoes.

"Yeah, hiking. We haven't been at all this year, and it's best in autumn. It's gonna be gorgeous."

"I'm in," Lisa says. "I haven't been in ages."

"Next week? Saturday?"

"Lemme check." Blake peers down at his phone calendar. "I guess. But nothing crazy."

"I was thinking a little light rock climbing?" Tony suggests.

Lisa swats at his arm. "Stop teasing. Can you drive us?"

With a grimace, Tony thinks of his rickety Toyota.

"I can drive," Daniel offers. "If, uh, if you want me—"

"Always," Tony says with a grin. "You want to go hiking?"

A flush rises on Daniel's cheeks, which might be the cinnamon bun lager he downed pretty quickly but also might be the words. "The jury's still out. But I could give it a try."

Tony's not entirely sure, but he thinks there's a *for you* at the end of that sentence going unspoken, and he likes it.

They order another round—Sprite for Tony, since he's driving now, although only Daniel has another cinnamon beer—and debate different trails to take. Tony will have to dig out his hiking boots from whatever storage closet his mom put them in. Maybe his running shoes could work if he doesn't get home in the meantime. He left those at Daniel's. They split an order of fries as they talk. Lisa hogs the ketchup. For the first time since this morning, Tony starts to relax a little.

Then the door opens and an all-too-familiar voice floats in.

"...just one, though, this place is way too expensive."

Lisa looks incredulously toward the source of the voice, coming from outside at one of the patio tables, and says, "This place has the only four-dollar beer in the state."

"College students." Blake follows her gaze, craning to see the culprit.

Daniel's posture straightens so fast his shoulder knocks into Tony's. "Please no."

Regretting most of his day, Tony looks outside as well. "Yup. Definitely college students." Dumbass college students, he adds in the privacy of his own mind because they're definitely drinking, and they're definitely here by car—the car Pa and Kyle spent half the afternoon fixing up.

"Hey, isn't that your sister?" Blake leans halfway out of his seat to see.

Tony's head whips around. He cranes a little to the left.

"Yup. That's...that sure is my sister." And his niece in her stroller, Gianna carefully rocking her as she laughs at something Sean says.

He seemed so innocuous in the shop, a lost, scared student barely out of his teens. Here, drinking beer with Tony's little sister, he kind of looks like a dick.

"Oh, shoot." Daniel sinks lower in his seat.

"Hm?" Tony doesn't look away from the scene outside.

"Those are my students," Daniel hisses. "And I'm...not sober."

"I'm so glad that can't happen to me," Lisa crows in delight.

Daniel glares. "Don't count your chickens before they're hatched. I'm told eighth graders drink cough syrup to get buzzed these days."

"Oh, yeah, I have a few who definitely would. But not in public, where I'm drinking."

"Fuck." Daniel sinks even lower.

"Are they okay?" Blake asks.

"Huh?"

"Are they...nice?"

Daniel blinks. He straightens a little. "Oh, yeah. I mean, Lily's great. She's had a rough time of it. I saw her this morning actually, and she's turned a corner. Sounds like she's finally got a decent support network at school with her friends and her boyfriend. And I mean, academically, she's...good. Really good. This year is her second chance at junior year, and I'm sure she'll be brilliant. Frank, in the jean jacket, is all right too. He's a lit major. Struggled with his math requirement and wound up taking a summer class, but a lot of kids in the humanities have trouble with math. I don't know the third one."

"Sean," Tony says.

"Oh, did Gianna introduce you?"

"No," he grates out. "Sean was in an accident today, and his car got towed to the shop."

"Was it his fault?"

"Unclear."

The deer wasn't anyone's fault, but Tony still doesn't get how the flat tire happened. Watching Sean grandstand now, wide smile on his face and his arms flailing about in all directions after being a chickenshit about calling his mom earlier, Tony wonders if the deer was even real. Judging by how anxiously Lily's eyeing Sean, he's not the only one.

"Oh." Blake gives him a knowing look. "And now you're concerned he'll be a bad influence on her."

"That's not..." Tony starts. "I mean, she's... I'm not..."

"If it helps, I think he's with Lily." Daniel squints through the window to where Sean has now slipped an arm onto the back of Lily's chair. "Must be the boyfriend she told me about."

It does help, which Tony hates himself for. Gianna's a grown-up, and she can make her own choices. "So, Lily's doing better?"

Daniel nods. "A little case of start-of-term jitters, but otherwise, I haven't seen her so even-keeled all summer. She seems ready for a new start."

Tony looks outside. Gianna's laughing again. She didn't do much of that for a while there last year. He should be glad to see it. He is when he's not being an idiot. "Yeah, I'm glad for Gigi too. Still a weird support group, but..."

Daniel nods.

"How's Gianna dealing with it all, anyway?" Blake asks. "I mean..."

Tony shrugs and then sighs. "About as well as she could be. She doesn't complain about anything but the lack of sleep, and she's great with Lia. She loves that kid so much. I think...I think she misses him."

Daniel looks away.

Tony's certain he misses Mario as well. Daniel doesn't talk about it much, not with Tony, but Mario was his friend before he was Gianna's...not-boyfriend. And Mario's dead now, murdered by Stacy, who Daniel was also friends with. It can't be easy. Tony's selfishly glad Daniel doesn't seem to need or want sympathy about it. What would he say? "Sorry for your loss; wish he had lived for me to throttle him per-sonally"?

They sit in awkward silence as everyone debates what to say.

Tony wishes it were the first time in the last eight months that there was awkward silence surrounding this topic and not the billionth. Out-side, Lily shifts in her seat, slightly out of range of Sean's hand, which was resting on her shoulder. For a moment, she looks over toward the waterfront, and her expression goes dark and clouded. Her hands clench to fists.

Then, Gianna says something, and Lily looks back to her group with a smile.

Tony forces himself to stop watching them.

One fry remains in the communal basket, the fry of decency no one wants to be greedy enough to eat. Tony takes it.

Outside, Gianna gets up. She shrugs on her jacket. It's too warm for a jacket, but she runs cold, and it drives Tony nuts because she always nudges the thermostat up a degree or two too warm. He checks his watch. It's almost eight. Way past Lia's bedtime. She'll be fussy as all hell.

The other college students drain their drinks as she gets up to go. They leave an assortment of loose change and dollar bills on the table to cover it. Students.

As they leave, Tony spots Sean handing his car keys to Lily. They did only have one beer, but a drink after an accident does not a safe driver make, and it looks like Lily was drinking a diet soda. The sight makes Tony feel a little better. Maybe Sean isn't so bad, especially if, as Daniel says, he's had such a good influence on Lily. Tony was overreacting before. There probably was a deer, and maybe there was some glass or rough gravel on the shoulder when Sean hit the guardrail.

They head out not long after. It's still a weeknight, after all, and they all have jobs to get to in the morning. Tony drives Daniel's car, leaving his own parked near Mike's. He's a little ashamed of how relieved he is to be driving a car where the steering wheel doesn't jam when he parallel parks.

"You good to drive me over tomorrow morning?" he asks Daniel, who folded himself into the passenger seat and appears ready to fall asleep.

"Yeah." Daniel yawns. "No classes till noon tomorrow, and if I get to be late for faculty council because I have to drive you places, I will reconsider giving road head."

Tony chokes on a laugh. "I mean, I won't. It's a safety hazard but noted."

Daniel chuckles, a warm, comforting sound, and Tony breathes it in. He likes how familiar it is to hear Daniel laugh, to make him laugh.

He looks over for a second at a red light, and Daniel is watching him. No. Studying him, examining the lines of his face and the cut of his jaw.

"What?"

"Nothing," Daniel says. "Just...wondering."

Tony forces his shoulders to stay relaxed, though instinct would have them up around his ears. He's been weird today, and he knows it.

The heavy cloud of his annoyance after work still follows him, and he can't quite make it go away. Daniel can ask him anything, of course, but Tony doesn't want to explain why he's in such a funk; he doesn't know if he can.

"How do you know so much about dick pics?"

Tony breathes an internal sigh of relief. "Blake doesn't know everything about me."

"Oh?"

"I did download Grindr once."

Daniel doesn't say anything, but he doesn't have to. Tony can feel his eyes, questioning, curious.

"It was last summer when I thought I was going to move out. I had a place lined up in downtown Kingston, and I thought...I thought it would be my chance to finally do something about..." Tony gestures toward himself.

"Hmm." Daniel hums in agreement. "Did you meet up with anyone?"

"This feels like a trap." Tony doesn't think it is. Daniel's not a person who gets jealous. But Tony would rather have the lighthearted, bantery relationship talk than try to explain his own sexual history. He's never had the right words for it.

"I know you were with other people before we met, Tony. It's not a big deal. I guess I want to know more about you."

"Oh." Tony hadn't thought about that. He knows a bit about Daniel's dating past, in large part because he met his ex not too long after Tony and Daniel started seeing each other. Jeff is a nice guy, and Tony likes him despite being very glad he moved to Ohio. "I met one guy. It was...fine, I guess."

"A ringing endorsement."

Tony shrugs. "It was pretty clear we were meeting to hook up, so we did. I didn't think much about it before or after."

For a moment, Daniel doesn't answer. Then, he says, "If I hadn't come back to the garage after we met..."

"I was thinking about you." Tony's glad he has to look at the road.

It feels strange to admit even though Daniel knows how Tony feels about him. He must. "I was thinking about you all the time."

He chances a glance over.

Daniel looks smug. "Sorry to pry," he says. He doesn't seem all that sorry to Tony, but Daniel is nothing if not polite. "If you don't want to talk about it, that's fine. I just... You had a whole life before I came along, and I'm sure seeing other people was part of it."

Tony shifts uncomfortably. "Not really. I mean, sometimes, I guess, but nothing serious." Nothing more than a quick fuck every now and again is what he means, but he doesn't want to say that in so many words.

"You weren't...dating?" Daniel asks, picking up on the subtext like he always does.

Tony shakes his head. "I...never felt that way about anyone." They're on the bridge now. He loves driving the bridge when it's dark, the water sparkling beneath them with the reflection of the lights on the bridge and absolutely no one around for miles. "You know, I used to think I was bi." He didn't enter this conversation intending on telling Daniel this. He's never told anyone. But Daniel's willing to listen, and the night is quiet and mellow with the first hints of autumn creeping up on the Hudson Valley. Some combination of all these things has put Tony in a sharing mood.

Daniel makes an amused sound. "I think a lot of us went through a phase of hoping we could still pass as straight."

"No, I mean..." Tony tries to find the words. "I didn't want to date anyone when I was a teenager. And I thought, well, I don't want to date girls, and I don't want to date guys, so I guess I like both equally."

"Oh. Oh, I see. What changed?"

"I started being attracted to people even if I wasn't too into the whole...dating thing." He doesn't quite mean attraction in the way he's seen it in movies or read about it in books, but he can't figure out how to make the words work to explain how he felt as a teenager. He was so confused all of the time. When he imagined the future, it was him in a nebulous marriage, modeled after what he knew from his parents. But when he tried to apply that to anyone his own age, he didn't want it. Sex, sure, he was interested in sex on a conceptual level, but not with anyone in particular and definitely not with anyone he tried dating.

"You know," Tony continues, "I dated Blake G for, like, two weeks in high school. Before he was Blake. We were friends and spent a bunch of time together, and I thought maybe that was what a crush was. But I didn't want...anything. Kissing, or sex, or even holding hands." The experience messed them both up more than Tony wants to let on right now. He spent the entire time feeling wrong for not wanting to kiss a pretty girl, and Blake G felt wrong for not being a girl. To this day, hanging out with Blake G alone is weird for Tony. Daniel doesn't need to know all that, at least not now. "And then a while later, I could at least picture hooking up with Blake W, so I figured I wasn't into girls."

"Really? Blake? W, I mean?"

Tony grins over at Daniel. "Highly strung, overthinks everything, ringing any bells here?"

"Shut up. I am not like Blake W."

"No." Tony never once wanted to sleep cuddled up with Blake or spend time together on the couch, touching for the comfort of it, nothing else. He didn't especially want to do anything sexual with Blake either. It was more that he wanted to have sex in general, and Blake was attractive. "No, you're definitely not. Eventually, I figured out I was attracted to men in general, but I still couldn't see myself dating anyone."

"Makes sense," Daniel says. "But you decided not to follow up on...the attraction and see if romantic feelings happened afterward?"

"It wasn't an active decision. I...never developed those feelings for anyone." Shifting in his seat as much as he can while driving, Tony adds, "I was a bit of a late bloomer in terms of...sex and all that."

Twenty wasn't necessarily late in the grand scheme of things, but at the time, it felt late to Tony. Only afterward, when he drove home after an unmemorable blowjob from a classmate in the classmate's shitty apartment toward the end of community college, did he realize he hadn't done it because he especially wanted to. It was something he thought he should want to do. It scratched a physical itch, but Tony didn't feel any particular way about it.

"Sounds kinda lonely."

Tony's foot slips on the accelerator.

He gets the car under control again, the back of his neck burning. "Yeah. I didn't...I didn't know that until you came along though."

It's an understatement. The dormant part of his brain or his heart or his dick, or all of the above, came online when he met Daniel and couldn't stop thinking about him. He wants to say as much. Before, he pursued some casual flings and had one-night stands now and again and never thought about it afterward, never needed more until Daniel walked into the shop, and Tony tripped over his tongue and his feet until Daniel kissed him. He doesn't know how to find the words without it sounding like too much.

Tony thinks the conversation might be over as he follows the winding roads toward Rhinebeck, safe in the dark from having to be seen so thoroughly in all ways at once.

"You did know a little," Daniel says just when Tony thinks he might let it go. "Or you wouldn't have downloaded Grindr."

"I guess. But I didn't get it. You know, I love Gianna, but I didn't understand then."

"Understand?"

"Why she couldn't leave well enough alone and not keep seeing Mario," Tony explains. "It was so clear to me whatever she had with him wasn't worth it. Every time she saw him, especially once she was pregnant, she was miserable, but she kept going back. I didn't understand why she would until..."

"Until I fucked up and made you miserable. And you still came back."

So, Daniel does know how special he is to Tony, even if neither of them can quite say it.

"Come on. It wasn't that bad," Tony says. It's not true, strictly speaking, but Daniel feels guilty enough about Mario, and Tony forgave him for everything he did last fall the minute he asked.

"I thought you helped Gianna kill a man."

"Okay, it was kind of bad," Tony revises. "But you more than made up for it."

"Or I'm lucky you're a very forgiving person."

Tony can hear Daniel's smile in his voice.

"Thanks for telling me about this," Daniel says.

"Yeah." Entirely without him intending it to, Tony's voice sounds like it was raked over hot coals. "I want you to know this stuff about me."

"One more question. You and Blake W. Did that ever happen?"

Tony groans as he pulls the car into the lot by Daniel's apartment building. "We kissed one time and then decided once was enough. You cannot ever tell anyone. We made a pact."

The sound of Daniel's laughter follows him out of the car and to the door.

"Hey, how are you, anyway?" Tony asks as they troop up the stairs. "I feel bad. We talked about me for ages. How's your first week as official dean of the department going?"

The college unofficially promoted Daniel last semester because someone had to pick up the slack left by Stacy's absence. She might have been a murderess, but she was also a very effective administrator. Now the dust has settled, Lobell changed Daniel's job title to encompass all his new duties. The actual process involved some more stuff about tenure and letters of recommendation, but Tony didn't follow past the point that it is, in essence, a promotion.

Daniel shrugs. "It's the same as being the unofficial dean of the department last semester. A lot of red tape."

"Red tape?"

Daniel unlocks the door and kicks off his shoes. "I mean, look at Lily. She couldn't do her finals last winter, but she was in classes all semester. Now, half her professors won't take a late final, and the other half will, so what do we do with her credits? And she was too late to withdraw from classes, so do the classes where she can't submit a final count as failed classes or incomplete? What will that do to her GPA?"

"Christ, I haven't thought about a GPA in years." Tony unties his shoes and follows Daniel into the living room. "So figuring out administrative headaches is your job now, huh?"

"Yeah." Daniel lets himself fall onto the couch. "Apparently, the registrar's office doesn't know what to do with Lily either."

This is at least the fifth time Daniel has mentioned the registrar since they started seeing each other. Tony vaguely remembers the word from his time at community college in Poughkeepsie. But he only went past the office with the word emblazoned on the door once in the two years he spent commuting for classes, and it's way too late to ask Daniel what it means.

"Lily was talking about heading to her psych professor's office and outright begging for her grades to be accepted. I had to convince her that wouldn't go over well." Daniel sinks into the couch until he's practically lying down. "I think she took it okay, but it must be frustrating, especially after she put in the hours with summer school and all."

"I forget how stressful it is being a student," Tony says. "All the insecurity about what will come next, depending on your professors for your future. I never had that."

"Must have been comforting, having built-in job security."

"I mean, so long as the shop keeps running," Tony points out.

"But you have skills and a trade, and experience." Daniel rolls onto his side to look at Tony. "Most college students don't, you know. They're looking to get a foundation for their futures from us, and we can't even give them any guarantees."

Tony thinks guiltily of Gianna and Lia. Gianna has most of her degree, but she's getting a BA in psychology, which is apparently worth nothing without at least an MSW, and she has a baby to support. She needs all the help she can get, and there he is, complaining about having to go to work a little more while she studies. Tony can't imagine having her ambition.

He studies Daniel, his tousled sandy hair, and how tired he looks. It's odd. Something about the bags under his eyes and the way he's lying there, propped up on one elbow, his whole body curled toward Tony, makes him appear both younger and older at the same time.

Maybe Tony feels vulnerable, soft-boiled, and he's looking to find the same feeling in Daniel.

Maybe Tony can imagine them lying like this after a long day years and years from now.

"I'm so old." Daniel turns onto his back and stares up at the ceiling. "Two beers on a weeknight, and I'm totally done for. And did I tell you my mom called today? Apparently, my dad is getting a hip replacement next week. I know I'm an adult and everything, but I was not ready to feel this ancient."

Tony chuckles and draws him close. "Wanna get ready for bed and watch some *Criminal Minds*?"

Daniel presses a wet kiss to his cheek. "You read my mind." He heads off to the bathroom to brush his teeth.

Tony watches him go, then pulls out his phone and checks it.

Sorry if this is out of line, Blake texted at some point in the last hour. *But if there's anything any of us can do to help you and your sister, I hope you know we're there for you.*

Tony swallows around the sudden lump in his throat.

He sends Blake a string of heart emojis. He can't imagine how he could possibly turn what he's feeling into words.

Then, Tony opens his text thread with Gianna. She last wrote him three days ago, a GIF of a dog in a funny hat.

How's your first week back at school going? he texts her. *U need a babysitter to get homework done or sth? lmk*

Chapter Three

Lia gurgles happily and reaches up to bat at her toy octopus.
        Tony bought it for her when Ma took Gianna to the hospital after her water broke. He realized suddenly that though he'd taken Gianna to Planned Parenthood when she first found out she was pregnant, to doctor's appointments all along the way, and to Lobell to figure out how she could pick up her studies again when the baby was there, he hadn't thought about what it would be like when the baby was born.

So, Tony took a detour to the toy shop on his way to the maternity ward, where he searched painstakingly through all the stuffed animals trying to find something cute, not weirdly gendered, and without huge, hard plastic eyes.

The octopus was his best bet.

Apparently, it's a winner because Lia loves it. Sometimes so much she cries when Gianna takes it away at bedtime. There's something about all the arms, Tony thinks, that make it a comforting toy to hang on to. He lowers it a bit so she can reach it, and she squirms with delight as she grabs on.

Tony hasn't been around babies much, at least not since Gianna was one. Given he was only five when she was born, his experience is limited. It's all been a surprise—from those first weeks when Lia could see so little of the world and barely understood what was around her, through her (mercifully brief) bout of colic in the summer when she couldn't stop crying, up to now when she wants constant interaction and reassurance but also a rigid schedule of twice-daily naps and walks.

The most shocking thing, to Tony, has been how much personality he thinks he can glimpse in Lia at only seven months. Her eyes sparkle with love when she spots Gianna, and her chubby little cheeks dimple right up. And she never makes as much of a mess with pea mash as she does with spinach. Tony knows she'll be a laugh riot when she's old enough to crack a joke.

With her arms full of octopus, he's free to tickle her belly.

She shrieks with laughter.

It segues quickly into the other kind of shrieking, and he picks her up and holds her against his chest, rocking gently.

"I got you, baby girl," Tony tells the top of her head as Lia starts to settle against him.

Tony loves being an uncle and getting these quiet moments with her. He'll get to watch her grow up from one step removed, from the room right next door, or sometimes from across the river.

He takes a deep breath of the sweet milky scent from the top of her head Ma calls "new baby smell." He could be in Rhinebeck. He's there often now, it's true, but he could be there more. He could come here for babysitting sometimes, but he could have a different key ring and maybe a better car. Then Gianna would have more space here, and Lia could have her own room when she gets older. Maybe someday, things will twist around and Gianna will cross the river to visit Tony's kids.

The thought must make something tense up in Tony, either with fear or desire, and the baby starts to fuss again.

She's finally quieted down properly for her nap when the key scrapes in the lock. Tony winces as he looks toward it, but it's just Ma coming in with the groceries. She spots them instantly and tiptoes through to the kitchen. Tony follows with the baby on his left arm and helps her put away the groceries one-handed. Trying not to wake Lia, he moves so slowly his help is practically counter-productive.

"How'd you end up on babysitting duty?" Ma whispers, taking a packet of spinach off of him and putting it in the crisper. Good thing Lia's asleep. She might bring the house down if she saw the spinach.

"I offered. It's my half day, and Gigi could do with a few baby-free classes."

Ma reaches up to cup his cheek. "Uncle of the year."

They get the groceries put away between them, and by then Lia's settled enough he can try to put her down in her crib in the living room. With the baby monitor on, they retreat to the kitchen for a cup of coffee.

"How are you doing?" Ma asks. "I feel like I haven't seen you in weeks."

Heat creeps up the back of Tony's neck. "I haven't been gone that much." He's not sure it's true. He slept here last night, at least. And Tuesday last week. And the Thursday two weeks ago when Daniel had a dinner thing with the faculty council.

She shakes her head. "You've been so busy at the shop, it happens. I'm glad you're making time for your niece and your sister."

"Always. They're my best girls."

"I always knew I'd be replaced by the younger generation." She sighs dramatically into her coffee cup.

"Aw, Ma." Tony comes around the kitchen table and wraps her up in a hug from behind. "You know I love you."

"Doesn't hurt to hear now and again." She pats at his arms. "I love you too, Anthony. And I know we're all pulling together to make this work, but I miss having us together as a family sometimes, you know?"

"I know. I know."

He thinks guiltily of his half-empty dresser upstairs. Earlier, he went looking for clean clothes after he gave Lia the bottle Gianna left in the fridge, and she spit up half of it all over him. He discovered his favorites are in Rhinebeck. Now, he's wearing a pair of basketball shorts he hasn't used in at least five years and a *Little Shop of Horrors* T-shirt, a leftover from when he halfheartedly helped out in the high school scene shop because Lisa decided to try acting, and he wanted to be supportive.

He ought to sort through his things and—

And.

"Ma... You know we probably won't all be living here forever?"

She rolls her eyes. "Of course I know. It's convenient now though. Until Gianna has a job that can support her and Lia, at least, she ought to stay here where there's plenty of help."

"Of course," Tony agrees hurriedly.

"Anyway, I didn't think I'd be having my grandkids living so close. Let me enjoy it."

Tony kisses the top of her head. None of them counted on Lia, but she's still perfect. There will be plenty of time to talk about Rhinebeck and all the T-shirts Tony left there some other time. He should probably cool it, anyway. Who knows if Daniel's on the same page? Maybe he's sick of Tony's stuff ending up in his laundry.

"Do you mind if I head over to the shop for a while?" Ma asks when they've finished their coffees. "Kyle's wife has a doctor's appointment, and he wants to leave a little early."

"Go for it. Lia and I are doing fine on our own."

One cool thing about dating a professor is Daniel's massive collection of books, both in his office and at home. It's ridiculous, and if he ever wants to move house, it'll be a pain in the neck, not to mention the one bookshelf in the living room Tony's been eyeing for weeks, fully expecting the shelves to crack under the weight any day. Still, Tony likes to browse Daniel's shelves and choose readings at random. He started something by Faulkner the other day, and it's been pretty interesting so far. Tony hasn't read many books that change who's telling the story partway through.

He settles in to read on the comfy chair in the living room while Lia naps, but only a few minutes later, the door slams shut. His head jerks up on instinct, and the baby starts crying.

Tony curses under his breath and then curses himself for cursing in front of Lia as he goes to pick her up and shush her.

"You woke up your daughter," he hisses to Gianna when she comes in.

"Sorry."

"I thought your class went till four?"

"I thought so too." Gianna frowns. She re-dyed her hair recently, and it's completely black. In conjunction with her expression, it makes her look very bleak. "Apparently, Professor Lawrence is in the hospital."

Tony blinks. "Wait, what?"

"Yeah. We all turned up for class at two, and no one showed up, and then Lily went to check her office and didn't come back. Next thing I knew, the police and an ambulance pulled up outside."

"Holy shit."

Lia loudly protests Tony's sudden pause in bouncing her, and he rocks her up and down again.

"Yeah." Gianna drops her bag in the corner and holds out her arms for Lia.

Tony hands her over reluctantly, and she quiets instantly. Of course.

It drove Gianna nuts at the start how Lia was attached to her at all times and rarely calmed down for anyone else. "I thought I was getting my body back," she complained once, six weeks in at four in the morning when nothing would soothe Lia but cuddles from mom. At the same time, Tony can tell she takes a little pride in being needed. She gets impatient when Lia starts to cry in someone else's arms and takes over immediately. And she always smiles just a little when Lia quiets for her.

Tony stuffs his hands in his pockets. "Are you okay?"

Gianna shrugs. "I'm not the one in an ambulance."

"I mean with...um..." He's not entirely sure how to broach that the last time she saw the police, she was taken in for questioning about the murder of Lia's dad.

"I'm fine. I gotta call Lily though."

Gianna hoists Lia over her shoulder and pulls her phone out of her pocket.

As she heads for the stairs, scrolling for Lily's number, Gianna says over her shoulder, "You can go now if you want. I got her."

Tony blinks at her retreating back. "I live here."

Already on the phone, she doesn't hear him. Or doesn't want to.

With his babysitting duties over more than an hour before he thought they would be, Tony's free afternoon is at loose ends. He could sit in the living room and read some more, but he's not calm enough anymore.

Instead, he does the mature thing and follows Gianna up the stairs, ignoring her previous brush-off. He wants to ask about the professor who was hurt and whether Gianna finds out anything on her phone call, whether Lily is all right. He wants to ask again whether Gianna is all right, and again and again until she tells him the truth.

Except he can hear her voice on the phone, and the cadence does not sound like she'll keep this short.

"Are you okay?" she asks, and then says, "Mm-hm, yeah," as Lily answers.

Tony's uncomfortably aware he's standing on the landing, listening in on his little sister's phone call, but he can't quite make himself leave. The dismissive look she gave him—as if he was waiting for her to let him leave the house when he's the one who offered to babysit—gnaws at him.

Behind the door, he hears the telltale sound of Lia fussing.

"Hey, hang on a sec. I need to put you on speaker," Gianna says. After a beep comes the clatter of the phone being set down, and then Lily's tinny voice fills the air, interspersed with Lia's cries.

"It was nuts, G. There was so much...so much blood. I don't even..."

"Shh, baby girl, shh," Gianna says to Lia, and then to Lily, "That sounds really scary."

Lia cries out again, swallowing half of Lily's answer.

"...you think she'll be okay?"

"I don't know. Will you?"

Lily sighs heavily, a crackle in the phone's speaker. "Sean's coming over. He says he can help."

The hubris of a man in his early twenties to think his presence (or his dick) can solve this particular problem. Apparently, Gianna agrees.

"You sure that's what you need right now?"

"Yeah." Lily's voice sounds more even, sure. "Yeah, it'll get me out of my head. Are you okay?"

"Why wouldn't I be?"

"Come on, Gianna. A professor getting attacked? It's..."

"It's not the same. Last year...he wasn't on campus, and he was shot, not stabbed. It's awful, but at least it's nothing to do with me."

Tony's breath catches in his throat. He never thought about it in that way, but Gianna's not wrong. Stacy did what she did out of some misguided desire to avenge Gianna. He never considered Gianna might feel guilty.

She shouldn't, of course, but he can hardly break down the door and tell her so.

It's a moment before Lily responds. "I'm having a hard time remembering it's nothing to do with me."

"Shit, yeah. Well, you found her. But it's not the same. You didn't have a *relationship* with her."

"I went to her office hours."

"But not like with..."

"No, nothing like with him."

Gianna nears the door, and Tony freezes at the sound of her footsteps. She walks away again. She must be rocking Lia to keep her quiet. "I'm sorry this happened to you."

"Me too. And seriously, if you need someone to talk..."

Daniel is right about Lily. She's a sweetheart.

"You, too, okay? I know you have Sean, but he's..."

"Yeah, he's not much of a talker. About this stuff anyway." Lily laughs. "But hey, you've got your family, too, right?"

Tony doesn't need to break down the door to know Gianna's rolling her eyes. "Yeah, yeah. They're all here. They don't get it, but they're here."

They don't get it. Of course they don't. When has Gianna ever given them the chance to? She's said more to Lily about Mario in the last two minutes than she's said to him all year. Tony turns and sneaks down the stairs. For a moment, he considers waiting around for her to get off the phone and then trying to talk to her again, but apparently, he *doesn't get it*, so why would she? Before he knows he's going to do it, Tony pulls on his sneakers and heads for his car.

"Guess I'm proving her right," he mutters to himself, but it doesn't stop him throwing the car into reverse and pulling out of the drive. He barely notices the funky moment when the wheel doesn't turn quite right because he's so lost in thought.

Tony pulls up at Daniel's building in Rhinebeck before he realizes that is where he intended to head. It's three thirty. Daniel won't be home for at least an hour yet, and Tony didn't tell him he was coming over. For a second, he debates shooting Daniel a text or driving over to Lobell to see how he's doing. Maybe he can find something out, or maybe Daniel will have already talked to Lily since he's advising her, and maybe—

Maybe Tony will be more in the way at Lobell than he was at home.

Maybe Daniel won't want him around when he's in the middle of work. Tony can't help. What does he know about how to react to a violent attack on a colleague? The closest he ever got was when Mrs. Cooper's wiener dog hid in the back seat and tried to bite Pa.

The thought of his own uselessness makes him itchy and restless, and given he's basically dressed in workout clothes anyway, there's only one thing to do. Tony drops his phone and wallet in the glove compartment, gets out of the car, locks up, and starts to run.

He's gone on runs this side of the river a couple of times, so he knows the way in theory. Usually, he has his phone with him to help him navigate. Usually, he has his earphones and his well-worn running playlist.

The silence is a comfort today.

It takes a mile or so before he starts feeling guilty for leaving Gianna and Lia alone. He should have stayed and kept babysitting, even though Gigi did send him away. She could probably use the help, and she'll need to process eventually. That's when she'll need him—when she's sent him away a few times, and he hasn't let it go.

It's been a little more than a year since she told him about Lia.

Of course, Lia wasn't Lia then. Lia was a collection of cells in

Gianna's uterus that she didn't know what to do with. Tony knew something was up for a while by then, Gianna had been withdrawn and secretive for months. Then one week in mid-July, Gianna stayed in her room for days, feigning a stomach flu. By Thursday, Tony was sure something was wrong, more wrong than her frequent trips to the bathroom to throw up. Usually, when she was sick, Gianna made it everyone else's problem and moaned loudly about her misery; usually, when she was sick, she got better in a day or two.

The night she told him, it was too hot to sleep despite the rickety AC in his room. Tony lay awake, staring at the ceiling, listening to Gianna's footsteps pacing around on the landing and wondering if he should go out and say something when she finally knocked on his door.

It's September now, and the taste of the air has changed. The fresh air of early summer turns musty and unbearable by fall. The heat is still cloying despite it being two months later, though, the sweat creeping down Tony's neck and chest and slicking his hair when he runs.

Those first days and weeks, the haze of summer made it hard to think clearly and make decisions. Maybe it was because the situation was so hard, but thinking back, Tony can't find a good reason why it took them so long to tell their parents. He should have as soon as he knew, as soon as she told him anything, but he didn't. He waited and waited for her to tell him what she wanted, and in the end, it took until September before their parents found out.

Tony remembers sitting in the boiling-hot car outside Gianna's doctor's office, waiting for her to get her vitamins and an ultrasound. Before Ma and Pa knew, he was on high alert the whole time, afraid one of their friends or neighbors would see them and rat Gianna out. Hanging out in parking lots, trying not to be seen, made him feel like he was there for a drug deal instead of for support.

He remembers listening while she talked about dropping out of college, about how she couldn't go back when *he* was there.

The road twists to the left, and Tony follows the forest trail off of it, welcoming the shade.

He remembers his parents' faces when they found out. Their

disappointment was the worst of it. They've never been the kind of parents who yell about serious things. Tony got in trouble more than once for not cleaning up his room to Ma's standards, and she yelled then. But when it was serious—when Tony got in trouble for punching another kid in school who called Blake G something he refused to repeat to them—they were calm, grave, and sad it had come to this.

The day Gianna told them she was taking a leave of absence from college, almost exactly a year ago, was a very quiet day. Gianna cried for an hour, afterward, big wracking sobs that made her whole body shake with the effort to keep them quiet. He sat next to her on the squeaky-springed twin bed she'd slept in for fifteen years, stroking her shoulders and unable to do anything to fix this. The next morning, Gianna pretended she was fine, and he pretended with her.

Tony's certain she's doing the same thing now, pretending, and he should go home and get her to talk it out, to let it out. In their relationship, his role is to be there for her until his presence is so obnoxious she tells him what's wrong. He sees it as his sacred big brother duty.

He remembers lying on Daniel's couch a few days ago, how empty and replete he felt once he got the chance to talk a few things out. It didn't change or do much of anything, but it made him feel like a whole person instead of a collection of different faces for different situations. Gianna deserves to feel like that too.

Heck, Gianna's studying psychology. She should know how important it is not to bury this stuff.

Maybe it's not him she wants to talk to. He can learn to be okay with that. Maybe Lily's the right person for her to talk to, although Tony gets the impression she's not as stable as Daniel wishes she were. They went through something somewhat similar, after all. Tony can't relate to how it feels to be in school with everyone knowing you were seeing a professor; he can't relate to losing someone you love to a sudden and violent death.

He can, a nasty voice in the back of his head says, relate to dating a professor in general, and he *nearly* lost Daniel to a sudden and violent death last year. But Tony tries his best not to think about how close he came to losing Daniel, and anyway, Gianna's never asked about his relationship. In fact, she does her best to ignore Daniel when she can. She talks to him when he's around, and she knows where Tony spends his time, but she never mentions they're dating. Gianna never mentions who he is to Tony, and she's never asked why Tony chose this, chose Daniel, now of all times.

Tony doesn't know if he wants her to.

His feet pound into the pavement harder as the road goes slightly uphill.

It's not that he's angry at Gianna, he reasons. He just always thought it would be a bigger deal when he finally came out. Not that he came out in so many words. He's never called Daniel his boyfriend in front of her. But she knows. She must have wondered over the last years why he stayed at home, why he never talked about dates or girlfriends. Maybe she suspected, but she never asked, and he never told.

With the way things panned out, no one had to ask, and Tony never had to tell anyone. It's a relief except in all the ways it isn't. He doesn't want a big fuss or a heart-to-heart with Ma. He has the latter all the time, and the idea of the former makes his skin crawl. Tony doesn't need to hear Ma say she doesn't mind he's gay. She shows him in the way she treats Daniel and how she insisted on meeting his parents when they were in town this summer. She shows him in the way she still treats Tony—like nothing at all has changed.

At the top of the hill, Tony comes to a stop, panting. He hasn't run this far before, not in Rhinebeck. Looking around, he doesn't recognize any of the houses or roads. He'll have to return the way he came.

The way back is harder. He quickly gets a stitch in his side and has to pace himself.

Tony has all sorts of reasons why he didn't come out earlier. Daniel asked—of course he did. Still living with his parents at age twenty-eight strikes people as odd; never bothering to tell them he isn't straight strikes Tony himself as weird. Daniel seemed satisfied with the answers he gave, but Tony's not sure he's satisfied anymore. Tony told him he didn't want to rock the boat, that he was worried about Pa's regulars and

Ma's church friends, and he didn't want them to lose their community because of him. He said he always thought he'd wait until there was something worth telling. Something like Daniel.

Only, Daniel's here now, and Tony still hasn't told them anything.

Only, they know now, and there's nothing to talk about.

Only, now it's all said and done with nothing having been said or done, and Tony doesn't feel relieved.

Instead, he still has all sorts of things weighing on his chest, and he doesn't know what he'd have to say to get them off. The one time he felt anywhere close was in Daniel's car the other day, and even then, Tony's not sure he managed to scratch the surface.

It takes him much longer to wind his way into town in this direction. He takes a wrong turn once, and he has to pause to walk once or twice when the stitch gets to him. He could use some water. And a hat. The sun makes his head feel swollen and warm, or maybe it's the exertion.

Daniel's car is in the lot when he gets there.

Tony takes the stairs up two at a time with the last of his energy.

He has a key, technically. When Daniel and Colette had to go to a conference in Atlanta in April, Tony fed Worf and watered Colette's plants, and Daniel told him to keep the key for next time. Tony still feels weird about using it when Daniel's home. He presses the buzzer instead.

"Hey," Daniel says when he opens the door. He looks tired, the top buttons on his shirt undone and the little worry lines he's starting to get on his forehead more pronounced. "When did you get here?"

"An hour or so ago." Tony doesn't know how long he was running for. "Gianna told me something happened at the college?"

Daniel steps aside wordlessly and lets Tony in. While Tony's busy untying his laces and getting some water from the kitchen, Daniel collapses onto the couch, slumped over.

Worf trots over immediately as if he can sense Daniel's mood. He probably can, tiny gremlin. He jumps up onto the couch with one of his weird squawks and squats next to Daniel, purring like an unoiled hinge.

"Bad day?" Tony asks, padding over to Daniel once he's drained two glasses of water.

"Amelia Lawrence was stabbed in her office. We don't know by whom. The police shut the whole college down for the next who knows how long."

"Holy shit."

"Yeah." Daniel scrubs his hands over his face. "I don't know what to do... I mean, it's not safe on campus. Students only got here last week, and we're sending them home already."

Tony doesn't want to sit on the couch in his sweated-through clothes, but he also doesn't want to leave Daniel alone and head for the shower. He hovers awkwardly instead, trying to find the words. "That's awful." Those are definitely not the words. "Is she, um...I mean... Gianna said there was an ambulance?"

Daniel shrugs. "We don't know yet. We're supposed to hang tight and stay available."

"Fuck."

"Fuck is right. God, Gianna saw?"

"Oh shit," Tony says, realizing. "You probably didn't— Lily Peterson is the one who found her. Gigi was on the phone with her before. I know you were worried about her."

"Jesus fucking Christ on a tricycle." Daniel forces himself upright, much to Worf's displeasure, and reaches for his phone. "I'd better call her. Sorry."

"Go ahead. I'm gonna shower."

When he gets out of the water, freshly washed and slightly headachy from running before the heat let up, Daniel's still on the phone. Tony pulls on clothes while Daniel talks—he has six different shirts stored in Daniel's dresser, it turns out, and he should offer to help with the laundry sometime. He does try not to listen in on another of Lily's private conversations. In a small apartment, Daniel's voice carries, and Tony can't *not* hear Daniel's side.

"I'm sure no one thinks that," he's saying. "It was a coincidence. A terrible coincidence."

Daniel smiles at Tony as he sprawls out on the couch and thumbs open one of the awkwardly sized coffee-table books Daniel got from another academic and actually put on the coffee table. Mostly, they use it to put drinks on in the absence of coasters. Daniel really needs more shelf space and maybe a trip to Bed, Bath & Beyond.

"Listen, Lily, I've watched a lot of crime shows, and I'm pretty sure the worst that can happen is the police asking you a few questions. And I've met the police who work around here. They're not that scary."

Tony blinks. That's an odd twist.

"No, I'm sure— Listen, how about you stop by my office tomorrow or the day after, and we can talk about it? Yeah? Okay."

Daniel hangs up and flings himself onto the couch next to Tony.

"She okay?" Tony asks in what he hopes is a light but not flippant tone.

Daniel laughs without humor. "No. She's freaking out. Poor kid is retaking Lawrence's stupid class, and when she tries to be nice and go looking for her, she finds a bloodbath."

Lily attempted suicide last year, Tony remembers. She was in the hospital for a long time recovering. He doesn't want to ask about Lily's method. It seems like a gross question, but he hopes it wasn't bloody.

"I thought she was trying to get her classes from last year counted?"

"Mm-hm. Lawrence said no, and there was no summer school equivalent. Now Lily thinks people will assume she did it because she found the—because she found Professor Lawrence."

Tony winces. "I would say she has nothing to worry about, but..."

"But." Neither of them mentions Colette's arrest. They don't need to.

"What a shitty first week back for her." Tony wraps his arm around Daniel's middle and pulls him in close. Daniel turns slightly to bury his face into Tony's shoulder. He exhales heavily, hot against the fabric of Tony's T-shirt, and his shoulders relax.

For a guilty moment, Tony remembers Gianna, alone in her room in Kingston, taking care of the baby by herself. She needs this too.

"It's not even Lily's first week back. She was trapped in summer school trying to make up classes for two months with all the burnouts and drug users who're close to flunking."

"At least she met her boyfriend there." Tony thinks of the fond way Lily mentioned him to Gianna, as if his comfort is really worth something. With Daniel's body pressed tight to his, Tony can understand how that makes a difference. "It's good having someone to...having someone."

"Yeah. I'm glad you're here," Daniel says into Tony's shirt.

Tony lets his eyes close. "Me too."

Chapter Four

The next day is a Tuesday, and Tony has to go to work in the morning. Daniel checks his work email in bed, a bad habit Tony tries to wean him off whenever he can. These are exceptional circumstances. He announces campus is still shut down until further notice and flops back into the sheets.

Tony brings him tea in bed before he has to go.

He texts Gianna to ask if she's holding up okay before he leaves because it isn't one of her workdays, and he might not see her otherwise. But then he finds her sitting in reception when he gets there, rocking Lia in her stroller with one hand while she types with the other.

She looks up briefly when he gets in. "I'm fine, nerd. Stop worrying."

Suitably rebuffed, Tony spends most of the day buffing. He's grateful Gianna's here as it saves him the customer service work, but he's also not sure he wants to be as alone with his thoughts as he is.

He should be glad she's doing fine.

It's weird he isn't.

Mrs. Cooper's car has never looked so good.

He clocks out at five on the dot, stops for gas and groceries, and heads to Rhinebeck again.

Daniel and Colette are already halfway through a bottle of wine when he gets there.

"Do you want help?" Daniel calls as Tony brings the food to the kitchen and starts unpacking.

"That's okay," Tony answers. "Salad all right?"

"Please. You're a miracle."

Rolling his eyes at nothing, Tony starts on dinner. He cooks on Tuesdays, although he'd probably have volunteered today anyway, with the day Daniel's had. Distantly, he hears chair legs scrape and Daniel's voice moving farther away as he talks on the phone. Tony's in the process of chopping a bell pepper when Colette comes in with her wine glass, pulls all her rings off, and sets them next to the sink before washing her hands and grabbing a cutting board.

He offers her a cucumber. "You holding up okay?"

"Not really."

Tony blinks in shock. He expected a sarcastic brush-off, not honesty. He's still working out how to reply, if at all, when Colette continues.

"One of my advisees asked to meet today. A film student. He was...in shock, I suppose."

"This is one of the summer school kids?"

"Yes." Colette sighs, pausing on the cucumber. Her grip on the knife is tight. "Maybe I should have directed him to his actual faculty advisor now summer school is over."

"He came to you. He must have needed your support."

"That's just it. I have no idea how to give nonacademic support."

Tony studies the back of her head, the elegant line of her neck, newly revealed by the haircut. She doesn't come across as a warm or extroverted person, but he's never thought of her as in any way socially inept or distanced. On the contrary, he envies her poise and dignity. "I don't think that's true."

The knife thuds against the cutting board as she resumes chopping. "Sean—the student—he's only ever come to me for class-related issues. Today, he told me his girlfriend found Professor Lawrence, and he was worried about her mental health."

"Oh, shit, Lily's boyfriend?"

"Lily?"

"Lily, you know, from, uh, last year?"

"Ah." Colette dumps her cucumber in the salad bowl and starts on the tomatoes with perhaps more vigor than necessary. "Yes. Well, I suppose concern about her mental health is warranted. And his."

"How did he seem?"

"Confused. Frustrated. Scared. Very young."

"It's good you were there for him."

"But I wasn't! I don't know how to be. It's not *like* this where I'm from."

Colette's English is fluent enough that Tony barely notices her accent most of the time. Occasionally around a particularly sharp word, her voice seems to automatically soften, but otherwise, she could pass as American. She rarely talks about France, only about all the issues in America, and Daniel only ever mentions it to tease her for how French she is.

"It's better there, huh?"

Her laugh, when it comes, is humorless. "Some things yes, some things no."

"What things?"

"Well, health care. Worker's rights. Public transportation."

"Right." Tony remembers, once again, that he's very lucky he's employed by his father, who has a vested interest in providing health care and decent hours to his own son.

"But it's not... It's different. People talk more here. About everything, even the difficult things."

"Like what?"

"Race. It's a more open debate here. My sister called last week. She's been asked to conform to a more professional hairstyle at the firm she works in. Not in a way anyone could sue for, but the implication is clear. Here, that would be cause for debate. In France..."

Again, Tony studies Colette's profile. "The change in hairstyle wasn't just an adventure?"

"Not exactly."

He lets that percolate a while, but he can't help pushing. "So, all the advising stuff..."

"Is not a professor's job in Europe." Colette speaks evenly and slices the tomatoes precisely, regardless of the fact that it's essentially her only skill in the kitchen. "There's no such thing as a faculty advisor in a French university. At least, there wasn't in mine. If you're overwhelmed, or anxious, or struggling, you don't talk to your professors."

"Who do you talk to?"

"Friends. Family. A professional if you can find one."

"Who did you talk to?"

"I didn't."

Not for the first time in the last few days, Tony remembers the comforting darkness in Daniel's car while he tried to put into words the things he'd never had cause to say out loud before. How nice it was that he was driving so his hands and feet and eyes were all busy. How vulnerable and bruised he felt afterward, and how safe in Daniel's bed. In Daniel's arms. "Sometimes it feels easier, not talking about things," he offers. "Safer."

"Yes."

He pretends not to notice how she wipes at her eyes with the back of her hand.

"Going to university... My siblings all went before me, but for safe subjects, medicine or law. I was taking a risk, and I couldn't fail. It was my first time away from my family, and I wasn't entirely sure what I was getting into with studying anthropology, and I didn't know how to cook anything, and it was very...very..."

"Lonely?"

"I suppose. I didn't want to admit that at the time. I made it work."

"As far as I can tell, you did a pretty good job of that."

"I suppose." Colette smiles over at him. "I don't enjoy being out of my depth, not then and not now."

"Well, I'm sure Sean appreciates you making the effort."

They work at the salad in companionable silence for a while until Daniel wanders in.

"Hey! Why'd you let her help?"

Tony elects not to answer.

Daniel downs the rest of his wine, slumping heavily into one of the bar stools at his tiny kitchen island. "That was Fatou Nchama asking for a letter of recommendation for an application at CUNY."

"Not Fatou," Colette says. "I love her."

"I know. She's great, everyone loves her. She doesn't love the idea of being stabbed though." He lets his forehead lower to the flat surface of the counter and rests there, spine curved much too far to be comfortable.

Colette catches Tony's eye with a rueful twist of her lips. "Daniel's talked to three different junior professors today. All of them are considering looking for different jobs."

Tony's never gone job hunting a day in his life, but if violent crime were a frequent occurrence at Angel Automotive—yeah, he'd consider it.

When he says as much, Colette sniffs disdainfully. "A sign of a weak constitution, to run at the first indication of trouble."

"There's running, and then there's two professors down in less than a year," Tony points out. "Any news on what happened?"

Reluctantly, Daniel straightens. "Not much. Amelia—Professor Lawrence—usually kept her office unlocked. We don't know who might have done it or why. It's...I can barely believe it happened."

"It was broad daylight," Colette chimes in. "She was found in the middle of the afternoon. Only in America."

Daniel winces visibly.

"It's true." Colette sets her wine glass down, presumably to gesture more emphatically. "This is the least civilized country in the world, people here persist in acting as if these things are unpreventable."

"Okay, I see your point. But isn't that more about gun violence?" Daniel props his elbows up on the counter, ready to start a discussion.

"Violence is violence. If it weren't so normalized here, if there weren't school shootings every other day, do you think someone would simply walk into a professor's office and...and..." Colette breaks off and takes a big gulp of wine.

After a long moment, Tony asks, "So this wouldn't have happened in France, huh?"

"Who knows." Colette sets her glass down and returns to cutting tomatoes. "But the chance at safety is certainly a good reason to move back."

"Move back?" This is the first Tony's heard about her considering it, and given everything she just said, it's a little shocking.

Colette shrugs helplessly. "There are universities in Europe, as well. Some of them have tenure."

"Thought it was the sign of a weak constitution," Daniel snaps. "Running away."

"Daniel..." Colette doesn't add anything, but the way she looks down at the table reveals they've talked about this before. Maybe she told Tony about her sister and about Sean to contextualize what Daniel must view as a betrayal; maybe she's still protecting herself, trying to get Tony on her side. Daniel can be a little intense when he's worried about something.

The only thing Tony can think to do is change the subject. "So, stabbed in her office. Who would be that..." Tony trails off. He wants to say "nuts," but given last year's events from Lily's mental health crisis to Stacy Allan and the student she was manipulating, he feels it would be insensitive. Instead of finishing the sentence, he turns to the fridge to get out the mustard for the salad dressing. Daniel knows what he means.

The bar stool creaks as Daniel shifts on it. "We don't know yet. It's not like Lobell is on the cutthroat edge of academic intrigue or something. There isn't even much infighting in the faculty."

"She's in psychology, right?" Tony asks as if he doesn't know.

"Yes." Colette dumps the tomatoes, now much smaller than Tony would have bothered dicing them, into the salad bowl. "Something to do with zebrafish and their egg sacs. She told me all about it once at an interminable mixer, and I forgot everything she told me."

"Behavioral psychology," Daniel adds.

Tony raises an eyebrow as he shakes the salad dressing. He should ask Gianna more about her studies. Based on today, she would only give him one-word answers, but he wants to know what zebrafish have to do with psychology.

Daniel shrugs. "That's all I know."

With the salad ready, Tony slides the fresh loaf of bread from the bakery across the street out of its paper bag and slices it. "And it's not...the way it was last year?"

Neither of them answers him.

"I mean." He looks down at the cutting board. "There are no...students involved?"

"Not unless one did it," Colette says grimly.

Tony swallows.

"We're not going there." Daniel's voice is tight and harsh. "You know where that got us."

"Will you ever stop blaming me for Andrew Clayfield?" It sounds conversational, but the hunched line of Colette's shoulders tells Tony it's anything but.

Daniel rolls his eyes. "I don't *blame* you."

"Really."

"Yeah, really, Colette. I just wish..." Daniel doesn't need to finish. Halfway through the summer, news reached the faculty email server about Andrew Clayfield, whom both Daniel and Colette had suspected of committing Mario's murder last year. He never recovered from the psychosis Stacy Allan's relentless manipulation caused and committed suicide in the allegedly secure facility he was being treated in.

Daniel took it hard, though he rarely talks about it.

"We don't know anything yet," Daniel says. "Not even if she's going to be okay. Is Gianna? Okay, I mean."

The cupboard door slams louder than Tony intended when he shuts it with his elbow after getting out the plates. "She says she is. Dinner?"

They eat on the couch. Daniel doesn't have a proper table to sit at, and the kitchen island only seats two. The silence feels fraught to Tony. Usually, they talk about their days, play worst customer versus worst student question of the day. Today, there isn't anything to talk about. Or maybe there would be if Daniel weren't running on anxiety and Colette weren't trying to undo years of staunch independence, and Tony had any fucking clue what he could possibly say to make any of this better.

Tony turns on the TV and sets it to Spotify to protect himself from the noise in his own head. He picks one of the premade playlists at random and lets the twangy acoustic guitar from one of Daniel's favorite bands fill the silence.

They finish eating to the dulcet sounds of whatever the algorithm decided Daniel wants to listen to this week. When Colette's phone starts buzzing, breaking the conversational lull, Tony breathes out in relief. She glances at it and sets it to speakerphone with a wry smile.

"I'm not coming to New York to bail anyone out this time," Jeff's tinny voice warns.

Colette makes a face at the phone. "You didn't bail me out. You thought I was guilty."

"The evidence was compelling." Without so much as seeing his face, Tony can hear how prim he sounds.

"No one is getting arrested this time." On the couch between them, Daniel's hand balls into a fist.

Tony lets his own hand rest next to it, pinky outstretched just enough to reach it.

Of all the parts of last year's shitshow, Colette's arrest was the worst for Daniel. He doesn't dream about getting shot. He doesn't dream about dangling off the side of a boulder with nothing but Tony's slipping grip stopping him from plunging into the Hudson a mile below. He doesn't dream about the fight that nearly stopped him and Tony before they ever started. He doesn't dream about Stacy Allan, literature professor turned murderess, handing out cookies on this very couch as if she wasn't the reason Mario Lombardi was dead.

Daniel dreams about Colette, stuck in prison because he couldn't get her out.

He dreams about the phone call he got about Andrew Clayfield.

"I'm glad to hear that," Jeff says. "But I have very little faith in you."

God, Jeff is blunt. Tony likes that about him, though he doesn't want to admit his grudging respect for Daniel's ex. He says, "I promise to keep them from breaking and entering into any crime scenes."

Daniel shoots him a look.

"Will you also not get yourself kidnapped whilst snooping?" Jeff's voice is so dry it balances out the fact that he uses 'whilst' and 'snooping' in the same sentence.

Daniel nods vigorously. "What he said."

"It was barely a kidnapping." Tony has argued this point before. He's aware it's ridiculous and incorrect, but it makes him feel better. "I was only missing for an hour."

"Some would argue any amount of time missing is too much." Colette examines her turquoise-painted fingernails studiously.

Short of any other defense, Tony admits, "Some would."

"Anyway." Jeff is business-like and firm down the phone line. "I'm going on a two-week retreat to Malta with Tatyana, so please don't get into trouble."

"We'll do our best." The corners of Daniel's lips twitch up as they do every time Jeff says anything about Tatyana. Tony doesn't have any experience with exes, but as far as he's concerned, it's both a little weird and a little sweet that Daniel and Jeff are so mutually invested in each other's relationships. "Have a good time."

Colette picks up the phone, switches off speaker, and proceeds to ask Jeff a series of increasingly personal questions about his trip and presumably his girlfriend. She stands in the entryway, nearly out of earshot to do it, but it must be serious because she switches to French partway through.

Tony takes her departure as his cue to start cleaning up dinner.

He's almost through loading the dishwasher when Daniel shows up with the breadbasket.

"And again, you don't let me help," Daniel complains.

"Sweetheart, you don't want to help." Tony hip checks him a little to the side so he can rinse the worst of the salad bits off the last plate before loading it up. Daniel's dishwasher is a tragedy, the cheapest model IKEA has on offer. He doesn't know how to clean the drain out properly by himself, and it's Tony's least favorite chore. All the better to avoid the damn thing getting clogged in the first place.

Daniel pouts, arms crossed as Tony finishes up. "I do want to help."

"If you did, you wouldn't ask."

Tony grabs a rag, gets it damp, and heads to the living room to wipe down the coffee table.

Daniel follows, spluttering. "That doesn't make any sense. If I didn't want to help, why would I ask?"

"To be polite." Tony gathers up the crumbs in his cloth. "You want people to say no." He's watched Daniel execute this maneuver with his ma over and over again. He offers about three times to be polite, she shoots him down every time to be polite back, and Daniel never even has to get up off his chair.

In a testament to how far gone Tony is he thinks it's kind of cute how transparently Daniel has no real interest in helping around the house. He'll do it if he has to. He makes Tony dinner every other day, and while his apartment does have a sort of standard clutter to it, it's reasonably clean. But if Daniel has the option, he'd rather not.

Someday, Tony thinks, it might bug him how much Daniel likes to stay put and let himself be served.

That'll have to be the day he says yes when Daniel asks if he needs help.

Tony tosses the rag into the kitchen sink and laughs when he turns to find Daniel clearly upset, sitting on one of the bar stools and watching Tony clean. "You'll know when I really need your help, baby."

Daniel's mouth shifts downward, a half of a frown. "Promise?"

"Cross my heart. C'mere."

He holds out his hands. The playlist has switched from Vampire Weekend, a band Tony reluctantly recognizes based entirely on the front man's vocals to "Twist and Shout." While Daniel holds strong opinions about Spotify's algorithmic playlists (he thinks they signal the downfall of the music industry), Tony can't help but feel smug to hear his own influence on Daniel's account.

Apparently deciding to let the question of household chores go, Daniel takes Tony's hands and lets Tony pull him up. He tugs Daniel out to the living room, elbowing the light switch off on the way there so the little side lamp on the bookshelf gives off mood lighting. Tony needs to ask Daniel about that shelf, one Penguin classic away from losing its structural integrity. He has some ideas on how to improve it, but he needs to see if Daniel wants him to fix it or if he'll let Tony to get a little creative and make it pretty.

"You're not as cute as you think you are," Daniel informs him as Tony pulls him close and shimmies his hips and shoulders to the beat.

Tony kisses his cheek. "Lies and slander."

"Am I interrupting?" Colette asks as she comes back in.

With a grin, Tony turns to her. "No way. *Come on and shake it out, baby!*" He sings along, gesturing to her.

Tony would bet money she only joins in with no protest because of the amount of wine she and Daniel have drunk. It's worth it, though. Daniel's grin goes a little goofy as they dance around the living room. Tony likes him this way, self-consciousness at the door. They should go dancing again sometime, properly. Colette lets herself be spun around by each of them in turn, laughing as they do.

The playlist switches to "A Hard Day's Night"—apparently, the Beatles kick Tony went on last week has had some rough consequences for the algorithm—and all of them sing along on instinct.

Tony hums along, reaching for Daniel's hand again. On accident, their eyes catch and lock.

Heat flushes up his neck, and Tony lets Daniel's hand drop.

Soon after, the playlist opts for a moody indie cover of "I Want to Hold Your Hand," and Colette decides to head downstairs for the night. The door closes behind her with a quiet click, and suddenly, Tony finds himself with an armful of professor.

"Hi." He kisses the tip of Daniel's nose.

Daniel's arms snake around his waist. "Hey."

Not too long ago, kissing was a rare novelty reserved for the few times Tony found someone to meet up with. Now, it's a regular fixture in his days, and he's shocked it's still just as exciting each time it happens, the slide of their lips a little spark in the jumper cables forming Tony's spine.

He tugs Daniel closer by the hips, tilting his head to the side to deepen the kiss. The wine left a sour note on Daniel's tongue, but Tony stops noticing it after a moment. Idly, he's only aware they're still swaying side to side in the living room to whatever's playing on the TV, close and tight as they make out like they're teenagers at a high school dance.

For a second, Tony wonders what how it would have been if he'd gone to school with Daniel, if he'd met someone he wanted to be with that much earlier.

It's a stupid thought, and the pang it brings with it is forgotten the second Daniel's hand slips under the hem of Tony's shirt.

He tugs Daniel backward, opening his eyes as they keep kissing. When his calves hit the couch, Tony lets himself fall onto the cushions, knees at the edge and feet still touching the floor. The springs somewhere under them protest, especially as Daniel follows him down with a surprised gasp.

Daniel catches himself on his wrists, propped up above Tony, splayed out on top of him.

Tony takes shameless advantage and grabs his ass with both hands, tugging them together, hips aligned.

"This is nice," Daniel mumbles against Tony's lips.

"Nice, huh?" Tony hitches his hips up, and Daniel groans.

"Maybe a bit more than nice," Daniel corrects.

"I'll show you nice." With the leverage of his one leg propped on the floor, Tony twists, and Daniel rolls off him to the side so Tony can crawl on top of him instead and really make him crazy.

Daniel's neck isn't as sensitive as Tony's, a fact which Daniel takes ruthless and repeated advantage of, but Daniel loves having his nipples played with. Tony unbuttons Daniel's shirt and, with one thumb and forefinger, pinches at the right one while his mouth descends on the left.

A huff of air escapes Daniel, nothing loud, but it's the first sign Tony's going to make him lose his mind tonight. Tony doesn't know when the idea took root, only that he wants it badly enough he can taste it, Daniel begging for him. The reminder stabilizes him. No matter how at loose ends he feels otherwise, this, right here, him and Daniel? This, he feels good about. This, he feels right about.

Tony sets to it with a purpose, tweaking and tasting at Daniel's chest until Daniel's hips are shifting under Tony minutely, and Daniel's gasps have turned into little, tiny sounds at the back of his throat. When Daniel pulls away, Tony's beard has left lightly raised red marks all around Daniel's chest.

"Did I hurt you?" he asks.

"Feels good." Daniel's voice has gone soft and deep, and the reverberations of his tone throb in the pit of Tony's stomach.

With his thumbs, he traces across Daniel's nipples again and relishes the way Daniel hisses.

"Get your shirt off." Tony leans back to pull off his own shirt. "And the rest."

"Bossy," Daniel says, but he does as Tony asks, pulling off his shirt in half a sit-up before squirming out of his pants and socks.

It's more cute than sexy, but Tony's weak either way. He considers, for a moment, getting all the way undressed himself. Playing with Daniel's chest got him hard, cock pushing up against the fly of his jeans, but it's nothing urgent. Nothing that can't wait.

Instead, he pulls the lube out from the drawer in the coffee table.

Daniel's forehead pinches—he thinks it's improper to keep the lube there, which Tony thinks is ridiculous. The living room happens to be where they need it most often—and Tony sets about making the expression go away with his mouth on Daniel's hipbones.

"Ah!" Daniel cries out, a shocked little exhalation. Tony slips one hand between Daniel's legs, fingertips rubbing soft, barely-there circles into the skin of Daniel's thighs.

It's a neat little trick he figured out over the summer when the shop was closed for Ma and Pa's yearly trip to Florida to visit Aunt Bianca. At the same time, Daniel finally handed in his grant proposal, and they spent half the week naked. With the temperature well into the nineties every day, the AC unit in Daniel's apartment could only do so much, and spending all afternoon lying around on the couch in various states of undress wasn't only pleasant, it was necessary. One day, when they'd already fucked once but hadn't bothered to get up afterward, Tony let his fingertips chase across Daniel's skin until Daniel grabbed him by the shoulders, eyes wild, pushed him down into the couch and fucked him for a second time that day.

Since then, Tony frequently takes advantage of his sensitivity.

"Fuck, Tony," Daniel says, legs splaying open as he squirms for more touch. "You know what that does to me."

"Why do you think I keep doing it, sweetheart?" Tony hides his smile against Daniel's skin and keeps his touch light.

It doesn't take much more for Daniel to harden fully, his cock flushed red and pulled tight to his belly. Quick enough that Daniel can't see it coming, Tony leans in and runs his tongue around the head.

"Fuck!"

Grinning with his mouth around Daniel's dick is tricky, but Tony gives it the old college try. He swipes his tongue around the head a few more times, tonguing the ridge at the joint of head and shaft. It compels him, the sharp line of it where Daniel's circumcised and he isn't, and he spends more time than is kind, teasing.

"Tony," Daniel whines above him.

"Yeah, baby." Tony squirts lube onto his fingers and reaches between Daniel's legs again, this time with a firmer touch.

They might not go any further tonight. Daniel's strung out and gasping by the time Tony's got two fingers hooked snug and tight up against his prostate, and he doesn't always need more than that. Fully hard in his jeans now, Tony is turned on and impatient, and he could just as soon jerk himself off while he takes care of Daniel.

But then, Daniel looks up at him, blue eyes hazy. "Come on, Tony. I want you."

Tony's breath catches. His cock throbs.

"Whatever you want." His voice has gone rough and harsh.

They stopped using condoms a few months ago, and right now,

Tony misses the barrier. He needs all the help he can get to hold out. Wrapping a slick hand around himself is an exercise in self-control when he could fuck his fist until he's coming all over Daniel.

He doesn't.

He keeps it to a few unsatisfying pulls until he's sticky-wet with lube and so keyed up it's hard to remember he's doing this for Daniel.

"Ready?" he asks.

Daniel nods.

Tony remembers the first time they did this when he'd set himself a challenge to satisfy Daniel as thoroughly as he could because he didn't have the words to explain that he wanted to see Daniel again, that he wanted to keep seeing him over and over till Daniel was sick of the sight of him. Instead, he tried to show it with his hands and his mouth and his body.

Since then, Tony's ability to say what he wants has improved. But sometimes, he still feels like this, like his thoughts have gotten so tangled up in his head that it becomes easier to tell Daniel what he wants without talking.

Right now, what Tony wants is to make Daniel feel everything Tony feels for him, wanted and cared for and needed and fucking cherished with nothing more than the touch of his hands and the use of his body.

He starts slow. The couch cushions give under Tony's knees as he shuffles into place between Daniel's spread thighs. His hand is still covered in slick, and he can barely get a grip on Daniel's leg. When Tony starts to sink into Daniel properly, he has to pause to keep himself in check.

Daniel shifts under him. "Tony," he says, almost a whine.

"Baby."

Daniel's about to answer something, but then Tony pushes in the rest of the way and the breath leaves Daniel's lungs in a rush.

Tony keeps it steady, an even rhythm of push and pull. He's propped up over Daniel, smearing lube on the couch with one hand, but he doesn't care. His focus is fully occupied by the way Daniel's eyes clench shut, how his mouth drops open.

Tony's thighs ache with the slow movements, his knees and wrists, too, with holding himself up.

He slips up and thrusts hard, once.

Daniel groans, a deep, guttural sound.

Tony does it again, once, and then stills.

Daniel's eyes blink open. "Tony. Please."

So, Tony does what Daniel wants, hard and thorough, putting his back into it. The friction on his cock makes him bite his lip to have something painful to concentrate on, or else the feel of Daniel underneath him and all around him will overwhelm him.

Melting into the couch cushions, Daniel luxuriates in it. "Feels good."

"Yeah." Tony breathes hard. His pulse throbs in his cock. "So good. Daniel, I—"

"Not yet?" Daniel asks. "Please, Tony, it's so good. I need—"

Tony stills, balls-deep inside Daniel.

Daniel stares at him for a long moment. "Good," he says finally. "God, that's so good, honey. You're doing so good for me."

Tony lets his eyes slip shut. He starts moving again, as deep and hard as Daniel wants but slower. Slow enough he can keep it going.

"That's it," Daniel hisses. "Like that."

"I can't—" Tony shivers all over. "You gotta touch yourself, baby. I can't reach."

"Don't worry about it. Just keep—keep it up. That's it. You're fucking perfect—"

Tony has to pause again.

He's on a fucking hair trigger from all of it, the sound of Daniel's voice, pleasure thick on his tongue, the way he knows what Tony needs to hear. It's too much. He needs to get Daniel there.

"Can I—" he starts, but he doesn't know how to finish it. Words aren't working right now. Instead, he grabs Daniel's thighs, presses them toward his chest.

Daniel moves with him, half surprise, half pleasure. Bless the yoga class Colette drags him to every other week because he hooks his heels over Tony's shoulders, and when Tony moves the next time, he shouts.

"Fuck." Daniel tips his head back, his neck and chest flushed pink. "Fuck, fuck, fuck, Tony, right there."

Tony can't hold on for much longer. His cock leaks so much it feels like he's about to start coming every time he thrusts forward. Daniel's tighter in this position, slick and hot, and Tony thought it was a turn of phrase, but there are literal stars sparking in the corners of his vision as he grinds his teeth to hold on. Daniel wants right there, and he'll get right there for as long as Tony can give it.

"I can't," Daniel gasps, and "I need." He gets a hand between them, cupping the head of his cock, and it's just that, just that little touch. But the next time Tony thrusts in, the orgasm boils over, come spilling thickly out of the red head of his cock all over his stomach and chest.

Tony's balls ache so much it hurts. "Daniel. Daniel, please, can I—"

"Yes," Daniel says, "yes, yes, yes—"

Tony's gone before he can say anything else. The world swirls around him and pleasure shoots up his spine and knocks him nearly senseless as he falls headfirst into orgasm and into Daniel. It lasts so long he thinks he might start crying, his abs crunching tight with it.

"Fuck." He collapses over Daniel, mouth buried in Daniel's shoulder.

His mouth is parched dry, and he's wrung out. Blissed out. Fucked out.

"Wow," Daniel says.

They separate in clumsy increments. Tony can barely support himself on his wrists anymore. Daniel hisses at the stretch in his thighs when Tony puts them down.

"Here." Tony grabs his T-shirt off the floor and wipes Daniel's stomach down with it.

Daniel's gratifyingly shaky on his feet when he gets up. "We'll have to clean the couch."

"I'll do it." Tony remembers seeing some fabric cleaner somewhere on the shelf under the kitchen sink. He doubts Daniel would go that far, but a damp towel will not solve this problem satisfactorily.

Daniel gives him a look. "Tomorrow. Come on. I want to shower."

They don't talk under the water, leaning into each other's space as they get clean. Only after Tony has rescued his hair tie from the cat again, when they've lain down in bed, front to back facing the wall, and Worf has hopped up and made a space between their legs like a fuzzy paperweight, does Daniel talk.

"Hey," he says. "I...I don't wanna push, but if your sister needs someone..."

Tony makes a noncommittal sound. Gianna wouldn't admit it if she did. "Are you okay about what Colette said? About going back to France?"

Daniel shrugs. Tony feels the movement more than he sees it, cocooned as he is in Daniel's arms. "She says that, sometimes, when she's upset. It probably doesn't mean anything."

"What if she—"

"She won't."

His voice is firm, but Tony's not convinced. He wonders if he should tell Daniel what he and Colette talked about in the kitchen earlier, how much she's struggling. He could get them to compare notes on how Lily and Sean are doing, at the very least, which would calm some of Daniel's nerves about Lily.

Then, Tony remembers the hint of vulnerability Colette let him see and reconsiders. If he shares that with Daniel now, breaks that trust, Daniel will probably want to talk it out with Colette, and Tony can't see the conversation going any other way than her shutting down entirely.

Daniel bats at Tony's shoulder until he twists to look at Daniel. "I'm serious though. If Gianna needs someone, or if you need someone, that's okay."

Tony swallows against the burning behind his eyes, in his nose.

"You should get to need someone more."

Daniel's hand is a warm comfort on his hip, even through the blankets. "It's not a competition."

Tony falls asleep before Daniel takes his hand away.

Chapter Five

The detective rings the doorbell less than a minute after Daniel gets up to make his tea.

Tony, who hasn't made it out of bed yet, groans when he hears the buzzer. Daniel's going to be grumpy. He likes his calm mornings.

When he hears the knock at the door, quickly followed by her voice, he struggles upright and rummages for whatever clothes they left on the bedroom floor last night. If he leaves Daniel to his own devices, he'll spend the entire conversation glowering at her, in part because she couldn't have waited ten minutes for the kettle to boil.

The other part is that he hates her.

Daniel would never say so, of course. He's very polite, even when she isn't there, and they're talking about last year's events in the privacy of the few people who witnessed the full story. Daniel always makes sure to mention she was just doing her job. That's how Tony knows Daniel really, truly hates her. He says meaner things about Colette than he ever would about Detective Taylor.

"We had nothing to do with Professor Lawrence," Daniel says before the detective can get a word in edgewise.

Tony, still in his glasses and the basketball shorts he wore over earlier this week, peers around the corner. "Hi, Detective."

"Mr. d'Angelo. This is a surprise. May I come in?"

She doesn't wait for an answer. Tony can practically hear Daniel grinding his teeth.

She also doesn't take off her shoes.

"I half expected to find Professor Ravel here as well." She examines the apartment as if Colette will appear from behind the dumb table with a foot like a bird's. "What a shame. I'll have to speak to her separately."

Daniel smiles blandly. "How about I go get her quickly, then you won't have to."

Tony interprets that to mean, *fuck if I will let you anywhere near Colette alone.*

"That would be great." The detective sounds and looks equally bland. Tony's positive her feelings on Daniel and Colette are as vitriolic as Daniel's.

"Do you want some coffee?" Tony asks when Daniel's gone, the door falling shut behind him.

Detective Taylor smiles at him. "Sure, thank you."

If Tony takes a small amount of pleasure in spooning out Daniel's god-awful instant coffee, he won't say it. Worf trots up at the sound of the kettle boiling; Daniel always feeds him while he's making tea.

"Hey, boy."

Purring, Worf squeezes his way between Tony's legs, rubbing his cold, wet nose along Tony's calf.

"Gimme a second," Tony laughs. He fills up Daniel's strainer with his tea leaves and pours hot water over Daniel's cup and the one he prepared for the detective. Then, Tony grabs the cat food out of the fridge and puts a spoon and a half in Worf's dish.

Worf keeps purring while he eats, which is ridiculous and adorable.

Tony sets out both mugs on the coffee table as Daniel returns with Colette in tow.

"Wonderful." The detective pulls out a notepad. "The gang's all here."

Colette's smile is poisonous.

"So." Detective Taylor is apparently unphased by the open hostility and the bad coffee. "Professor Amelia Lawrence. Any connection to you three?"

Daniel shrugs. "We work for the same college."

"Did you know her?"

"Is she dead?" Daniel asks.

Detective Taylor frowns.

"You were speaking in past tense."

The detective takes another sip of her coffee. "Professor Lawrence passed away in the intensive care unit last night. I can't share any more information about an active case."

"Well, what are you here for, then?" Colette asks.

"Just...making sure none of you are involved. Or intending to be involved."

"Getting involved in an active police investigation sounds like a terrible idea," Daniel says with an entirely straight face.

Tony meets his eyes and raises an eyebrow.

Almost imperceptibly, Daniel shrugs. It *is* a terrible idea, something Tony has told him seventeen times since he did it. Daniel always argues the point that his and Tony's involvement is what stopped Colette from going to jail.

"It does, doesn't it." The detective sets her mug down. "Similarly, I would hereby caution you against interviewing potential witnesses. Or potential murderers." The last, she says with a pointed glance in Tony's direction.

It's Daniel's turn to give Tony a smug look.

"Gee, ma'am. Sounds pretty dangerous. Who would do something like that?" Tony widens his eyes as far as he can.

Speaking entirely to her coffee mug, the detective says, "An excellent question."

After a pause that drags on too long to be comfortable, Colette pushes away from the counter. "Given I have done none of those things, I imagine my presence in this conversation is superfluous."

The detective doesn't have an answer for her. Colette is right. Colette is absolutely, 100 percent correct. She did go to a crime scene she shouldn't have, but the detective doesn't know about that, and anyway, Daniel started it. The only thing Colette is guilty of is being framed for murder by an insane literature professor.

Detective Taylor seems to know she's on thin ice because she gets up and straightens her blazer. "I'm glad we've had this conversation, given I found this on your front door." She slaps a sheet of paper onto the counter.

Daniel flinches.

It wouldn't be out of place in a Nancy Drew book or a particularly campy episode of *Murder, She Wrote*. Someone actually used letters clipped from newspapers or magazines to spell out "Don't look into Lawrence."

Tony can't help it. A laugh bubbles up from somewhere in his chest, sounding unhinged. He only manages to stop when Colette glares at him.

"Isn't that evidence?" Daniel asks. "Shouldn't you check for fingerprints or something?"

"You'd like that, wouldn't you."

Colette cocks her head to the side, brow furrowing.

"I may not be Sherlock Holmes," Taylor says, "but I can tell when I'm being pranked."

Daniel frowns. "You think...we did this?"

"It's an obvious way to insert yourself in an ongoing murder investigation. Again."

"We didn't even know Amelia Lawrence was dead before you came here, and you think we sat down to make a collage?"

"I think you would have called me if I hadn't come."

Daniel stares at Taylor blankly.

"Well," Colette says tartly. "You've clearly made up your mind."

"I have. If any of you think of anything *actually* important, call me." For a moment, Taylor pauses, perhaps tempted to add something to the tune of *before you get involved*. Then, she seems to think better of it and says instead, "Oh, Mr. d'Angelo?"

Tony winces. He hoped this was over.

"I'll need to speak to your sister, as well, since she was taking Professor Lawrence's class. Is she still living at your parents' house?"

"We both are. She'll be there or at the garage until classes start back up at Lobell."

The detective nods firmly and strolls out the door.

Daniel waits about two minutes before turning on Tony. "*Gee, ma'am?*" he repeats incredulously. "What are you, an extra from *West Side Story*?"

"Oh, come on." Tony rolls his eyes. "She was speaking in past tense, huh, Sherlock?"

"I think you both made equally clear you have no intention of taking responsibility for your actions after Mario's death." Colette shakes her head at them, but her mouth is twitching.

"And she has no intention of apologizing to you for wrongful arrest," Daniel mutters.

"Nor should she. As much as it pains me to say it, it was her job."

"She should have thought about that before she chose her job."

Tony sighs. "Maybe she did. Drink your tea, sweetheart."

Daniel lifts out the strainer, picks up his mug, and takes a deep sip. It's probably way too strong and lukewarm, which is how he likes it, the weirdo.

"So." Daniel sets the mug down carefully. "I'm guessing none of us crafted the fun little message on the door, huh?"

"Nope."

Colette steeples her fingers. "Is it a threat?"

"Sounds like it." Tony studies the sheet of paper. "Why not type out the message and print it?"

"Maybe the person doesn't have a printer?"

"If it's someone at Lobell, they'll have access to a printer." Daniel considers. "Then again, it's not the sort of thing you want to get caught printing at the library."

"Could it be someone who was on Stacy's...side?" Colette grimaces at the word choice.

Tony is dubious. "Was anyone?"

"Not that I know of. And her husband and kids don't live here anymore. They won't have heard about Amelia Lawrence."

"So, it was probably the murderer."

Tony swallows hard. "Great. So. The murderer was here. And knows where you live. And the police won't take it seriously. That's...that's comforting."

"Is it too early to start drinking?" Colette asks.

Tony wants to say no and get out the wine, which means she's been a bad influence on him. "Do you think...do you think maybe the detective should know about Lily?"

"What about Lily?" Daniel sets his mug down.

"For one, she's worried people will think it was her."

"She thinks *what*?" Colette asks sharply.

Ignoring Colette, Daniel says, "What would we tell the detective? This key witness is afraid you might suspect her? Knowing Taylor, she'll get the handcuffs out immediately."

"I'm sorry. Lily thinks she'll be a suspect?"

Daniel drains his tea. "Yes, since she found Professor Lawrence, and they'd had a...disagreement via email."

"That would have been good to know."

"Why?"

Colette rubs her hand over her forehead. "Sean, her boyfriend—he was one of my summer advisees. He came to see me yesterday and was very concerned about her. I told him he had nothing to worry about."

Daniel and Tony both wince.

"And, uh..." Tony considers his word choices, trying not to piss off Daniel. "We're sure it wasn't one of them who left the message? Trying to keep you from talking to the police about Lily's concerns?"

"I hope it was," Daniel says.

"Why!"

"Because then it wasn't an actual murderer at our home."

"Ugh," Tony sighs. "Well, we can at least hope they'll be more careful about who they arrest this time? So even if the detective does follow up with Sean and Lily, they should be fine." Tony guesses it was probably embarrassing for Detective Taylor, last time around.

Colette's mouth quirks downward. "I wouldn't bet on it."

Daniel starts angrily putting the mugs in the dishwasher. It's an easy tell he's thinking about something that pisses him off. Otherwise, he'd probably leave them out until tonight. "Police reform—" he starts, but both Tony and Colette shake their heads.

"You do not need to convince us about the necessity of reform," Colette tells him.

Daniel opens his mouth.

"Or," Tony adds hurriedly, "about all the other social structures more in need of funding than the police."

"I wrote the grant proposal for the crime show project with you," Colette reminds Daniel.

"And I watch all the crime shows with you two as punishment for my sins," Tony throws in.

Really, he doesn't mind. Tony likes a good police procedural as much as the next person, although they're slogging their way through *Bones* right now, and the later seasons are dire, both politically and from a storytelling perspective. Watching it is kind of torturous, what with Daniel on one side complaining about war crime apologia every time Booth is on screen and Colette on the other complaining about poor representation of the field of anthropology every time Brennan opens her mouth. Collectively, Tony would estimate they spend about 80 percent of each episode's runtime complaining.

Personally, he thinks Angela's character assassination is the worst part of the later seasons, so that takes up the remaining runtime.

If their *Bones* marathons are what academic research is usually like, maybe Tony is smarter than he thought.

It takes a moment to get into the swing of their morning routine. Daniel has to head into college today for meetings with some council he's on—Tony loses track sometimes—so they get dressed in a hurry while Colette makes toast in the kitchen.

Worf hops up onto the bed and chirps inconsolably to make sure they know he doesn't want them to leave. Tony pets his flat head in apology before threading his belt through the loops of his jeans.

"Gotta do laundry this week," he says.

"Mm," Daniel agrees. "Here or Kingston?"

Tony shrugs. "Probably here. I'll let you know. Promised Ma dinner today though."

"If you—"

"Nope, you're coming."

"Honey." Daniel pauses to look at Tony, three buttons still undone at the top of his shirt. "If there's a lot going on, with Gianna and Lia and your parents, especially now, I get it. As much as I love your mother's cooking, I can stay home alone."

Tony swallows. He pads over to the bathroom and unscrews the little plastic dishes his contacts rest in overnight. He can't talk while he's putting them in; for some reason he needs to open his mouth while he does it. It gives him time to look for the words he's not sure he has. Gianna being questioned by the police about a dead professor again isn't a small deal. It's awful, and on top of the hectic pace at the garage with all of them switching up their schedules to make it possible for her to go back to college, the stress will get to everyone.

But no one's talking about it.

No one's said anything except Tony and his big dumb mouth, asking Gianna over and over if she's all right. Spending another whole night not talking about it while no one in the room seems to understand that he's gasping under the strain when Daniel could be there and know— Tony doesn't want that.

"I want you there" is all he says in the end.

To his credit, Daniel nods with no further protest. "I'll be there, then. Pick me up?"

"Of course."

Tony sleepwalks through work, leaving customer interaction to Gianna at the front desk. It's Pa's day off, and he's taking it, which teaches Tony to be thankful for small mercies when the detective shows up. At least Pa doesn't have to see this happening all over again.

He's not sure if his parents have forgiven him for keeping Gianna's secrets for as long as he did.

Kyle doesn't ask questions about the brief and seemingly friendly conversation the detective has with Gianna, which is also kind. Tony can still feel Kyle's eyes on him as he immerses himself in the inner workings of a middle school teacher's Audi, but he tries to ignore it.

It works until closing when Gianna steps through the door into the garage with the baby on her hip. "You coming home tonight?"

Tony bangs his head on the hood of the Audi as he straightens up. "Yeah, for dinner."

"Okay." Gianna's voice is so even, so untroubled Tony has no alternative but to believe her. "I'm heading out. You'll lock up?"

"Yup."

After a few minutes, the decisive jingle of the bell in the front office announces her departure.

Tony closes the hood and wipes it down.

It's only when he hears Kyle's voice that he realizes they haven't talked all day. "You doing okay, kid?"

Tony knows he should appreciate it. It's the question he wishes Gianna would answer. It's the question he wishes she would ask *him* sometimes.

"I'm not a kid."

"Just checking. That's me done for the day too."

"See ya."

Daniel texted him some time in the afternoon to let Tony know he's out of detergent, so Tony detours through Red Hook on his way back from Kingston. It would be way faster to hit up the Target at the Kingston Mall, but the Hannaford's in Red Hook has the bougie brand of pesto Daniel likes and also a significantly lower likelihood of Tony running into someone he vaguely knows and has to make small talk with. Anyway, if he's picking Daniel up at work, he'd have to cross the bridge either way.

It seems a solid idea all the way up until he remembers the road works blocking the direct road from Kingston, which means he has to drive through Red Hook proper. Red Hook is the worst. The intersection by the gas station collects all the rush hour traffic running between Rhinebeck and Germantown. When the road was built, apparently no one remembered people sometimes turn left at intersections, so there are ten- to fifteen-minute waits at a red light every time Tony ends up here because some bozo in a pickup has essentially parked in the middle of the road. For a hot second, from a distance of half a mile, Tony thinks he'll get lucky. But sure enough, the light turns red before more than two cars can get through. Tony gets stuck behind the goddamn Lobell college shuttle at the worst intersection in the state.

He's not kidding. Based on this intersection alone, he cannot fathom someone got paid to do urban planning in this town.

"Swear to god," he mutters to no one in particular, grinding to a sudden halt behind the shuttle, right next to the dinky little tea shop Gianna loves. "I'm gonna petition Andrew Cuomo personally to build a fucking left-turn lane."

Behind him, someone honks way too close for comfort.

Tony gnashes his teeth, lifting his foot off the brake and rolling forward the scant few inches between him and the shuttle.

He checks the rearview mirror.

It's that goddamn '07 Toyota Camry. Ironic mustache Sean sits in the passenger seat, and Lily rolls to a stop way too close for comfort. In the mirror, he can see she's been crying. Even after nearly rear-ending him, her eyes aren't on the road. Instead, she's staring at her boyfriend and gesticulating wildly. Her hands are still on the wheel, but she slaps it several times in quick succession as if to make her agitation disappear.

A wordless sound of frustration makes its way out of Tony's throat.

Neither of them should be behind the wheel. They're a danger on the roads. And why the fuck Lily's the one driving when she found her professor stabbed less than three days ago is a mystery for the ages. She seems as though she's unstable enough to leave threatening messages on her professor's door.

After another two full cycles of the traffic lights up ahead, Tony to makes it around the corner, and he spends the entire interim staring at Lily in the mirror. She's obviously upset, talking nonstop, hands flying around. Sean's mouth barely moves in response, but his hand is on her shoulder. As far as Tony can tell, this does not calm her down. A pang goes through him. He wonders if he would have been that calm, that stable at Sean's age. He doubts he would have been able to keep it together for someone else to the extent Sean is. At least Sean has Colette to talk to. It's good he knows to seek out help. Whatever Lily is going through, he can't carry it for her, and by the looks of it, trying is making it harder on them both.

Tony hopes he's never too much for Daniel to carry.

Tony shakes himself out of his reverie when traffic starts up again, and he can finally get to the store. He rushes through shopping, then dumps the detergent and some things for dinner tomorrow in the back seat.

Daniel waits for him in the big parking lot at the back of the lecture hall at Lobell. He's dressed for work in a light blue button-up, beige pants, and the leather briefcase Tony laughed at the first time he saw it. The shirt brings out Daniel's eyes. If Tony didn't know better, he'd think everything was fine. But he knows Daniel well enough by now to read the troubled tension lingering around the corners of his mouth.

"How was your day?" he asks as Daniel gets into the car.

Daniel sighs, rubbing his palms over his face. "Not great."

Tony reverses out of his parking space, ignoring the little sputter the motor does every time he switches gear. Time to check under the hood again soon. This car, it's killing him. "You gonna elaborate?" He switches to drive and exits the lot.

"Do you want me to?" Daniel shifts in his seat. "It's all about…"

"I'd rather know."

Daniel doesn't immediately start talking.

"Look, you have way more reason than me to be upset. You knew Amelia Lawrence. You're—"

"It's not a competition."

He's so fucking calm.

Tony takes a shaky breath, switching on his turn signal and making a left onto Campus Road. "Please."

It's so quiet in the car he hears the click of Daniel's throat as he swallows.

"We have to resume classes. After last year, we can't afford to have a big gap in education going on. But administration wants a police presence on campus while the culprit is still on the loose."

"Can't see that going over well."

Daniel is by no means alone in his deep skepticism toward the police as an institution, not at a liberal arts college in upstate New York.

"What about Campus Security?" Tony asks.

"You mean the three middle-aged guys whose job is to stop college kids from smoking pot in public?"

Tony winces. "They all do that anyway." He's walked across campus often enough, waiting for Daniel to be finished with a class or a meeting. The times he doesn't catch a whiff of weed are rare.

"Oh, yeah. Clint's been known to take a hit in exchange for his silence."

"Right. So. Police presence."

"Yeah. We've got parents wanting to pull their kids out of class and get a refund on tuition since campus 'isn't safe.'" Daniel even does the air quotes; Tony spots it out of the corner of his eye.

"It's not." Tony wasn't expecting his voice to sound so harsh. He clenches his fingers on the steering wheel.

Daniel doesn't answer.

"Aren't you scared?" Tony carefully keeps looking straight ahead at the road. His contacts itch.

It's a long moment before Daniel says anything. When he does, he sounds defeated. "No."

Tony glances over at him incredulously.

"You know," Daniel says, "last year, I was so scared the first night after it happened?"

It's rhetorical, but Tony didn't know. For someone who tends to overthink himself into anxiety attacks, Daniel always seems ridiculously sanguine about everything related to crime—except for the part where he thought Gianna might be a murderer.

"Couldn't leave my apartment at night all week," Daniel continues, "in case the killer was out there waiting for a second try. But then…"

"Then the killer was out there and shot you."

"Yeah. The worst already happened, so how bad could it get this time?"

It takes Tony significant effort to keep his voice level. "That is insane. If the letter is genuine, the killer is threatening you, personally."

"Believe me, I know." Daniel scrubs a hand through his messy hair. "I'm sure I'll get scared eventually. It will hit me, and I'll be a mess, but I…haven't gotten there yet. Objectively, that could be a good thing because—don't take this the wrong way—it kind of seems like you're the one who's freaking out this time."

Tony bangs the heel of his hand against the steering wheel. "I don't know what's wrong with me."

"Pull over."

"What?"

"Pull over."

Tony does, gravel spraying out behind the wheels as he comes to a rough stop on the shoulder.

"Look at me."

Tony swallows heavily and does.

"Tony," Daniel says gently. "You know you went through something incredibly traumatic, right?"

Tony opens his mouth to protest—*he* didn't. It was Gianna who lost someone important to her. It was Colette who was wrongfully arrested. It was Daniel whose friend was murdered right outside his building by his other friend. And Daniel was this close to falling into the river from a distance at which water becomes harder than concrete. But Tony can't get the words out.

"Stacy's gun was pointed at you. She kidnapped you after everything Gianna and I did got you dragged into her orbit. You have every right to be scared and to need people in your life to support you right now."

Tony takes a few deep, measured breaths, but in the end, he can't manage more than a nod.

"Want me to drive?" Daniel asks.

"You hate driving my car."

Daniel shrugs. "True. But I also hate seeing you upset."

They switch, and Daniel cursing about the way the key sticks in the ignition and the squeaky noise the windshield wipers make when it starts drizzling keeps Tony distracted for the rest of the drive.

He hasn't talked about it much, the hour or two after Stacy Allan pointed a gun at his chest with shaking fingers and walked him into the woods to kill him. Tony went through it with the police, of course. They had to write down an account of everything that happened, but otherwise, he didn't think it worth mentioning.

He remembers sacking out in the hospital waiting room with Jeff while Daniel was in surgery after Stacy shot him in the hand. Jeff knew enough of what happened to give a rough account of events when Detective Taylor showed up with Colette.

The detective reviewed the story with him over weak hospital coffee, and Tony told her about it, feeling as if he was hovering above his own body. He remembers burning his tongue on the coffee; he doesn't remember any of the words he said.

He does remember how it happened, of course. He was in Stacy's office, asking her a series of innocuous questions about how to get Gianna back into school after her education was summarily halted by her pregnancy. Stacy gave him a whole series of tips and pamphlets, all of which turned out to be useful. Tony found them in the inside pocket of his jacket after it was all done and saw no reason not to use them. He left them on the dining room table for Gianna. Stacy might have murdered a man, but no one could accuse her of being bad at her job.

That was how he got her. When Tony realized she wouldn't give him anything useful about Mario's murder based only on questions about accommodations for students who were single mothers, he tried a different tack. He told her how angry he still was at a dead man for getting his sister in the situation she was in. It wasn't a lie. The anger still chokes

Tony sometimes, how Mario derailed Gianna's life so thoroughly, and he didn't even live to deal with the consequences.

And Stacy—Stacy agreed. Vehemently. So vehemently, it shocked Tony.

He and Daniel planned for Tony to press her for information because she had access to the emails being used to frame Colette. Neither of them thought, until that moment, she had anything to do with the murder. But Daniel has this thing he says when he gets frustrated at his own tendency to overcomplicate everything, this theorem—Occam's razor. The simplest answer is often the correct one. Faced with a woman ranting on and on about how terrible it was when men took advantage of their students, a seed of doubt started to grow in Tony's mind.

Like an idiot, he pushed it. He asked if maybe, possibly, Stacy thought the murderer did the right thing. Next thing he knew, she whipped a handgun out of her green fake-leather purse and told him he really shouldn't have asked.

The rest of it was logistics. Stacy took his phone off him, had him unlock it with his fingerprint, and texted Daniel to throw him off the scent. She hid the gun in the folds of her coat as she marched him out of her office and down toward the woods. During winter break, Lobell campus was mostly deserted, so it was easy to act as if they were going for a walk.

Tony didn't think to be scared until he stood over the water with the gun in point-blank range of his face.

Maybe Tony has worked too hard to forget it because now Daniel has brought it up, he can't find his way back to equanimity, to forgetting how scared he was when reality sank in.

Tony thinks of Daniel saying the worst has already happened, so he can't summon fear. He thinks of Lily's face, tiny in his rearview mirror, shaking and crying and trying so hard not to let this ruin her second chance. He thinks of Sean, projecting calm and nonchalance and only letting Colette know he's secretly worried. Tony thinks of Colette trying her hardest to never need anyone. He thinks about how, last time, they stumbled on the murderer by accident. This time, the murderer left a fucking note on the door.

There's nothing he can do about any of it, and that's what he hates most of all. He doesn't know how to handle not being able to fix things.

They finally get to his parents' house, and eating dinner with them feels like trying to breathe underwater. Tony talks shop with Pa—it's slow going now summer break's over, with fewer people driving up to Boston or down to the city every other day. Tony agrees with Ma about making up another get-well-soon basket for Kyle's wife. Apparently, her doctor's visit revealed she has what might be early stages of arthritis as a consequence of Lyme disease, so she's not out of the woods yet.

Gianna asks Daniel if there's been any news.

Daniel tells her it's probably not dinner conversation with a sidelong glance at Tony.

"Are you going to the memorial thing for Professor Lawrence on Thursday?" Gianna asks.

"Yeah," Daniel says. "I was planning to. You too?"

Gianna shrugs. "If I can find a babysitter. I only took one class with her, but still."

"You can bring Lia," Tony offers. "I'll hang out with her outside."

"Thanks."

Daniel bumps their knees together. "You don't have to come."

Tony feels, ridiculously, as if he's being protected from something he doesn't understand. "It's okay. I didn't know her, but you both did. I can be supportive."

Under the table, Daniel rests a hand on Tony's leg.

Tony presses into the touch, trying to communicate that a memorial won't be the straw that breaks the camel's back. He can handle a memorial. It might actually be a relief, to be there with Daniel and Gianna, to keep an eye on them. To make sure whoever did it isn't getting close to them, making good on their threat.

Tony never told his family about that afternoon, he realizes. They know Daniel got shot. They know who did it. They don't know about the part where Tony nearly got killed. He never thought it was worth mentioning until right this moment. Stacy never cared about him as a person; he just happened to be in her way. Now that Daniel has pointed out why it was so important that Tony was losing his shit because of it, Tony can't understand why he ever thought it wasn't.

For a moment, he considers reaching for Daniel's hand resting on the tabletop, right where everyone can see it, and telling him he'd rather they stick together all the time. It's what he'd do if they were at home, turn it into a romantic gesture instead of an admission he feels most safe when they're together, when he can keep Daniel in his line of sight.

But he's never held Daniel's hand in front of his parents. He's never let himself need comfort so obviously in front of Gianna.

It'll keep. Daniel will let him fall apart when it's only the two of them, when Tony can find the words he needs to say, and that will need to be enough.

Chapter Six

The science building is an easy thirty years newer than every other building at Lobell Tony has been in. The sleek glass exterior and long, twisted shape, not conceived of until the 2000s, make it stand out on an otherwise cozy and overgrown campus. It's very impressive, even if it lacks the antiquated charm of Daniel's office.

Tony tugs at the top button of his black dress shirt, undoing it. The relentlessly muggy weather makes it too hot for long sleeves. He doesn't own any short-sleeved button-ups, though; they look too much like something his dad would wear.

In front of him, Lia gurgles in her stroller, batting at the pacifier dangling from the top of it. She's gotten really good at understanding cause and effect, and she follows the motion as the toy sways after she hits it.

After the noise and bustle inside got to be too much for her, Tony took her outside by the back entrance, away from the reception but still in the protective shade of the building. It does absolutely nothing to help with the humidity. The only thing worse than upstate New York this time of year is the city, where the air not only feels like soup, it smells of garbage.

Tony is maybe a little biased. He hates going to memorials for people he didn't know. Which isn't something he has to do often. It *is* weird it's happened twice in a year. Attending this one has been less painful than Mario's, at least. That was a trial to sit through, from Gianna crying quietly next to him to Colette presenting the story of Mario's life as if his death was a horrific tragedy. Retrospectively, Tony understands it was, but at the time, he was filled with so much rage toward Mario it was hard not to cheer when the students started asking questions about the rumors going around that he behaved inappropriately toward his students.

On the whole, this one has been much more bearable, not least because he's spent most of it outside with Lia.

At least Tony managed to snag a champagne flute full of orange juice and a cup of olives from the servers setting out refreshments for after the speeches. He doesn't remember Mario's memorial being catered. On the other hand, if memory serves, that event was organized by his killer. It stands to reason she would cheap out on the amenities.

Then again, Tony doesn't know who organized this shindig. It could easily be the killer, and it could easily be a ruse to get their next victim to the scene of the first crime. Daniel might be ignoring the letter threatening him, but Tony can't forget about it.

When the noise level inside begins to rise, the speeches now replaced by the low hum of conversation, Lia starts to complain. Tony pushes her stroller back and forth slowly, trying to get her to relax.

"C'mon, little girl," he mutters to her. "It's only boring grown-up talk."

She gurgles a little, squirming in place, one chubby little arm stretched, her tiny fingers spreading apart.

"You're still so small." It's embarrassing how, despite his best intentions, Tony always starts baby-talking to her. "How are you so small, huh?"

She gurgles at him again, which is close enough to an answer for an eight-month-old.

"Oh, hey, man," a voice says behind Tony.

Lia stills.

Tony flinches at being caught out in his sentimentality and turns around.

"Sean, right?" Tony plasters his customer service smile onto his face. "How's that Camry doing?"

"Huh?" Sean frowns briefly. "Oh, the car. Yeah, it's fine, good as new."

"Great."

Sean pulls out a pack of loose tobacco and cigarette papers and starts rolling. "You want?" he asks after he finishes making his own cigarette and sees Tony staring at him.

"No thanks." What Tony wants is to take Lia and go for a long walk away from the secondhand smoke. Unfortunately, he promised Gianna he'd stay close. Also, this guy is her friend, and he's probably going through some shit right now. Tony makes it a rule not to be rude to people whether or not they deserve it. Sean doesn't deserve it.

"Yeah." Sean lights up, takes a drag, and exhales a long breath of smoke. "Probably better. I'm not actually a smoker, y'know. Just, like, at parties and stuff."

Tony eyes the mix of academics and students in black and gray through the door, milling around and making small talk. "Not sure I'd call this a party."

Sean laughs. The upward curve of his mouth makes the mustache even less fitting on his face.

Tony reminds himself he doesn't hold a monopoly on facial hair. If some guy younger than Tony's baby sister wants to experiment with looking like *Magnum P.I.* in puberty, that's his prerogative.

"Nah, man." Sean leans against the building in a way he probably thinks makes him look cool. "Not my idea of a good time in there."

"What brings you here, then?"

Sean sighs, flicking ashes onto the ground. "My girlfriend made this whole thing about it."

"Lily, right?"

"Yeah. Good memory, dude."

"My, uh—" It seems weird to mention his boyfriend in this context, especially given Sean might not even know who Daniel is, let alone that he regularly tells Tony personal information about Sean's girlfriend. Worse, he probably doesn't know Daniel and Colette are friends. No one wants to be reminded that people talk about them behind their back, but Tony imagines it would be especially brutal to hear about a trusted advisor telling two other unconnected people about your relationship difficulties. At the last second, Tony changes tack. "My sister said Lily found Professor Lawrence."

"Oh, yeah, I forgot you were Gianna's brother." Sean says it like a revelation, as if he barely bothers to remember personal information about his friends.

Tony takes a breath and tries to stop himself from judging. He knows way more about this guy than he should, a guy who has so much going on he has no reason to remember Tony. "Seems traumatic. No wonder she wanted to be here."

"I guess." Sean sounds doubtful, as if discovering a stabbed woman doesn't count as a life-altering event in his book. "She's a little..." He gestures at his temple with his free hand, drawing lazy circles to indicate insanity.

Sean leans in, too close for comfort. Tony smells the cigarette smoke on his breath and notes how unsteady he looks. The skin under his eyes is red, and something about them doesn't seem right; the pupils are the wrong size.

"Just between us, dude," Sean says, "there was no fuckin' deer on the road when she lost it and crashed the car. Had to tell y'all I did it so she'd stop fucking crying."

It takes supreme effort for Tony to keep his expression neutral. "I figured. Story didn't quite add up." The deer story didn't add up, and an absence of deer still doesn't explain how they got a flat tire hitting the guardrail. Tony didn't guess that Lily was driving, though, and Sean covered for her. Presumably, she's not insured to drive his car. It's nice of him to lie for her. Illegal and bound to get them both in trouble, but nice.

"Yeah, well." Sean shrugs. "Storytelling's not my thing. I may be a film major, but I'm more interested in, like, autobiographical filmmaking. Was hoping to screen this short film about my parents in this cool theater in Germantown, but that place went up in smoke."

Last semester, Daniel took Tony to a screening of student films—not an experience he looks to repeat. Colette threatened to take them both to similar screenings in Germantown. Tony's never been so happy to see a small business die.

"So, Lily is..." Tony starts, trying anything to distract Sean from the topic of his films.

Sean drops the stub of his cigarette and crushes it with the heel of his dress shoe. What kind of college student has dress shoes lying around in his dorm room? The rich kind, probably. "She's not even here."

"Huh."

"Yeah. Texted something about how she was feeling sick, and it was too much for her when it was too late for me not to show up."

"Sounds tough." The customer service voice turns out to be a good trick for expressing sympathy and condolences while simultaneously prodding for information. Tony thinks it's probably tougher for Lily, but he's still curious to hear what Sean has to say.

"Yeah. It's...hard. I want to support her and stuff, but it's hard when she keeps changing the tune on me, y'know?"

"Mm-hm."

"And I need to do better at school this year, and it's all getting to be too much right now."

Tony nods sympathetically. "Do you have anyone to lean on?"

"Huh?" Sean looks up at him with a frown.

"It sounds like your girlfriend needs support, and you're doing your best to give it to her. It's a lot to take on though. You probably need someone to talk with too."

"Oh." Sean looks as if it's the first time he's considered that his own emotional needs are also worth taking care of. As much as Tony suspects he's a spoiled rich kid who needs to rethink his major and his grooming choices, he gets it. He knows intimately how it can be more comfortable to offer support than to admit you might need some yourself. "I have this professor. She's...she's been helping me out."

Hoping Colette will forgive him, Tony says, "That's great. Maybe you should make an appointment with her to talk about it?"

"Good idea, bro. Thanks." Sean starts rolling another cigarette, and Tony decides he's out of energy for comforting people he doesn't know and also out of patience with secondhand smoke.

Tony knocks into Lia's stroller accidentally-on-purpose. She starts crying immediately. "Sorry. I'd better take her for a walk, calm her down."

"See ya."

Tony waits until they're around the corner to breathe a sigh of relief. "You," he tells Lia, "are the best wing woman on the planet."

She doesn't stop crying, so he picks her up and starts to rock her until she settles a little. They'll do a quick loop around the building, enough time for Sean to finish his cigarette and fuck off but not so much that Gianna will come looking for them and freak out.

"What a mess," he mutters, still holding Lia. "Don't tell your mom I said that about her friends. It's true though. None of them are ready to be in relationships." He thinks guiltily of Daniel and wonders if he's ready to be in a relationship with all the baggage he's carrying from last year and all the years before. Tony hopes he is. He hopes he doesn't lean on Daniel so hard Daniel crumbles.

By the time they pass the front entrance, Lia calms down enough to go into the stroller again, and Tony realizes it's a very bad idea for Sean to cover for Lily. He shouldn't let someone who isn't insured drive the car. He'd be the one on the line for the money as far as the insurance company is concerned if they found out. If Sean and Lily tell the truth, they have a chance at getting partial coverage. Tony knows much more about car insurance than either Sean or Lily, so they probably think Sean is getting her out of trouble. Someone should let them know that's not the case. Not now, when they're both struggling, but maybe Tony can find Sean's number in their shop files on Monday to let him know he ought to change his statement for the insurance company. What a fun conversation to start his week with.

He feels bad for Lily. After everything she went through last year, she deserves an easy start to the semester, not all of this. No wonder she's struggling. Tony wonders if maybe she'd have been better off starting fresh somewhere else. The country has more than enough tiny liberal arts colleges dotted around it. Returning to the one she almost died at might not have been the best choice. Especially given Lily was on edge before Professor Lawrence was killed.

Tony feels bad for Sean as well. The guy has probably never taken responsibility for anything in his life, not if he's the kind of kid whose parents can pay for this place out of pocket, buy him dress shoes for college, and not bat an eye at a hefty bill for a car accident. He's trying, at least. Telling him about the insurance will be a load off Sean's shoulders. But now also seems to be a bad time to add more fuel to the fire of Lily's stress.

Mercifully, Sean has left when Tony returns to his spot by the back door, saving Tony from making the decision of when to let him know about his insurance. Even better, he didn't spot the olives where Tony left them in the shade past the door. Lia's playing with her pacifier again. Tony sits on the steps leading down from the paved walkway surrounding the building to the parking lot, one hand on Lia's stroller and the other free to nibble.

He makes it about halfway through his olives before the noise inside escalates again. Preemptively, Tony rocks the stroller, hoping the motion will keep Lia calm. She already made her preference for constant motion known when she was a fetus. Whenever Gianna was up and walking around, Lia was calm and quiet, but as soon as Gianna sat down, she'd start to kick. Tony remembers the first time he felt it. Gianna called him into the front from the workshop. She sounded so freaked out he sprinted to her in the office. He found her slumped in the office chair, hands cupping her belly under the thick high school sweatshirt she stole from Blake W when he went to college and forgot it at their house.

"C'mere." Gianna waved him over impatiently. "Touch."

"You hate when people touch your stomach."

She rolled her eyes. "Yeah, strangers I didn't ask. Come on!"

He put his hand on her stomach tentatively and, only seconds later, was rewarded by the reverberation of the person who would one day be Lia. "Oh my God."

Gianna nodded wordlessly. She'd been feeling it for a few days, but no one else had been able to yet.

"Hey," Tony whispered, rubbing the baby bump. "Hi, little person."

It was the first time he fully realized Lia was going to be real, and the sense of awe hasn't diminished since then.

From behind, the door opens, and a wave of noise crashes over them. Lia cries out in discomfort. It's bizarre because she doesn't mind the godawful Top 40 station Gianna likes to play in the front office at full volume or the sounds of the workshop. Lia naps there with no problem, but this memorial appears to be an issue.

Tony struggles to his feet and picks Lia up, shushing her softly.

The door closes, the noise diminishing.

Moving slowly so he doesn't jar Lia, Tony turns to see who it is. Hopefully, not Sean.

"Sorry," whispers a little girl barely as tall as the door handle. "Am I allowed to be here?"

"Of course." Tony tries to school his face into something calm and welcoming. "Are your parents in there?"

She nods. A black bow fixed in her hair leans a little lopsidedly, hard to see against the tight, dark coils of it. "My dad's inside."

"He knows where you are?"

Again, she nods. Her dark purple dress, with its little flowers, pairs with a white blouse. She probably doesn't have any black clothes. Why would she? She can't be older than five.

"I'm Tony, and this is Lia," he says, and Lia chooses to mark the moment by pulling at the top button of his shirt. "What's your name?"

"Francie," she says.

"Nice to meet you, Francie. You seem a little young for college."

She gives Tony a look. "I don't go to school here," she says with supreme dignity, and she's right to. Tony should obviously have known better. "My mom is a professor."

"Oh yeah? What does she teach?"

A little frown line creases on Francie's forehead. "Sigh..." she tries. "No, puh-sigh... Something with Zebrafish."

Lia fusses again when Tony tenses up.

"Zebrafish, huh?" he says, jostling the baby. "They sound pretty cool."

Authoritatively, Francie nods. "They're called that 'cause they have stripes. Like zebras. And their brains do stuff like human brains."

It could be a coincidence. Probably lots of psychology professors do research with Zebrafish. It's 5:00 p.m. on a Thursday, not the easiest time to get childcare. Maybe her parents brought her today because she met Amelia Lawrence too.

Except, she said only her dad was there. And she said her mom was the professor of the two of them.

Tony sets Lia down. Her nap time has been and gone. Gianna was supposed to get out in time so she could nap in the car, but at this time of day, a nap will mess up her bedtime. If her fussing over the last half hour is any indication, she's close to meltdown. Tony offers her the pacifier to tide her over.

"What's that?" Francie points at the string of beads it's connected to.

"That's her pacifier. We keep one for her in the stroller so she always has it when she needs it."

Francie comes a little closer and peers over the top of the stroller to watch Lia suck at the pacifier. "Where's her mommy?"

"Her mom is my sister. She's inside. She wanted to go to the memorial. She'll be out any minute."

Francie doesn't look away from Lia. There's something unnerving about how steady her focus is. "They're talking about my mommy in there."

"Mm-hm." Tony doesn't know what else to say. He doesn't want to reach out and touch Francie. It seems too familiar for a little girl he doesn't know. At the same time, her being out here alone feels very wrong.

Francie turns to look at him. "Why are they talking about her like she's not here?"

Panic grips Tony, tightening around his throat. "What do you mean, sweetie?"

"Daddy said she wasn't coming home yesterday, but he didn't say *when* she would. And everyone keeps talking about her like she won't come back to work, but she *loves* work."

This is not a situation Tony is even slightly equipped to handle.

Thankfully, the door swings open again, this time on a disheveled, unshaven man in his mid-thirties.

"Francie, there you are." The man runs a hand through his thick, dark hair. Francie must get it from him. "You can't run off, *querida*."

"I told you I was going outside." Francie pouts. "I don't like it when you get loud, Daddy."

The man winces. His tie is a little crooked, and the suit doesn't fit him too well. He must have gained a little weight since he bought it. There are deep circles under his dark eyes.

"You must be Francie's dad." Tony holds out his hand to shake. "I'm sorry for your loss."

"Thanks." The man who must be Mr. Lawrence attempts a smile. "Sorry about her."

"No, she's been great. Clever kid."

Mr. Lawrence's grimace of a smile becomes marginally more real. "Don't I know it. Hey, kiddo, you want your book until Dad's ready to go?"

Francie nods and holds out her hand.

From the inside of his suit jacket, Mr. Lawrence produces a *Magic Tree House* book. Francie grabs hold of it, sits on the steps, and immediately opens to somewhere in the middle. The font is enormous; Tony should have gotten his prescription checked six months ago, and he can read it over her shoulder.

With a sigh, Mr. Lawrence leans against the side of the building. He loosens his tie. It doesn't help his generally disheveled appearance. "Sorry," he says to Tony. "We'll leave in a second. I just need—I need..."

"Take your time." Tony risks a glance at Lia. Her eyes have fallen shut. Her bedtime will be fucked for today, for which he sends a silent apology to Gianna. "I can go, if you—"

Mr. Lawrence shakes his head. "No, no. It's fine. I need to catch my breath or something."

"Can I get you anything? Some water? Coffee?"

"Nah. Had enough of that in there."

"That bad, huh?" Tony can't imagine listening to other people give eulogies for his dead wife. If it was Daniel, he's not sure he'd have shown up to this. It would hurt too much.

Mr. Lawrence snorts. "It's a memorial for my wife, man. Of course it's hard to take. All of them talking about Amy's work here like...like it didn't...like this place wasn't why." The last he says with an eye on his daughter, clearly aware she doesn't understand what's happening yet.

Tony's not sure how to respond, so he makes a vague sound of agreement and hopes for the best.

"You work here?"

"No. My sister's a student." On a whim, Tony adds, "And my partner's a professor."

"Tenured?"

"Yeah." At least, Tony thinks Daniel is tenured. He's tenure-track, whatever that means. The way he said it when he told Tony made it sound as if the college gifted him a baby unicorn.

"Lucky, then." Mr. Lawrence lets out a long sigh. "Amy was trying for it. For years. They kept giving her more classes and responsibilities and putting off the tenure for next year. She worked late every night the week before...before... And what did it get her? Some whacko with a knife. You know she was alone in her office for hours before anyone found her? She went in early. Thought this was her semester. And none of them are even sorry."

"Jesus." Tony doubts the college's tenure policies are to blame for what happened to Amelia Lawrence. They weren't the ones holding the knife, unless there's another psychotic administrator hiding in the woodwork. He understands the rage though, especially since there's no one else to blame right now.

"It's all, oh, she was such a hard worker, she gave so much." Mr. Lawrence pulls his tie all the way off. "Never what she gave up. She didn't get to say goodnight to Francie the night before...and the morning before, she left before Francie was up. I've had to do her hair all week, and I *suck* at hair."

Silently, Francie nods at her book.

"I think you're doing pretty good," Tony offers. "Better than I would. And I know they're doing their best to find the person who..."

"Yeah." Mr. Lawrence gives him another weak smile. "Yeah, I know. I have no idea what we'll do without her. We live here for her job, you know? I took her name when we got married. Everything is just...her."

"I can't imagine," Tony lies. He can imagine how he would feel if Daniel were gone, did for one brief, horrifying minute in January. He's not in a hurry to repeat the experience.

"C'mon, I don't exactly look like a Lawrence." He barks a laugh, mis-understanding entirely what part of it Tony can't imagine. "And the in-laws won't let me forget it either. More jobs in IT for a Lawrence than a Martínez though. It all made sense with Amy. Now nothing does."

Tony claps him on the shoulder. "Give yourself some time. You don't need to know what to do right now. Take each day as it comes, and you'll get there."

"Yeah." Mr. Lawrence manages a slow, steady exhale. "Thanks, man. I'm really...this is really hard."

"Anytime," Tony says, although he doubts they'll see each other again.

"C'mon, Francie. Let's go home."

Francie gets to her feet, brushing off her dress. "Dad?" she asks. "When's Mommy coming home?"

For a moment, Tony's sure Mr. Lawrence is going to crumple to the ground, knees cut out from under him. Instead, he keeps himself steady, his back ramrod straight.

"I don't know, querida." He rests a gentle hand on her cheek. "I don't know."

Tony watches them set off across the parking lot with a lump in his throat. He never thought Lia was lucky to have lost her father before she was born, but it might be better than having to go through it when she's old enough to remember it.

He feels strange, as though he's floating above his body. Over the course of the last hour, he said a bunch of helpful and supportive things to two people who needed it much more than him, but what he can't work out is why it was him who said them. What qualifies him for that? He doesn't know anything. He's totally adrift and clinging to Daniel like a lifeline.

Maybe he should take his own advice to Sean and find someone to talk to.

It doesn't take long for Gianna, Daniel, and Colette to come out.

"Oh, shoot, she fell asleep already?" Gianna winces as if it's Tony's fault she stayed much longer than either of them thought she would.

"Sorry." Tony isn't sorry. He also isn't in the habit of using his customer service voice on family. There's a first time for everything.

"It's fine. I gotta get her to the car though." Gianna takes off toward the lot, carefully maneuvering the stroller down the steps and not asking for help. "Thanks." The last is thrown over her shoulder, barely an afterthought.

Tony rolls his eyes. "Anytime. Happy to help."

She can't hear him anymore.

"What a nightmare," Colette announces.

For a second, Tony wants to defend Gianna—she's a pain in the ass, but she's not *that* bad. Then, he realizes Colette's talking about the memorial. "I only caught the Cliff notes out here. What happened?"

"Amy's husband happened," Colette says sourly. "That is a man with anger management problems."

A bad feeling sinks low in Tony's gut. Francie did say she didn't like when her dad got loud. He wonders what Mr. Lawrence said or did when his daughter couldn't hear it.

"He's going through something awful." Daniel's more measured, but he doesn't deny the anger issues. "People react to grief all sorts of ways." The last, he says with a pointed look at Colette.

"I suppose that's fair." She sounds begrudging about it at best. "Still, I never yelled at three separate faculty members in front of the entire student body."

Tony raises his eyebrows. "Guess I missed some pretty wild stuff."

"Eh." Daniel makes a weighing motion with his hands. "Extreme emotions happen at funerals. To be honest, it seemed like he and Amelia had been having some issues for a while. She was working too much, he didn't approve, you know."

Colette crosses her arms and inspects the fingernails on her right hand closely. "If you ask me, he should be the prime suspect after the show he put on."

Daniel doesn't protest.

Tony shakes his head. "I don't see it."

"You didn't *hear* it," Colette points out.

"He came out this way after." Tony wonders if he should repeat the things Mr. Lawrence said, the naked desperation in his tone. He doesn't think it would help. "He didn't seem like a killer, just a grieving husband."

Colette sighs, put-upon. "All those seasons of *Bones*, and you learned nothing."

"Sure, I did." Tony grins. "Police violence is justified when it's the good guys."

Colette scoffs in disgust, heading for the car. "America," she mutters under her breath as she goes.

Daniel follows her. "You don't mean that."

They bicker across the parking lot about the merits and lack thereof of the USA, the tone light and teasing to hide their unease. It's familiar, which is why Tony started it. Familiarity is comforting. He wonders if he's been hiding behind it for too long now. Maybe he should have broken up the slow, steady routine at the garage to have a real conversation with his father about Daniel. Maybe he should have broken up his weeknight routines with Daniel to talk about Stacy and Mario properly. Maybe he should have broken up his own routines to find someone professional to listen to all the things he didn't know he needed to say.

Tony considers breaking up this routine to tell Colette about Sean needing more hands-on counseling or about Mr. Lawrence and his utter devastation. Instead, Tony says nothing as he slides into the passenger seat, still thinking about Francie and her father.

When they pull up in front of the apartment, Tony's shocked out of his daze by the sight of a knife taped to the door.

"Um," he says.

Colette doesn't hear him as she passionately defends something by Rousseau as being "easily a better foundation for democracy than the Federalist Papers." Daniel, occupied with listening closely to Colette's argument and trying to find the holes in it, hears him but doesn't respond.

"Guys," Tony tries again.

When neither of them responds, he slides out of the passenger seat and walks up to the door. Masking tape, fraying at the edges, attaches the knife to it—a hunting knife with a flat blade and, from what Tony can see around the tape, a stupidly ornate handle. The kind of thing people who are really into weapons would get, or someone who enjoys the Ren faire a little too much or who genuinely wants to kill deer. The blade is clean, but that doesn't mean anything.

There's no note, no cutout magazine letters. It feels much less like a student prank and much more like a threat.

"Daniel," Tony says. He should probably raise his voice, but as soon as someone else notices, this will be very, very real.

Tony tears his eyes away from the knife and glances at the car, where Daniel and Colette are getting out. Daniel grabs his briefcase from the trunk and looks over to Tony, to the door, and freezes.

Colette stares at the knife over Tony's shoulder. "That's..."

Tony clears his throat. "I think we found the murder weapon."

Chapter Seven

Tony's working on his Toyota. It's not an '07 Camry, which is pretty much the only thing in its favor right now. Still, he can make it run smooth again with a bit of elbow grease. The first thing he does is take out the fuel pump and clean it up. Corollas get that—janky fuel pumps. This is Tony's second pump, and he hopes some TLC can keep it running a while longer without replacing it. Every repair on a twenty-year-old car is a gamble as to whether it's worth it, so the less parts he replaces the better Tony can justify it to himself.

"You ever think maybe buying a new car would be cheaper than all the money you spend on repairs?" Charlie asks mildly.

They're sitting on the stool by the workbench, spinning circles while they wait for Tony's half day to end and Daniel to pick them up to go hiking.

"No one should buy a new car," Tony says to the inner workings of the Corolla.

He can practically hear Charlie rolling their eyes. "Fine, then. There are plenty of functioning used cars out there not in need of a complete overhaul every other month."

"It's not a complete overhaul; it's only a few fixes." Tony ignores the fact that he's switched out most of the major parts of his car at least once.

The stool squeaks as Charlie twists in another circle. "Tony. My dude. Have you heard of the ship of Theseus?"

"Yeah, Charlie. I was in the same high school classes as you. My car is the same as it's ever been."

He ignores Charlie's muttered, "I know, that's the problem."

Cleaning the fuel pump should fix the awkward moment when the car protests being put in reverse and the way it complains about accelerating too fast. Now, Tony needs to switch out the wiper pads for the squeaky windshield wipers and oil the ignition slot. It's fine. It's only another few minutes of work.

He ignores steadfastly that if he were getting paid for the amount of work he puts into this car, he'd probably recommend trading up. When the reception door opens slowly, he's just started peeling off the old wiper pads.

Lisa stands in the doorway, waiting for Blake, who's dawdling in the front office, to catch up. Tony can barely hear his voice, talking to Gianna out of his line of sight.

"That's rough," Blake says.

"It's whatever," Gianna answers.

Tony rolls his eyes.

"No, seriously." Blake rarely sounds so earnest and serious. "I nearly dropped out of college sophomore year because picking a major stressed me out, I can't imagine doing it all with a baby."

As if on cue, Lia gurgles, which makes Tony smile. He can picture her happy little face, but he doesn't want to come around from behind the car right now to let Gianna know he's listening.

"Well, I'll make it work," Gianna says staunchly.

Tony wonders what she'll do now that one of the classes she needs for her major might not happen due to unforeseen stabbing.

"Anyway, I can always pick up shifts here if things get tight," Gianna adds. "It's a great place to study between customers."

This is news to Tony. He wonders how she would feel about picking up the extra shifts he took on so she could go to class. He doesn't want them or need the half pay he gets for them. Much like her, he lives with their parents. He knows for a fact Gianna doesn't have extra expenses as their parents cover all of Lia's food and clothing. So, beyond future savings, the money she earns here doesn't impact her life too much. Great to hear the business he works himself to the bone for means fuck-all to her besides a place to study.

"That's cool," Blake says.

"Yeah. Anyway. I gotta go. Have fun on your hike."

"Thanks." Blake is letting the hotter air from the front office into the garage, and Tony wishes he would wrap this conversation up already. "Hey, maybe next time you and Lia can come."

Tony grits his teeth as he rummages through the storage containers against the wall in search of new wiper pads. The door to the front slides closed behind Lisa and Blake while he's looking.

An engine revs in the lot, and Tony breathes out in relief. It means Gianna and Lia have taken off for the day. As soon as Daniel gets here, Tony can lock up and start his weekend.

"Your niece is the cutest baby on the eastern seafront," Blake announces.

Tony squints. "I mean, I know, but didn't your brother have a baby a month ago?"

"I said what I said. We're not driving in that, are we?"

"My car is perfectly fine and perfectly roadworthy."

No one answers.

"Not that any of you have any idea what you're talking about," he continues, "because I am the only mechanic in the room. But Daniel's picking us up."

"Oh, thank god," Lisa says much too fast.

Tony shoots her a middle finger over the top of the car.

Lisa blows a raspberry in his direction. "When are we heading out?"

"Whenever he gets here. He had a thing at work today, but he'll be here any minute."

"It's Saturday," Charlie points out. "He's a professor, right? What's he got to do today?"

Tony bites the inside of his cheek until it hurts enough to distract him from his brain. "There was, uh... A thing happened. Um. One of the Lobell professors was found stabbed in her office on Monday. Daniel did extra office hours for all his traumatized students this morning."

In point of fact, Daniel did extra office hours for one Lily Peterson today, by himself with no one else there.

Tony was violently against this course of action. They spent half of Thursday night debating what to do with the knife taped to the door. Tony pried it off carefully, wearing a pair of work gloves to avoid leaving fingerprints. As they talked, it sat on the table between them, a silent fourth participant in the conversation. Daniel and Colette were against calling detective Taylor. She already didn't trust them and was more likely to arrest them for having the murder weapon than to take them seriously.

When Tony made the mistake of pointing out Lily was markedly absent from the memorial while her boyfriend attended without her, Daniel decided he needed to talk to her. Colette and Tony argued that was dangerously close to investigating the crime, and Daniel argued Lily was, in his opinion, definitely not the killer, just a troubled student.

Unfortunately, Daniel is chronically good at arguing. All that practice he gets doing it with his own brain pays off. He reminded them they didn't know the knife was the murder weapon, and they didn't know Lily was the one who left it there. Both were, at most, conjecture, and even if Detective Taylor was inclined to believe they hadn't planted the knife themselves, they had nothing to offer but guesswork.

The compromise they reached was that Daniel would talk to Lily and try to see whether she was a crazed murderer, and he would check in via text every half hour. So far, he has. The second compromise Daniel and Tony made after Colette went downstairs to bed was to triple-check all the locks and not talk about how long they took to fall asleep.

Tony checks his phone now. Daniel texted fifteen minutes ago. In the wake of his announcement about the newest violent crime to shock the Lobell community, the garage is blissfully silent except for the satisfying tear of plastic backing off the new wiper pads as Tony gets them ready.

"Holy fuck," Blake says, which confirms that Gianna somehow didn't find this information noteworthy while they were catching up.

Charlie asks, "Is your sister okay?"

Carefully, Tony aligns the new pad on the wiper and sticks it on, pressing down to make sure it adheres properly. "You heard her; she's fine." It's what she would say. It's what she's been saying, but it tastes like a lie on his tongue.

"She can't catch a break," Blake says, and Tony emerges from behind the car to see Blake shaking his head. "First, that asshole professor who knocked her up, now this..."

Tony snorts. "Yeah, she was actually taking a class with this one, too, believe it or not."

"Wow. Is there anything we can do? To, like, help?"

Because he might as well while he's at it, Tony changes out the pad on the rear wiper. "I'm gonna be honest," he says, a feat he can only manage with his back turned. "She's not telling me what she needs right now, so unless you're down to babysit, I don't know how. I appreciate the offer though."

It's quiet long enough for Tony to sort the wiper.

Tentatively, Lisa asks, "She's...not talking to you?"

Tony wipes his hands off on a rag. He's out of things to do with the car and also out of reasons not to look at his friends. "She's talking to me. She's not mad or anything. She's not...she isn't telling me if anything's up."

"Maybe nothing's up," Blake suggests.

Charlie and Lisa both skewer him with looks.

"Maybe she doesn't want to add more to your load," Charlie suggests.

"What load?" Tony fishes his phone out of his pocket to check how far away Daniel is. He doesn't want to talk about this in the garage. He's the only one here, sure. Gianna leaving means they're closed officially, and no one else will come in on their day off. It still feels weird, like his dad will suddenly pop out from under a car to ask a semi-pointed question about who made Tony's lunch today.

Lisa's voice is so kind it grates on Tony's last nerve. "You've all been through a lot this year. First the baby, and I mean, you came out. That's huge. Maybe she wants to give you space."

"Don't forget all the murder," Charlie adds. "Also, pretty significant events."

"Right." Lisa pulls a face. "How could I."

"Did I come out? Must have missed that." Tony hates himself as soon as he's said it. He chose not to say anything in as many words, which is his own way of doing things, and he doesn't regret it. It still stings that this is the first time his friends mention it.

Charlie sighs, obviously done with his shit.

It's fair. They've put up with more of it than most people through the years. Before Daniel came along, they were the only person who could make an informed guess about where Tony stood on the Kinsey scale (largely because they were the one who explained the Kinsey scale to him in the first place).

"That's up to you," Charlie says. "We can't decide for you. If you want to...change the way we perceive you, you're gonna have to use your words."

Tony rubs a hand across his face. "Sorry. Sorry. I—I didn't think I'd have to figure out the right words."

"Because you didn't know?" Lisa doesn't sound curious or angry or anything at all, and it's what makes answering bearable.

"No, I knew. I didn't feel strongly about anyone, and it was never—it was never something real enough to be worth all the fuss."

He catches the look Blake and Charlie shoot each other.

"Does Daniel know he's worth the fuss?" Lisa asks.

Unbidden, a smile stretches across Tony's face. He can't help it.

"Gross," Blake mutters. "He'd better know."

Thankfully, Daniel chooses that moment to pull up in the lot and honk his horn. Tony sets about closing up the shop.

Lisa, Blake, and Charlie crowd into the back seat of Daniel's car, leaving Tony the front. He doesn't think much of it, sliding into place as usual. If they were alone, he'd lean over and kiss Daniel hello. As it is, he smiles and physically restrains himself from asking about Lily explicitly.

"All okay?" he says instead.

Daniel shrugs.

"Tony told us about your colleague," Lisa says.

With everyone in the back seat peering at him in obvious concern, Daniel shrinks in on himself.

"Yeah. It's been a lot this week. Where are we headed?"

Tony takes Daniel's phone out of its holder, types in the security pin (it's Worf's birthday; Daniel is a softie), and enters the address into Google maps.

"Don't get your hopes up," Tony warns his friends. "It's not a real hike. We're doing Overlook Mountain."

"Wow," Daniel says. "And you call me an elitist?"

"You don't have real hiking shoes." Tony's mostly kidding. A hike is a hike, and Daniel's shoes will be fine either way. While Overlook Mountain is steep as fuck, especially to start with, it's a pleasant enough hike for beginners and athletes alike. He just enjoys messing with Daniel.

Daniel glances down at his sneakers and doesn't answer.

"Overlook Mountain is more than enough for me. It's two p.m., and we can't do too much more today." Blake's not wrong, but he also hates most forms of exercise passionately.

Charlie saves Tony from having to point that out. "And you want your post-hike beer. Provided by Blake G, which is why he can't be here with us."

"We'll definitely be done in time for that."

It's a great day for it, clear skies and fresh air, not as oppressively hot and humid as it sometimes gets in September. If it were a little warmer, it would be unbearable as there's so little shade, but the worst of it is the steep incline.

"This isn't a real hike, huh?" Daniel huffs part of the way through, his cheeks now red and his hair starting to stick to the back of his neck with sweat. Tony still thinks he looks good, which is further proof of how very gone Tony is on him.

"No." Tony only keeps his face straight because he's wearing sunglasses, and Daniel can't see his eyes. "It doesn't count unless you need some rope and mountaineering equipment."

"Oh, fuck you." Daniel stomps ahead in mock fury.

Tony watches him go with no small pleasure.

He draws to a halt soon enough, anyway, at the ruins of the old Overlook Hotel. They're more overgrown than the last time Tony was here, and the end of a summer season means jackass tourists have left trash in all the corners.

The ruins still make something ache in Tony's chest.

"Never seen anything like this in the US." Daniel surveys the surroundings quietly, taking it in the way he does with things he thinks are beautiful. Tony's had that look directed at him, and it makes his heartrate pick up.

Blake, heedless of nature's beauty and the awe it inspires in other people, walks right past them and through the door leading to nothing but rocks and dust.

"Never seen them in Europe," Tony murmurs.

Tony sometimes wonders if Daniel would bring him to one of his conferences farther away or if they could go somewhere together to relax, like a real couple.

Daniel takes a deep drag from his water bottle. "It's different. When I was in France, the ruins were...they're a tourist attraction, you know? To remember history by."

Tony swallows. "Ruins around here are just failures." He thinks of downtown Kingston, of all the historic buildings in different states of disrepair. As proud as people are of being part of Kingston, no one's pumping money into making it a real destination.

"It's not a failure. It's something manmade that's been given back to nature."

Tony could say something about the empty soda bottles in the corner, the paper napkins piled up and mixed in with the dried leaves. He can't quite find the words, though, and then Charlie asks Daniel about Lobell and his work. Daniel steps off and into the ruins, and Tony follows.

Daniel talks about Lily as they walk on. Lisa and Charlie asked, so he explains the story so far in broad strokes. Tony tunes out the parts he knows already and only begins actively listening when Daniel describes this morning's events.

"It was strange. She was upset all week, and today, it seemed suddenly as if she hadn't even processed that she found a woman bleeding out on the floor of the science building. She kept asking me about her grade."

"It's the second week," Charlie says. "How would she have a grade?"

"Oh, she took the class last year." Daniel waves his hand dismissively. "She dropped out of the semester before handing in the final paper, so it counts as a flunked class on her transcript. She managed to make up the rest over the summer, but that one class wasn't available. I think she's hoping now the professor's...gone, someone will reconsider. It was wild, actually. She was talking a mile a minute and kept laughing about the idea."

"That's cold," Charlie says.

Tony frowns to himself. It doesn't add up, not when two days ago, she was so grief-stricken she couldn't attend the memorial, according to her boyfriend. But why would she pretend not to feel anything in front of Daniel? Perhaps as a smokescreen to hide her guilt after killing someone and taping the murder weapon to Daniel's door? That seems unnecessarily complicated. To make him think she's as stable and ready for the new semester as he did a week ago? Maybe Sean was reading her wrong on the day of the memorial. Maybe her reasons for not attending had nothing to do with grief and everything to do with egotism.

Tony thinks of how Lily looked in the rearview mirror of his car, all bloodshot eyes and panic.

"I wouldn't call it cold," he says. "It sounds like she's a mess right now. Probably doesn't know what she's doing." Leaving threatening messages and weapons on people's doors, for example.

Daniel sighs. He's caught the subtext. "I know, right? I tried to convince her to go to counseling, but she kept saying it was fine."

Tony shakes his head to himself out of Daniel's line of sight. So, Lily gave him nothing, and Daniel went to his go-to, trying to herd his students to counseling as if counseling has any more appointments left to give. Tony wonders if Daniel's ever thought of going himself, if they really can help. He likes to think they can. Someday, when Gianna gets her degree done, she'll be the one with an overcrowded schedule and not much she can do besides listen to other people's troubles. He can barely imagine it.

"Well," Lisa says. "It's been less than a week. I think her mental health will stabilize if you give her some more time."

Tony doubts it after everything he's seen and heard about Lily, but it's a nice thought.

"Yeah. You're probably right," Daniel rubs across his forehead with his shirtsleeve. "Something happens, and then you get a million emails about it, and everything seems so important."

Tony turns to look over his shoulder at Daniel. "Like the stupid spring festival thing last semester, when I had to stop you from driving to campus in the middle of the night?"

"Right. Right, right. Yeah, nothing is as urgent as a three a.m. email makes it sound. I guess I feel responsible for her."

Biting down on the comment that Daniel feels responsible for everything, most especially for students, Tony walks on ahead. It won't do any good to tell Daniel he takes on too much—that he can't save people from themselves, not Andrew Clayfield and not Lily Peterson. It will do even less good to tell Daniel he shouldn't be worried about saving them from themselves. He should be worried about saving himself from them if the knife on the door is any indication. Maybe Tony should make Colette talk to Daniel about her approach to advising students since it sounds like she has a healthier distance when it comes to Sean.

"I don't know." Lisa is pensive, probably thinking about her own students and how different that would be. She'd have to plan lessons about this kind of stuff. Eighth grade is too young to be left alone with it. "This is two murders in one college in less than a year. Sounds urgent. But the mental health stuff takes time. You can't fix it for her in one advising session."

She doesn't intend it, but Lisa's words comfort Tony a little. Maybe it's okay to not be okay. He lets the conversation pass him by as they walk farther up the trail, lets himself be still and quiet as he takes in all the green around them, the crunch of the gravel under his feet.

They reach the top in good time. Blake immediately groans in relief and falls into a seat on a boulder overlooking the river. What a drama queen.

Charlie unbuckles their backpack and takes out some water, and Lisa follows suit.

Tony makes for the water tower.

His feet still itch, and he can't quite settle down. He doesn't want to sit and talk about how nice the view is. He wants to keep going, even if it's on a manmade structure instead of through the woods.

Daniel follows him.

They climb in silence, only their footfalls on the steps and the wind in the trees around them. Tony's out of breath when they reach the top, which is as good a reason as any to stay quiet as he leans on the railing.

Coming up to stand beside him, Daniel lets their elbows brush together. He offers Tony some water, and Tony takes it, realizing he's parched.

"So. No dice with Lily?"

Daniel shakes his head. "Nothing. I really don't think it was her."

"The murder or the knife?"

"Well...both? I mean, whoever did one did the other."

"We don't know that." Tony reminds Daniel of his own argument, maybe a little snidely.

Daniel sighs. "Okay, you got me. Look, even if Lily did do both, I don't think I'm in any danger from her."

"And you don't think she did it."

"I think she's upset and confused, and if she's a danger to anyone, it's herself."

"Which isn't something you can live with."

There's no answer forthcoming, but Daniel leans more heavily into Tony's space.

"Is it worth me pointing out that we didn't think we were in any danger from Stacy either?"

"It's always worth making a good point."

Tony glares.

"I promise I had my hand on my phone to dial 911 every minute of the meeting today. I'm not taking this lightly, Tony. I just…" Daniel sighs in frustration. "I let her down last year. I can't do it again."

"I wish I could say I didn't understand." Tony's spent much of the last year feeling like he let someone down, be it Gianna because he didn't see earlier what was happening to her, his parents for not telling them about it sooner, or Daniel for not being outer and prouder with him.

"So what do we do with the knife?" Daniel asks,

"I still think we need to tell Detective Taylor. At the very least, it's a threat."

"Maybe."

"Think about it?"

"Yeah."

"And not to pressure you," Tony adds, "but maybe think about it fast? The longer you take to tell her, the worse it will seem."

"Yeah, yeah." Daniel looks away. Tony knows he's not going to call the detective. "Are you holding up okay? I know this is asking a lot of you, on top of everything."

Tony looks out over the valley. The hills beneath them are still green, dark and deep. They haven't begun to turn the rich cornucopia of orange, yellow, and red the next few weeks will produce. Beyond the forest, the Hudson glitters in the distance.

"Did you go to the ocean much in California?" Tony asks.

Daniel shrugs. "Sometimes, I guess. It's pretty cold around the Bay Area, so we didn't do a whole lot of swimming there."

"That's a shame."

"Eh." Daniel makes a weighing motion with his hands. "I went a few times when I was in undergrad in LA. I ended up getting knocked on my ass—the waves out there were so intense. Not a fun time."

"That tracks. I can picture baby Daniel refusing to have fun at the beach."

"What can I say?" Daniel's grinning his most self-satisfied grin, the one Tony doesn't want to admit he finds seductive. Tony can hear it in his voice, though they're both looking toward the Hudson and not at each other. "I'm a river guy."

Tony shakes his head in mock consternation. The effect is probably ruined. He can't quite pull his eyes away from the view, the broad expanse of the Hudson snaking its way past the forests lining the banks. "It always looks so calm, this far away."

"That's what I'm saying. The Hudson's way calmer than the ocean. They're both nice to look at, but I'm partial to the river."

"Sure," Tony agrees. "I mean..." He loses the words for what he's trying to say.

Daniel turns away from the river and focuses on Tony entirely.

With substantial effort, Tony makes himself look Daniel in the eye. Usually, he loves this—the way Daniel looks at him, the clarity he gets from being with Daniel. But when he's feeling unsure, or worse yet, unmoored, the clarity with which Daniel sees him can be hard to take.

"You think the Hudson's safe and placid, right?" Tony asks. "I mean, I know *you* don't. You think too much, but...people think so."

"Sure." Daniel nods slowly.

"But then when you get close, the water's way too deep, or it's polluted, or you're right next to a shipping route, and the waves might drag you into a motor or something."

"Okay." Daniel drags the word out, clearly unsure where Tony's going with this. "No skinny-dipping in the river. Got it."

For a moment, Tony lets the thought distract him. There are places they could go for a swim, and the idea of Daniel's pale shoulders and back freckling under the late autumn sun as they sneak into the water is unreasonably tempting. It sounds like an escape.

"I mean, we could—" he starts but then stops. "Um. No, what I mean is, the water doesn't choose that, does it? The way some bits turn to poison, or the way the boats drag it in and it turns treacherous."

"No." Tony's pretty sure Daniel isn't saying a bunch of pedantic things about how water isn't sentient and can't choose things.

"I feel the same, sometimes. Like someone or something else came along and made me into something wrong and poisonous or pushed me up against some rocks or a boat until I had to give way and break into pieces."

One of Daniel's broad hands rests casually on the railing of the fire tower. "Fluids don't break," he says. It's exactly the sort of comment Tony thinks Daniel would make, except his voice is soft and kind. "They reform themselves over and over, and if you give the water a chance, it can clean itself of any poison."

Tony looks out over the Hudson again and lets his hand rest on the railing next to Daniel's. "It's so hard though." Tony's voice cracks a little, making his cheeks heat. "To keep putting yourself together again."

In an instant, Daniel's hand covers his, warm and comforting. "I know."

He doesn't add anything else, but he stands there, body angled toward Tony, looking over the Hudson with his hand resting gently on Tony's until the sound of hiking boots on the metal rungs of the tower draws them apart.

There's no reason Tony shouldn't let himself keep touching Daniel. His friends all know. They talked about it two hours ago—how they all know. But something holds him back. Something keeps him a hand's breadth away from Daniel, where people in his life before Daniel entered it might see.

Tony wonders if it would be different if he were with a woman. If there was never anything to keep...not hidden, precisely, but unspoken. He tries to picture it, having a girl he goes out with sometimes. Could he hold her hand in public? Could he kiss her on the cheek? On the lips?

He could. He's sure he could. Absolutely. It would be easy because it would be a lie. It wouldn't mean anything, and it wouldn't reveal anything about Tony and who he is and what he wants.

He wonders when it got so hard for him to be honest about these things.

For a long time, he thought he was waiting, biding his time. But along the way, he turned himself into someone who hides away every vulnerable part of himself. Every part of himself that makes him *feel*, whether it's Daniel, or the panic still thick in his chest at the thought of what happened in January when they both nearly died. When Daniel nearly hit the harsh waters of the Hudson and somehow, Tony was the one who dashed up against the rocks and decided not to put himself back together for months on end because no one but Daniel could see he needed to.

You gotta work on this, Anthony, he thinks to himself. *Daniel deserves better.*

"So, college man," Charlie says, having reached the top at last. "What do you think of hiking?"

Daniel turns away from Tony with an easy laugh. "You know, some super pretentious people go on and on about the healing power of nature and how we need to get out there and forget our phones."

He pauses a second for dramatic effect, and Tony knows before he says it, what Daniel's going to say.

"I hate that they're right."

The group collapses into giggles, and they stay there for a while, looking out at the forest beneath them.

Chapter Eight

There's a package of Milano wafers in the back of the cabinet in the tiny faculty kitchen in Daniel's office building.

In a minute, or ten, or whenever Daniel gets to the office he's supposed to be waiting in, they're going out to dinner. Right now, the locked door means there's no hot professor for Tony to wine and dine, and Tony's starving—he packed one sandwich for work again today.

He fishes out the packet of Milano wafers and tries one. It's inedibly stale. Tony fills up a cup of water at the water fountain to wash away the disconcerting mouthfeel of crumbly chocolate.

The door to the building swings open. Condelmuir, being unbearably pompous, boasts a very big door. Not only do all the buildings on this campus have names as if they house British royalty, no, some of them also look like it, and Daniel's office building is one of the worst offenders. Wood paneling covers everything. The floorboards squeak. The windows in the entrance hall—an actual room—have pointed arches above them.

In this building, it would be hard not to be aware of the door bursting open.

The sound is quickly followed by voices—tight, raised voices. Tony would recognize Daniel's voice no matter the tone. He ambles toward the entrance, trying to make it seem as if he's casually walking in that direction.

No one is watching.

He feels ridiculous.

The door to Daniel's office slams shut as Tony reaches the hallway by the door, leaving Tony to wave awkwardly at the uniformed officer standing in front of it.

Through the door, Tony can make out the gist of what is happening.

"You seem to believe an unfounded suspicion is enough for administration to accept unconstitutional searches." Daniel sounds prissy, which is a clear sign he's very sure he's right and being ignored. He gets like this about Tony's approach to washing the dishes (nine times out of ten, Tony doesn't see a need for detergent). Tony doesn't care that much about the dishes. He does enjoy how Daniel starts overenunciating his consonants and picking unnecessarily long words.

"A woman is dead," an exasperated voice says though the door. Having seen her recently, Tony recognizes Detective Taylor's voice instantly. "I'm not looking to infringe on anyone's rights, Professor Rosenbaum. Just trying to make sure no one else dies."

"I understand your concerns." The dulcet sound of Daniel Rosenbaum at a level eight priss, minimum, cheers Tony. "But I don't think a mass search is the way to go."

"It's the only way to go. And if administration doesn't budge, I'll have to use my warrant."

Tony winces.

He wonders if Detective Taylor would see it Daniel's way if she knew the murder weapon is definitely not on campus but rather in the junk drawer in Daniel's kitchen. That would be a fun way to announce his presence. And torpedo his relationship, while he's at it. It would also be a fun way to get arrested for obstruction of justice.

The officer skulking by the door crosses his arms, eyebrows rising. It's the first he's acknowledged Tony's presence.

"Imagine a thousand of him, and every single one wants to debate you about the room searches," Tony says. "Now you've got the student body."

The officer frowns. "We're trying to—"

"I know. I get it, man. But this is not the right clientele for that kind of law and order."

"What other kind is there?" The officer looks honestly baffled, but his tone is curious, not judging.

"The kind based on open conversation and consent."

The officer snorts. "You don't debate with murderers."

Idly, Tony wonders whether this guy would debate with queers.

"What are you doing here, anyway? You don't seem like..."

Tony raises his own eyebrows and crosses his arms right back at the officer.

"...a student," the officer finishes.

"I'm not. Just waiting on Professor Rosenbaum." *We have a dinner date*, he could continue. Or even, *He's my boyfriend*, to see how this guy reacts. He's probably Hudson Valley born and raised. Why else would a cop end up here?

He probably has more in common with Tony than Daniel does.

At least in terms of the things you can see easily.

The door to Daniel's office bursts open. Detective Taylor stalks out, obviously frustrated, her hair coming loose from its standard twisty updo and her blouse wrinkled. Tony wonders about that. Is it the case? Two murders in a year in what's supposed to be a sleepy precinct? Or is there more to it?

"Mr. d'Angelo," Taylor says sharply. "Perhaps you can talk some sense into Professor Rosenbaum." With a jerk of her head toward the officer, she bites out, "Jeffries," and the officer follows her out of the building, giving Tony a nod as he goes.

Tony steps to the open doorframe of Daniel's office.

Daniel's slumped in his chair, staring blankly at the space where the detective was previously.

"Hey," Tony says.

"Hi. I'm guessing you heard?"

"Enough. They think it was a student, huh?"

"Yup."

Tony steps inside to lean against Daniel's desk. "Well, it's gotta be someone connected to the college. What else do you and Amelia Lawrence have in common?"

"I know." Daniel rubs a hand across his forehead. "I still don't want to believe it. I also don't want a riot on my hands when the students find out about the room searches."

"Or for the murderer to lash out at you when they find out."

If Tony weren't watching closely, he would miss the way Daniel's entire body flinches.

"Or that." Daniel's voice is calm. "Do you think I'm insane?"

"No more than usual. I like that about you most of the time."

"But not now."

Tony sighs. "Daniel, you can either not tell the police about the legitimate threats of violence against you and the murder weapon in the kitchen, or you can be anxious about how it will affect our relationship. Both isn't fair."

To his surprise, Daniel laughs. "You're right."

For a moment, they stare at each other.

This is where Tony should comfort Daniel, should let him know it's okay, that Tony supports him. Except the stakes are too high. Daniel's choices are too dangerous, and Tony can't do it.

Instead, he asks, "You think the students will riot?"

Daniel gives him a look. "Have you met Lobell students?"

"Christ, they'll go on the barricades to avoid the cops finding all their drugs and alcohol." Thinking of Lily, Tony's not sure. If she did put the knife on Daniel's door, she has nothing to hide. If she didn't, well, she was still worried about being a suspect. A room search would prove her innocence.

Then, he thinks of Sean and wonders if he would care or if he'd want this whole situation over and done with as soon as possible.

"Yup. Can't say I would have been different. At least it wasn't only me. The administration vote was about seventy–thirty against. Which doesn't mean anything if Taylor has a warrant. I don't know why she even asked us." Daniel leans back in his chair, exhaling in a long huff. He scrubs a hand over his face, and Tony decides not to present his theory that Detective Taylor is trying her best not to alienate the college completely. "I guess she's on me because she thinks I'll try to solve the case myself. Christ, I'm ready for pizza and beer."

"Great. I'm starving."

As they walk out the door, Tony adds, "Just checking—aren't you trying to solve the case yourself?"

Daniel draws to a halt and studies him seriously. "I'm taking my responsibility to the student body seriously by providing counsel and protecting them from unfounded police searches. There isn't any real evidence pointing to a student. We don't know anything about the knife. And Taylor wouldn't believe me either way."

So, they're sticking with keeping the murder weapon in the kitchen. Tony sighs and nods. It's not worth fighting about.

In retrospect, they should have chosen a place farther from campus. But Daniel's been craving the weirdly specific Cajun chicken pizza they do at the chain that opened right on the 9W across from campus. They also have an obnoxiously fruity IPA on tap, which is right up Daniel's alley. Tony orders the plainest pizza he can find on the menu and a side order of garlic knots along with an apology to his Italian ancestors.

Their order has barely arrived when Gianna and her friends get there.

"Shit," Daniel mutters and sinks low in his seat.

"Huh?" Tony looks over his shoulder to follow Daniel's line of sight, and when he sees Gianna's dark flannel shirt and bangs out of the corner of his eye, his stomach clenches. It's probably hunger.

"Do you think they saw us?" Daniel asks.

Instead of answering, Tony stuffs a garlic knot in his mouth.

Gianna and her friends are seated kitty-corner to him and Daniel, which gives Tony a clear view of Sean's caterpillar of a hipster mustache and the way Lily's knee keeps bouncing incessantly through the entirety of his and Daniel's meal.

"Should've known there would be too many students here." Even under the restaurant's dim lighting, Daniel looks a little pale, exhausted by the last few days. "I should probably say hi."

Tony shakes his head. "Eat your dinner, baby. If they see you, fine, but you need a break."

It gets them through maybe half of the meal, both keeping quiet.

Unfortunately, with no conversation distracting him, Tony can hear every inane college kid conversation happening around them.

"I swear," one girl at the bar says loudly. "Birkenstocks! With socks!"

Two tables over, someone else explains what a rip-off the campus bookstore is.

Most immediately, diagonally across from him, Sean, who seems the type to always be complaining, complains. "Room searches," he says seriously. "Are they fucking kidding? Room searches? That's, like, unconstitutional."

Daniel winces and bends over his pizza-shaped monstrosity. "They must have already sent out an email about it."

There's a high, nervous laugh from Gianna's table as Lily Peterson wraps her arms tightly around her middle. She sips at an iced water on the table in front of her. Tony didn't hear her order food. "They're seriously...they won't actually *search* our *rooms*, will they?"

Their other friend, the tall, skinny guy with the less obnoxious facial hair—the one whose name is the same as someone else Tony can't remember, Fred or maybe Frank—shrugs. "They sure said they would. And you know the Dutchess County police are gonna blame this on a Black kid who stole a knife from the dining hall or some shit."

Daniel closes his eyes with a pained expression, likely imagining that particular scenario.

"Ugh." Sean groans. "It's basically fascism in action. We should stage a protest or a walkout or something."

"You just don't wanna go to class."

Tony's proud Gianna isn't letting herself get dragged into this. The last thing she needs is more police attention.

"That's not the point. It's about *democracy* and freedom and shit."

Gianna's eyes narrow. "You sound like you're in the NRA."

Sean scoffs. "I mean, they have a legal right to bear arms. If the police started searching people's homes in Alabama or whatever for assault rifles after every school shooting, you can bet the NRA would drag them to court. The laws are shitty, but they should still count for us even if the dorm rooms aren't *technically* our property."

"Maybe they'll change their minds." Lily rests her elbows on the table, her fingers drumming against the linoleum. "If enough people speak out and tell them it's...it's..."

"Illegal and a blatant misuse of power?" Fred-Frank offers.

"Yeah. We could do, like, a petition. Stop this from happening." Interesting. Lily isn't acting like a cold-blooded murderer or someone who would relish the chance to prove she doesn't have the murder weapon. She's acting as if she has something to hide.

Sean sprawls out across the table, forehead resting on the sticky top. "That's so much work. God, Gianna, you're so lucky you live off campus."

Gianna snorts. "Bet," she says, which doesn't mean anything to Tony.

"Come on; it must be so chill." Sean looks up at Gianna balefully. "No shitty dining hall food, more than two square feet of space, no police presence searching your room..."

"It's such a drag." Gianna pushes her hair out of her face. She needs to get it cut, or tie it up, or something. Lia's always pulling at it. "Like, I'll be twenty-three in a month. I shouldn't still have my mom asking me if I want a hot drink before bed." She doesn't mention the detective's visit to the shop or that she's probably next on the list if the police find nothing on campus.

"That sounds kind of nice though." Lily has her arms folded around herself, and she sounds wistful. She's much too skinny. She should be eating something. "My parents barely talked to me when I was at home."

Sean snorts. "You could not pay me to move back in with my parents. Playing happy families in suburbia? No, thank you. Going on my dad's dumb wilderness trips? Double no."

Tony thinks of how his mom still makes enough food for four, though Tony stays at Daniel's more nights than not. How she sat Tony down before he started his associate's degree in Poughkeepsie and told him he was an adult, and he didn't have a curfew anymore. She didn't want to bother him by expecting him to be home for dinner every day, but she did want him to talk to her when he wouldn't be, so she wouldn't worry.

Sean's a dick.

"I wish," Gianna groans around some monstrosity with asparagus and hollandaise sauce this place sells as a pizza. "But my chances of moving out any time in the next five years are basically zero."

"Must be real rough." Tony says it before the words bypass his brain, way too loud and way too angry. "Paying nothing in rent and childcare to eat shitty pizza with your friends while Ma and Pa bend over backward so you can finish college."

He notices, in an abstract way, how Daniel freezes on the other side of the table. Tony doesn't make eye contact. Instead, he dips a garlic knot halfway into the marinara sauce until it glops out the side of the bowl and spills onto the table.

"Tony?" Gianna twists in her chair to see him.

"Hi." Tony stuffs the entire garlic knot in his mouth to avoid saying anything else.

Gianna rolls her eyes. "Guys, this is my big brother Tony. He's twenty-eight and still lives at home, so his opinion is worthless."

Tony chews methodically. There was an apartment in downtown Kingston, close to the water. Big windows, lots of light. A studio, but what more did Tony really need? He didn't have a boyfriend, then, just the vague idea of maybe wanting one someday. He filled out the application immediately after touring the place. He decided to sleep on it, scan it in on the work computer, and email it to the landlady the next day.

That was the night Gianna knocked on his door at three in the morning.

Nausea and anxiety kept her up, one feeling piling onto the next until she couldn't take it anymore. She told him everything then—that she'd fallen for a professor and still loved him, that she wasn't sure if she was eight or ten weeks pregnant because she didn't understand how people calculated pregnancies, and that she didn't know what to do.

The next morning, he wheedled his dad into letting him take the day off work and drove Gianna to the Planned Parenthood in Hudson.

He killed the engine on his car and asked her what she wanted.

They sat in complete silence for over an hour before she told him she didn't want an abortion.

While she and the baby were being examined by a harried nurse, he drove to the nearest CVS, crumpled up the application for the apartment and threw it in the trash can by the door. Then, he went inside, armed with a list of things the internet claimed were good for morning sickness.

"Tell me," Tony says when he's swallowed the last of his garlic knot, and Gianna's friends have stopped laughing. "Who's taking care of your baby right now?"

Gianna falls silent.

"Ma, right? You know we're all picking up extra shifts at the garage to make up for you not being there anymore, right? And that's on top of your tuition."

He regrets it before he's even done saying it. Gianna's tuition has always been a source of guilt. Lobell's one of the most expensive colleges in the country, and while she has a generous package of federal aid and student loans, her education still puts a hefty dent into their parents' savings. She was all set to go to community college instead, but Ma talked her around, said it was a once in a lifetime opportunity. Said she should be proud.

Tony never disagreed with Ma before now.

"Geez, lighten up." Sean's stupid, smug little caterpillar of a mustache twitches on his face. Did he always look this punchable? Why did Tony feel sorry for him the other day at the memorial? "It was a joke, man."

"Wasn't very funny." Under the table, Tony feels Daniel's ankle knock into his.

"Christ, you're the perfect fucking son." Gianna sounds disgusted with him. "Sorry I don't live up to your expectations or whatever. Guess I'd better go home and be a good little penitent nun since that's the only acceptable thing for me to do."

She grabs her jacket off the back of her chair—it's eighty degrees out; no one should need a damn jacket—and stalks off.

"Gianna," Tony calls after her.

"Hey, G, you didn't pay!" Sean cranes his long, goose-like neck to see after her, but she ducks between two twentysomethings in basketball jerseys and leaves out the door.

Lily elbows her boyfriend. "Shut up, Sean. We can spot her."

"She better pay us back."

"He's a real prince," Tony mutters. "I can tell why Gigi's friends with him."

"Tony." Daniel's voice is gentle, probably more so than Tony has a right to at the moment.

Sighing, Tony rubs a hand across his forehead. "Sorry. Sorry. I...I just..."

"Hey, it's okay. Wanna get out of here?"

Wordlessly, Tony nods.

Daniel takes care of the check. He nods to Lily and Sean and their friend as they leave, wishes them a nice night.

Tony wonders what they think of him and Daniel here together. If they can guess.

"Hope I didn't make you look bad in front of your students," he mutters in the car.

Daniel laughs. "Tony, I caught a murderer last semester. A little family argument can't kill my street cred."

"Your street cred," Tony repeats incredulously.

"I said what I said." With the sun setting around them, Tony can't see it properly but he thinks the tips of Daniel's ears are going red.

It's an effort, but Tony forces himself to relax, his shoulder blades pressed against the driver's seat instead of hunched up over the wheel and lets go of all the frustration coiled under his ribs with a short, forced laugh. "You're adorable."

"Excuse you." Daniel studiously examines his fingernails. "I am an adult, which means I am dignified and graceful."

Tony pulls into the tiny parking lot by Daniel's building, right under the streetlight that's been out since June but apparently isn't the landlord's job to fix. "Whatever you say, baby."

Daniel pokes him in retaliation, which means Tony has free range to slap his ass as he walks up the stairs in front of Tony, eliciting a squeak that belies Daniel's claims of dignity.

"Can't resist," Tony says when Daniel glares at him.

"A likely story." Daniel turns away to unlock the door. This leaves Tony free to crowd in close behind him, cupping his ass through his pants. He's aware, in a distant way, that Daniel's clothes are not sexy. He's wearing a slightly creased light green button-down and a pair of gray pants. It's not that they're tailor-made; it's that they look so much like clothes Daniel would wear they've become attractive to Tony because he likes the way Daniel looks.

Plus, he gets exclusive access to the ass under those pants, which is a bonus.

"You're a tease," Daniel accuses as he gets the door unlocked and steps out of Tony's grip.

"Trust me, sweetheart." Tony follows close behind, wraps his arms around Daniel's waist, and presses his lips against the side of Daniel's neck. "I fully intend on following through."

Daniel kicks off his shoes and tilts his head, giving Tony better access. "Tell me more."

Too busy kissing the juncture of Daniel's neck and shoulder, Tony doesn't answer. Instead, he slips his fingers into Daniel's shirt, unbuttoning it slowly. With his chest pressed to Daniel's back, he pushes slightly, propelling Daniel toward the living room. They should probably have sex in the bed at least sometimes, but why bother when the living room carpet is plush and soft, and Daniel's letting Tony unbutton and unzip his pants before sinking them both to the floor?

He can't say it's intentional, but he likes the picture it makes, Daniel sprawled across the carpet, a long line of pale skin, arms above his head with Tony hovering over him, kissing him senseless.

Daniel reaches out to touch him, and Tony stops him with a firm grasp on his wrists.

"No." The gravel in Tony's voice is a surprise, even to himself. "Keep them there."

Daniel's mouth opens and then closes as if he reconsidered saying something. "Make me," he says after a second's pause. Despite the words, he puts both arms over his head again.

Rearing back to balance on his knees, Tony undoes his belt buckle and pulls his belt out of its loops. Between his legs, Daniel shifts. Tony wraps the belt around both of Daniel's wrists and cinches it shut.

"Yeah?" Tony asks after he's finished, a little belated.

Daniel nods furiously, his head rubbing against the carpet under him, causing his hair to frizz.

There's no game plan here. Tony didn't start this with anything specific in mind. The last time they tried something in this vein, it was prearranged, discussed, and Tony knew exactly what he'd do. This time, he just goes for it. He runs soft hands up and down Daniel's sides, the way he knows will make Daniel squirm. He kisses and licks at Daniel's nipples until Daniel pants out little breathless gasps. He strokes Daniel's hard cock, slow and loose enough it won't get Daniel off so much as tease him mercilessly.

Tony still has his jeans on, and it's gone from mildly uncomfortable to downright painful in the time it takes Daniel to start pleading with him.

"Come on, Tony, please. Do something."

"I am." Tony says it lightly, guilelessly, as he continues to go as slowly as he possibly can. With his free hand, he unbuttons and unzips his pants. Immediately, his cock swells in the looser fabric of his boxer briefs.

For an instant, Tony tightens his hand around Daniel's cock.

Daniel's hips twist. *"Tony."*

Immediately, Tony takes his hand away.

Daniel *whines*. It's really gratifying.

Tony rocks back onto his heels and stands. He strips off his pants and socks, and then pulls his shirt off over his head. It catches on his ponytail, and he ends up pulling that out as well, but he can't say he cares. Not with Daniel shifting restlessly on the carpet, waiting for him. He grabs the lube from the coffee table drawer and settles over Daniel again, one knee either side of his hips.

The brush of his cock against Daniel's sends a shiver down Tony's spine.

Daniel's eyes go wide as Tony shifts his hips to start a slow, filthy grind. His mouth parts, and he lets out a stuttering, "Ah—ah, yes."

It's too dry and not nearly enough to get either of them there, but it feels good, heat and sweat trapped between their bodies. Tony dips down to kiss Daniel, arching his spine to keep their hips aligned as he does. Daniel kisses him back sloppily, a sure sign he's pretty far gone.

With Daniel distracted, Tony gropes for the lube and slicks up his fingers. He rubs them across his opening, quick, perfunctory, not terribly interested in drawing this out. When they first started doing this, when it was brand new for Tony, it was always kind of a production. He would make sure to shower thoroughly in advance, worried about any possible unattractive smell or sight. In a rare and uncharacteristically sanguine turn, Daniel assured him he didn't need to worry too much, and if a person were going to kick up a fuss about unexpected or unpleasant bodily fluids, they probably weren't ready to have sex in the first place.

At the same time, Daniel used to spend ages opening him up, fingering him and getting him relaxed, sometimes so thoroughly they didn't make it to the main event. It led to a lot of slow, sweet, romantic sex Tony loved.

That's not what he's after tonight.

He's gotten used to this, is the thing. He knows how to do a decent risk assessment of what he's eaten in the last day or two, when he last used the bathroom, and when he last showered. He knows he doesn't need much prep, not when Daniel's this hard, not when Tony wants to *feel* it.

He just needs to take it slow to start.

When Tony wraps his slick hand around Daniel's cock, Daniel's hips twitch upward so hard he nearly unseats him. Tony strokes Daniel the way he wants but only for as long as it takes to get him wet.

He lets his hips hover over Daniel for a long moment, rubbing the head of Daniel's cock against his hole until Daniel breathes out "please" in between hungry, panting sounds.

Finally, Tony grabs the base of Daniel's cock in a firm grip and sinks onto it slowly. He keeps his breathing steady, in and out, keeps relaxed against the urge to tighten up.

"You feel good," he sighs as he eases down as far as he can go.

"You feel..." Daniel's trapped hands flex. "You feel...God, Tony..."

Tony keeps it slow to start, teasing. He circles his hips gently until he can get the angle right, massaging his prostate with the head of Daniel's dick. It's not enough for Daniel, definitely not, but it feels fantastic. Tony balances on his knees, circling his hips in a slow rhythm, and wraps his hand around his own cock.

He groans and lets his eyes flutter shut.

"The way you look..." Daniel's one to talk. He's flushed under Tony, panting for air as his wrists strain against the belt.

"Yeah?" Tony sinks a little deeper, pushes his chest out, and arches his spine more. "Tell me."

"You look amazing. Fucking yourself on me, *using* me."

"You like that, huh, baby?"

"I like being yours," Daniel says, way too sincere and way too erotic.

Tony rests his hands either side of Daniel's face and gives up the game. He starts to fuck himself properly, harder as Daniel's knees draw up behind him, and his feet plant on the floor. "Come on. Give it to me."

Usually, Daniel would grip his hips and use the leverage to hold Tony still and fuck up into him. Without the option, all he can do is use his legs and ass, making the fuck uneven, hard and soft by turns. It's a tease as much as it's fucking hot. When Tony's knees skid on the carpet, his dick bounces against his own stomach, and rasps against the hair on Daniel's. Sticky drops of precome leak from the head in the sweaty space between their bodies.

Tony wants it so badly.

He scrambles for the belt buckle, tugs it out, and then he's got Daniel's big hand on his hip, holding him down while Daniel drives up into him.

Tony makes sounds he'll be embarrassed about later, moaning high and tight as he gets what he wants.

"I'm not gonna last," Daniel pants. "You feel too good, fuck, Tony…"

"C'mon. Take what you want. I want you to. Want to be dripping with you. I need you, Daniel, need you, don't—don't stop, don't leave me."

It's too much, too honest, and relief fills Tony when Daniel twists enough to get his other hand out of the tangle of the belt and between their bodies. He circles his thumb and forefinger around Tony's cock and fucks his hips in hard, right where Tony needs it.

Tony comes immediately, crying out against Daniel's skin when his knees buckle with the force of it, and he can't stay upright anymore. His cock still drools out slow ropes of jizz when Daniel grabs his other hip and fucks up one more time with a groan.

His face is flushed red, his eyes are closed, and his mouth is open. He's so fucking beautiful, and he's all Tony's.

After, it takes Tony a few tries to stand up properly. One of his feet fell asleep, circulation cut off from how he's been sitting on it. Rug burn covers both his knees. Daniel has to help him stay upright in the shower, snickering.

"Shut up," Tony mumbles. "Worth it."

"Not arguing." Daniel strokes a wet hand through Tony's hair. "Not sure why you didn't go for the handcuffs we specifically purchased for that kind of thing, but…"

"Oh fuck." In early August, they went down to the city to visit Daniel's grad school roommate, Paul. They took an afternoon to go to a sex shop, specifically because of how quickly they'd both come when Tony held Daniel's hands down against the bed one time. They haven't gotten around to trying the cuffs out yet. "I totally forgot."

Daniel laughs, letting his head fall back in the spray. "You were a little focused."

Tony drops his head forward to Daniel's shoulder and breathes for a while.

"Hey, Tony?"

"Mm?"

"I'm sorry I'm putting you through this."

"Don't wanna talk about it."

"Okay. But, um...about before, with Gianna..."

"*Really* don't wanna talk about it."

He feels more than hears Daniel sigh.

"Okay," Daniel says. "If you change your mind..."

"I'll let you know."

Under Tony's head, Daniel's chest rises and falls evenly. If he's very quiet, Tony can feel Daniel's steady heartbeat. He doesn't want to talk about it; he wasn't lying. He doesn't want to fight. But he can't quite let it go. "Hey, Daniel?"

"Hm?"

"Why's Lily so upset about the room searches? If she was the one who left the knife?"

Daniel's shoulders draw tight beneath him. "Good question."

"You still don't think she..."

"No." Daniel heaves a big sigh, hampered by Tony's weight. "I don't think she's the one who left it. It's probably normal student things she doesn't want the police to find. Alcohol and weed, right? She was worried about being a suspect just because she found Amelia Lawrence, remember?"

Daniel's hand settles heavily on Tony's head, rubbing softly against the shaved sides.

Tony leans into it. "I still have a bad feeling about her. You might be right about the knife, but I think maybe she needs more help than you can give her."

Daniel doesn't answer.

Like this, with his face buried in Daniel's chest, it's easy to add, "I think maybe I need more help than you can give me."

"Tony..."

"No, I mean...I was out of line tonight. I don't want to put all that on you."

Daniel's hand stays steady in his hair. "Let me worry about what I can take, okay?"

Tony wants to protest. A relationship should be a two-way street, and if all the restless, residual anger is too much for him, how can he expect Daniel to take it on? But Daniel's fingers stroke his head so slowly, Daniel's body is warm and safe under his, and Tony drifts off before he can.

Chapter Nine

M orning finds Tony flat on his stomach on the living room floor, trying to reach his hair tie.

"Worf," he growls out.

The cat blinks at him impassively from under the couch.

"C'mon, man. I'm gonna be late for work."

He shifts forward until he can move the couch just a little with his shoulder and grasps the edge of the hair tie.

"You have real toys," he tells Worf and boops his nose for good measure. Worf squawks at him in response.

Getting up off the floor is a mistake. His thighs burn, and his knees rub uncomfortably against the fabric of his jeans.

"Told you." Daniel watches the entire exchange from an elevated vantage point, leaning against the kitchen doorway and sipping his tea. "You sure you don't want some ibuprofen?"

Tony grits his teeth. Taking painkillers for sex-related injuries seems wrong somehow, like an admission of how desperate he felt last night for Daniel to stay with him, to stay safe. In the light of day, it's more than a little embarrassing. "I'll live."

"Mm-hm." Daniel takes a long sip. "You'll live to regret riding me into the floor after about two hours of your highly physical job."

Tony's fairly sure it'll be twenty minutes, but fuck if he'll admit to that. "Baby." He presses a wet kiss to Daniel's cheek. "I could never regret it."

Daniel scoffs, but he looks pleased enough that Tony counts it as a win. The good feeling carries him through the drive to Kingston, even when his engine starts making a wheezing noise partway across the river.

"Morning, Pa," he calls as he drops his wallet and phone in his tray by the workbench.

"Morning," comes from somewhere in the depths of the garage, probably where Pa is doing inventory. He's not under a car, which is progress. "How you doing, kiddo?"

"Fine." Tony's knees still ache, same as his hips. Sore enough that it'll make sitting down a little uncomfortable, he's not getting fucked again anytime in the next couple of days. None of these are things he especially wants to share with his father.

Pa ambles out from the storage closet in the back where they keep spare lights and wipers.

"Inventory?" Tony asks.

"Mm. Need to put in an order today or tomorrow. We're low on headlights."

Tony shakes his head. "The fucking kid from Lobell the other day with his deer story."

"That was one light. Carl brought us in another two last week, remember?"

"I guess." Tony can't blame Gianna's friends for absolutely everything stressful in his life. He wants to because he's angry at her, but he's self-aware enough to realize it's not a productive emotion.

"You sure you're okay?" Pa leans against one of the pillars, studying Tony too closely.

Tony looks away as he pulls a coverall out of the closet. "Uh-huh." He hides a wince as his hips protest the movement of getting into the coverall.

He's almost convinced himself this conversation is done when Pa continues.

"You seemed a little upset at dinner the other night."

The other night, Tony reminds himself. Before the weekend. After he broke down in his stupid car because his stupid feelings are all over the place. Before he yelled at his sister because he still hasn't worked through a goddamn bit of it.

"Is...Daniel all right?"

Tony freezes. Pa never asks about Daniel by name. He talks around it, mentions Tony staying over in Rhinebeck obliquely, or says "your professor friend."

"Yeah." Tony's voice is rough, which is weird. "I mean, sort of. The professor—the stabbing..."

"Scary stuff."

"Yeah." Tony forces himself to meet Pa's eye. "And he has a whole bunch of stuff to take care of now he's the dean. He's been pretty stressed."

"Right." Pa doesn't say anything else, but the way he keeps looking at Tony is enough to make Tony crack. He always gets that expression when he knows something is up.

The first time Tony drank a shitty, lukewarm PBR at a bonfire in the woods when he was fifteen, it took Pa all of three minutes. Waiting up in the living room with the manual to the latest Buick model and his reading glasses, he gave Tony that look, no disappointment, only endless patience. Tony folded instantly and told him all about the whole night, and Pa didn't get mad about the drinking. He just asked questions about fire safety, clapped Tony on the shoulder, and told him to be careful.

"It...kind of brought up some memories," Tony admits. "For both of us. About last year, and..."

"Mario." Pa says his name so blandly it's immediately obvious he's suppressing large amounts of rage.

Tony surprises himself by shaking his head. "I mean, I guess a little. But mostly...Stacy Allan. That day in the forest, she...she had both of us at gunpoint."

To Pa's credit, he doesn't flinch. "Christ, kid, you never said. I mean, I knew Daniel was shot, but..."

"Didn't want to freak you and Ma out. There was enough going on. I thought... For about an hour, I was sure I was going to die, and now..."

"Now you're thinking about it again."

"Yeah."

Pa rests his hand heavily on Tony's shoulder for a minute while Tony sorts through the inventory folder and fires up the computer in the office to make the orders. If he said one more word, asked one more question, Tony would spill everything—the note on Daniel's door, the murder weapon, Lily Peterson and her boyfriend. But Pa's never been one for too many words, and Tony keeps Daniel's secrets and tells himself it's better that way.

Gianna comes in at one for her half day, no baby in sight. The first thing she does is tell Pa he needs to go out to Kyle's because his motorboat won't start, and he needs a second pair of hands.

Tony retreats into the bowels of the garage. He's hit his limit on emotional conversations for the day. Even if he could fathom talking out their fight from last night, he has no idea how to tell Gianna what he's thinking, how he's feeling.

Probably, he should start with an apology. But the thought of it feels sour on his tongue. He's not sorry; he didn't say anything he doesn't believe. At the same time, it makes him feel like a petulant toddler. He wants her to acknowledge he went through a bunch of shit at the same time she did. He wants her to understand he missed opportunities for her sake. He wants her to understand it hurts him when she acts as if having a family that loves her is a pain. He wants so many things, and none of them are all that important, but he's not about to back down on them. That would mean admitting he feels vulnerable and stupid to want them in the first place.

Gianna must feel similarly unwilling to make the first step. She lets him work on stripping parts out of Mrs. Cooper's son's ancient Volvo in peace for most of the work day. It finally gave up the ghost a month ago, and he traded it in for a newer used car. Though not technically a dealership, they usually know when their regulars are looking to trade up, and it's easy enough to get buyers and sellers in touch with one another. The upshot is that every now and again, Pa ends up buying very used cars for very cheap. It's a good deal for everyone. The Volvo isn't roadworthy anymore, but there are things worth saving about it—vintage upholstery, wiring, and some of the parts under the hood are still in use in newer Volvos.

Tony's ripping out the upholstery when Gianna finally makes her way to the garage. Tony finds it therapeutic, cutting up along the seams and ripping it all out.

"So," she says, her voice loud in the quiet space since the radio's off today. Usually, Kyle turns it on, but it's his day off (or not, depending on how long he and Pa spend fixing the motorboat). "Are we gonna talk about it?"

"What's to talk about?" Tony keeps his back turned, bent over the car's seats.

"Hm, well, let me think." From the ironic tone of her voice, he can tell she's probably crossing her arms and cocking her hip. "Maybe how you embarrassed me in front of all of my friends? Lily and Sean aren't answering my texts. You made me sound like a freeloader."

"That's not what I said." Tony tries not to change his tone and reveal how angry he still is. He wonders for a second if this is how Pa feels when he talks about Mario.

Gianna's voice is thick, like she's fighting tears. "Is it so bad to want some time to be a normal college student? I wouldn't actually move out. It's not like I'm not grateful or like I regret Lia or anything. I just...want to be normal sometimes."

Tony doesn't answer, clenching his jaw as he tears out a tricky bit.

"God, what is *with* you?" Gianna says in disgust. "You didn't used to be this way."

"What way?"

"Emotionally unavailable."

Tony straightens and tosses the scraps of upholstery on the pile behind him. "I'm available. I'm available all the damn time. You're the one who's acting as if nothing's wrong when your goddamn professor got stabbed. At least your fancy college friends are pretending to care a little."

Gianna hesitates a moment. Her eyes go wide, and he thinks this will be when she finally opens up.

Then, her chin juts out. "Maybe I don't want to talk about that with you."

"Fine. Then don't come complaining to me about this."

"Fine." She stalks off, grabs her keys and phone off the workbench, and heads for the door.

"Where are you going?" he calls after her. "Day's not over."

"You can close up today." She's barely loud enough to be heard across the garage, not even doing him the decency of yelling. "I'm gonna go take care of my daughter since babysitting is such a burden to Mom."

The door slams behind her.

"Fuck," Tony says to no one in particular.

He goes back to the Volvo. Ripping out cloth and foam is less satisfying now that he feels guilty. Guiltier.

Eventually, he caves and gets his phone out.

All he has is one text from Daniel: *Emergency meeting w counseling this afternoon about the stupid police searches. home by six. maybe six thirty.*

Tony rolls his eyes. *Baby,* he answers. *You are not the only dean at the college. You're also not a counselor. Delegate or sth.*

He remembers what Gianna said about counseling at Lobell once, how they were no help to someone like Andrew Clayfield, who was veering into psychosis. They probably need all the support they can get. On the other hand, what help can Daniel be to them? He keeps trying to send Lily to them every time she comes to talk to him, and it's clearly not working. Counseling services at a small liberal arts college don't exist to handle violent crime, they're meant to tackle homesickness or stress from too much classwork. One meeting with Daniel will not suddenly equip students to handle the disaster on campus right now.

With his brain already on the Lily Peterson track, Tony can't help but retrace every concern about her he's had in the last few weeks. Every time he's seen her, she's looked anxious, even desperate. She was nervous the day "Sean hit a deer," but last night, she seemed all over the place. And who's there to help her besides Daniel? Gianna? Gianna has her own shit to deal with. Sean? He's trying his best, but his best is getting overwhelmed at the thought of handing out flyers. He doesn't seem like the kind of guy who's able to handle an unstable girlfriend in meltdown. All this new business with police searches is hardly helping.

What Lily could possibly have to hide from the police is beyond Tony. Maybe an embarrassing sex toy collection. Maybe pot. Maybe, the paranoid part of his brain adds, proof of the murder or a handy stack of magazines with the letters cut out. She *was* worried about being a suspect, which could mean she did it. If watching his way through several procedural crime shows with Daniel in the name of science has taught him anything, it's that if someone is trying to look innocent, they probably aren't.

Great, and now he's thinking like Daniel was last year when he started suspecting every troubled student who intersected with Mario of murder, including Tony's own sister. Daniel believes Lily didn't do it, and Daniel is the most suspicious person he knows. If she were going to do anything to him, she would have already done it.

"You're being ridiculous, Anthony," he tells himself firmly.

Daniel is a professor, not a psychologist, and it's clear Lily needs the latter right now.

Daniel doesn't get the text. The checkmarks at the bottom remain grayed out instead of blue. Tony reopens their thread more times than he wants to admit, just to be sure. He debates telling Daniel he fucked up with Gianna again. But he doesn't want to reopen night's conversation. Then he would have to admit there are things he needs to talk about and that maybe Lily isn't the only one who could do with a psychologist.

It doesn't seem fair to mention it to Daniel. Not right now, not with everything going on. There will be time enough to deal with all of Tony's shit when the killer has been caught and Daniel's home and workplace aren't literally life-threatening. Again.

Anyway, it's harder to talk about—harder to think about—in the cold light of day when he can't hide in Daniel's arms.

Instead, Tony texts again to ask if Daniel wants rice or pasta for dinner.

Tony closes up shop alone. Apparently, Kyle's boat was more messed up than he thought. Either that, or Kyle offered Pa a beer, and they got caught up. Good thing it's a Tuesday. There are less walk-ins in the middle of the week, so Tony's had the shop to himself. Lucky in that he doesn't think his customer service face is up to scratch right now, unlucky in that he's been alone with his thoughts all afternoon.

By the time he's locked up, Daniel still hasn't texted back. It's five thirty though. He's probably still talking to counseling. Tony has an easy hour and a half before it will be time to start dinner. Maybe he can sort things out with Gianna, if only so it stops weighing on his mind, and he and Daniel can enjoy a nice meal together after last night's failure. With that thought in mind, Tony heads over to his parents' house instead of across the bridge.

"Ma?" He unlocks the door and kicks off his shoes. "Gianna?"

"Gimme a second," Ma answers. He hears footsteps, farther away than usual, and then she's coming down the stairs. "Your sister took the baby on a drive. She wouldn't stop crying."

For a moment, Tony's uncertain if Ma means Gianna or Lia.

Ma chooses not to clarify. "She said you'd had a fight?"

Tony winces. "Yeah. I was hoping to apologize."

"Good kid." Drawing up close, Ma presses a kiss to his cheek. "She deserve it?"

"I think so?" Tony has no idea whether or not Gianna's to blame for their fight. The righteous indignation still burns under his skin. He's not interested in groveling. He'll do it, though, to keep the peace.

Ma gives him a look, part fondness and part exasperation. "Tony Baloney," she says, chiding.

It shocks a laugh out of Tony. "You haven't called me that in ten years."

"I was looking at some old albums in the attic. Thinking I should start one for Lia. I have so many pictures on my phone."

"Gigi would love that."

She pats him on the shoulder. "I think she'd love it if you apologized, whether or not you should."

He smiles weakly.

"You staying for dinner?" she asks over her shoulder as she walks toward the kitchen.

"Nah." He pulls out his phone to check the time. Past six already, Daniel's probably headed home. "Just a pit stop. I guess you don't know when Gianna will be home?"

"Sorry. You want to take anything with you? I made meatloaf."

Tony debates trying to explain how he can't bring meatloaf to Rhinebeck because Daniel tries not to eat meat on weeknights to lessen his carbon footprint. An incoming text from Colette thankfully distracts him from that Sisyphean task. She rarely texts him. "No thanks," he says, distracted. "We've got stuff at home."

Have you heard from Daniel? Colette has texted him. *He's late picking me up and he's not answering his phone.*

Frowning, Tony tries to call Daniel. It goes straight to voicemail. He texts a question mark. Only one check mark. Daniel's phone must be off.

"Hey, Ma?"

"Uh-huh."

"I gotta go. Tell Gianna I was looking for her?"

"You got here three minutes ago." Ma pokes her head back in from the kitchen door.

"Sorry." Tony pulls his shoes on with one hand, texting Colette with the other. "Something came up."

He thinks about Gianna while he drives. It's easier than worrying about Daniel. He's kind of glad he missed her, all told. If he had seen her, if she'd been there—Tony can imagine what would have happened. He'd have apologized, she'd have accepted, and then he would have left, still pissed off that she thought she deserved an apology.

By the time he's blown past the bridge, a little over the speed limit and his car complaining about it all the way, he's accepted that it wouldn't have helped. It would be a quick fix, a bandage on what's bothering him with the bullet left under his skin. His whole family seems to have moved on from everything that's happened in the last year and left him behind.

He finds Colette standing beside Daniel's car in the faculty parking lot. She has her phone out, frowning at it.

Cutting the engine and getting out of the car is less work than rolling down the windows, so Tony gets out. "Anything?"

She shakes her head. "You?"

"No." There's no point in saying it's not like Daniel to go radio silent or miss an appointment with Colette without giving her a heads-up. They both know, or she'd never have texted him. Instead, Tony offers, "We could check his office?"

Colette shrugs. "I went there before I texted you. He wasn't in."

Neither of them has a better idea, so they take the winding pathway to Condelmuir to check again. They walk—briskly, but a walk all the same. Running would be admitting there's something to worry about.

There are no voices to be heard in the hallway outside Daniel's office. Why would there be? It's past six, and classes are at an absolute minimum. No one wants to spend more time on campus when there's a killer around.

Tony raps on the door to Daniel's office with his knuckles.

No response.

He tries the doorknob. The door falls open with a creak.

He and Colette exchange a glance. Tony wonders if she's thinking what he's thinking—that going inside might be as stupid as the time she and Daniel decided to investigate an active crime scene with the murderer.

They do it anyway, of course.

Daniel's computer is still on, his cup of tea half-drunk, and an untouched glass of water sits on the other side of his desk, leaving a ring of condensation in the wood.

"He was meeting someone from counseling," Tony remembers. "Maybe he's still there?"

"Maybe there was an emergency?"

"I hope not."

Colette shrugs. "Sorry. I'm probably overreacting. After Mario...and then that knife..."

"No, I get it." Tony rests a hand on her shoulder. "Everything with...with Amelia Lawrence keeps reminding me of... Well."

"Of course it does." Colette leans toward him slightly, bumping their sides together. "It's a natural response to trauma."

They survey Daniel's empty office together.

"So now what?" Tony asks.

"Let me try calling counseling. Maybe he's still there."

Colette uses the landline in Daniel's office to call the counseling center on the other side of campus, pressing an extension to reach them. It's very old-school, matching the vibes of the building. Angel Automotive has had a dedicated office cell phone since the phone company jacked up the prices for the landline.

"Hello, this is Professor Ravel," Colette says smoothly. "I'm calling to ask if Professor Daniel Rosenbaum has been in this afternoon." There's a brief pause, and then, "Oh, no, not as a patient. He mentioned a meeting with counseling, and he hasn't come back to his office."

Tony runs his fingers across one of the bookshelves—solid wood, not some IKEA shit. Daniel should get shelves like this for the apartment, not what he has now.

Colette makes a series of listening sounds that remind Tony so intensely of his own customer service voice he wants to laugh.

"He didn't. No, of course, I understand completely. Thank you for your help." She sets the phone down in its anchor. "Daniel hasn't been in today."

"Great." Tony slouches against the bookcase. "Any other ideas?"

Colette stares at him blankly.

"He was here," Tony offers, "or the door would be locked."

"Maybe..." Colette hesitates. "Maybe Lily Peterson stopped by?"

"He promised he would text every half hour when he saw her." But that was on Saturday, and he didn't plan on seeing Lily today. On the other hand, Daniel decided she didn't do it, so maybe he also decided he could relax around her.

"I could try to email her."

"Odds on her answering in the next ten minutes?"

Colette snorts. Not likely, then. "I suppose…"

"Hm?"

"I could try her boyfriend. I do have his phone number."

At Tony's encouragement, Colette calls with the phone on speaker.

After a long while, Sean picks up, sounding confused and a little panicked. Which is fair; Tony would have been the same if one of his college professors cold-called him. "Professor Ravel?"

"Yes, hello Sean."

"What's, uh…what's up?"

"I'm afraid this is a very odd question, but you mentioned your girlfriend Lily to me?"

"Uh-huh?"

"She sees Professor Rosenbaum in his office frequently, and now I can't reach him. Could you get me in touch with her?"

"Um…"

"Just to ask if she's seen him."

Colette uses the same voice with Sean as with counseling services, as if she needs to psych herself up or practice her phrasing before talking to a student. Maybe she does. Tony's only ever seen her truly at ease when there's no one but him and Daniel around.

"She's…I mean, she's not answering me right now, so…"

"Ah." Colette pauses. "Is it because of what we talked about?"

Something loud happens on Sean's end, a door slamming or something else abrupt and startling. "No, no, I didn't…do it. Yet. But I think she knows I want to, and it's… I think she's doing worse. So, uh, if you can reach her, maybe that would be good. I'll text you her number."

"Thank you, Sean. Let me know if you need anything."

"Thanks, prof."

The number he sends goes straight to voicemail, same as Daniel's.

"What did you talk to him about?" Tony asks.

"Breaking up with Lily."

"Oh."

Colette tries Lily's number again and then types out a message on her phone.

"Is that..." Tony tries to think of the right words. "Is that a good idea? I mean, she's unstable..."

"And he's a student who needs to focus on his academics. Her mental health is not his responsibility."

It echoes everything Tony has thought about himself and Daniel so sharply it makes Tony flinch. "You're right."

"I know it sounds callous."

"I'm guessing you didn't just tell him to do it."

"No, of course not. It was his idea. I told him he should prioritize his own needs. No one else will do it for him."

"Sound advice." At the memorial for Professor Lawrence, Tony agreed with it wholeheartedly. The other night at the pizza place, he thought a little less kindly of Sean, but he had so much anger and resentment getting in the way. Still, Tony remembers those dress shoes and Sean's entitlement about room searches. "Although he doesn't seem to be struggling."

"Appearances can be deceiving. And many of our students are wealthy adolescents who've never been on their own before. That can be its own struggle."

"I guess. So no dice on Lily?"

Colette shakes her head. "She probably has nothing to do with this."

"Daniel would have said if he was meeting her."

Wouldn't he? Or would he hide it to protect Tony from his own worries? But then, surely, he would tell Colette she needed to take the bus home. And why would he leave his office unlocked and turn his phone off? It's not like him, and the only explanation could be—has to be—

"Tony." Colette's firm voice snaps him out of it. "We can't do anything now except wait. It's only been an hour or so."

Tony agrees shakily. "Sorry. My brain is...a mess. Let me drive you home. I'll make dinner, and we can wait up for Daniel together."

"The human brain often is messy. Thank you."

He makes pasta with store-bought pesto and some cherry tomatoes, and because he's feeling anxious, he toasts some additional pine nuts to go along with it. Pine nuts are too expensive to use regularly in Tony's opinion, but maybe eating something that costs as much as his wiper blade replacement will distract him.

Colette watches from one of the bar stools by the kitchen counter. "It was probably the husband," she says conversationally while Tony rinses the cutting board.

The board slips out of Tony's hands and clatters into the sink.

"Statistically, I mean," Colette continues. "Amelia Lawrence was probably killed by her husband, and Lily Peterson has nothing to do with it. Most violent crimes are committed by intimate partners."

"That sounds like you took it from *Bones*."

The stool creaks as Colette leans forward on it and rests her elbows on the island. "A stopped clock is right twice a day. It wasn't only the husband's outburst at the memorial. Amelia talked about how difficult it was raising a child when she had to work all the time."

Tony turns around to eye Colette suspiciously. "She told you that?"

Colette looks away. "She told other colleagues."

"You've been snooping."

"Staffroom exchanges are not snooping." Colette says it with a hefty dose of dignity, but she's lying through her teeth.

"Come on." Tony ladles a spoonful of the hot pasta water into the pan the pesto is heating up in before dumping the rest of the noodles into the strainer. "You're not teaching high school. You don't *have* a staffroom. You had to go all the way to the psych department to find someone to ask." In point of fact, he didn't know this about college professors until he started spending time with Daniel, but he does know now.

"I did not." Colette maintains the facade until Tony tosses the pasta into the pesto pan, stirs it, and then plates it up. He's dotting the top with cherry tomatoes and pine nuts when she finally admits, "I happened to chance upon a few psychology professors in the dining hall."

"You hate the dining hall."

"It's practically inedible. I don't know why anyone would eat there. I suppose hard scientists are gluttons for punishment."

Tony laughs and slides her plate across the kitchen island along with a fork. She digs in immediately. "So did you learn anything else?"

She swallows delicately. "Why should I tell you anything if you're going to judge me for it?"

"I'm not judging." He shovels a forkful of pasta into his mouth. When she doesn't answer, he finishes chewing before continuing. "I just want you to be honest about what you're doing. Trust me, I get it. I've been freaking out ever since that knife ended up on the door."

"Yes." She drums her fingers on the island's fake marble top. "I'm not anxious for police attention, and I truly think Detective Taylor would find a way to blame us. But either Daniel or I are definitely being threatened."

The idea of the threats being meant for Colette hadn't even occurred to Tony.

"Amelia Lawrence was well-liked among faculty." Colette picks her fork up and then sets it back down. "And she did too much in her efforts for tenure. She was at the least a decent professor, and her courses were reasonably popular. She had a young daughter and a husband who works from home, and she struggled to prioritize them over work."

"I don't understand the whole tenure thing," Tony admits.

"Neither do I, and I'm trying to get it. Academic jobs have become far more competitive with more people getting degrees, which means the few positions with a lifetime guarantee—"

"Tenure?" Tony checks.

"Yes. Those positions go to fewer and fewer of the applicants for them. Most positions are limited to a few years at a time and subject to contract renewals and negotiations. Conditions are terrible—too many teaching hours for too little pay and not enough time for your own research. I'm sure Amelia didn't want to move her whole family again for a different job, and her field of study doesn't exist in the private sector."

"Hm." Tony knows Daniel's tenure got fast-tracked in the spring when he took over most of Stacy Allan's responsibilities, and he knows

Colette is up for tenure soon as well. "So you and Daniel were pretty lucky." That aligns with everything Mr. Lawrence said last week, which keeps him out of the running as a suspect as far as Tony's concerned.

"Daniel is extremely talented at his job and occupies a very specific academic niche." Colette shakes her head. "He's very good at making his research seem like something anyone could think of, but it isn't, and that's part of what makes him such a good teacher."

Warmth suffuses Tony, which is dumb. It's not his accomplishment. It's Daniel's. He just enjoys hearing that Daniel's as good as Tony thinks he is. "And you?"

"I was very lucky."

Tony has a sneaking suspicion Colette is also very good at her job and downplaying her own accomplishments. He lets it slide. "You serious about moving back to Europe?"

She doesn't instantly say no, which is worse than he'd been hoping for. "I don't know. There aren't many positions for anthropologists in Europe either."

"What about your family?" It's something Tony's wondered about, on and off, since he met Colette, especially since she mentioned her sister the other day. He knows much more about Daniel's family and how Daniel ended up living so far away from them. He also gets to be around for more of Daniel's Skype calls to his family these days, so he knows distance is only an impediment if you let it be.

Colette hardly mentions her family.

"I wouldn't mind seeing my siblings more," she says. "Even if they're all doctors and lawyers."

Tony lets the silence grow longer while he eats.

Eventually, Colette continues. "My parents are...complicated. From a different time, a colonial time, in my father's case at least. They're not welcoming of...alternative lifestyles."

"Ah."

Colette's never talked about it specifically, and she hasn't dated anyone in the time Tony's known her, but Daniel confirmed Tony's gut instinct that she's not interested in the opposite sex. Maybe she's discrete about it. Maybe she's waiting until there's something worth talking about. Tony can relate. He remembers how his father asked about Daniel today, a little awkward but with his heart in the right place. He's suddenly, overwhelmingly thankful.

Colette spears a piece of fusilli on her fork. "On the other hand, France has less insane policies on gun control."

"I think you mean France has policies on gun control."

"Precisely." She leans against the uncomfortable metal cross forming the back of the stool. "I don't know. I like it here. I like my work and my home. I hate the politics. And...it's lonely sometimes, always being foreign. It's easier to play into it than to try to assimilate when you know you'll never pass as a native."

With a start, Tony realizes he's part of a couple that Colette is a third wheel to. He wants to comfort her, wants to say she always has a place with them, but it seems presumptuous.

Instead, he offers a weak smile. "Want to keep going on *Bones* while we wait for Daniel?"

Chapter Ten

Tony wakes with a start some time past three in the morning, leaned back against the couch, overstretched, his neck killing him. The DVD menu is on a loop. Colette sleeps slumped against the other arm of the couch. Her neck must be hurting too; she's bent forward, chin to her chest. The spreadsheet they were filling out rests on the coffee table precariously. It shows tracking on *Bones* for the locations, perpetrators, and frequency of violent crimes as well as whether or not they're solved.

Tony stumbles to his feet to check the bedroom.

Empty.

Daniel would have woken them up when he came home.

Tony finds his phone on the coffee table, his battery at 11 percent.

Daniel still hasn't read his messages.

With shaking fingers, Tony dials his number. It goes straight to voicemail again.

On the couch, Colette groans and stretches. "What..."

"He's not home." Tony's voice sounds awful. Dry and cracked and terrified. "Colette, he didn't come home."

She straightens. "Do we call the police?"

"I'm calling Taylor."

"It's the middle of the night."

Tony shrugs. Some of Daniel's deep and abiding skepticism toward law enforcement has rubbed off on him during the last year. Detective Taylor's handling of Mario's murder put Colette under wrongful arrest and Daniel and Tony in danger. The slow, slow seconds, when the only thing between Daniel and death were Tony's hands gripping his arms as he dangled over the Hudson River, altered a part of Tony that used to have optimism and faith in community.

The police should have been there earlier. They should have found the solution themselves. It shouldn't have been him and Daniel.

"She's still the only person who can actually help," he says anyway.

"We could call Lily," Colette suggests.

When she tries, it goes straight to voicemail again.

Out of options, Tony scrolls through his contacts for the personal number he was hoping he would never have to use. It rings and rings and rings, and finally, when he thinks it's time to give up and try 911, Detective Taylor answers, groggy and annoyed.

"Hi. This is Tony d'Angelo. It's about Daniel Rosenbaum. He's missing." Saying it out loud sends a bolt of fear straight down Tony's spine.

Tony answers a few questions Taylor asks distractedly—when he last saw Daniel, whether not coming home late is unusual for him, what he was doing when he went missing.

"He texted me around four and said he was in a meeting with counseling, but counseling says he never showed up. Anyone could have texted from his phone, though." Tony feels compelled to point it out. Daniel refuses to use a biometric lock on his phone. He says he doesn't trust them, but his pin is easy.

Not that a biometric lock is safe from criminals. Stacy had Tony press his thumbprint to his phone so she could text Daniel to stop him from looking. She was pointing a gun at him. He had to do it. If someone was pointing a weapon at Daniel, he'd have told them Worf's birthday.

Don't spiral, Tony tells himself firmly. *It won't help.*

There's probably a rational explanation: Lily Peterson waylaid

Daniel in a crisis; he took her to the hospital; his phone ran out of battery; he doesn't know anyone's number by heart except the landline in the New York City apartment he used to share with his grad school roommate, Paul Weintrob.

It will be fine, and Detective Taylor will be pissed at them for wasting her time.

She shows up half an hour later, wearing her dress shirt inside out, badge pinned to it haphazardly.

Colette grabbed her coffee grounds and cooker from downstairs, which is a mercy. Tony has no idea what he would have done with the time if not sit there and drink coffee. Worf reads the nervous energy in the room and hides under the couch, purring incessantly as if it will calm them all down.

"Walk me through it," the detective demands as she sits on the chair she always uses to interrogate them. "You last saw him yesterday morning."

"We left here around eight," Tony confirms. "I went to work in Kingston. Daniel and Colette drove to Lobell."

Colette nods. "We got there at around twenty past, I believe. I went to my office. Daniel went to a meeting with the president. He texted in the afternoon to say he would drive us home at six."

"And he texted you as well?"

"Yeah." Tony thumbs open his phone to show her. "He said he was meeting counseling to talk about the room searches, and he'd be home by six or six thirty."

The detective says nothing as she writes down the information.

Unable to stop himself, Tony adds, "He has a student who's seemed increasingly unstable. Lily Peterson."

"Lily Peterson." The detective makes another note in her booklet. "That's the girl who found Professor Lawrence."

"Yes. Daniel is her academic advisor."

"Mm-hm. And he sees her frequently?"

Tony and Colette exchange a glance.

Tony clears his throat. "More often since...what happened with

Professor Lawrence. From what Daniel has said, she hasn't been doing well." He doesn't mention that Daniel wants to believe she's doing well and resisted mentioning her to the police on several occasions. Tony hopes Daniel will forgive him later for mentioning Lily and potentially getting her into trouble after Daniel has tried so hard to keep her off the police's radar.

Taylor taps her pen against the notebook. "She was involved last year as well, wasn't she?"

Colette looks away, toward the dark windows. It's still a sore subject for her, what Mario did with—to—his students. Tony's not sure if she and Daniel have talked about it. Heck, Daniel barely talks to Tony about it, probably because he knows Tony still can't let go of the anger toward Mario for what he did to Gianna. It wakens another layer of guilt in Tony that Daniel's still grieving a friend, and Tony can't even empathize.

He can at least take the heat off Colette. "She had feelings for Professor Lombardi. It's unclear whether they were returned. She said the relationship was never physical, but after his death, she attempted suicide."

"Right." Detective Taylor scrubs a hand through her hair, pulling it out of its updo. She curses, drops her pen on her lap, and tries to fix it. "Did Professor Rosenbaum say anything else about these counseling sessions with Lily?"

"Advising sessions," Colette corrects. "He's concerned."

Tony adds, "Lily struggles with her mental health. Daniel's trying to encourage her to seek counseling."

"I hate to ask, but do either of you think there might be something...inappropriate between her and Professor Rosenbaum?"

An undignified snort escapes Tony's nose.

Colette shakes her head instantly. "Absolutely not."

The detective raises an eyebrow. "She has a history."

"As does Daniel, with men, exclusively. He's also adamantly against relationships between professors and students." Colette sounds bored, as if both these things should be extremely obvious.

To a certain degree, maybe they should be. The detective should certainly be aware by now that Daniel and Tony are together. Then again, in her line of work, she probably sees all sorts of relationships end all sorts of horrible ways. Daniel has never talked to her about his orientation. It wouldn't be unreasonable to think he's bi.

Someone who has met Daniel and spent significant time with him would find the idea laughable. Not Daniel being bi, but Daniel being unscrupulous enough to take advantage of a student. He would never.

"Lily was concerned about the police searches," Tony remembers. "She was trying to start a petition against them."

Colette and the detective both look at him blankly.

"And she was focused on whether she could get an automatic pass on Professor Lawrence's class or something. She didn't even go to the memorial. But she was also worried she'd be a suspect because she found the professor."

Detective Taylor closes her eyes as if asking for patience. "I thought I told you *not to investigate.*"

"You told Daniel not to investigate. I just...happened to be in the room."

She gives him a cold, hard stare. "That was a general encouragement to all of you."

"It's suspicious, though, right?" he pushes.

"*If* it were, I wouldn't be able to say anything about an ongoing investigation."

Tony's patience snaps. He yanks open the junk drawer in the kitchen and throws the plastic bag with the letter on the table, the one she dismissed only last week when this all started. "And what about this? This still isn't suspicious?"

Taylor opens her mouth, then closes it again.

"Or this?" Tony slams the second baggie, the one with the knife, on the table next to it. "This was on our door last Thursday."

"Why didn't you call me *then*?"

"Daniel refused. He thought you would arrest him or Colette for it."

"I wouldn't—"

Tony crosses his arms.

"Well, at least he'd have been safe in custody." Detective Taylor has the good grace to at least look sheepish. "It's not uncommon for people to get a taste of adrenaline chasing criminals, and then start creating their own crimes."

"It's not uncommon for innocent people to end up in jail in this country because the police won't do their fucking jobs." Tony slams the junk drawer shut with more force than necessary.

Choosing this as her moment for some reason, Colette leans forward. "What about the husband? He and Amelia were having difficulties, and he made a scene at her memorial. He yelled at Daniel."

"You didn't tell me he yelled at Daniel." Tony turns to her, frowning.

"He didn't want to worry you." Colette's mouth twists. "Clearly, that worked well."

The detective throws her hands up. "Are all of you incapable of following basic instructions?"

Tony opens his mouth to deny it; he wants more than anything to tell her she's the one who's incapable. It's her fault for alienating Daniel so thoroughly he put himself in danger again. Tony stops short, clinging to the belief that at least now she knows, she can do something to save Daniel.

"Right," Taylor says, voice grim. Despite her disheveled appearance, she's all professionalism. "Well, this has been illuminating. Call me if you hear from him."

"Wait." Tony follows her to the door. "Do you think it's connected? Do you think Daniel's in danger?"

"Mr. d'Angelo," the detective says firmly, not unkindly, but unbending. "There's no way I can give you an answer right now. I'll let you know when I have more information."

"But what do we *do*?" It comes out plaintive, desperate, which Tony hates. "I have to do something." This isn't anything like when Mario Lombardi died. At the time, there was nothing more *to* do. The event passed, and Tony had no reason to expect anything else to happen. His role was clear: Support Gianna and do what was best for her.

"The best thing you can do is stay where he can find you. If he can,

I'm sure he'll come home. Are you in touch with his family?"

Tony nods.

"You could let them know. If we haven't found him by the end of the day, you could make flyers."

Tony wants to scream.

With a tight smile, Taylor leaves, the evidence held between her pinched thumb and forefinger.

It's still only five in the morning. Daniel's family on the West Coast won't be awake for hours. Tony and Colette drift into the kitchen for more coffee. Neither of them can think of anything to say. Eventually, Tony gets too jittery to sit, so he takes a shower. He uses Daniel's shampoo, letting the smell of it fill the small bathroom. It's generic—of course it is, it's three in one—in the way bottom-of-the-shelf men's hygiene products always are. They made no effort to make it smell like something that would occur naturally. The label says it's "fresh and clean," and it does smell like both of those things.

Mostly, it smells like Daniel.

Tony keeps his bag of toiletries in the mirrored cabinet above the sink. Daniel mostly uses it to store his huge bottle of Advil for tension headaches. Tony brought his kit over sometime in January, and it's stayed here ever since. He needs it for beard care every other day, and he's been here at least that often. Since it's still early, and he can't think of anything else to do, Tony gets out the circular beard brush and starts methodically brushing out his beard. He hasn't had time or energy to trim it in at least a week or two, and it's starting to get a little wild. He usually goes for a sleeker look. By now, he's edging closer and closer to hipster territory.

Daniel never had a beard. He says he tried in his teens, and it was such a patchy disaster he never wanted to repeat it. Tony thinks it would be worth a shot now. If Daniel doesn't come back, they'll never know.

The thought takes Tony out at the knees, and he has to sit on the closed toilet lid for a long moment, just breathing.

Today isn't the day for a trim. He doesn't trust himself with the scissors right now. Best to leave it at a thorough brush. Halfway through, he pats in some beard oil. It's neutral, so it won't mask the scent of Daniel's shampoo.

Colette knocks while he's trying to brush out the stubborn swirl of hair on the left, under his jawline.

He has a towel wrapped around his waist, so he opens the door. "What's up?"

"Do you want breakfast? I can get something from Bread and Basket."

"Sure." The bakery's across the street, and he and Daniel often go on weekend mornings. "I love their quiche."

"Quiche is not a breakfast food."

He shrugs.

She stays where she is in the doorway.

"I'm not changing my order."

She laughs, which is nice to hear. "No, no, sorry. I've never watched this process before. I hadn't imagined it being so involved."

"That's probably the real reason Daniel never grew a beard." Tony snaps his fingers in realization. "Can't use three in one on a beard." Probably Daniel would try, but it would be awful.

Colette's smile dims a little. "That does sound like him."

"He'll be fine." Tony wishes his voice didn't crack on the words. "Right?"

"I hope so." Colette sounds as helpless as Tony feels.

It doesn't comfort either of them.

Neither, it turns out, does the third cup of coffee or the flaky pastry filled with cheese and spinach. Although Tony takes any excuse to eat it otherwise, this morning, it tastes of nothing. Food is only another way to kill time.

After breakfast, they try Lily again. Still no response. Fortified with what must be her fourth coffee, Colette calls Sean again and asks if he's heard from Lily. He hasn't. With all of their avenues of research exhausted, short of doing something Taylor would probably arrest them for, they have nothing left to do but wait.

They don't talk much. Tony's thankful Colette takes at face value that they will stay here, together, to wait this out. She makes no attempt to return to her own apartment. Instead, they fuck around on their phones as if anything on there could calm the buzzing of Tony's nerves. He toggles between the same three apps, scrolling blindly and not taking in anything he sees.

"Look at this," Colette demands, turning her phone screen toward him. The black-and-white website has blocks of color down the left side, denoting different scores, and the bold letters R M P at the top.

Amelia Lawrence's name jumps out at him immediately.

"What is this?"

"Rate my professor."

Tony blinks. "What."

Colette grimaces, mouth pulling wide and tight. "I know, I know. It's essentially word of mouth, but for the digital age. Anonymous users leave reviews of their college and their professors, possibly to help students decide which courses to take."

"Hm." Tony peers at the screen. "And the categories are—'for credit, would take again, grade, and textbook'? What does 'textbook' mean?"

"Whether the class requires you to buy a textbook. This website does not use a scientific metric." Colette makes another face. "They used to allot little pepper symbols along with academic quality to indicate physical attractiveness."

Tony snorts. "It's nice to hear about students objectifying professors instead of the opposite for a change. So, what am I looking at here?"

"Amelia Lawrence's page."

There are five ratings on the page with a combined score of 2.0, which, based on the fact that it's colored red, is not a good thing. Three of the ratings score her as a 1.0 or a 1.5, while the other two situate her at a 4.0.

The three low ratings all appear to be for the same class: Psych 218. Research Methods, apparently. The first one reads: *Professor Lawrence only cares about her Zebrafish. She wouldn't lift a finger for a student if they were drowning in a lake. I hope someone teaches her a lesson on research ethics.* The listed grade is "NA."

"Sounds like a threat," Tony says.

Colette nods. "My thoughts exactly."

Just to check, Tony scrolls to the positive reviews. They rate different classes and offer fairly generic praise, saying Amelia Lawrence was good at her job, friendly, and helpful.

"So...where does this leave us?" Tony asks.

Colette takes her phone back, studying it briefly before turning off the display. "I'm wondering if Lily wrote those."

"Daniel did say she was only interested in whether or not she could get an automatic pass on the class now Professor Lawrence is dead."

"That's a motive."

It's a shitty motive. "I don't know. Is she that callous?"

"A few hours ago, you were trying to convince the detective she's a suspect, despite Daniel's beliefs to the contrary." Colette's cadence reminds Tony of the way she speaks when she and Daniel get into academic debates, detached and analytical, but Tony knows her well enough by now to hear the tight coil of anger in her voice.

"And you were sure it was the husband. It's not our job to figure out—"

"You were doing it anyway, though, weren't you?"

Tony rolls his eyes and is instantly annoyed at himself for having done it. Too much like Gianna. "They left a knife on the door! Sue me for feeling threatened. Anyway, it's not as if I was investigating on purpose. I happened to hear her say some stuff. You're the one who was going out of your way to—"

"Forgive me if my faith in the Dutchess County police force is not high." Colette bites out the words, harsh and angry, and Tony instantly feels bad.

"Sorry. I know what they did to you—"

"Me!" She snorts. "I was at least being credibly framed. They nearly let you and Daniel die last year. Who's to say they won't do it again if we don't..."

"If we don't do something," Tony finishes. It makes a horrific amount of sense. He doesn't want to think about Daniel, alone with a killer, possibly injured, waiting on rescue only for Detective Taylor and her miles of red tape to be too late this time. Tony considers the idea from every angle he can think of. "Daniel would hate it."

"If it were you, Daniel would be staking out the Lawrence's family home like a character on *CSI*."

Tony draws in a shuddering breath. "Okay. I see your point. Let me...uh...let me call his family first, and then we can...we can figure something out."

She shrugs. "I can always go on my own."

"You absolutely cannot. If you think I'll let you be next, you're out of your mind."

They discuss logistics idly in the time it takes for 9:00 a.m. to roll around. Watching Mr. Lawrence is the easiest and safest course of action, which makes Tony more inclined to try that out instead of the alternative. This is in no small part because the alternative would be breaking into Lily's dorm room to figure out what it is she's so scared of the police finding. Counting on his fingers, Tony easily comes up with five reasons not to do it: One, figuring out where her dorm room is will alert the college of what they're up to. Two, chances are Lily is in her dorm room and would be shocked, if not further traumatized, by them showing up at her door. Three, if she weren't there and they didn't find anything, she would report the break-in, and Tony and Colette would get arrested. Four, if she weren't there and they did find something, they would have to tell Taylor and get arrested. Five, Tony's ma would be so disappointed in him.

Besides, some part of Tony still feels it would be a betrayal to go after Lily. Daniel was so sure of her. Tony already feels bad for telling the detective about her and about the knife, though he thinks it was the right thing to do. Which he also feels bad about. It's a sentimental train of thought and nowhere near as practical as he needs to be if it really is down to him and Colette to keep Daniel safe. There's a reason Tony's not a detective, and this is it.

Finally, he can't reasonably put it off anymore, so Tony searches his phone for Leah Rosenbaum's number. He only has it because of the time

Daniel's cell phone ran out of battery while he was in Albany with his parents last summer, and he left it too late to double-check with Tony about dinner plans. He called Tony from his mom's phone, and Tony saved the number, just in case.

They had dinner at a sushi place in Tivoli that night. Daniel taught Tony how to use chopsticks properly. It was delicious, and they've been meaning to go back since, even though Daniel's dad complained afterward it was nothing compared to Japanese food in the Bay Area.

Tony hopes desperately they will go again. He hopes Daniel can take him to California someday. He hopes he and Colette won't be too late.

Mrs. Rosenbaum—Leah, Daniel's mom—picks up on the fifth ring. "Hello?"

"Hi, uh, it's Tony. D'Angelo?"

"Tony? Is everything all right?"

Of course she'd ask immediately. Why else would he be calling? He doesn't call her; he hangs out in the background when Daniel calls.

"Uh, no," he manages. "You...have you heard from Daniel?"

"Not since last week. Has something happened?"

"He's gone missing." It feels like someone else said the words, far away through the buzzing in his ears.

"Oh my god."

He doesn't know Daniel's mom well enough to understand her tone of voice, what it might mean to her to hear this news. He will someday, maybe, if he and Daniel are still together years from now, but it's too soon.

"Is it...anything to do with the man who was killed last year?"

Jesus fucking Christ, Tony thinks and immediately feels guilty. It makes sense for her to make that leap, even if it's the last thing he wants to think about. If everyone could stop mentioning Mario in conjunction with the current case, it would be great for Tony's mental health.

"Um, probably not. Another professor was injured on campus last week. It might be connected."

"Might?" Her voice is climbing in pitch, headed for hysterical, and Tony can't blame her.

"The police don't know anything right now. But, uh, they wanted me to get in touch to see if you've heard anything."

"Oh my god," she says again. "We should be there."

"I—" Tony starts and then realizes he has nothing to say.

"Aaron's getting his operation today. How are we going to...oh my god."

A distant bell rings in the depths of Tony's mind. It feels like months ago, Daniel mentioning his dad's hip replacement in passing, but it was only last week.

"Maybe wait on telling him until after the operation?" he says.

"I hate lying to him. And we should be there."

"Flying with a bad hip, though—"

"Oh, I know. It was already bad in the summer, not that he would admit it to Daniel. What will we do?"

Selfishly, Tony doesn't want them to fly out. He doesn't know what he would possibly say to them, how he could bridge the gap of their missing child. They should wait to come. Until Daniel is home, safe and sound. Until they know what's happened.

"What about Meredith?" he suggests. Daniel's sister is sensible, almost to the point of being cynical. She'll talk them out of getting on any hasty flights.

"Meredith!" Daniel's mom sounds cheered by the mere mention of her name. "I'm sure she can make it out. Benjamin can watch the kids for a change. That would be perfect. Thank you for calling, Tony. I'll let you know as soon as we've figured out travel plans."

"She doesn't need to—" Tony starts, but the line has gone dead.

Chapter Eleven

The Lawrence family rents a three-bedroom, one-story house on the outskirts of Germantown. The faculty addresses are all on a mailing list, out in the open on a shared server for any staff member to access. Apparently, the college cares far more about protecting a student's privacy than a professor's.

"I'm just saying, I would have thought about changing that when one of your staff murdered another." Tony feels this point should be obvious, but what does he know? He's only the driver in this situation, and it's taking up a larger part of his concentration than it ought to. He never drives to Germantown, and stretches the car isn't used to are getting harder and harder to manage.

From the passenger seat, Colette makes a disgruntled noise. "Stacy didn't murder Mario at his home."

"That is the barest technicality—"

"Take a left here."

Germantown isn't big enough to have suburbs, but these sure look like the suburbs. Half of the lots are active construction sites for new single-family homes.

"There," Colette says. "Right over there."

Tony parks at the curb in front of an empty lot across the street from the house Colette indicates. They're far enough away they shouldn't draw too much attention but close enough they can see into the back yard.

"How do you know your way around here?" Tony asks, irritated by the abruptness of the directions and the shitty parking job. As far as he knows, Colette doesn't drive, though she has a car. When she has to go anywhere, she takes Amtrak or has someone drive her.

"The Continuum," Colette says, which means absolutely nothing to Tony. She must see as much on his face because she adds, "The movie theater I used to go to with...you know—"

"All right." Tony cuts her off before she can continue. The last thing they need is to start talking about Mario. "Did we bring snacks?"

Colette elbows him.

"What? In the movies, the cops always spend hours on stakeouts. They change the lighting between shots and everything!"

"They also conveniently cut out all the parts between the beginning of the stakeout and the part where something interesting happens."

"Not true." Tony takes a deep sip of the coffee in his to-go mug. "There have been at least five episodes of *Bones* where the people on the stakeout have a meaningful heart-to-heart right before the suspect does something."

"I blotted those from my memory."

Tony laughs at the blatant lie. She complains about the show too often to have forgotten anything. Then he sobers immediately. He shouldn't be laughing. Daniel's missing, possible injured or—or something. He looks over at Colette and sees the guilt on her face as clear as it must be on his own.

They lapse into silence for a while, watching the house.

It's a perfectly normal house. The yard is maybe a little overgrown, but the local HOA will have to accept extenuating circumstances for Mr. Lawrence forgetting to mow the lawn. The kitchen window has those little lacy half curtains Tony remembers from his grandma's place. A cutout of a pumpkin in transparent paper hanging above them must color the room light orange in the evening, something Francie made in preschool or kindergarten or wherever she goes.

A half an hour passes before a family-sized Subaru pulls up in the driveway.

Quickly, Colette snaps a picture of the license plate.

The cruel, cynical part of Tony wants to point out there's not a lot they can do with a license plate. If the car belongs to Lawrence, they're already watching him. If it doesn't, getting the numbers run would involve letting Detective Taylor know what they're up to.

A middle-aged woman in a black coat gets out of the driver's seat as the front door to the house opens. Francie runs out and throws herself bodily at the woman. She bends to hug Francie, and the movement turns her face toward Tony.

"That must be Lawrence's mom," he says.

"They do look alike," Colette agrees.

They mostly both look heartbroken.

Mr. Lawrence appears in the doorway. He appears worse than he did a few days ago at the memorial. He still hasn't shaved, and Tony's willing to bet he's wearing the same shirt, the buttons now misaligned and a stain near the collar.

The woman pulls away from Francie to draw her son into a hug. He crumples against her like a puppet with its strings cut. For a moment, Tony thinks they'll both fall, but Lawrence catches himself before he can put too much weight on her, stepping back and away.

From behind the door, he pulls out a purple suitcase, followed by a laundry basket full of stuffed animals and pillows. The last thing is a ludicrously tiny backpack with one of the *Paw Patrol* dogs on it.

The woman starts loading things into the trunk of the Subaru while Lawrence crouches in front of his daughter.

Francie won't even look at him.

His hands are tight on her shoulders, perhaps too tight. He says something they can't hear, but it must be important because he's impressing it on her so intensely. When he finishes, he pulls her into a rough hug she doesn't return.

Francie gets into the car with her grandmother, and the Subaru drives off.

Lawrence watches them go, leaning against the doorframe as if it's the only thing keeping him upright.

"See?" Colette says. "He's incredibly suspicious."

Tony turns to look at her incredulously. "Are you kidding me right now? He's *miserable.*"

"Guilty people often are."

"No way. That's a man who just became a single father. That's a man who just lost the love of his life."

Colette purses her lips. "And he's sending his daughter away right after a tragic loss because…"

A sharp tap on the window makes them both flinch in their seats.

Lawrence peers at them through the glass.

Feeling very much the way he did the time his dad caught him sneaking in late from a party, Tony rolls down his window. "Hi."

"Hi." Lawrence studies them both. "You were both at Amy's memorial, weren't you?"

"Yup, we were."

"What are you doing here?"

Tony glances over at Colette. She's stock-still, frozen solid, staring at the dashboard.

Nothing for it but to go for broke. "You know Daniel? Daniel Rosenbaum?"

Lawrence squints. "That's one of the guys who does admin at the college, right?"

"He's a professor," Tony corrects. "And a dean, now, I guess."

"Right." Lawrence straightens, pulling his face away from the window and giving Tony slightly more breathing room. "I probably owe him an apology, huh?"

"Have you seen him?"

"Huh?"

"He's missing. And we think it might be…connected."

"Connected," Lawrence repeats. "I...listen, you'd better come inside."

He turns on his heel and heads toward his house.

"We can't go in there, right?" Colette asks. "If he's a suspect..."

Tony shakes his head. "We can't not go in there now. And thanks for all your help."

"I'm an academic, not a spy!"

"Yeah, well, we're all trying new things." Tony unbuckles his seatbelt and gets out of the car. "Come on."

"This is how Stacy got you." Colette still opens the door and slides out.

"Totally different situation." Tony fumbles his phone out. "Look, there's two of us. What could possibly happen? I'll record everything as a voice message to you. It'll be fine."

"All right. All right."

Kid's shoes litter the floor of the Lawrence house's hallway and stacks of unopened mail cover the side table. Two letters have fallen down the crack between the table and the wall, and no one has bothered to pick them up.

"I know it's a mess," Lawrence says, ducking out of the kitchen. "Coffee?"

"Sure." Tony's bloodstream is probably mostly caffeine at this point, but nothing matters, so he might as well.

Colette elbows him sharply. "None for me, thank you."

Right. She probably thinks it's full of sedatives or something.

They follow Lawrence into the kitchen. He dumps a used coffee filter into the overflowing trash and rummages in the cupboard for a clean cup. His own cup, he picks seemingly at random from the graveyard of used dishes piled up by the sink.

This man does not strike Tony as a criminal mastermind.

"So." Lawrence leans against the counter while the coffee brews. "You were parked outside my house because a college dean went missing, and you think it's connected to Amy. You think I did it, right?"

Blood shoots to Tony's head, flushing his cheeks and his neck so fast he gets dizzy.

"The thought had crossed our minds, Mr. Lawrence." Now of all times, Colette manages to be cool as a cucumber, perfectly collected.

"Call me Emilio." He doesn't sound even a little angry. Mostly, he sounds tired. "I didn't, but I guess that's what my wife's murderer would say."

Tony manages to find his voice. "You don't seem surprised."

"The police have been here four times in the last week. Doesn't take a genius to know I'm the prime suspect." Emilio rubs across his forehead. "Guess losing my temper the other day only put fuel on the fire, huh?"

The coffee machine beeps, and he turns to pour a cup. "Milk? Sugar?" he asks Tony over his shoulder.

"Milk, thanks." Deciding there's no way out but through, Tony adds, "I'm sorry."

Emilio grabs the milk from the fridge and pours a splash into Tony's mug before handing it over. "People have thought I was bad for Amy since the day I met her. What else is new?"

Colette clears her throat. "I don't know if Amelia told you about Professor Lombardi, last year?"

"The other dead professor." Emilio shrugs. "Sure."

"I was arrested for his murder." Colette says it plainly, openly, as though it's something she talks about frequently. It isn't. Much like the time Tony spent being forced around at gunpoint by Stacy Allan, they talk about it obliquely, if at all, in jokes and references, not in plain fact. "Wrongfully, of course."

Emilio takes a long sip of his coffee, studying her.

"We're here because we don't trust the police to be fast enough for Daniel," Colette continues. "It's not personal."

"Fair enough." Emilio spreads his arms out wide. "Look around. I'm not hiding him in the closet or anything. If you have any other leads, let me know. My faith in law enforcement is reaching new lows."

"All right." Colette sets her purse down and walks down the hallway, opening doors as she goes.

"Seriously, feel free." Emilio gestures at Tony to follow. "I'm past the point of being angry or insulted."

"No kidding." Tony rolls up the sleeves on Daniel's UCLA sweatshirt he borrowed this morning. "You look exhausted." He turns to the sink and starts running hot water. "Sit down, man."

"What are you doing?" Despite the question, Emilio sits.

"Your damn dishes. It's the least I can do for barging in here and accusing you of murder and kidnapping."

It's not until he turns off the tap that Tony hears Emilio's quiet sobs.

"Your daughter's with her grandparents?" Tony keeps his voice steady and his back turned as he starts with the cups.

"Yeah," Emilio says, hoarse and choked, trying not to cry audibly. "For the week. Until the...until the funeral. Got a week to get my shit together and be a good dad."

Tony hums in assent. "Sounds like you're being a good dad to me. Might be good for her and good for you."

"She just...won't get it. I keep trying to tell her mom's not coming home, but she won't stop asking." Emilio draws in a shuddering breath. "I lost it last night. Yelled at her that her mom is dead, and she's not coming home, and she...she won't look at me."

The water is hot enough to burn on Tony's hands. He welcomes it; he hasn't been feeling much of anything recently. "She's, what, five? She'll forgive you. She's going to need you so much."

"Christ." Emilio's chair creaks. Tony chances a look over his shoulder. Emilio, head tipped up to the ceiling, takes deep breaths. "She will, won't she."

Tony gets through all the cereal bowls in silence. There are too many cereal bowls. He has a suspicion Fruit Loops have been easier than cooking a meal for Emilio these last few days.

"Tell me about Daniel," Emilio demands eventually.

Tony swallows heavily. "He's, uh... Well, he's a literature professor at Lobell. Dean of the department since the last one turned out to be a murderess." Tony almost leaves it there, but with Daniel gone, missing, he can't not say what it means to him. What Daniel means to him. "He's my...we're partners."

"You must be worried."

"Yeah."

Worried is an understatement. Tony goes out of his mind every time he manages the full thought: Daniel is missing, possibly kidnapped, possibly by the murderer. And now that he's seen Emilio, Tony gets the feeling the police's prime suspect is a dead end. Banking on his one and only experience meeting a murderer isn't a solid foundation of evidence, but Tony trusts his gut, and his gut tells him Emilio had nothing to do with it. Which means he and Colette are back to square one: cold-calling a college student who won't pick up the phone.

"Worried enough to go check out some guy you think might have done it."

Tony laughs humorlessly. "When you say it like that, it sounds dumber than it is."

"Oh, it's very dumb. Academics, man. Where's your common sense?"

"Not to burst your bubble, but I'm a mechanic."

Emilio tuts. "You should definitely know better."

It's not funny, but they're both still chuckling about it when Colette returns.

"Daniel not locked in any closets?" Tony asks her.

"Not that I could find." She picks up a dish towel and wipes off a clean dish. "If Emilio here is our culprit, he's too smart to keep Daniel in his home."

"Hm." Tony hands her a plate. "Shame. Would have been easy."

"Say I didn't do it, for the sake of argument. What other ideas have you got?"

They explain about Lily as they move on to straightening the kitchen. By the time Emilio's caught up, it's a livable space again.

"Is there a reason no one told the police about this girl earlier?" The way Emilio's looking at them makes the question seem totally reasonable, and suddenly, Tony can't quite remember why they didn't. Helplessly, he looks to Colette.

"She's a student."

"And...?"

"Daniel feels...responsible, I guess," Tony tries to explain. "He's her advisor, and as far as he could tell, she was a troubled kid in need of professional help."

"Yeah," Emilio says, as if it should be obvious. "Which he is not. Isn't there some sort of emergency service? One-800-this-crazy-chick-might-have-stabbed-someone?"

"The counseling staff on campus doesn't have many availabilities."

"Don't tell me my wife died because of a fucking booking problem."

Tony freezes at the counter, the words cutting straight through him. He glances at Colette and finds her similarly still and stricken. If Lily did do it, they have a lot to answer for.

"It wasn't like that." Even to Tony, it sounds weak as he says it. "Before—before it all happened, Daniel thought she was getting better. She had a therapist off campus, and she was looking forward to the school year. After...he thought...he thinks Lily was spiraling after she found your wife, which would be traumatic enough. For all we know, her issues are unrelated to your wife's death. We have no evidence to the contrary. And if she did want to harm Daniel, she's had ample opportunity before yesterday."

Every word is true. On the off chance Lily has nothing to do with the crimes at stake, it's still going to be a miserable story for her since finding a stabbed woman is traumatic whether or not she was involved. Tony can't help but wonder if all of this could have been prevented if she had better care. If someone had intervened before Lily went over the edge upon finding Professor Lawrence, stabbed and dying in her office. Tony just doesn't know who could have done it, if not Daniel.

A more bitter, jaded voice in the back of his head says that maybe Daniel, and by extension Tony and Colette, are clinging to the belief of her innocence because if she did do it, it would be a failure on Daniel's part to see how close to the edge she really was.

At least Emilio seems to accept Tony's excuses. "I think Amy said something about her. You know, not that I think your whole investigative duo thing is a *good* idea..."

"But?" Tony prompts, leaning against the counter and draining his lukewarm coffee.

"But I work in IT. And I know most of Amy's passwords. I could probably find a paper trail if there is one."

Colette opens her mouth to say something—probably something about how they can't involve a suspect in their investigation, which would be true but, in Tony's opinion, a moot point given neither of them are professionals in the first place—when Tony's phone starts buzzing in his pocket.

He wipes his still-slippery fingers on his jeans and pulls it out. Guiltily, he ends the voice memo to Colette. Even more guiltily, he makes sure it's sent.

He has five messages from his dad. Why was his phone on silent? What if Daniel tried to call?

"Shit." Tony scrambles to return the call. "Shit."

The phone only rings once before Pa answers. "Tony? Where the hell are you? You're never late."

"Shit," Tony says again. "I'm so sorry. I—"

"Is everything all right?"

Abruptly, tears start to burn behind his eyes, in his nose. Colette and Emilio's eyes are too heavy on him.

Tony escapes to the hallway. "Daniel's missing." It's no easier for it being the third or fourth time he's said it. "He never came home last night, and we don't know if—the professor, the one who was killed—"

"Oh, fuck."

Tony's never heard Pa say the f-word. It sounds wrong. Upsetting.

"I guess I forgot to come to work with everything..."

There's an impatient, guttural sound from the other end of the line. "You're not coming to work today, kid. Or for the rest of the week. Stay in Rhinebeck. Do what you gotta do. Your ma'll be there soon."

"She doesn't have to—"

"She'll be there soon."

Tony doesn't bother trying to protest.

Returning to the kitchen, Tony tells Colette, "I have to get back to the apartment, my parents..."

She nods. "We should probably be there, anyway. In case he comes back. Or the police do."

Tony gives Emilio a once-over, still slumped on the kitchen chair with deep bags under his eyes, listening to their every word. "You got a laptop you can bring, Mr. IT expert?"

Emilio looks up, shocked.

"C'mon, man. You gotta get out of this house for a bit. Anyway, if you did do it, better we keep an eye on you, huh?"

Colette gives him a look, but Tony meets her gaze, defiant. Emilio knows what they're thinking anyway. They can at least give him the respect of saying it out loud.

"Such a soft touch," she mutters. "Just like Daniel."

They wait around for as long as it takes Emilio to find his laptop and charger, to put on shoes and a clean T-shirt. Colette even lets him sit in the front as they drive back to Rhinebeck.

Tony's ma makes it to the apartment ten minutes after them. At a conservative estimate, she's brought half the food in Target.

"Ma," Tony protests as he lets her in.

She drops all her bag to hug him. "Tony, baby, why didn't you *call*?"

"I didn't think..." He rests his chin on top of her head. "I'm not thinking straight."

Case in point, the door's still open, and the cat's peering around the corner, interested in the scent of freedom. Tony pulls away to shoo Worf inside before closing the door.

"Oh, I forgot to bring treats for him." Ma sounds crestfallen, like it's actually a failing on her part.

Tony takes her jacket and picks up three of the four grocery bags. "We have cat treats. And food. You didn't have to—"

"Don't you dare finish that sentence." She immediately starts handing him things for the fridge. "We're not leaving you alone with this; are you kidding? Come on. Give me that." She takes the eggplant she saw fit to bring out of his hands, puts it on the counter, and shuts the fridge. "Go lie down, baby. You look dead on your feet."

Between waiting up for Daniel last night and waking up at three, Tony's running on caffeine and nerves at this point. She's not wrong.

He peeks out into the living room. Colette and Emilio stare at Emilio's laptop screen together, going over whatever it is they're looking for.

"Hey, Colette?"

"Hm?"

"You guys okay if I take a nap for an hour?"

"Go ahead." She gets up from the couch and peers into the kitchen. "You must be Tony's mother. I'm Colette, Daniel's neighbor."

"Lovely to meet you." Ma ignores her outstretched hand and pulls her in for a hug. "Daniel told us so much about you. Now, Colette, do you eat meat?"

Tony leaves them to it. He heads for the bedroom, pulls off his jeans, and roots around for the sweatpants he left in the bottom of Daniel's dresser sometime in April when it got warm enough to sleep without them. He pulls his hair loose from its ponytail and sinks on top of the covers.

It feels like gravity is pushing him down harder than usual, like the weight of Daniel being gone is a stone on his back pressing him into the mattress, like he'll never be able to sleep from the fear pulsing in the pit of his stomach. But the second his eyes close, he drifts off all the same.

By the time Tony wakes up, the whole apartment smells delicious.

He stumbles out of the bedroom, groggy and confused, until he finds his phone on the coffee table. It's well past two in the afternoon. "Y'should've woken me up," he mutters to whoever is in the living room.

"You needed rest." Ma's in the armchair, leafing through the coffee table book of ayahuasca-induced photos Paul from New York somehow managed to sell to the academic world as an anthropological project. He sent Daniel a copy to his campus PO box, which meant Daniel got called in during the summer to pick it up because the package was too big for his slot. Paul cited this as revenge for Daniel always calling him on the landline and nearly giving him a heart attack every time since no one ever uses the landline. Daniel, in turn, does this because Paul might be as New York as they come, but his parents were born and raised in Indiana and drilled an intense fear and respect of the city into him. This meant that when he and Daniel moved in together, Paul forced Daniel to repeat the number over and over until they could both remember it, in case one of them got mugged. Daniel complains about how much unnecessary space the number takes up in his brain every time he calls Paul, and therefore, he insists on calling the landline instead of Paul's cell. Tony does not understand their friendship. He imagines having to call Paul and invite him to a funeral. The thought nearly sends him right back to bed.

There are no messages from Daniel on Tony's phone. He spots one from an unknown number, and for a moment, hope climbs Tony's throat, until he opens it.

Hi Tony, this is Meredith. I caught a flight to Albany. I should be there by 6:00 p.m. Can someone pick me up?

Tony pushes his hair out of his face. He tries to imagine a trip to Albany in his shitty car within the next four hours. "Daniel's sister is flying in."

"JFK or Newark?" Colette asks.

Meredith could take Amtrak if it were that easy, those are better and more connected airports.

Tony grimaces. "Albany." The airport and train station in Albany are about an hour apart, and Meredith would have to find the right bus. Much faster to drive. "You have a car somewhere in this country, right? Could I borrow it?"

"Your father will pick her up," Ma interrupts.

Daniel shakes his head. "Ma, I can't ask that. I'm already not at the shop—"

"No arguments. Are you hungry? I made mac and cheese. We have enough time to eat before Gianna's shift ends."

Tony closes his eyes for a second. "Fine. Mac and cheese sounds good."

It's delicious, of course, it is. Ma leaves twenty minutes later, announcing Gianna and Lia will be by soon.

As soon as the door is shut behind her, Tony turns to Colette. "Anything from the detective?"

Colette shakes her head.

Tony turns to Emilio. "What about you? Anything on Lily?"

Emilio grimaces. He hasn't done much more than pick at his mac
and cheese, which would be a grave insult if the man hadn't lost the love
of his life and then been blamed for her murder within the last week. "I
found her email to Amy. Nothing you didn't know in there. Amy told her
she had to retake the class she dropped out of last year, and Lily never
responded."

Tony considers. "What about Daniel's emails?"

Neither of them answers him immediately.

"Are you sure?" Colette asks eventually.

Pushing his hair out of his face again, Tony says, "Look, I think he'll
forgive the breach of privacy if he ends up not dead."

"Not that." Colette waves away the thought of the potential invasion
of privacy with a lazy hand. "I've seen Lily Peterson. She's tiny. Could
she really have the physical strength to stab someone? Or kidnap someone?"

"Stacy Allan was tiny, and she kidnapped me just fine."

She also had a gun, which helped. Tony's not sure he'd have been as
intimidated by a knife, especially given Lily might not have another one
after taping the murder weapon to their door. Still, he's not about to un-
derestimate anyone.

"I think we should check," he reaffirms.

Emilio shrugs. "Do you know his password?"

It's probably Worf's fucking birthday.

"I can give it a shot." His hair is in his face again. Tony sighs. "Hey,
could you two get up for a second?"

Baffled, they do it.

Tony lifts the couch, forcing Worf to trundle out from underneath
and into the safety of the little cubbyhole halfway up his cat tree.

"Dude," Tony tells him. "Give me my hair tie."

Yellow eyes blink at him from the dark cubbyhole.

"Come on. I'll give you a treat."

Worf inches forward. The hair tie is still in his mouth. He must have stolen it right from off the nightstand.

"C'mon," Tony cajoles.

Worf inches forward again, and Tony grabs his hair tie, the cat's jaw no match for opposable thumbs.

"Gotcha," Tony crows and puts his hair up.

Colette and Emilio stare at him again.

Tony shrugs. "He does this. If I had an explanation, I would give it, trust me. Let me give Daniel's email a try."

Emilio hands over his laptop with Daniel's standard-issue university email username in the top field. The cursor blinks away in the password box, and Tony gives it his best shot.

It's not Worf's birthday.

It's also not 'worf0720' or any variation thereof Tony can think of.

"Fuck," Tony eventually sighs in resignation.

"I can try forcing it," Emilio says around a yawn. "If you're sure..."

"Yeah, I'm sure. But only after you've gotten some rest."

"Can't sleep."

Tony looks him over. "Try. Bedroom's next door. Sheets are reasonably clean."

Emilio looks set to protest. But he came over here in Tony's car. He's got no way home and nothing waiting for him there but household chores and grief.

"Come on," Tony cajoles, trying not to talk to him the way he talks to the cat. "You'll feel better."

"That's what I'm afraid of." Emilio grimaces as soon as it's out of his mouth. Out of the corner of his eye, Tony sees Colette's eyebrow raise.

"How about this," Tony offers. "Lie down for half an hour, and if you can't sleep, I'll forget about it."

Emilio's out like a light within five minutes, doesn't so much as twitch when Gianna rings the security doorbell at the building entrance.

Tony buzzes her in, dread settling in his stomach along with the anxiety. "You don't have to stay for the invasion of my entire family," he tells Colette. "If you want some space..."

"It's kind of your family to care so much." Colette busies herself putting their plates in the dishwasher.

Tony opens the fridge to inspect the damage. It's full to bursting. What he and Daniel could possibly use four whole mozzarella blocks for is a mystery, but apparently, Ma is planning on a round-the-clock d'Angelo presence, which is as comforting as it is invasive.

"After Mario..." Colette stops, takes a breath, and then forces herself to continue. "After Mario, I thought being alone would help. It didn't. All I did was isolate myself and Daniel, and I regret it. I'm not leaving, and I'm glad we won't be alone in this."

"Oh yeah? Even with a suspect in the other room?"

Colette is poised to answer, but Gianna's knock on the front door interrupts her.

When he opens, Tony finds Gianna also not alone.

There's Lia, of course, nestled against Gianna's chest in the snug wraparound Ma bought the week she found out about the pregnancy. Standing next to the two of them, though, huffing slightly from the effort of carrying the stroller up two flights of stairs, is Blake.

"What..." Tony asks blankly.

Gianna shrugs. "I figured you'd rather have him here than me."

"I got off night shifts this morning. I have a few days off," Blake adds.

Sighing, Tony stands aside and lets them in.

"I left Lisa a voice message." Blake kicks off his shoes before pushing the stroller into the living room. "Who knows when she'll hear it, but she should be off work soon too."

"She hates voice messages," Tony reminds him. "As does every rational person over the age of twenty."

"My mom loves voice messages."

Tony gives Blake a look. "Is she rational?"

They both know the answer to that question.

"So, what do you know so far?" Gianna asks. She sits down on the couch, Lia still wrapped up tight and, as far as Tony can tell, fast asleep.

Colette sits beside her and starts filling her in on everything, from Daniel's last messages to calling the detective to Emilio, asleep next door.

Tony pulls out the pitcher from the very top cupboard and busies himself filling it up with filtered water. He sets out glasses on the coffee table just as Gianna interrupts the story.

"Wait, you think Lily might have something to do with it?" She leans forward on the couch, dark hair swinging in front of her face. "Lily Peterson?"

"Yes." Colette sounds utterly guileless as if Tony hasn't *told* her Lily is Gianna's friend. "Why?"

If Tony had room in his brain for complex emotions, he would be in awe of how well Colette can play a room.

Frowning, Gianna pulls out her phone and examines her recent text messages. "She hasn't answered me since yesterday. I thought it was because..."

"I made a scene and got her pissed off at you," Tony finishes.

Awkward silence descends on them, only interrupted when Blake exits the bathroom, beelines for the kitchen, and cries out, "Sick! Is this your mom's mac and cheese?"

"Help yourself, Blake," Tony says wearily. "Dishes are on the top left, silverware's to the right of the stove."

"Have you tried calling Lily?" Colette asks.

They haven't tried since this morning, and maybe Gianna will have more luck since she isn't calling from an unknown number,

Gianna wrinkles her nose. "I mean, I didn't want to seem desperate."

Colette makes a sound in the back of her throat, which Tony takes to mean, *this generation is ridiculous.*

Gianna presses the call button.

She shakes her head. "Straight to voicemail." Tapping out something quick, she adds, "And texts aren't going through."

"Same as Daniel." Tony looks over to Colette. Same as when they tried yesterday and this morning. If it was Lily—if she took Daniel—

"What if Lily got kidnapped too?" Gianna asks.

Tony swallows around nothing. He didn't consider that possibility. It's certainly kinder than what he currently thinks about Lily.

"It's possible," Colette says. Her face gives nothing away. She must have been a poker player in a previous life. "Has Lily been acting abnormally recently?"

Gianna tilts her head to the side, considering. Lia grumbles at the sudden movement. "She's been pretty anxious. Coming back was harder than she thought, and she feels like everyone is judging her. She's been kind of flaky. Keeps forgetting to answer texts, and then she talks about how stressed out she is about it all. Sometimes, she seems really good, though, like, incredibly good, given everything. Then she phases back into not answering messages. I don't know if she was this way before...everything though."

"How long have you guys been hanging out?" Tony should probably feel guilty for acting as if it's an idle question and not mining Gianna for information. He comforts himself with the knowledge that if he's wrong, she'll never know.

"Just over the summer." Gianna looks down at the top of Lia's head, jiggling her a little. "We texted some in the spring when she was gone. She was here doing makeup classes in summer school, and we hung out toward the start. Then she met Sean in one of her classes and started spending more time with him."

"So, she bailed on you for a guy."

Gianna eyes him warily. "I mean, I guess? Or she wanted the normal college experience instead hanging out with a baby all the time."

Guilt clenches in Tony's stomach. He's been so focused on how hard everything is for him when he should have spent more time worrying about how hard it is for her.

"Hm." Colette folds her hands together, the first tell that she's trying to play Gianna. "Do you know where her dorm room is? We could see if she's there and why she isn't answering her phone. Maybe she forgot to charge it, or it broke."

Gianna considers. "Yeah. Yeah, that sounds like a good idea."

Chapter Twelve

Blake crashes on the couch, the night shifts getting to him, about an hour after Colette and Gianna head out to investigate Lily's room. Tony's a little upset they left him behind, but it makes sense because his family decided to camp out in Daniel's apartment. Anyway, someone needs to watch Lia while Gianna is gone. Plus, no one wants Emilio waking up to an empty apartment.

Ma spends the late afternoon in the kitchen, cooking up something much too complicated for dinner, and Tony dragged extra chairs up from Colette's apartment when it became clear the apartment would be stuffed to the limit tonight. Now, he sits in the kitchen, one eye on the baby monitor, one eye on his phone. Lisa's made it in as well and sits on the corner of the couch not occupied by Blake's sprawled-out form, trying to convince Worf to be friends with her. So far, she's gotten him to sniff her fingers and rub up against them, after which he promptly turns around and smacks her hand with his claws, even though he's the one who asked to be petted.

Pa and Meredith should get in any minute. Her flight got in on time, and Pa texted before they hit the road.

There's still nothing from Daniel.

Tony's phone battery is almost drained again. He's been checking it so much, reading and rereading Daniel's last message, looking for a code or a hint or anything that could be a fucking lifeline. The police haven't gotten in touch either.

"No news is good news," Ma says, bending over the oven.

"Yeah, they haven't found a body yet." Tony's aware his voice sounds detached, caustic. No one here deserves that. They've all shown up for him, for Daniel, but he can't help himself. The longer they hear nothing, the more it itches under his skin. He wishes he could translate his irritation into something more tangible, into tears or rage or *anything*. Where's all the emotion that was sitting under his skin for days at a time beforehand? Why can't he work it up for Daniel, when Daniel's— when he feels—when Daniel means...

"Tony." It takes a moment for him to remember what Ma is chiding him for.

"Sorry."

"Where are Daniel's spices?" Ma asks, already busy over the stove again.

Tony points. "Cupboard right above you." Calling them "Daniel's spices" is a bit of a reach. When Tony started cooking here, all Daniel had was salt, paprika, and dried sage. Tony's been fixing that, one shopping trip at a time, and by the look Ma gives him over her shoulder, she can tell it's his doing. It would be a big coincidence if Daniel stocked the same brand of spices she always buys.

While her back is turned, Tony checks his phone again.

Colette has sent him seven pictures of a narrow dorm room cluttered with things. Tony zooms in to see beyond the general detritus. Laundry sits heaped in one corner. A silver laptop balances precariously on top a stack of textbooks covering the desk. The bed is unmade. All of the dresser drawers hang open. A prescription pill box sits on the windowsill by the bed, next to a plastic bottle of cheap vodka and an open can of soda.

Surely, a cold-blooded murderer's lair would look less like a normal college student's room. There's also no sign of Daniel anywhere.

What are the pills? Tony texts Colette.

Xanax, comes the response.

The doorbell startles Tony up from googling the side effects of Xanax and trying to figure out whether they could cause someone to kidnap a professor.

It's chaos from the start: Woken by the bell, Emilio wanders in and tries to talk himself out of staying for dinner since he feels so bad for overstaying his welcome; Blake shoots upright and blearily tries to help while getting in everyone's way; Lia squalls at the sudden uproar; Colette and Gianna pretend, badly, that they only went to Hannaford's to pick up more drinks; and there, in the entrance, Meredith Rosenbaum arrives with a carry-on suitcase in one hand and an expression on her face painfully reminiscent of Daniel's at the end of a long day.

Tony sets the extra chair he's carrying down. "Hi, Meredith."

"Hi," she says. "You look bigger when you're not on FaceTime."

It's barely a joke, but he snorts with laughter anyway. "Thank you for being here. Come in. Let me take your bag."

"Are you kidding? Of course I'm here. Have you heard anything?"

Wordlessly, Tony shakes his head. He pulls her bag down the hallway and leaves it in front of the bedroom. "Fuck," he mutters to himself. He has no idea where Meredith will sleep, especially if Emilio sticks around.

They'll figure something out. Maybe his family will go home.

Dinner is hectic. None of the chairs are the same height, and the only tables in the apartment are Daniel's desk and his second overflow desk, both of which are full of crap they have to clean off.

It's a chance for Tony to catch Colette alone, to ask if they found anything.

"Nothing," she says with a grimace. "It looks like her room was ransacked, but..."

"But she's a college student. It might just look like that. How did you even get in?"

"Gianna knew the RA and asked for the master key."

Hopefully, the RA didn't find that at all suspicious.

"It might be good," Colette offers. "There were no weapons. Nothing strange or dangerous, besides cheap vodka."

"She might have taken everything with her."

"Tony."

Tony ignores her and sees about getting the desks to the living room.

"He's going to be so pissed," he groans as they carry out the proper desk from the office. "Took him all summer to get through all his papers and find the surface of the tables."

"I think if he comes home safely, the state of his desk will be the least of his worries." Colette means it to be encouraging, but the "if" doesn't fill Tony with hope.

Somehow, between 5:00 and 7:30 p.m., Ma managed to produce a salad and two separate lasagnas, one vegetarian and one with meat. She also made her own garlic bread. It's the tearaway kind, and it would be impressive if Tony didn't know most of her kitchen cheats—she lets it do the second rise in the preheating oven so she can make it in under two hours.

The makeshift tables can barely fit all the plates, so they serve themselves in the kitchen and eat as best they can in the living room.

"I keep telling Daniel we need to get a real table," Tony apologizes to no one in particular. "Sorry."

"That's fine." Meredith smiles like her brother, all crinkly eyes. "Reminds me of college."

"Right...well, I guess, in a way, Daniel still is in college."

They discuss what they should do over dessert (brownies, quick and easy, and Ma's one concession to the fact that whipping up a full meal for nine on a moment's notice is actually a ton of work). Everyone kindly pretends there is anything tangible they can do.

Lisa offers to use her school supplies to get missing posters copied. Blake says he'll tag along with her to work so he can start hanging them up immediately, which means they need to make the posters tonight. Gianna offers to make something on photoshop; Meredith finds a good picture of Daniel on her phone. Colette helps Ma with the washing-up while Tony and Emilio put the furniture back where it belongs.

Tony pauses to catch his breath when they've got the desks in the office again.

"You all right, man?" Emilio looks better for the sleep, his eyes sharper.

"Should be asking you that."

Emilio laughs. "Pretty sure I'm not gonna be all right for a good long time."

Tony's throat dries out. "Yeah. Yeah. I'm fine. It's just a lot."

"All that love and support. Must be rough."

"Fuck you, dude."

Unrepentant, Emilio shrugs. "They're all here for you, and for Daniel. Means something."

"Makes me feel as if I'm not...worrying enough." Tony looks away as he says it, stuffing his hands into the pockets of Daniel's sweatshirt. "I should be thinking about Daniel, not...wondering when we last washed the spare sheets."

"You'll have enough time to feel like shit later," Emilio says grimly.

Tony's head snaps in his direction.

"I mean, if... Look, you have no reason to feel like shit *now*."

"Yeah." Tony tries to nod, tries to look as if Emilio's choice of words didn't make him suddenly remember, all at once and viscerally, that Daniel could be dead. "Sure."

It's too late. Emilio mutters, "Sorry," and heads back to the living room.

Tony gives himself a second to breathe before he follows. It's a harsh reminder of what he could have already lost. He tries to be a realist, to acknowledge his fears without letting them rule him. Of course Emilio would know how it feels. Of course he would be able to rip away Tony's attempt at distance with a few choice words.

The chill down Tony's spine isn't Emilio's fault, but it makes it hard to look him in the eye.

The impromptu group project for the poster sits crowded on the couch. Gianna looks up when Tony comes in. "Hey. Is there a computer we could use?"

Wincing at the thought of the desktop in the office, the monitors, keyboard, and mouse now on the floor with the cables tangled up hopelessly, Tony digs in the drawer under the coffee table to pull out Daniel's laptop. He hopes no one spotted the bottle of lube in there.

"Yeah, let me get you set up." He pulls the charger cable out from under the couch, where Daniel shoves it when they're watching TV and Tony complains about the damn cable always being in the way.

The password is "worfsforehead." Daniel is such a nerd.

"Here you go." Tony passes the laptop to Gianna.

From where he's been scrutinizing the bookshelves in the hall, Pa says, "Hmm."

Tony wanders over to him. "Something the matter?"

"Nah." Pa looks back at the shelf. It's the classics shelf, the one Daniel thinks looks the most pretentious because of all the matching Penguin logos on the spines. "You're here a lot, huh?"

"Yeah."

"Guess you know where everything is."

"Yup."

There doesn't appear to be more to say, so Pa continues his perusal of the shelf, frowning slightly.

Nonplussed, Tony follows Pa's sightline to Daniel's copy of *Of Human Bondage*. "Uh, that one's not about what you think."

"What's it about, then?"

Tony grimaces. "Mostly about how doing good things for other people is worthless if it makes you feel good about yourself. There's some stuff in there about love, too, but to be honest, I gave up about halfway through."

"Sounds like a blast. Daniel recommend it?"

"Nah, he never tells me what to read." Tony smiles faintly. "Just asks what I thought of it after." Which doesn't mean Daniel is relaxed about Tony's reading material. When Tony set *Of Human Bondage* back on the shelf, it turned out Daniel had a whole speech prepared on why he hated it, as if he had been bracing himself to talk Tony out of enjoying it. He gave an impromptu lecture about virgin-whore complexes and W. Somerset Maugham's biography, and Tony got lost in listening to Daniel talk about something he was passionate about and forgot most of the details.

"Hmm." Pa runs a finger along the shelf. "He should stabilize this. Shelves are starting to bend."

"I was gonna do that sometime this month." Tony picked up a few two-by-fours at the hardware store and borrowed a drill for a quick and dirty solution against the weight of Daniel's ever-expanding collection of books and journals. He was debating if it would be worth getting wood paint to match the shelf and if he should add some low-level lighting to it for the evenings. It seemed daunting, before, to talk to Daniel about making purposeful changes to the apartment. Tony was scared of asking too much. Now he wishes he was braver. Maybe if Daniel knew Tony was waiting for him at home, at their home, he wouldn't have stayed at Lobell for so long, and no one could have kidnapped him. "Was gonna talk to Daniel about it sometime soon."

Out of the corner of his eye, Tony catches Pa's smile.

"What?"

Pa shakes his head. "Nothing. I...nothing. You think he'd mind if I borrowed something?"

"Nope. The stuff he needs for work is at the office anyway."

"All right, then, recommend something."

Tony eyes the shelves. He hasn't read many of Daniel's books, at least not in comparison to the sheer number of them, but he does have a solid hold on what his pa reads. He pulls one of the less oppressively long Brandon Sanderson novels out from the fantasy section and offers it to Pa. "Give that one a shot."

"Thanks."

Pa settles in the comfy chair while work on the poster proceeds next to him. Colette and Ma are talking in the kitchen, a low murmur of voices. Tony debates going to help, but Emilio's already there, drying dishes, and Tony doesn't want to risk another disturbing conversation.

Instead, he goes for the hallway closet and pulls out the spare bedding. He can make up enough for two extra people to sleep here tonight, so long as they don't mind sharing the couch. If anyone else is planning on staying, they'll have to share the bed with him. Tony hopes that will be enough of a disincentive to drive everyone else away.

By the time he's finished sorting out the sheets, cleanup is finished in the kitchen. Emilio's on his phone in the hallway and seems to be talking to Francie if his sudden abrupt change in tone to soft and gentle is any indication. Gianna's in the office with Lia, who's about ready to be put down for the night. Colette and Meredith are drinking wine in the kitchen, and it looks like they've just about convinced Ma to join them for a glass. Blake and Lisa are bickering over the poster.

Tony lets himself fall into place beside them on the couch and pulls out his phone. Still nothing from Daniel, of course. Colette's forwarded a text from Detective Taylor, a simple *No news yet*.

With nothing better to do, Tony googles Rate My Professor. He checks Amelia Lawrence's page again and rereads the negative reviews left for her. There's the one with the implicit threat, of course, but the other one isn't what Tony would call grounds for suspicion. *Take this class if you love zebrafish and robotically handing in every assignment exactly on time. If you're human, tough luck.*

Honestly, it's kind of funny. Not that Tony was ever the type of student to need an extension. He's proud of his school record of pervasive mediocrity, right down to being punctual if not prepared. He wrote most of his essays the night before, and the worst it did for him was a D-plus in World History in eleventh grade.

Still, he knew many people like Lily Peterson. Charlie was a similar student when they all still went to school together, anxious, overprepared, and somehow underperforming, despite their intelligence, because the pressures of their brain were too big.

Tony gets it.

He's eternally grateful he didn't have unlimited access to the internet when he was growing up. This is exactly the shit he'd have thought would be witty to post about his high school chemistry teacher.

It's not a good look, but it doesn't scream murder either. Anyway, there's no way to prove Lily left these messages, not without tracing her IP address or something else Daniel would probably know about.

With nothing better to do, Tony looks up Daniel on the site. He has a 4.1 rating. It's lit up in green, so it must be a good score. The first commenter complains about all the reading but says *Professor Rosenbaum makes up for it with interesting classes and good essay prompts.*

The second one gushes about how available he is even outside of office hours.

The third one calls him cute.

Tony doesn't disagree with any of these assessments, but he feels weird about strangers online leaving such detailed, personal descriptions of what they like about him. It's almost a relief when the next commenter gives Daniel a 2.0 and calls his class boring.

Colette has a 3.8 rating. Apparently, she's strict, but her classes are "worth it." Tony wonders what that means. He's debating screenshotting some of the funnier reviews—pro: it will be hilarious to tease Daniel and Colette about; con: Tony hasn't checked the shop's Google ratings in a while, and who knows what ammunition they might find in return—when his phone starts ringing.

He doesn't recognize the number, but it has a New York area code. Frowning, Tony gets up to take the call in the bedroom.

"Hello?"

"Tony? Is that you?"

"Yeah." Tony knows the voice, but he can't quite place where from.

"Oh, thank fuck. You would not believe the journey I have been on to get your number."

"Uh," Tony tries. "Who is this?"

"Fuck, sorry. It's Paul. Weintrob? Daniel's—"

"Paul!" Tony's heart jumps into his throat. "Have you heard from Daniel?"

"Maybe."

Tony blinks. "What the fuck does 'maybe' mean?"

"About an hour and a half ago, I got a text on my phone."

"Okay." Tony's running out of patience quickly. Paul is a weird guy at the best of times, and right now, Tony doesn't have the stomach for it. "From Daniel?"

"On the *landline*. Frankly, I didn't know it could do that."

"Oh, shit. It's the only number Daniel knows by heart."

"Right," Paul agrees. "And he never lets me forget it. My own parents never use the landline anymore, only him."

"So he texted you?"

"He sent a text to the landline, or at least I think he did, and an automated woman's voice read it out loud. She said the number it was from, too, but it's not Daniel's number."

"What did it say?"

"Tony. Germantown. Come alone. No 911." Paul recites it by rote, like he's reading it off something. But that's Tony's name. That's information straight from Daniel. That's proof he's not dead, or at least he wasn't when he sent the message.

Relief gets Tony right in the knees, and he's sitting heavily on the bed before he realizes what he's doing. He can barely breathe. The vague, heavy fear he's been carrying since this morning crystallizes into an anxious desire to get to Germantown right now, to end this.

"Tony, what the hell is going on?"

Oh, right. Tony hasn't told him. "Daniel's been missing since yesterday. No one has heard from him. He left his car. His phone isn't on. And, uh. Someone stabbed a professor at his college last week."

Paul lets loose an impressive string of profanity. "'Why couldn't you find a nice cushy job at a rural college, Paul,'" he mocks. "'The city is so dangerous.' I am never taking my parents seriously again. What the fuck is happening upstate?"

Tony laughs shakily. "I wish I knew. This is the first we've heard from him."

"Okay," Paul says. "Okay, okay. So, I listened to it three times, and then I accidentally deleted it. But I'm about eighty-nine percent certain those were the exact words. Tony, Germantown, come alone, no 911. You're the only Tony I know, and Germantown is pretty close to you guys, so it has to be Daniel, right?"

Germantown. No police. That's...ominous, at best.

"And you might be getting some concerned calls," Paul adds. "I had to call Mari, who called Daniel's parents to get your number, to send it back to me."

"Daniel's parents know. At least his mom does. His dad was in surgery today, so you probably didn't catch him."

"God, you two are domestic."

"Thanks, I think. You're sure the message didn't say anything else?"

"Nothing."

There's a long, awkward pause in which Tony tries to think of a good way to end this conversation.

"Christ," Paul says, "Um, do you need anything?"

Tony has more help than he can deal with. "Thanks, but not right now. Let me know if you get anything else. This is actually really good."

"*How*?"

"He's still alive."

It takes another three minutes of Paul expounding on the dangers of living outside of Williamsburg, but Tony manages to extricate himself from the call.

It's dark out already. Every light in the apartment is on. The kitchen is spotless. The living room is quiet, as though everyone has tired themselves out by acting busy, and all that's left is the anxiety drawing them together.

For a brief moment, Tony considers telling everyone the good news: Daniel's alive, or he was an hour and a half ago. They have a place to go. They have a goal.

Immediately, he reconsiders.

He doesn't want his family knowing he's going to Germantown alone, and he's definitely not calling the police if Daniel doesn't want him to. He justifies it to himself on the pretense that the police are informed about Daniel's disappearance and Lily's likely involvement, and so far, it's achieved jack shit in finding Daniel. But no one else was here last year; they wouldn't understand. Tony's not even sure Blake and Lisa would take it well. Colette will get it. Colette, he would take with him, but Emilio has joined her discussion with Meredith, and he...

He's the one link to Germantown Tony can think of.

Suddenly, the chills Tony got when Emilio told him he would have plenty of time for grief later return tenfold. Tony spent all day being sure Emilio didn't do it after seeing how honestly wrecked he is. But he doesn't know Emilio. For all Tony knows, he could be the world's best actor. If Tony tells everyone Daniel is alive, Emilio will know Daniel got a message out, and that could put him in danger if Emilio did it.

Instead of an announcement, Tony starts with a yawn. "So." He keeps his mouth open pretending he's too tired to stop yawning while he talks. "I'm getting pretty beat. How do y'all want to do this?"

"We'll head back to Kingston," Pa says. "Let you get some rest."

"We'll be here again in the morning," Ma threatens.

"I can come into the shop." For a moment, Tony feels guilty. He has absolutely no intention of going to work tomorrow. He knows his parents care too much to let him do it. He's offering so they can turn him down, and he's so thankful they will.

"Absolutely not. Let Kyle earn his keep." Ma's expression bodes no dissent.

Tony holds his hands up in surrender.

"You good to stay here if I take my car?" Gianna asks Blake.

Right. She brought him over this afternoon.

"I'll catch a ride with Lisa tomorrow morning. But you gotta let me say goodbye to the princess." Blake gestures to Lia, sleeping in her stroller, briefly angelic.

While he coos over her, Gianna pulls Tony into a brief, tight hug.

"Right, then," she says. "I'm headed home too. I'll see you tomorrow."

He blames it on the mess that has been this day, but tears spark briefly behind his eyes. Despite everything they've said to each other recently, he still has this.

"Yeah," he says roughly. "Glad you came."

She ruffles his hair. "'Course."

It takes another twenty minutes for them all to get their shoes on, for Blake to give Gianna a hug goodbye (and since when have they been so close?), and for Lia to be picked up from her nap so Ma and Pa can fight over who will carry the stroller. (Pa's back is acting up, but he still doesn't like it when his wife carries things.) In the end, Emilio carries it downstairs for them. Pa will be so grumpy tomorrow when he has to open the shop after getting less than his full eight hours of sleep.

Guilt twinges in Tony's gut. He should probably have told them the truth.

After, it's just the six of them, standing around the too-well-lit living room.

"So," Tony starts, wondering if he can get everyone to leave but Colette.

"It's cool if we crash here, right?" Blake yawns.

"Um." Is there a polite way to point out that Daniel's sister has first dibs on the couch? Or that Blake and Lisa both have their own apartments twenty minutes away? Tony doesn't really care; he gave up on being polite to the two of them long ago. But he'd rather get to know Meredith a little before she finds out what he's usually like.

"Actually, I was thinking..." Colette says. "Maybe Meredith would be more comfortable on my guest bed." It sounds as if it's an idea Colette came up with in the last five minutes, but Tony tracks her and Meredith sharing a glance and guesses they were talking about this before.

"If you'd rather, sure," he says. "We've got enough bedding and space for two people on the couch. So, if these two"—Tony jerks his thumb toward Blake and Lisa—"are staying, it'll probably be better. You can always have the bed though. I can drive back to Kingston." He adds the last as an afterthought, a gesture to the fact that he doesn't live here. It feels strange after he's spent all day playing host, telling people where to find the silverware and the cups.

Meredith shakes her head. "No, no, I don't want to put you out."

"You're not, not at all. I'm so glad you came—"

"Tony," Meredith says firmly. Her hair is darker than Daniel's, pulled up to a braid gone messy after a day of travel. It's less curly too.

Her eyes, though, are the same, and the way she looks at Tony, half gentle, half chiding—that's Daniel all over. "It's okay. Get some rest. We'll have all the time tomorrow to be awkward in-laws, yeah?"

In-laws. The word sends a shoot of fear and longing straight through Tony. "Yeah, all right. Thanks, Colette."

Colette gives him the same kind of look. She's been spending too much time with the Rosenbaums. "My contributions have been vast. Eating your mother's cooking and drinking your wine."

She leaves her coffee maker on the stove when she and Meredith slip downstairs for the night, a clear sign tomorrow will be more of the same as today, with the apartment full of people who care about Daniel. And Tony. If he makes it back from whatever's waiting for him in Germantown. Especially now he's missed his chance to tell Colette about it.

Emilio clears his throat.

"Right," Tony says. "We gotta get you home, huh?"

"I don't wanna put you out, but you did drive me here." Emilio shrugs. "I'm kinda short on other options. Unless you'd rather I call a cab."

"It's twenty minutes, man. It's fine." Tony turns to Blake and Lisa. "Bedding's in the bedroom. You can throw all the pillows off the couch onto the floor."

Blake salutes.

By quarter to eleven, Tony's in the car, peeling off onto the 9G toward Germantown with Emilio in the passenger seat, and by some miracle, no one thinks it was his idea.

Of course, there's the minor matter of being alone with a man who might have killed his wife. *Germantown*, Daniel's message said, and *Come alone*. It doesn't mean anything to Tony. Before Daniel, he didn't spend much time this side of the Hudson, and Germantown isn't known for its social scene. Mostly, it's known for having a big trailer park. Or for being another dot on the map on the way to Hudson (the town, not the river).

What other connection could there be besides Emilio?

"So, no new leads, huh?" Emilio asks. It's dark in the car. Tony can't make out his expressions while he watches the road.

"Not exactly." Tony drums his fingers on the steering wheel. "Sorry to waste your time."

Emilio laughs humorlessly. "You got me out of the house. And you got to watch a prime suspect nap all day. Still think I did it?"

"After last year, I don't trust my own instincts." Tony never for a moment suspected Stacy until he knew it was her beyond a shadow of a doubt. Which means his gut instinct in ruling Emilio out as a suspect is meaningless. Ever since Daniel's message told him to go to Germantown, everything Emilio says has sounded suspicious.

"Fair enough."

"You're still shockingly chill about people thinking you killed your wife."

"Tried getting angry. Made it worse."

"Ah. The memorial."

Emilio rubs his hands across his face, scraping against his stubble. "Yeah. Apparently, yelling at a bunch of people makes them think you're volatile or something."

"Did it feel good?"

"When does it not feel good to get pissed off?" Emilio asks it as if it's natural, as if everyone enjoys feeling rage.

After the last few days with Gianna, Tony can't relate. Anger makes him miserable.

"God, the fights I used to have with Amy..." Emilio mutters.

"Yeah?" Tony prods. This is what got him in trouble with Stacy in broad daylight on a college campus. Now, he's in a moving car, in the dark, and the only people who know where he is have no way of following them. This has "bad idea" written all over it, and Colette would tell him so, but she's not here. Daniel would tell him so, but Daniel's why he's here, speeding to Germantown in the middle of the night.

"Yeah, man," Emilio continues. "I was practically raising our kid alone as soon as the semester started. Of course we fought about it."

"Sounds rough."

There's a smile in Emilio's voice. "You and Daniel aren't the kind of couple that fights, huh?"

"There was one time." Tony wouldn't call it a fight so much as the catalyst of their relationship. They could have fallen apart over it; instead, Daniel found the courage to be honest about what he wanted, and Tony found the faith to trust in what they had. "But otherwise, no, not really our style."

"Amy loved a good discussion." Emilio sighs wistfully. "The night we met, we spent all night arguing about whether women are underrepresented in STEM fields. By the time we agreed on anything, the rest of the party around us was over, and it was nearly dawn."

Tony's not one to judge. Emilio apparently cherishes the memory. To Tony, it sounds awful. "Sounds different than fighting about your kid."

"Well, yeah. We'd have worked it out though. We always do. Did."

They pass through Red Hook and Tivoli while Tony chews on that. "Not something you can tell the police," he says eventually when he can't let the silence go on.

"Nope. Not you or your friend either, huh?"

Tony winces. He's being too obvious.

"It's cool. I wouldn't trust me either. Hell, I don't right now."

"Comforting."

Emilio shrugs. "I never thought I was the kind of guy who yelled at strangers. Turns out I am if enough shit has happened around me. Never thought I'd send my kid away because I can't take care of her. Who knows what I could do."

They're closing in on Germantown now. With no other plan of how to find Daniel, Tony takes the turnoff to Emilio's house. "You'll be fine. You'll get Francie back next week, and you'll make it work for her."

"Sure." Emilio's eyes are heavy on Tony, making him want to squirm. "Someday. Anyway, I wanted to say thanks."

"For suspecting you of murder?"

"For getting me out of the goddamn house. And cleaning up my kitchen. I needed that. I'll take being a murder suspect if it gets me out of my own head."

It startles a laugh out of Tony as he pulls up to the curb next to the Lawrence house. "If you say so."

"I do." With a grin so sharp it's wolfish, Emilio undoes his seatbelt and gets out of the car.

"Hey," Tony says before he can get too far away.

Emilio turns.

"Look," Tony says, "I have one more lead for you. It's a long shot, but someone was leaving bomb reviews of your wife on Rate My Professor. Maybe you can trace them. Might be something to incriminate Lily Peterson." At least it could keep Emilio occupied while Tony gets Daniel the hell out of this town.

"Probably not. But thanks. Come back anytime. Seriously." Emilio raps his knuckles on the roof of the car, and then he's vanishing into the dark of his empty house.

Tony watches lights turn on and off in the windows as Emilio climbs the stairs, uses the bathroom, and goes to bed, until a lone lamp upstairs stays lit. He wonders if Emilio will sleep. Probably not, not in the bed he and Amy shared. Tony couldn't. He'd be sleeping on the couch if anything happened to Daniel. Unless Emilio's that cold, and he likes to sleep in sheets still smelling of a woman he murdered.

Tony can't stay here, watching the house like a creeper. Emilio knows his car; he caught Tony staking him out once today. Anyway, Daniel's not in the house. Colette checked everywhere. Unless there's a secret basement or something, Daniel must be somewhere else.

He pulls away from the curb and cruises through Germantown. It's pretty depressing. A two-year-old billboard for the school's baseball team looms to the side, and otherwise, only ads for shops in other towns line the roadside. Maybe in daylight it would be green and tranquil, but at this time of night, Tony can't help but find it eerie.

Germantown by darkness is nothing besides the 9G winding through it. The only thing still open is the gas station with a lone teenager behind the till, eating a candy bar and scrolling on his phone. Tony exhausts every road in town he can drive down, headlights sweeping across darkened houses and empty parking lots.

214 - S.B. Barnes

He's just finished another pass by the Lawrence house (Emilio's light is still on upstairs) and is about to give up for the night when he spots it. To his left, a parking lot looms in front of a building with dilapidated neon lettering barely illuminating it. Only a *C*, an *N*, and two *U*'s announce that it used to be a movie theater called the Continuum. And there, all alone in the parking lot, sits an '07 Toyota Camry.

Chapter Thirteen

Tony doesn't park in the lot. He drives to the Lawrence house again and leaves his car at the curb. If anything happens, Emilio will see the car eventually and come looking. Or if Emilio's involved, the police—more likely, Colette—will know where to start looking.

Fuck. Who is he kidding? Emilio isn't involved. Tony should have trusted his gut, which has been protesting Emilio's innocence since the memorial service. It's been evident since they met that Emilio had nothing to do with this. Over the last few hours, Tony flirted with the simple solution, imagining he might have done it. It was easy in the way the resolution of an episode of *Bones* often is. Emilio has a motive and a complicated relationship with his wife. Emilio wouldn't need to be pitied if he did it. It would make sense.

It would be wrong. Tony might not easily understand Emilio's relationship with his wife, but he loved her, and he loves his daughter. His grief is making him harder and harsher than he was before. Tony understands more intimately than he wants to. He has from day one even if Colette can't quite see it.

No, the solution is much more obvious and a lot harder to take.

Since the very beginning, Tony thought there was something off about Lily. The first couple days of the semester, she put up a good front that she was doing better, and she was ready to be back in school. But after Amelia Lawrence's death, Lily's downward spiral was so obvious Tony noticed it from two degrees of separation. He let Daniel's firm, almost desperate desire to help her blind him to the danger of Lily's instability, and now, they're paying the price. Now, Emilio and his daughter have paid the price.

The only thing stopping Tony from calling 911 is that Daniel's message said, "No police," and Tony has no idea why.

He uses his phone flashlight to return most of the way to the Continuum. Germantown needs to invest in some streetlamps. Some infrastructure. Something. When Tony can see the empty theater in the distance, he shuts his light off. No need to alert anyone to his presence.

Empty beer cans and fast-food wrappers litter the parking lot and pile up high beside the overflowing trash can. The place has probably become a favorite hangout for local teens since it shut down. Tony and his friends used to do that as well, find empty spaces no one was using and claim them for their own. He likes to think he was a little more conscientious about cleaning up his trash, but he knows for sure no one in the vicinity appreciated the elongated Eminem phase he and Blake G went through when they were about fourteen, so he really has no legs to stand on.

The main entrance is padlocked. If he had the proper tools on him, Tony could easily crowbar it open, but he doubts it's a good idea. At the very least, whoever took Daniel—and at the moment, Lily is looking likely—got rid of his phone and made him come here, which tells Tony a threat was involved.

Tony wanders around the outside. On *Criminal Minds*, they would call it "casing the perimeter." On *Bones*, the FBI characters would be angry at the scientists for going to a possible crime scene without backup.

Tony's neither a scientist nor an FBI agent. He's just a run-of-the-mill idiot.

The building barely has any windows, which is probably convenient for a movie theater but annoying for people trying to see inside. The back door has no lock. Tony tries the handle, but it doesn't budge as if there's something blocking the way.

He pushes a little harder, and an awful, grinding scrape screeches as though something shifted minutely, but the door stays shut.

Almost immediately, he hears footsteps inside.

"Hello?" a thin, high voice calls.

Low, aggravated whispers follow, and then what sounds like furniture shifts behind the door, loud and sudden.

Tony races around the corner of the building and makes for a section of greenery on slightly higher ground between that side of the old building and the fence encasing the whole property. He drops to his knees and scrambles into the underbrush growing wild there, which scratches at his face, hands, and neck.

The light of a cell phone flashlight sweeps around the asphalt by the back door. Thank fuck, Tony was paranoid enough to park somewhere else. He can't make out the owner of the phone, not in the dark with the light from it blinding him to everything else. He can take an educated guess though. Especially when the person, obviously agitated and frustrated, sparks up a cigarette as they continue their search.

Sean.

He and Colette talked about how out of his depth he was, that Lily was dragging him down. But for some reason, Tony didn't expect to find him here. He looks incongruous, like a teenager in a suit he borrowed from his dad, the wrong shape to fit.

Colette said it days ago, didn't she? Amelia Lawrence and Daniel aren't the only ones who have been pulled under by the tide of Lily sinking into her struggles. Sean has also been affected, and Tony has done him the same disservice he does himself: pretending that because he acts unaffected, he's doing fine. They should have pushed more on the phone with him, should have asked him if he was really okay, if he was sure he hadn't heard from Lily. He must have been scared.

Sean sweeps the whole of the parking lot, checks behind the

building, and for one agonizing minute, the light of his phone shines across the bushes hiding Tony. He covers his face with his arms. The whole thing is over fast enough that he doesn't even rediscover Catholicism through panicked prayer, which is a pleasant surprise.

After Sean's done, both with the search and the cigarette, he returns to the building. Tony can't see or hear a single thing happening inside. But it's only a matter of minutes before Sean exits again, this time wearing an unseasonably warm duffel coat and a baseball cap that, unfortunately, does nothing to disguise his distinctive facial hair. Sean chains a second lock into place over the back door.

Then, he gets in his car and drives away.

"Fuck," Tony mutters to himself as he scrambles out of the bushes and heads for the door. He should have said something. Gotten Sean's attention. Sean is the reasonable one here, the one who doesn't want to be in this mess. If Tony talked to him... But who knows how deeply Lily has her hooks in him. What if Sean thinks he needs to keep helping her or she'll hurt him? It's too risky. Tony's first priority is Daniel.

He should have brought a toolbox. He should have brought fucking anything. No way he's getting through that lock with his bare hands. It's a bike lock (of course it is; these are Lobell students), and with the right tools it would be easy to crack, but Tony doesn't have anything helpful on hand.

"Daniel?" he hisses. He doesn't dare raise his voice too much. Who knows if Lily is still in there, or how dangerous she is. At least Sean was free to leave. But their third friend might also be part of this. Tony is unarmed, and he's no closer to getting Daniel out.

A scrambling noise comes from the other side of the door. "Tony?"

It's been a day and a half since he last heard Daniel's voice. Not much time in the grand scheme of things, but the sound of it makes Tony's entire body feel so light with relief he thinks he might float away. His joints turn to water. He sinks to his knees by the door.

"Daniel," he repeats dumbly. "Are you all right? I mean, are you hurt?"

"I'm fine," Daniel says hurriedly. "I mean, they have me in some terrible Party City handcuffs, and I'm losing circulation, but otherwise."

"They have a quick release? I can't get the door open right now, but give me an hour or so to get some tools. Then I can—"

"No, listen." Daniel's voice through the door is urgent. "You can't break me out yet."

The information doesn't register in Tony's brain at first.

"What?"

"Look, this has gotten...complicated."

Tony lets his head thunk against the door. The adrenaline of finding Daniel, the relief he's alive and reasonably unharmed, fades quickly. "Tell me why I'm not calling Detective Taylor out here right now."

"It's Lily."

Great. Just as Tony suspected. "She did it? Amelia Lawrence?"

An ominously long pause follows.

"She showed up at my office yesterday looking as if she hadn't slept in years. She was talking about the knife, Tony. I think she...I think she probably must have."

"Of course she did! She taped the murder weapon to your door!"

"She was freaking out though. Totally off the wall. I couldn't understand half of what she was saying. Next thing I know, she's pulling out a *hunting rifle* she could barely hold up on her own and pointing it at me and telling me I had to go with her."

"Jesus." Tony waits for Daniel to continue, but when no further information is forthcoming, he has to ask. "Seriously, though, why no police?"

He can hear the huff of Daniel's sigh through the door. "I think she's high."

This still doesn't sound like a reason to Tony, but he bites his tongue.

"And the boyfriend is helping her," Daniel continues. "He took my phone, threw it out the window somewhere on the road. Brought us here. He had the pills they both took before."

"She has a Xanax prescription. Shouldn't that help—"

"Not those kind of pills."

Ice creeps down Tony's spine. Lily has been getting more and more unstable ever since the start of the school year. Tony saw, and he barely knows her. What did Gianna say? Lily was "flaky." Not responding to messages. Moody.

"You think that's why she did it?" Tony asks.

"Maybe. I mean, she's barely responsive half the time and totally over the top the rest of it. And, well..."

"Hey." Tony leans in so he's as close to the door as he can be when Daniel trails off, seeming unwilling to say the rest. "You can tell me. It's *me*, Daniel. I came out here alone because of a *text* you sent to Paul's *landline*."

"I had no idea if that would work," Daniel admits. "But, uh... Look, I don't know enough about all this, but one or both of them is... After they took the pills, she got all...hyperactive. They, well, they...went into the bathroom. Together. And...I don't want to say it."

Tony swallows. "You think *he's* taking advantage?" Of the two students, Tony has a pretty good idea who is trying to keep it together and who caused this mess. The drugs are a bad look, but they're *students*. Of course they're doing drugs.

"I have no idea who is taking advantage of whom." Daniel's voice is clipped and angry. "But I do know she has been taken advantage of before, and she's my student and my responsibility, and I can't call the cops on her. You remember what happened to Andrew."

That's who Daniel's angry at, then. Himself.

"It wasn't your fault." Tony tries to be as gentle about it as he can, but he already knows Daniel doesn't want to hear it.

"I should have done better by him. And I should have done better by her, last year. I should have known."

Frustration boils over. "Lily *kidnapped you* at *gunpoint*. She's been threatening you for weeks. She's dangerous. Daniel, you could have died."

"She needs help."

Tony wants to shake Daniel by the shoulders. Just because Lily needs help doesn't mean it has to be from Daniel. Just because Daniel is carrying all this guilt for things out of his control doesn't mean he should put himself in danger. It doesn't mean he should put Tony through this.

Tony wishes he'd met Mario so he could have done more than shake him for starting all of this. If he'd known what consequences his actions would have, not only for Gianna but for Lily, for Daniel, for Colette, would he have acted differently? They'll never know. "So how did you get the text message out?"

"Right." Daniel clears his throat. "Lily left her phone out when they went to the bathroom. I used the quick release on the cuffs and texted the only number I know. Gotta hope she's a real Gen Z kid and doesn't check old-school SMS logs. I'm going to have to tell Paul he was right to make me memorize the damn thing."

"Jesus," Tony says again. So much for not rediscovering Catholicism.

"And I always knew this place was creepy as fuck," Daniel continues. "I told Colette every time she and Mario wanted to come here that it's always cold, the chairs are covered in scratched-up stickers and gross old gum, and it's not a fun place to watch a movie. They never showed good movies anyway. It was always weird arthouse shit—"

"Sweetheart, I love you so much, but this is *not* the time."

There's nothing but the hum of cicadas and distant cars passing on the 9G for a moment.

"I love you, too, Tony," Daniel says.

Abruptly, Tony starts crying. The tears have been lying in wait for him all day, and hearing Daniel say those words to him reminds him he told himself twenty separate times he might never get the chance.

"And I'm so sorry, but I can't leave her," Daniel adds. "Not now. It's dangerous. They're both high, and she's been swinging that damn rifle around like a toy. She shot a hole in the wall and then *laughed*. She's... I'll never forgive myself if I leave her here for the police to take care of and she doesn't even get a chance, or if she hurts herself, or..."

"I'll never forgive myself if you *die* when I could have saved you." Tony's voice breaks as he says it.

"Tony..."

"It's not going to change what Mario did if you get hurt over it. It's not going to bring Andrew back to life."

"I know."

Tony takes a deep, unsteady breath. "Look, I...I need you to be safe."

"Well, he left, and she's totally out of it right now."

"So, we'll get you both out. We'll get you both out, and we'll figure out how to help her, and *then* we'll call the police."

"That's the problem though. I don't think she'll come with us. Not while she's like this."

"Have you asked her?"

Daniel shifts against the door. He must be leaning his head on it. "I tried earlier. She kept saying it was all her fault, and that I didn't understand. I'm scared she'll hurt herself. And what if she goes into withdrawal or something?"

Tony thinks for a minute. "I have some ideas. Can you sit tight here for, like, an hour?"

"Can't do much else," Daniel says wryly.

"You think Sean'll be back?"

"He said he was going to his dorm. Honestly, I hope he doesn't come back. They seem to bring out the worst in each other."

As much as it pains Tony to say it, Sean is probably completely out of his depth here. "It's probably better for him if he isn't involved anymore. As an accessory or whatever. He'll be in enough trouble."

"I didn't even think about that." Something hits the metal of the door dully. Probably Daniel's head, more self-flagellation. "You're right. If you make it back early enough, we'll probably be able to leave before he returns. That might...protect him."

Early enough. Tony's not getting any fucking sleep tonight. "I don't want to leave you here."

"Is this where I say something brave and cinematic like 'the sooner you leave me, the sooner you get back'?"

Maybe it's the situation, maybe it's the lack of sleep, maybe it's the idea of Daniel as a movie damsel in distress, but Tony laughs. "I guess."

"I don't want you to go either."

"I'll get you out as soon as I can."

"I love you."

Tony's heart does something truly stupid in his chest. "I love you too. I want to see your face the next time you say that."

"You will."

It's a wrench to leave, to hurry to his car. Tony looks over his shoulder at least twenty times. Every set of headlights down the road, every sign of life disrupting the tiny slot of time he has to get Daniel out of there sends his pulse racing.

The trip to Rhinebeck is some of the worst driving Tony's done since he got his license. He's lucky it's so late, and the road is largely empty. By the time he gets home, he's walked through the facts in his head so often they've stopped feeling real.

He should call the police. He can't call the police. He has to call the police. It's the only rational thing he could possibly do, and Daniel is totally blinded by—whatever. Tony can't call the police without getting all of them into more trouble. With any luck, Detective Taylor found some incriminating fingerprints on the knife, and she'll arrest Lily without Tony having to lift a finger. Then, they'll only have to explain why they didn't call. Again.

The thought drags a high-pitched laugh out of Tony. Christ, he's losing it. Maybe it's because it's past midnight, and he's running on about four and a half hours of sleep since Daniel first went missing.

The lights are still on in the apartment when he gets in. Lisa and Blake are under the covers on the foldout couch. Lisa's got her hair in a scrunched-up bun on the top of her head and her knees drawn up tight. They're both still sitting up, neither of them trying to sleep.

"Having a slumber party?" Tony asks as he sets his keys down by the door.

"Tony!" Lisa struggles fully upright through the blanket. "Where have you been? We were getting worried."

Tony lets himself fall into the chair beside the couch. "It's a long story. And I'm going to need your help."

"Literally what we're here for."

"Okay." Tony leans forward. "I found Daniel."

It takes longer to summarize the whole story than Tony wants when he can barely stop himself from turning right back around to Germantown to make sure Daniel's still all right, from Lily's increasing instability to Daniel's crazy text message plan to the difficulty they now find themselves in.

"Daniel doesn't want to call the cops?" Lisa frowns. "It sounds like Lily definitely did it though. And like she's...unstable to begin with."

"Yeah." Tony clenches his jaw. It takes real effort not to get mad that he's sitting here defending this incredibly stupid choice. "I think he wants her in a better place to advocate for herself at the very least. Last year...last year, Andrew was institutionalized, Colette was arrested, and Daniel couldn't do anything to help either of them. I think he wants to help as much as he can before it's too late. Especially after..."

"After?" Blake prompts.

"After Mario."

Neither of them says anything, but their bated silence might as well be a question. Beyond his existence and his name, Tony hasn't told them much about Mario. It's sweet they still aren't pushing him to.

"Lily...she was in love with him. She said he never...got physical with her, but we don't know how much he encouraged her feelings. It seems likely he did, at least in some way."

Blake picks at a loose thread on the blanket. "What a shitstain."

"My thoughts exactly."

"Okay." Lisa considers. "So, you have an extremely vulnerable girl—young woman—whatever, on some drug. She's armed, violent, and presumably not in her right mind, and your mild-mannered professor boyfriend is... Okay, he's not trapped, but he feels responsible for keeping her safe, and the goal is to get the girl and the professor out unscathed."

"When you put it that way that, it could be a video game."

"I am in the process of writing a proposal for Bethesda as we speak," Lisa assures him. "I'm also wondering what we can possibly do to help. I'm happy to call in sick to work and come to Germantown with you, but I'm also no good in a fight."

"No fighting," Tony says instantly. "We do not want any fighting to happen this time."

"This time," Blake repeats faintly.

Tony glares him into silence. "There are two problems. First, we need to get them out. I can do it with a decent crowbar and some bolt cutters. Daniel says Lily doesn't want to leave and get help, though, so we need to convince her."

"One problem is solved with bolt cutters," Blake says. "Something else for your video game proposal, Lisa."

"No, that wasn't one of the problems."

Blake groans.

"We don't know what she's on. We don't know if she'll go into detox, or come down badly, or whatever else once we get her out. That's where you come in."

Blinking and turning to Tony in bafflement, Blake repeats, "Me?"

"Are you or are you not an in-house social worker in a mental health ward?"

"Oh, right." Blake laughs nervously. "I nearly forgot."

"Encouraging."

"So, Blake takes care of her and gets her back to herself once she's here," Lisa says. "But how do we get her here?"

Tony shrugs uncomfortably. This is the one part he hoped they'd sort out for him. "I was hoping you two would be able to convince her?"

Lisa looks over at Blake doubtfully. "We can try."

Blake's lips thin to a narrow line. "Tony."

"What?"

"You know who you need for this."

"I do?" It's news to Tony that he knows anything at all.

Blake rolls his eyes. In the last half hour, Tony has told him he intends to rescue both a kidnapping victim and his kidnapper by himself without informing the police, and it's only now Blake starts to look annoyed. "Yeah, man. You do. Lisa and I can come along, sure. We might have enough experience with troubled kids to help out, but Lily doesn't know us, and she won't trust us. You know who she does trust. You know who definitely shares her awful taste in men."

Tony swallows hard. "You mean Gianna."

"Yeah, I mean Gianna," Blake says as if it should be obvious.

Shifting on his seat, Tony avoids meeting Blake's eyes. "I mean. I guess. But she won't be awake or here in time. And I don't wanna—"

"*Dude*," Blake interjects impatiently. "Get over yourself and whatever dumb fight you and Gianna are having. If anyone knows what Lily's feeling—like returning to college with everyone knowing about their stupid fling with an asshat professor—it's gonna be Gianna. If anyone can get through to her, it's gonna be Gianna."

"It's still the middle of the night." Tony knows it's a weak protest, but he can't quite deal with the piercing way Blake is staring straight through him.

Lisa rests a gentle hand on his knee. "She's going to pick up the phone. She'll always pick up the phone for you."

Tony lets his eyes fall shut. "Okay. All right. I'll try."

Gianna picks up on the third ring. Her voice is sleep-soaked and groggy, but she picks up. "Tony? What is it?"

"I found him," Tony says. He moved to the kitchen to make this call. It gives him the illusion of privacy, although he knows Blake and Lisa can hear everything he's saying anyway. "I need your help."

"I can be there in half an hour."

"Lia—"

"Ma will take her. She was gonna tomorrow morning anyway."

Tony wants to ask if she's sure. Why would she drive out here with no more information than Tony needing her help, especially after everything he's said to her in the last few days? He wants to apologize, to tell her he loves her, to explain everything going around and around in circles in his head.

All he ends up saying is "Thank you."

All Gianna says in response is "Of course."

It takes her twenty-five minutes. She must have been speeding.

Her hair isn't straightened, and she's not wearing makeup. Tony hasn't seen her like this since two weeks after Lia was born when they were all still getting used to life with a baby.

She's wearing an old flannel shirt of Tony's.

Tony can't stop himself from hugging her for much too long, so filled with gratitude he can hardly speak for the first few minutes.

"Hey," she says, gentle in a way he rarely gets to hear anymore. "Tony, what's going on?"

He tells her in bits and pieces between getting coffee brewed much too strong in the hope it will keep them going for long enough to get through the night. He pours it into a thermos and dumps towels, tools, and whatever else he can think of into the trunk of his car while Blake and Lisa fill in the blanks, things he'd told them a half hour ago and already forgotten.

"Are you *sure*?" Gianna asks more than once. "I knew something was wrong, but..."

Tony can't offer her more than a helpless shrug. "I guess the pressure was too much for her?"

Gianna's lips tighten, but she doesn't say anything. She slides into the passenger seat, and they take off.

It's only him and Gianna in the car, headed to Germantown. Blake rightly pointed out that if Lily does need medical attention, Daniel's apartment is severely low on supplies. He and Lisa will pick up all the materials Blake's lifted from work over the last couple of months.

According to Blake, it's fully within his rights as an employee to take along the odd bandage or syringe every time he gets thrown up on, someone yells slurs at him, or he gets "accidentally" scheduled for back-to-back shifts. Beyond the possibility of it getting him fired, Tony can't find anything wrong with his argument. Ever pragmatic, Lisa is thrilled she won't have to steal materials from her job since the missing poster has become a moot point.

"All that work on the poster," Gianna sighs as they pull out of the tiny lot under Daniel's apartment in Rhinebeck.

"Imagine if we actually had to go around hanging them up though."

"Yeah, would have been a pain."

They're silent for a stretch of dark road.

"Why didn't you tell me you thought she had something to do with it?" Gianna asks Tony. "She's my friend. I was trying to, like, support her. If I had known..."

He freezes, foot slipping on the accelerator.

"You would have, what? Called the cops?"

"I mean, maybe?"

Even Gianna knows it would be the sensible option. And she's closest to Lily of all of them. The things Tony is willing to do for Daniel...

"Seriously though. Why didn't you tell me?"

"We...weren't really talking," Tony mutters.

Gianna crosses her arms under her chest. "Yeah. Why was that?"

Tony can't quite meet her eye. "Because I was being a dick?"

"I'm not sure you were." Gianna twists toward him, tangling her seatbelt the way Ma always told her not to. "Talk to me."

"I..." Tony tries to remember when he got so angry at her and why he couldn't let it go. "When it happened, with Professor Lawrence, I kept asking if you were all right."

"Yeah," Gianna says slowly. "I didn't want to talk about it. Brought up a lot of things for me I haven't had time to work through, with Lia and everything."

"I get that." To his own surprise, he does. It makes sense, and it's understandable. "It...brought up a lot of things for me too. Things I didn't tell you about when they happened."

"Like what?" It's the first time in days he hasn't read irritation or boredom in her voice when she talks to him, only open curiosity. She probably wasn't annoyed or bored, looking back on it. She just wanted him to stop asking when she wasn't ready to answer, the same as him.

"Stacy Allan nearly killed me too." Tony's thankful he's staring straight ahead at the road and can't see her expression, or he wouldn't be able to keep going. "And Daniel. And Colette nearly went to prison for Mario's murder. It was...intense when it all happened. I know you knew about Daniel getting shot, but she was about to shoot me first when Daniel found us. I never told you about...about me because you were already going through so much. I didn't want to put that on you or

Ma and Pa. But when this happened…"

"It started reminding you of all the things you were trying not to think about," Gianna finishes.

"Yeah."

"Guess I should have asked if you were okay."

"You couldn't know I had any reason not to be. I never told you." Admitting out loud that he hasn't been okay and part of it is his fault for not leaning on her, on his family when he needed them, is a weight off his chest.

Gianna picks at a fingernail. "You know you're the best big brother I could have asked for, right?"

Tony blinks, surprised. "I don't think I'll be winning any awards after the last few weeks."

She shakes her head. "Forget about that. All the rest. Our whole lives. Lia. You always did your best for me, took care of me."

"That's my job."

Looking up at him, Gianna forces him to meet her gaze head-on for an instant before he turns to the road again. Even without her makeup, she's fierce, undeniable. "I love you so much for that. But I want to take care of you, too, sometimes. I'm not a kid anymore. You gotta give me a chance to be there for you."

He lets out a long, shaky breath. "You're right."

"Wow." A faint smile loosens her expression. "I'm gonna need that in writing."

"Ha, ha."

They're quiet for long enough that Tony starts to consider logistics again—whether they'll be on time or if they can get Lily into the car by force if necessary.

"Is there anything else?"

The question draws him up short.

"C'mon, Tony Baloney." Gianna grins at him, a shadow of the know-it-all twelve-year-old who used to follow him around the whole house when he was seventeen and thought he was so much cooler than her. "License to be fully honest."

"I wanted to talk to you about Daniel," he admits.

She doesn't say anything in response. Strangely, it makes him want to say more.

"It's not on you." He forces his shoulders to drop, his jaw to unclench. "Not at all. I never knew how to start the conversation. I never...I didn't know how to talk about it with you or with Ma and Pa. And before him, I kinda...gave up hoping I would feel like this about anyone."

"*Tony.*" She reaches out. For a moment, he panics, wants to duck away, but he's driving and has nowhere to go. Her hand is soft on the top of his head, stroking across his hair where it's coming out of its ponytail. It makes it easier for him to keep going.

"I never...I never got what all the fuss was about. I mean, I knew I preferred men. But I never wanted to *be* with someone the way I want to be with Daniel. Thought there was something wrong with me." He laughs humorlessly. "I was gonna move out, before Lia. Try dating; see if that would fix me. Then..."

"Then, Lia."

"Yeah."

Gianna rests a hand on his on the steering wheel, not long enough to affect his steering, just so he knows she's there. "There's nothing wrong with you."

"I know. I—"

"Even if you hadn't met Daniel, even if you never met anyone you cared about romantically. We'd still love you. You know that, right?"

He nods. He can't seem to speak.

"Idiot," Gianna adds to make them both smile.

"I also felt kinda shitty about...about being with a Lobell professor after..."

That makes Gianna laugh. "Don't be dumb, Tony. Daniel's nothing like Mario."

He doesn't tell her how comforting it is to hear that.

"Plus, you weren't ever his student." She pauses a moment. "Hey, he was *your* customer. Did you—wait, did you *hit on him* at the *shop*?"

Involuntarily, Tony remembers the first time Daniel came to the shop, how he felt an attraction so sudden and abrupt it felt as if he put on glasses for the first time after living in a blurry world. How he hadn't been able to stop himself from flirting, how they kissed up against a customer's car. He doesn't need to say anything; his face gives him away.

"Oh my *God*." Gianna cackles. "You didn't! In front of all of Pa's tools!"

"Shut up." Tony's glad it's dark, and she can't see how red he's going. God knows what she'll read in his face if he starts thinking about the *second* time Daniel came to the shop when they did have sex on the premises.

"So, do I need to bleach the entire shop?" Gianna asks lightly.

Tony did bleach parts of the shop afterward, suddenly paranoid Pa or Kyle would find suspicious stains on the floor. It was one of his more ridiculous moments. It's a goddamn auto shop. There are so many motor oil stains that cleaning up was probably more suspicious than doing nothing.

"Please stop talking."

Mercifully, they reach Germantown, and Tony pulls into the Continuum's parking lot. He throws the car into park a little too suddenly, so the brakes squeak in protest for a long minute after he turns off the ignition. He locks the car and raps on the hood in apology before heading for the door. Oil time is coming up again whenever things calm down.

After she gets out of the car, he holds his arms open for Gianna.

She walks straight into his hold. He buries his face in the top of her head. She smells like shampoo and baby powder. Her arms snake around him to squeeze him tight.

He takes a deep, steadying breath. "All right. Are we ready to do this?"

Chapter Fourteen

Tony's Toyota is the only car in the Continuum's empty lot. Sean hasn't come back, then. That's a relief; one person at least will be spared whatever is about to happen.

"Daniel?" Tony asks the closed back door.

No response. Maybe Daniel's asleep. Maybe something else happened in the meantime. Maybe Tony should have saved his heart-to-heart with Gianna for after they got Daniel to safety and driven faster.

He takes a steadying breath and gets to work on the bike lock with the bolt cutters.

"Shoulda gone to the shop," he mutters to Gianna. "Gotten a damn angle grinder or something."

"Guess you're gonna have to start keeping power tools in Rhinebeck." She looks over her shoulder anxiously, monitoring the road. "Hurry up, will you?"

"This isn't exactly easy." It comes out as more of a grunt than a sentence. Tony winces as the lock gives under his hands. "Got it."

The door opens minutely, forcing them to shove until the gap is wide enough to pass through.

Tables and chairs piled up haphazardly right behind it shift away, likely Lily's idea of a barricade. Given Daniel was right up by the door before, it isn't all that effective.

"Daniel?" Tony calls into the space.

Colder inside than outside, the musty air smells of mildew and stale beer. No wonder Daniel hated watching movies here.

From a distance, Tony hears a voice.

He and Gianna wrestle the chairs and tables aside to get through. The furniture legs scrape loudly against the linoleum floors. One of the stacks of chairs wobbles dangerously when Gianna pushes it. For a moment, Tony's half convinced it will crash to the floor and alert every last resident of Germantown what's going on in here.

Gianna manages to steady it.

Their breathing is loud in the room.

"Come on." Tony turns on his phone's flashlight and searches for other doors. The bullet hole in the wall Daniel mentioned taunts Tony, right above the emergency light.

"Tony?" a voice calls from the far side of the room.

They sprint through a door and into a hallway to the main entrance. More emergency lighting dimly illuminates the space, pointing the way out.

They find Daniel waiting for them in the doorway leading to the bathrooms. His hair is a mess, flat on the sides and piled up at the top of his head in a tangle. He's pale, washed out, with deep circles under his eyes. His chinos have a rip at the knee—the second pair he's lost to violent crime this year, and he hates clothes shopping—and his shirt is crinkled and sweat-stained.

He's the best thing Tony's ever seen.

The air leaves his lungs in an instant. Tony lunges across the hall, breathless and elated and desperate. Grabbing Daniel by the front of his shirt, he pulls him in close and twists his head in time so he can kiss him without their noses bumping.

Daniel follows him easily. He cups the back of Tony's neck in his hand, the other arm wrapping around Tony's middle, easy and warm.

Stubble covers his cheeks, unfamiliar and rough, scratching against Tony's skin. Tony welcomes it as proof Daniel is here, real and warm in his arms.

"Hey," Daniel whispers when they pull apart. "Hey, it's okay. I'm okay."

Tony shudders a little and buries his head in Daniel's shoulder. He smells awful, of sweat and this horrible building, but somewhere underneath it, there's his three-in-one body wash.

Behind them, Gianna clears her throat.

She's studying the wall beside them carefully.

Tony wrenches himself away from Daniel's grasp. "Um," he manages. "Where's—"

From inside the bathroom, retching answers the question before he can finish asking.

Daniel grimaces. "She's thrown up a few times already. I'm trying to help, but she keeps panicking, and it isn't getting better. Whatever Sean gave her, it's not agreeing with her. She's hyperventilating, and I think she needs real medical help. Had to take these off." He pulls the handcuffs out of his pocket. They're terrible quality, so cheap they might as well be plastic.

Gianna squints at them in the half-light of the hallway. "You know how to get out of handcuffs?"

Daniel demonstrates the quick-release, and Tony makes a concerted effort not to think about the pair they got the last time they went to the city.

In the bathroom, Lily vomits again, ending with a sob. At this rate, they shouldn't only be calling the police, they should be calling an ambulance.

Tony opens his mouth to say as much, but before he can, Gianna pushes past Daniel into the restroom.

"Lily?" she calls.

The sobbing intensifies.

Tony sets his phone face down on the counter by the mirrors, the flashlight illuminating the room somewhat.

"Lily, hey." Gianna crouches beside Lily, hunched over the toilet. "It's me, Gianna." Tentatively, she puts a hand on Lily's back.

Tony can see how Lily shivers from across the room.

"Hey, it's going to be okay," Gianna croons. "It's gonna be fine, okay? Take a few deep breaths."

Lily tries. They come out shuddery and uneven.

"Follow my lead." Gianna demonstrates a deep breath in and a long breath out, one at a time. Lily follows her, hesitantly and offbeat at first, but gaining confidence as she goes.

Beside Tony, Daniel sags against the bathroom counter.

"You think you're gonna be sick again?" Gianna asks, managing to keep her voice soft, a simple question instead of a medical checkup.

Lily shrugs.

"Okay, how about some water. Think you can get to the sink?"

Together, Gianna and Daniel manage to get Lily standing and over to the sink.

Lily rinses out her mouth twice before she tries to drink. The water seems to help, which is the first time anyone has ever said that about Hudson Valley tap water. She's steadier on her feet afterward. She must also be thinking more clearly because she finally grasps that Gianna and Tony are here.

"Oh no," Lily groans. "How did you find us?"

It's a good thing she doesn't wait on an answer. Tony's not up to explaining Daniel's text message scheme a third time tonight.

"He's going to be so pissed, oh fuck, oh fuck, oh fuck, I'm getting him in so much trouble..."

She must mean Sean, and she's not wrong. She has gotten him into a lot of trouble, but there's not much to be done about that now. Lily should have considered the consequences before she stabbed someone. She should have thought of the ramifications before she kidnapped a professor and called her boyfriend in to help.

"We can leave while he's gone." Tony realizes it's the wrong offer to make as soon as Lily starts breathing much too fast. She's going a little green around the nose again.

"Hey." Gianna snaps her fingers in Lily's face. "Breathe, Lily. Remember, slowly, in and out." She demonstrates again, and Lily follows the pattern. "Come on. It's only Sean. You can leave here."

Lily shakes her head. "He says I can't. He says then everyone will know I—will know—"

"About Professor Lawrence?" Gianna speaks softly, no trace of irritation or anger in her voice. It's such a far cry from how she talks to Tony or even to Ma and Pa that it's eerie.

"He says...he says if I talk to anyone, they're going to know I did it."

"Lily..." Gianna settles an arm around Lily's shoulders, part comfort and part to keep her in place. "They're going to find out anyway. You know that, right? Especially after everything with Professor Rosenbaum."

"I know. It's all my fault. I should never have come back here. I should have— If I hadn't messed it all up last year, none of this would have happened."

A trickle of unwanted sympathy keeps Tony from agreeing wholeheartedly. It's true Lily is not so much a victim of circumstance as she is the perpetrator by now, but unlike Stacy, she never had a plan. She never tried to cover her tracks, to blame someone else. She's just sick and desperate.

"I was so angry about the grade from last year, you know, and...and I went to her office. He helped me with what to say because it's so hard not to give up and agree with whatever professors say, and he's so much better at it. But then, I forgot everything he said, and the knife—"

"Why did you bring a knife?" Gianna asks.

It's a valid question.

"I don't *know*." Deep worry lines, too deep for someone her age, ravage Lily's forehead before she buries her face in her hands. If Tony asks her now why she left the knife taped to Daniel's door, he suspects she would say the same thing. Maybe it wasn't a threat, as he's been assuming; maybe in her muddled mind, it was a confession.

"We'll figure it out." Daniel sounds firm, calm, and nowhere near as incredulous as Tony's feeling right about now. How are they supposed to figure anything out when she can't even remember why she did what she did?

"But I—when I— Everyone knows I'm totally nuts. I can't—"

"Yeah, well, you're not." Gianna rubs Lily's arm comfortingly, still holding her. Belatedly, it strikes Tony that maybe he should be concerned about his sister being so close to a murderer, let alone blatantly lying to one to make her feel better. "Look, you need some help. You need—"

Lily wrenches out of Gianna's grasp. "I'm *tired* of needing help! Everyone looks at me like I'm...like I'm broken, or an idiot, or *both*. This year was supposed to be my fresh start, my second chance, and I thought if I got all my grades from last year, I could finally stop thinking about— about—"

"About Mario," Gianna finishes.

Lily nods wordlessly, looking away.

"You know, Mario was really good at making me feel as if everything was my idea."

Tony freezes in place, not daring to look at Gianna. He's never heard her talk about Mario or their relationship beyond the barest of bones.

Lily, though—Lily looks up as if every word Gianna says is the lifeline she needs.

"The first time he kissed me," Gianna continues, "he got mad right after, said it was my fault. I mean, I wanted him to, and I thought he wanted to, as well, but he acted like I tempted him or something." Gianna shakes her head with a forced laugh. "It took me a while to work out the pattern. Too long. He'd start something and then pretend I was the one who forced his hand. Made me feel guilty about it. Made me feel like I couldn't tell anyone because I was the one who wanted him."

Tucking her hair behind her ears, Lily quietly says, "When I went to his office hours, he would say I should stop looking at him 'like that,' or he wouldn't be responsible for his actions. He said it as if it was a joke, but I still felt bad."

Gianna nods. "Exactly, yeah. You know, I was actually excited when I first found out I was pregnant. I thought he'd take me seriously then. I thought maybe we would really be together."

"What did he say?"

Tony leans in closer. This is the part Gianna never told him about. First, she said he hadn't decided yet what he wanted to do about the baby. Later, he was dead.

"He said..." For the first time, Gianna looks down, away from Lily. "He said it was my fault. I should have been more careful. I was going to get him in trouble. He wanted me to get rid of it. Of her. Of Lia."

Tony thinks back to the parking lot at the Planned Parenthood in Hudson. He'd been waiting to hear what *she* wanted. She must have been going over it in her head, around and around in circles, what *he* wanted.

"And I mean, I understood," Gianna barrels on. "It would have probably been the smart choice. But I couldn't—I mean, I *loved* him, or I thought I did. And I already loved that kid so much. I wasn't—I couldn't—"

Tony wants, more than anything, to reach out, to support her. She's not looking at him right now, though, she's looking at Lily.

"It wasn't fair of him to put that on you." Lily is quiet, but her voice is steadier, less panicked than before. "She's his kid too. Even if he didn't want to be involved, it wasn't just you."

"It wasn't just you who was interested either." Gianna says it matter-of-factly, as if it doesn't hurt that the man she loved was busy seducing other students at the same time. "It wasn't your fault he was flirting with you, and it wasn't all in your head either. I don't think you're broken or an idiot for falling for him. I think that's what he wanted you to feel."

Lily wraps her arms around herself. She's so skinny, her black and gray striped shirt clinging tightly to her narrow frame. She must be freezing. August might be muggy and awful in the Hudson Valley, but it's also cold at night, and the old theater is drafty and unpleasant.

"I will think you're an idiot if you still let him ruin your life *now* though. He's not making you do any of this. This is all you."

"*Gianna*," Daniel hisses.

Internally, Tony cheers. Finally, someone isn't treating Lily with kid gloves. It's risky, maybe dangerous, depending on where Lily's hiding the rifle and how drugged-up she still is. It's also absolutely what Lily needs to hear.

"Seriously, you're better than this," Gianna insists. "You made it through Mario. You made it through what he did to you. Don't let it ruin you now."

None of them say anything, but Gianna stares Lily down.

If Gianna does end up becoming a psychologist after all of this, Tony is never going to let her forget that what convinces Lily to give them a chance, to leave this building, isn't any of Gianna's well-thought-out arguments, it's her death glare.

They get Lily and Gianna situated in the back seat of Tony's car. Thankfully, Tony remembers to toss Gianna the roll of hefty bags in glove compartment in case Lily's nausea returns.

The car's not big enough for everyone to have enough leg room, but the drive is short. In the open on the parking lot, Tony feels exposed and rushed as if the minute some commuter sees them, they'll all get arrested. He wants to get this over with as quickly as possible.

"For the record," Tony mutters to Daniel before they get into the front of the car, "you know we could both get in trouble for this? Real trouble? With the law? This is technically aiding and abetting a criminal." Guiltily, he thinks of the murder weapon, now in police custody. Even if this plan weren't enough to get them all in trouble before Tony handed the knife over to Detective Taylor, it sure is now.

"The law isn't always right."

"Damn it, Daniel, we aren't actually on *Bones*. Actions have consequences."

Daniel doesn't answer, but his jaw is set, so there's nothing left to do but get in the car and leave.

Tony slides the key into the ignition, and the engine sputters.

"Come on, not now." He tries again.

Dawn is breaking behind the empty shell of the movie theater, illuminating the door they left open, the broken bike lock on the ground.

The car still won't start.

"Should've taken my car." Gianna's not wrong, but she's also not helpful.

Lily shifts nervously in the back seat, looking around as if she's waiting for someone to catch them.

Tony pops the hood and slides out of the driver's seat. At a glance, he can't find anything wrong, all the cables where they should be, the tank still half full. The car is just being dramatic.

If the battery isn't dead, of course—a problem Tony has no hope of fixing, not without a donor car in the vicinity.

On the 9G, headlights sweep across the street in the predawn light. Rush hour, such as it is in this part of the world, will start soon, all the people driving from here out to their jobs in Hudson, Catskill, Poughkeepsie, and Albany. Tony doesn't want them to be seen here, not before Lily's ready, before she's *sober* and able to talk to the police. Selfishly, it's nothing to do with Gianna and Daniel's priority to protect Lily. Tony really, really doesn't want to try explaining to anyone why he put a murderer and her kidnapping victim in his car with his sister. The only explanation is that it would have made his boyfriend sad to do anything else.

He gets in the driver's seat and tries the ignition again.

Nothing.

"Fuck."

"What do we do?" Daniel tries to sound in control and not like he's been made very nervous by this development. He's probably fooling Lily, maybe Gianna, but Tony can hear the uncertainty in his voice.

It's a great question.

There might be someone at the gas station who can help, maybe someone nice enough to let Tony start the engine using their car. It'll take a while, though, and if this whole plan goes to shit, there will be witnesses saying Lily was making a hasty exit, accompanied by the rest of them. There will also be witnesses saying Daniel, Tony, and Gianna were aiding and abetting a murderer. Because they are.

Tony has only one other option he can think of, and it's an even worse idea.

"I shouldn't go with you." Lily's voice is high and tight and anxious.

Tony decides he's already committed to some awful ideas tonight, and he might as well keep it going. "Stay put. Don't move. I'll be right back."

They aren't actually in a hurry. The police don't know where they are, nor does anyone else besides Lisa and Blake. It's more that Lily is a flight risk, and now that Daniel and Gianna have both committed to helping her— Well, Tony can't let her get away with not experiencing a single consequence. He's going with the worst idea he has, and they'll all have to deal with it.

He hasn't been running in a week, and he's wearing the wrong shoes for it. At least he's still in sweatpants. It takes Tony ten minutes to get to Emilio's all the same, going as fast as he can. The pace seems to get progressively slower the longer he goes, but it's still quick enough that he can't second-guess this incredibly stupid idea.

Of everyone in Germantown, Emilio's the one person who would have a reason *not* to help Tony jumpstart the car. Of everyone in Germantown, he's the one person who would and could instantly call the police on them.

The part of Tony that thinks he should have called the police the second Paul got in touch with him reminds him that of everyone in Germantown, Emilio is the one who has the right to know what's going on.

It's a dick move, but Tony leans on the doorbell.

Emilio takes precious minutes to get to the door. He's changed clothes, which is progress for him. "When I said anytime..."

"Not now," Tony snaps. "I need your help. We have Daniel. We know who killed your wife. But we need to get out of here. Where's your car?"

"Garage. What the—"

"Get your keys."

The drive to the parking lot is tense, Tony's knee jiggling the entire time, his breath still coming in pants from the brisk run. It's almost fully light out.

"Park across from me," he instructs. "Hood to hood."

Tony tries to look relaxed and calm when he gets out the jumper cables from the trunk. He's done this enough that it's a quick process to connect the cables to his battery and to get Emilio's hood open and ready. It still feels like every movement draws out for hours, Emilio's eyes heavy on him and on the car, where Daniel's fully visible in the passenger seat, though at least the back is shrouded in darkness and hidden by the front seat.

"Come on, come on," Tony mutters to himself.

Finally, the engine springs to life.

He leaves it running as he disconnects the cables and closes the hood.

"Tony?" Emilio asks as Tony slides into the driver's seat. "Tony, are you gonna—"

Tony could tell him now. He could say everything, and Emilio would absolutely call the cops instantly, and it would be a savage satisfaction to have it over with, to have someone explode in anger about all the things Tony's keeping his temper in check about.

In the passenger seat of the Toyota, Daniel's twisted around to watch Lily, concern etched across every inch of his face.

Once again, Tony takes a deep breath and reins in his temper.

"I'll explain everything later." Tony's not surprised when Emilio's expression darkens as Tony pulls the door shut. Emilio never gave him a phone number.

The car squeaks violently in protest as Tony throws it into reverse. He pulls away from Emilio's car, barrels onto the 9G, and doesn't slow down until they hit Red Hook.

No one in the car speaks.

When they pass the sign for Rhinebeck, Tony says, "I think I need to get a new car."

In the passenger seat, Daniel bursts into laughter. "Finally." He looks at Tony so fondly that Tony forgets for an instant Amelia Lawrence's murderer is in the car, and they need to figure out how to get her in a place to hand her off to someone who knows what they're doing so they'll no longer be harboring a murderer. He forgets Amelia's husband saw them all together, and this is far from over. He has Daniel back, safe and sound, the lines around his eyes crinkling with joy and his jawline devastatingly handsome with that hint of stubble.

Blake and Lisa beat them to Rhinebeck. It's not surprising, given their errand probably involved less crises. They don't have a key to Daniel's apartment, though, so they've stationed themselves in Colette's, where they waylay Tony and Daniel as soon as they hear them coming up the stairs. They're followed immediately by Colette.

Colette, who is blindingly furious with Tony for not waking her up.

With Lily behind them, blinking in the overhead light, confused and probably still high, Tony figures he'll have to do some damage control. He hands his key over to Gianna, and she and heads for Daniel's apartment with Lily in tow. Tony watches them go, wondering if he can really leave Gianna alone with Lily before facing Colette.

"Someone would have had to call the cops if we didn't make it back," Tony tells her before she can start. "And you were—"

"You should have woken me up anyway," Colette insists.

"Why? So you could stay up and worry?"

Meredith peers out onto the landing. She wears pajamas and glasses, looking barely awake herself. "She was doing that anyway."

In the next instant, Meredith catches sight of Daniel and barrels out to hug him.

"Meredith." Daniel braces against the banister so the impact doesn't knock him down the stairs. "What are you doing here?"

"What do you mean, what am I doing here? You went *missing*. You're lucky Mom and Dad aren't here too."

"Oh, shit, wasn't Dad's surgery—"

"Yes, and it went fine, and that is *not* the point."

"As heartwarming as this all is," Colette interrupts, "can we maybe take it inside so you can all explain yourselves?"

Tony exhales in silent relief. Five minutes is too long to leave Lily alone with Gianna. They pile into Daniel's living room again, reminiscent of yesterday's full house. Exhaustion has replaced the nervous tension they were all carrying then, but it's like staring at a spot-the-difference painting and finding nothing but the change in lighting.

Gianna and Lily must be in the bathroom; the shower is running. Tony roots through Daniel's dresser for a change of clothes for Lily and sets them out in front of the bathroom door.

Colette makes coffee. Tony's starting to get sick of the stuff.

"Is there a reason you haven't called the police?" Meredith asks when Daniel's told her everything.

Tony glares at Daniel. Maybe if everyone says it, he'll reconsider.

Daniel sighs. "We're trying to get Lily to a place where she can actually...tell us what happened. I'm still not clear on some of it, and she's not yet able to advocate for herself. We need to get her a lawyer. If the police had found us and come in, guns blazing, and she hid or, worse, shot back..."

Tony frowns. Daniel said she had a rifle, but there was no sign of it in the theater.

"She did it though," Meredith says. "If she stabbed that professor, she should—"

"She's a traumatized twenty-one-year-old, and she's been taking drugs," Blake interrupts. "She needs to be sober at the very least."

Colette snorts. "I need to not be sober."

"Yeah," Blake says. "You're not wrong. This is a mess." He has a bag full of supplies, including bandages and an IV drip poking out the top.

When he catches Tony staring, Blake says, "Look, I bought the drip myself, okay? It's not stolen. Stop judging me."

Tony holds his hands up in surrender. That wasn't what he was thinking; he was wondering if Blake knows how to lay an IV, given he's a social worker and not a nurse, albeit an in-house social worker at a hospital. Discretion appears to be the better part of valor in this case though.

When Lily gets out of the shower, trailing behind Gianna in a sweatshirt three sizes too big for her, Blake takes over easily, making her comfortable in Daniel's bedroom.

Blake shuts the door behind Lily and Gianna, nothing to be heard from them but the murmur of indistinct voices.

"So what's our angle?" Colette asks. "How do we proceed?"

"Can we at least tell the police Daniel's safe?" Meredith suggests. "They're still out there looking for him."

Daniel makes a weighing motion with his hands. "How do we do that without incriminating Lily?"

Colette's mouth twists. "She killed someone, Daniel. That will incriminate her. Because it's a crime."

"Thank you," Tony says.

Daniel glares at him. "Yeah, well, I'm not willing call the police until I know she won't be—" Daniel looks away abruptly.

"She won't be what?" Colette asks.

"She won't be abandoned like Andrew was, or like she was last year, all right?" Daniel snaps.

Colette's fingers go to her shoulder, looking for a braid to toy with only to find it gone. "I knew you blamed me for that."

Daniel stares at her, incredulous. "I don't blame you. I blame *myself*."

"He was my student."

"And you didn't think he needed counseling. I did!"

"Yes, you were right, and I was wrong. But—"

"It's not *about* right or wrong, Colette—"

The buzzer snaps through the incipient argument.

Tony answers the door on autopilot.

"Hey," Emilio's voice says, far away at the bottom of the stairs and, at the same time, very close. "Are you gonna tell me what's going on?"

Chapter Fifteen

"I was meaning to ask how you met Tony." Daniel makes Emilio coffee, seeming for all the world like a friendly, calm host and not someone who was kidnapped at gunpoint a day ago. He fumbles over Colette's coffee maker, but everyone else is too frozen solid with nerves to do it for him. "Thanks for helping us start the car, by the way, Mr. Lawrence."

"It's Emilio." Emilio leans against the kitchen counter. "Glad you're okay."

"Me too."

"You got a lot of people here who care about you."

Daniel gives Tony a shadow of a smile. "I guess I do."

"Well." Emilio crosses his arms over his chest. The unimpeded view of his biceps highlights that he's easily the biggest and strongest person in the room, and it's a little ridiculous how this concern occurs to Tony *now*, when they've fully eliminated him as a suspect. "Colette and Tony, here, were trying to find you, and obviously, they succeeded. They searched my house in the process though."

Daniel's eyebrows climb up his forehead. "You did *what*?"

"To be fair, he invited us to," Tony says. It's a weak defense for impoliteness, and if Ma were here, she would tell him so.

"Their original plan was to park right across the road and watch me, I think."

Daniel rubs a hand over his face. "You promised not to get involved in any more murder investigations."

Utter shock at the hypocrisy stops Tony from forming meaningful thoughts momentarily.

"Technically, it was a kidnapping."

"Thank you for the distinction, Professor Ravel."

"Daniel—" Tony tries.

"No, no." Colette waves him off. "Daniel is angry, and he has every right to be. Everything is my fault."

"I didn't say it was your fault." The coffee maker bangs against the stovetop as Daniel sets it down.

"No, you said you blamed yourself, which is ridiculous. I was far more at fault than you."

"That's not fair. You're putting words in my mouth—"

"You're not being fair."

Daniel turns his back and turns the burner on. "Do you take milk or sugar?" he asks Emilio.

Emilio shakes his head wordlessly.

"Hey, you think you could give me your key?" Meredith asks Colette. "I'm just gonna shower and freshen up."

She escapes down the stairs, and Lisa, the coward, goes to check on the patient in the other room.

Tony barely dares to think her name, not with the situation in the kitchen set to explode.

Daniel hands Emilio his coffee.

Emilio takes it, thanks him, and asks, "Daniel, who kidnapped you?"

Daniel's Adam's apple bobs as he swallows. "I don't know if..."

"It's an easy question, unless you were blindfolded or unconscious or something."

When no one responds, Emilio continues. "And given no one here is racing you to the hospital, I'm guessing you weren't. So, I'm thinking you know exactly who it was, and you don't want to tell me. Which is weird because, last I heard, I was helping you guys out and tracking IP addresses off of Rate My Professor, which was also pretty weird."

"Christ." Tony rubs a hand across his eyes. This is his fault. He shouldn't have gotten Emilio involved. He's so tired. "Emilio, man, this isn't about you—"

"If you all know who killed my wife, it sure as fuck is."

"It's not that simple." Daniel tries to stay rational and light, but Tony hears the steel in his voice. He's getting angry, and if Tony is supposed to be the last remaining voice of reason in the room, he might as well start hiding the sharp knives.

"Sounds simple to me. My wife gets stabbed, you get kidnapped, you know who did both, they get arrested. Boom. Easy."

"She's just a kid, Emilio," Tony tries. Lily is only seven years younger than him. Gianna's old enough to be a mom, and she's only a year older. Lily can vote. She can drink legally.

She's old enough to own her fuck-ups, no matter how bad things get.

But at twenty-one, Tony had finished his associate's degree and started working full-time in the shop. All his friends were doing four-year degrees or work placements in other towns; they were dating and having regular sex with whomever they wanted. Tony was right where he'd always been and exactly as unsure of what and whom he wanted how.

He would have given anything for anyone in his life to think he was worth protecting.

After everything Lily's done, he can't give her that grace anymore, but he knows why Daniel thinks she deserves it. He suppresses the part of himself that violently disagrees.

"I don't care who the fuck she is, she—" Emilio says.

"I know!" Daniel bursts out. "I know, all right? And we'll get there. But she—I—look, this is my fault."

Colette scoffs.

"She is *my* student, and my responsibility," Daniel continues. "She's been taking drugs, and she's been through a hell of a lot, and I will not watch another kid get institutionalized and die over what fucking Mario did to them."

"So we tell the detective." Colette inspects her fingernails, trying to look cool even though she's trembling as if the tension is rattling through her entire body. "They have suicide watch protocols. They can—"

"Do you know how inhumane that is?" Daniel turns on her. He hasn't slept in about as long as Tony, probably. "I mean, you've been reading those articles I sent you, right, about—"

"Remember which of us was arrested last year? You're not responsible for this country's draconian nightmare of a criminal justice system."

"If you hate the country so much—"

"This is not about that!"

"You're right. It's about protecting students who need help."

"Your savior complex can't cure mental illness!"

"*Hey!*" Emilio yells, his voice a thunderclap through the kitchen.

Everyone stops to stare at him.

"I don't give a shit about the criminal justice system. I care about my dead wife and our kid. Tell me who did it."

Daniel's chin juts out. "Not until I've found her a lawyer."

"Fine." Emilio takes a long sip of his coffee. "Then I'm staying right here until you do."

It's understandable, if not reasonable. Emilio has no reason to trust them. Tony doesn't trust them either right now.

With nothing better to do, he makes breakfast.

Bigger pan, he puts on his mental list of things to talk to Daniel about getting. Ma made sure the fridge was stocked to bursting, but he can only fit so many eggs into Daniel's shitty Jamie Oliver pan (three for two on Amazon the week Daniel moved into this apartment, which makes Tony cringe almost as much as the scratched-up Teflon on the smallest one in the set. Ma always says you have to pick a pan up before you buy it), especially if he's frying up hash browns in the biggest one.

Emilio takes up residence at the island, watching him cook. Colette and Daniel abscond to the office, presumably to get in touch with Jeff.

"You realize this is insane, right?" Emilio asks Tony eventually.

"Yeah. I know."

"Why are you going along with it?"

"If he hadn't been around last year, it could be me." Gianna bumps Tony aside to grab a plate from overhead. She fills it straight out of the pan.

"It wouldn't have been you," Tony says.

"You don't know that."

"I do." Tony makes a plate for himself. His appetite is all over the place and nowhere to be found right now, but he should probably eat anyway. He fills a third plate and offers it to Emilio.

Emilio eyes it skeptically, but he takes it all the same.

Gianna could never have ended up where Lily is now. She's too smart to get hooked on drugs, too good to do the things Lily has done. Tony would never have let her get so lost.

Maybe she's a little right.

"How's it going in there?" Tony asks.

She shrugs. "Blake's good with her. But he thinks she's gonna need a hospital and a real doctor sooner rather than later."

Emilio's fork clatters to the floor. "She's *here*?"

Tony closes the kitchen door.

"The woman who killed my wife is *in this apartment*, and you want me to, what, sit still and eat some fucking eggs?"

"Yeah. That's what I want." It's not though. It's not what Tony wants, not even for a second, and the lie tastes bitter on his tongue.

For a moment, Emilio stares at him. Then, he says, "Fuck no," and makes for the door.

Tony blocks his way. "What are you gonna do?"

"I'm gonna—"

"You're gonna go in there and threaten a twenty-one-year-old girl? You're gonna hurt her? That's gonna look great in court, man. A good lawyer will get her off the hook if you do."

"I'm not just *waiting here*."

"You're not. You're having some breakfast, and you're sitting down, and you're taking a fucking breather." Tony pushes Emilio lightly by the shoulders, getting him situated on the bar stool Tony usually sits at when he and Daniel eat in here.

"Look," Tony says, "I know this doesn't make a whole lot of sense but think about it this way. You know who did it. You know where she is. She's going to get arrested sooner or later. And yeah, maybe sooner would be better, but the smartest person in the room thinks we should wait. No one else needs to get hurt."

Emilio takes a deep breath. "Give me a minute."

Tony grabs his plate. "Sure thing. We'll be in the living room."

He closes the kitchen door behind himself and Gianna and tries not to sigh with relief too loudly.

"You're good at that," she observes. "Calming him down."

"I get how he feels." He felt the same much of the time this last year. First, about Mario when he was still alive, then, about Daniel, briefly, when Daniel thought Gianna had killed Mario. Then, about no one in particular when it was all over and there was no one left to be angry at. "Hey, you were amazing with Lily, you know." Tony bumps their shoulders together as they sit on the couch between the mess of bedding Lisa and Blake never ended up needing.

Her lips twitch into the start of a smile. "Thanks, I think."

"I never knew how you felt about Mario. About everything that happened with him."

"How could you? I didn't."

"But you—"

Gianna pats his shoulder. "I didn't know when it was happening, or last year, when I was busy freaking out about him being dead and me becoming a mom. It took me a while to work through everything."

"Well, if you need someone to talk to..." He's not sure he should be offering himself as a resource right now. They both know he has his own stuff to work on.

She must catch where he's going, though, because she says, "Maybe we both do. Maybe we should make coffee dates or something."

The thought makes him smile. "We could do it when we do customer logs. Busywork and trauma, the two things that will keep Dad and Kyle out of the front office."

She laughs. "I'm down. You bring the drinks."

"Deal. Pastries on bad days."

They bump fists, a gesture they haven't done since Gianna still had braces.

"Did you make breakfast?" Colette asks, emerging from the office. "Bless you."

"Yeah. Maybe wait a minute, Emilio's cooling off in there."

She nods and falls into place next to them on the couch.

"Any luck with Jeff?" Tony asks her.

"He's furious we interrupted his holiday. He gave us a number for a colleague in the city. Daniel's calling right now."

Tony grins.

"What?"

"I knew he didn't have to come out here himself last year. He wanted to help."

Colette blinks. "Oh. I hadn't thought of that."

"Yeah. There had to be a heart buried somewhere under those suspenders."

"Tony..." Colette shifts awkwardly on the couch. "Should I..."

"Hm?"

"Suppose Daniel is right about all this. Suppose we should have kept a closer eye on Andrew and on Lily. Should I... I suppose I am responsible for Sean?"

"I don't know if you're responsible for him. He's an adult. But you could see how he's doing. Daniel says he was there for most of...everything."

Gianna nods. "He's kind of a dick, but he probably needs some help to get out of this."

"He's definitely neck-deep in the drugs part of it."

Colette groans. "I've never even smoked marihuana. I'm not qualified to help. I don't... What do I say?"

It's not a question Tony can answer. He's glad Gianna's here, just as firm and clear as she was with Lily before.

"You can tell him we know about Lily, that she's safe and getting help, and he can too. Also, he's probably better off if he comes forward and explains what happened."

"All right." Taking a deep breath, Colette pulls out her phone. "Why does the thought of calling a student make me so nervous?"

Tony pats her shoulder. "It's not something you usually do. But he'll appreciate it. And it's a good thing to do. Maybe the whole advisor thing will work out better than you think."

For all the buildup, Sean's phone number goes straight to voicemail. It's disappointing, but Colette leaves a well-spoken message all the same. Tony hopes it's enough.

Meredith joins them shortly after, freshly showered and looking much less exhausted than Tony feels. Lisa comes out of the bedroom and tells them Blake is trying to get Lily to sleep. After a careful knock on the kitchen door, Tony starts handing out plates and food and getting everyone situated somewhere in the mess of the living room. Eventually, Daniel emerges from the office.

Tony's filling up a plate for him when the buzzer sounds. It's probably his mom, back to cook some more. She'll be annoyed he made breakfast already, but she'll pretend she isn't, which will be comforting in its normalcy. He buzzes her up without checking on the intercom.

Tony expects her with such certainty that when he opens the door to Detective Taylor, he wonders whether she's a sleep deprivation hallucination. Did he wish for her to intervene so strongly that she showed up as a badly dressed, poorly tempered Mary Poppins?

She looks about how he feels, no less disheveled than she was at 4:00 a.m. the day before.

"You people, I swear," she mutters as she pushes past him into the apartment.

"Uh, Detective," Tony tries, but she won't let him.

"I told you all specifically not to get involved, to let us do our damn jobs. You ignored everything I said, got yourselves in trouble, made it my problem *again*, and now, here Professor Rosenbaum is, no worse for wear, eating breakfast?"

"Hi," Daniel offers weakly. "Sorry for all the extra work."

"Detective, would you like something to eat?" Meredith offers.

"No, I would like some goddamn answers."

Meredith gives her a coffee anyway, and she takes a quick gulp.

"So," Taylor says pleasantly. "Explain to me why my prime suspect had to tell me the kidnapping was solved and not any of you."

Tony purposely doesn't look at Emilio.

Emilio shrugs. "No one else here was going to make the call. Couldn't do nothing."

Fierce satisfaction nearly bowls Tony over. He wasn't expecting to feel so pleased about it, but he wanted Emilio to do it. He hinted at it; he's the one who got Emilio to come here to force Daniel into facing the consequences of Lily's actions. Guilt follows closely behind the satisfaction though. Is this why Tony had to use Emilio's car to jump-start the engine? Was Tony planning this in his subconscious?

Unable to stop himself, he looks over at Daniel.

Daniel's looking back.

He's not happy.

"Well," Daniel says tightly. "I guess we're doing this then."

"Great. Start now," Detective Taylor demands.

"I..."

"Let me give you some pointers. Why didn't you tell me about the murder weapon on the door? Why were you kidnapped? Is it connected to the murder? What was the motive for either crime, and how did your friends know where to find you?"

Daniel sighs. "Do you know what happens when you send a text message to a landline?"

The detective looks close to apoplexy.

"Daniel managed to get the kidnapper's phone to text a friend's landline," Tony translates. "The friend called me."

"And you ran to Germantown, guns blazing, and didn't think to inform me."

"Pretty much. I don't have a gun though. The murderer does, but we don't know what happened to it."

A frown line draws tight between Daniel's eyebrows. He didn't think of that yet, then. Just as he hasn't considered how he places his own guilt and sense of responsibility higher than Emilio and his kid, higher than Sean, higher than how insane Tony has felt since the last time he and Daniel were in a room together.

"God, I should arrest all of you for obstruction of justice."

Tony shrugs uncomfortably. At least he won't get fired for having an arrest record.

Stiffly, Daniel says, "We're just trying to help."

"No, you're all putting yourselves in unnecessary danger and not helping me at all."

The door to the bedroom clicks open. Blake slips out. "Could you all keep it down in here? I finally got her to go to sleep."

Detective Taylor rolls her eyes. "And who is this one?"

"Blake Walia." Blake holds out his hand for her to shake.

She does no such thing. "Who are you hiding in the bedroom?"

No one responds. Not even Emilio, though he shifts uncomfortably.

The detective walks toward the bedroom, and Daniel looks to Tony, panicked. Tony can't offer him anything. What are they supposed to do, stop her? She's armed, and she can, in fact, arrest them. She probably should.

Taylor pushes open the door, looks inside, and stops dead.

She looks back at them and lets the door fall closed quietly. "That's Lily Peterson. The girl who tried to kill herself last year."

Daniel nods slowly. "Yup."

Detective Taylor rubs a hand across her face tiredly. "Okay. Okay." She goes to the kitchen, takes a plate, and piles it high with scrambled eggs and toast. Then, she sits on the only chair available in the living room and says, "Go on. Explain yourselves."

Hesitantly, they crowd around her. Daniel takes a seat on the edge of the foldout couch. Everyone else follows suit, perching on the available surfaces or right on the floor.

"Lily came to my office two days ago," he starts. "She was confused and panicked. She mentioned the murder weapon, said she'd given it to me, and wanted to know why she hadn't been arrested yet. She wasn't speaking coherently, and I didn't know if it was a confession to the murder or to the threats against me. I tried to call you—"

The detective gives him a look.

"Okay, I tried to call Tony. Before I could, though, Lily drew out a shotgun, or a rifle or... I don't know anything about guns. Something about a foot and a half long, way too heavy for her—"

"Drew out from where?" Tony asks. Lily was wearing a long-sleeved T-shirt and jeans last he remembered.

"She had this big duffel coat on. I thought it was weird when she walked in because it's been so warm, but I didn't think much of it until...well. She threatened me with the gun, told me I had to come with her. I did, and her boyfriend was waiting outside."

They didn't bring any duffel coat with them from the theater. Lily was shivering in her thin clothes every time Tony checked the rearview mirror. He's only seen one coat like that today, and Sean was wearing it when he left the old theater. If he took the coat and the gun, trying to hide the evidence to protect Lily, he'll be in so much more trouble than he already is. Tony wishes he could travel back in time and warn Sean. He shouldn't have hidden in the bushes. He should have talked to Sean. Hell, he should have said something at Amelia Lawrence's memorial, and then maybe he could have stopped this.

Unaware of Tony's turmoil, Daniel continues, "He made me give up my phone. He took us to the Continuum, the—"

"I know," Taylor says around a mouthful, "the independent movie theater in Germantown. Damn shame it shut down."

Tony can't take his eyes off of how the detective eats her food. She carefully places a piece of egg on the corner of her toast before taking a bite and then repeats the process ad nauseam.

Colette looks put out that the detective frequented the same movie theater. "You knew it?"

"I have hobbies. Keep going."

"They must have planned something, or he wouldn't have had handcuffs. Actually..." Daniel pats down his pockets and pulls out the handcuffs. "And he had a lock for outside the back door. He gave Lily something, pills, to calm her down and keep her quiet, and he took some himself. They got really intense. I guess they were both high. She waved the gun around and fired it at the wall. There were more pills. I didn't hear everything they said when he took her to the bathrooms, and they, uh..."

Daniel looks around awkwardly. Tony remembers what he said before, and he guesses Daniel doesn't want to repeat it in front of so many people. He's still trying to protect Lily, though it's the detail most likely to raise everyone's sympathy for her, which she desperately needs.

Daniel must realize that as well. "I could only hear it, but I'm fairly certain they were having sex. I don't think she wasn't able to consent because of the drugs, and I wasn't sure about him either. I was worried about them. I used the quick release on the handcuffs and took her phone—she left it out. I only know one number by heart, my friend Paul in the city, so I texted him. He called Tony, and Tony came and found us."

"Why didn't you call 911?"

Daniel sighs. "Honestly? Lily was barely coherent all day. After what happened to Andrew Clayfield and to her last year, I didn't want her to get arrested without some idea of how to get her stable and thinking clearly. I was worried it would do more damage to her."

"And you didn't trust us to—"

"No," Daniel interrupts. "No, I didn't. Not after last year." His eyes flick toward Colette, and the detective looks down at her eggs.

"All right, fine. Mr. d'Angelo shows up. What then?"

"The boyfriend left. Tony and I talked. Tony went out to get help. Lily got sick. She was vomiting for about half an hour before Tony got back with his sister and the tools to break open the lock on the door. We convinced Lily to come with us, got out of there, and came here."

The detective sets her plate on the coffee table. "And why did Lily, the alleged murderess, need convincing to flee the scene of the crime?"

Slowly, Blake raises his hand. "I might be able to help with that one."

Everyone turns to him.

"Sheesh," he mutters. "So, from what Lily told me, she has a Xanax prescription to help manage her anxiety. She's been on it way too long, though, honestly, and she's overusing, which means her therapist should have—"

"Blake," Gianna interrupts.

"Right. So, coming back to Lobell has worsened her anxiety, for obvious reasons. The Xanax wasn't cutting it, and her boyfriend started trading her. Weed at first, over the summer, but weed's a depressant too. Neither of them was doing great, and they got in a car crash when he was driving after doing both at the same time. They switched to molly."

There's the car crash again. Tony debates saying something about what Sean told him at the memorial, but ultimately, Lily's in enough trouble. What good would it do to tell everyone she was driving? He's sure Sean will mention it as soon as the tiniest hint of pressure is put on him.

"She didn't happen to know how he was getting all these drugs?" Taylor asks.

"I didn't ask. Not my department."

"What exactly is molly?" Colette asks.

"Uh, a type of MDMA. Like ecstasy," Blake explains. "It's an upper. He gave her molly when she was on a downward spiral, to make her happy. But MDMA basically uses up all the serotonin in your body, and when it wore off, she'd crash into depression and need the Xanax again."

"Christ." Daniel leans forward. "Will she be okay?"

"She hasn't been doing this for long. It's only been, what, a week or two since that car accident? It's not good, but with proper care and reliable mental health providers, she'll be all right physically. I'm more worried about the reliance on Xanax right now."

It's rare seeing Blake in professional mode. Tony has known him for so long it's hard to imagine Blake as anyone other than the kid who dyed his bowl-cut hair black in sophomore year of high school and thought it was the height of fashion even though his hair was naturally so black you couldn't tell the difference. Goofy as he might be, though, his heart is in the right place, and Tony is incredibly thankful to know him.

"And it was in one of these states that she attacked Professor Lawrence?" Taylor asks.

For a moment, no one answers, and Tony realizes he still doesn't know how the actual murder happened.

Gianna volunteers. "From what Lily said before, I think what happened is she went to Professor Lawrence's office to try to get her to agree to accepting last year's coursework for a grade. She probably didn't mean it to be a big deal or anything, but she got nervous. Sean—the boyfriend—gave her tips on what to say, but something went wrong. When Professor Lawrence didn't agree, something happened, and Lily... She mentioned the knife, but it was like she didn't remember doing it."

Taylor raises an eyebrow. "Professor Lawrence was stabbed four times."

Abruptly, Emilio gets up and goes into the kitchen.

Tony winces and makes to stand, but Lisa puts a hand on his elbow. "Let me. You don't need me for this."

It's a fair point, so he lets her go.

"Lily is definitely sure it's her fault," Daniel says. "She kept saying it was and waving the gun around. I have no idea where she even got it."

"Sean's family hunts." Gianna's lips twist in disapproval. "I'm sure that's where she got the knife as well."

"If she's been using drugs regularly, especially combining them, it definitely affected her ability to make choices," Blake throws in. "It could also be affecting her memory, although trauma affects memory as well, so who knows. I doubt she had a fully worked-out plan. In my professional opinion, she's not in any state to complete a premeditated crime, but I don't know why she went after Daniel either."

Daniel shrugs. "I'm her adviser. She'd been talking to me about how scared she was and how bad she was feeling. She probably thought I knew more than I did."

Taylor nods slowly. "All right, then. Lily's sleeping?"

Blake nods. "She's crashing hard. I'd like to get her to a hospital and, ideally, into treatment with a psychiatrist who can wean her off the Xanax and onto something less addictive."

"She trusts you," Taylor says. It's not quite a question.

"She trusts Gianna. Me by proxy."

"We're going to need a police presence at the hospital. She'll want familiar faces with her." Taylor turns to Gianna. "And you should be the one to ask her if she wants to do a rape kit." The detective is blunt about it, and the words are a heavy, leaden weight in the room.

"She took a shower before," Gianna says. "We kept her clothes, but—"

"She can still get the kit done, but it might not be as conclusive. Put the clothes in a plastic bag and keep them as evidence. If she wants to submit it, she can. She doesn't have to press charges, but if she gets the kit done, it will be easier. Still can't promise anything, especially if he was on drugs too."

The detective drains her cup of coffee. "I will leave you this. When you get yourselves involved in a criminal investigation, at least you get competent help."

Blake's chest puffs out ever so slightly. Tony's going to have to start taking him seriously now.

"In your opinion, is the boyfriend a threat?" Taylor asks. She doesn't seem to be asking anyone in particular. Daniel makes a doubtful face, while Colette shakes her head minutely.

Tony snorts.

Detective Taylor's laser focus turns to him.

"Sorry. I just get the impression he's mostly an idiot."

"Yup," Gianna agrees. "He's obnoxious as shit, and the drugs are concerning, but as far as I know, he's not a big-time dealer or anything."

"Hm. Miss Peterson didn't seem like a threat either, did she?"

Tony winces.

"If he's where she got both the drugs and the weapons," Taylor continues, "he's at least an accessory of some sort."

"I'm sure the college can tell you where to find him," Daniel says. "His dorm or address will be on file." He sounds utterly resigned to yet another student whose life will be ruined by the fallout from Mario.

Colette pulls out her phone again. Tony tries to lean in to see what she's doing, but she angles the screen away before he can catch more than Sean's name at the top of the screen. It doesn't matter. He knows it's a warning. Daniel must have really gotten to her. Now, she's following his example of the overly attached mentor.

"As far as I've understood from Sean," Colette says delicately once she's put her phone away again, carefully out of the detective's line of sight, "he's doing his best to support someone he cares about in crisis. It shows integrity for someone so young."

Detective Taylor absolutely levels Colette with a harsh glare. "I think we'll have to agree to disagree about what integrity means in this case, Professor Ravel."

She sighs, leaning back in her seat. "You're all going to have to come down to the station and make statements. That includes Mr. Lawrence in the kitchen, by the way. We'll have to look for this Sean and any physical evidence before charges can be made. And we'll need a statement from Miss Peterson as well when she's able. Chances are when this all goes to trial, you'll have to explain your actions to a judge and jury."

"You don't sound terribly concerned," Colette says.

"Unfortunately," Taylor gets out through gritted teeth, "I am well aware some juries will likely view your decisions as understandable and compassionate rather than foolhardy. Some judges might consider a fine. Some won't."

"Would some judges consider fining a police officer who accuses people of planting evidence without any investigation?" It slips out of Tony's mouth, caustic and irritated. "We could have skipped a whole lot of this if you'd done your job."

Taylor stiffens. She doesn't answer.

It might not have changed anything. Daniel was always going to prioritize his own guilt.

"We'll have to consult our lawyer about the legal consequences." Colette is serious and grave. If Tony didn't know she just means she'll call Jeff again whenever he gets home from Malta, he might be concerned.

Detective Taylor gets to her feet and pulls out her phone. "You do that. I have work to do. Mr. Walia, would you mind giving me your contact details so I can arrange a police escort for you and Miss Peterson to get to the hospital?"

"Uh, sure." Blakes eyes are wide as he gives the detective his full name and number.

Taylor punches in the info, then starts making calls as she heads out the front door. The words "you're not going to believe this" echo in the hallway as her footsteps retreat down the stairs.

"Whew." Daniel sinks back into the couch. "Well, that could have gone worse."

Meredith shakes her head. "You are extremely lucky I came and not Mom and Dad."

"I love you, too," Daniel says, dry and sarcastic and nothing like when he said the same thing to Tony only hours ago. "What about your kids, anyway?"

"Won't kill my husband to take care of them for a few days."

"Are you *sure*?"

Meredith doesn't dignify that with a response, which is, to Tony's mind, answer enough. Daniel refers to his brother-in-law exclusively as "fucking Benjamin." This is probably why. Meredith starts picking up coffee mugs instead and takes them to the kitchen.

Beyond the open door, Tony makes out Emilio on one of the stools by the island with his head hung low. Lisa stands next to him, her hand resting gently on his shoulder.

"Think he'll be okay?" Blake asks.

"No," everyone else in the room says immediately.

"Sheesh. Just a question." Blake's thoughtless comments are a universal constant. It's good to return things to the status quo.

The escort to get Lily to the hospital arrives soon after. Gianna and Blake pile into the police car to accompany her, and Tony sets about stripping all the bedding in the apartment and starting a load of laundry. So many people have slept and sat on every surface that it feels necessary.

Lisa leaves next, saying she's going to see Emilio home safely and then try to catch some sleep herself. She promises to call later.

Finally, only Colette and Meredith remain. In a rare fit of sensitivity, Colette helps to clean up the kitchen while Daniel showers and doesn't say much of anything. Meredith tidies the living room, and Tony suspects it's more so she has something to do than because she wants to.

Daniel exits the shower, clean and unfortunately also clean-shaven once again, leaving the bathroom free for Tony. Tony hasn't focused on how gross he feels. He's been wearing the same clothes for over twenty-four hours, and he smells of stale sweat and cooking fumes. The shower is a blessing.

The apartment is empty when he gets out.

Daniel sits on the couch, petting Worf, who finally emerged from his hiding spot in the cat tree. "Alone at last," Daniel tells Tony with a smile. It doesn't meet his eyes.

"Sorry," Tony says.

"You don't mean that."

"No, not really. I wish I did."

"Do you?"

Tony takes a seat next to Daniel, not quite close enough to touch. "I wish you understood what it felt like when you were gone. I wish you'd seen Emilio when we got to him."

"I understand. Last year, with Stacy, it was terrifying—"

"No, you don't understand. It was more than a day, Daniel. I thought you had died. I thought I'd never— And Emilio, he's a wreck. Their kid will never see her mom again. That's on Lily. She should have come to you sooner, or gone to anyone else, or—"

Daniel shakes his head. "I was supposed to help her. I was supposed to take care of her."

"For fuck's sake, you're a professor, not a therapist!" With energy he didn't know he had left, Tony springs to his feet. "You're supposed to teach her, not save her from herself or fix problems you didn't even know she could have. You keep saying you're responsible, but you're not. You just want to stop feeling guilty."

Daniel's eyes are wide when Tony looks over at him. His mouth is open a bit, his cheeks flushed with anger. "I—" he starts, and then he crumples in his seat. "You're right."

The shock stops Tony in his tracks. "I'm not. I'm angry and scared and so fucking tired. And I know you're smarter about this stuff than me—"

"No, you're right." Daniel laughs ruefully. "I've been trying so hard to do everything right that I did wrong with Mario, you know? Being there for Lily. Being there for you. Being compassionate and helping and fixing everyone. I didn't realize I was making it about me."

"You weren't. I needed you. You were there."

"Yeah, but I can't fix everything for you."

"I don't want you to. I just like when you listen." Slowly, Tony lets his shoulders drop and his jaw unclench. He sits next to Daniel. "I know why you did it. I know why you want to protect her, and it's good. It's right. But you can't do it on your own, and even if the systems we have suck and don't work, sometimes, they can do more than you can by yourself."

"How do I trust that she'll..."

"You visit. You check up on her. You see how you can help within the system. Even if it sucks. You let *someone else* be responsible."

Daniel chokes on a sob as he leans into Tony. "I'm sorry you were so scared."

"I'm sorry I told Emilio to call the police."

"We were both doing what we thought was best, I guess."

"Yeah."

"Can this day be over now?"

"*Please.*" Tony presses a kiss into the top of Daniel's head. "Wait, what about Meredith? I'm sure she—"

"Colette offered to take her out, show her the campus and stuff."

Worf drops his whole head into Daniel's hand, demanding scritches.

"I think they could both tell I'm about to keel over," he says.

"Yeah. You must be running on no sleep."

"I dozed off for a bit in the theater. But no real sleep, no. Can we—would you—"

"I haven't slept either. Let's go to bed."

"*Thank you.*"

The sheets are still in the washer, so they lie right on the mattress topper, under the uncovered duvet.

"Hey," Daniel says as Tony's eyes fall shut.

"Hmm?"

"I told you I'd say it next when you could see my face. I love you."

Tony snuggles in tight until he can wrap his arms around Daniel's middle and bury his nose in the base of Daniel's neck, where his damp hair still smells of his stupid three-in-one shower product. "I love you too."

Chapter Sixteen

Daniel's making tea in the kitchen.

He's making tea in the kitchen, and Tony hears him whistling through the door, and the sound heals a fractured part of his heart worn thin with worrying the last few days.

Tony pushes the comforter off and pads to the kitchen, where he wraps his arms around Daniel's middle and kisses Daniel's cheek.

His skin is still sleep-warm and cozy.

"Good morning." Daniel reaches back and pats Tony's hip through the thin material of his boxers.

"Morning," Tony mumbles into Daniel's T-shirt. "No, wait. What time is it?"

"Like, three p.m. Sleep well?" The kettle clicks off and Daniel pours hot water over his tea leaves.

Tony makes some a noncommittal sound that means he won't have to let go yet.

"You okay?" Daniel asks.

Tony nods and burrows his nose deeper into Daniel's shirt. "I just missed you." It comes out more honest, more heartbroken than he expected.

White-hot panic floods Tony for an instant as he remembers all the thoughts and worst-case scenarios he went through while Daniel was gone, making his grip on Daniel go tight.

"Hey." Daniel's hand is light on Tony's hip, brushing against it to offer some comfort. "I'm okay. I'm here."

"Yeah." It's hard to stop shaking, to loosen his hold on Daniel. Tony does it anyway. He doesn't want to leave anything unresolved between them. "I'm still sorry I got Emilio involved. I should have talked to you about it instead of getting angry and not...saying anything."

Daniel pulls him close again and cards his hand through Tony's messy hair. "Who's to say you weren't right? Maybe I should have used Lily's phone to call the police in the first place. Who knows if I did anyone any favors?"

"You were doing what you thought was right."

"I was thinking about me. I thought I could fix everything by myself better than the police, and I dragged you and Gianna and everyone else into trouble."

Tony buries his face in Daniel's shoulder. His voice is barely audible. "I was thinking about me too. I was so scared and so angry, and I knew Emilio would...I knew he would do something."

Daniel cups his cheek. "Angry at me?"

"No." Tony takes a deep, shuddering breath. "Maybe a little. But only because you wouldn't let me save you."

"I'm sorry I put you through so much."

"I'm sorry I got Emilio involved."

"Don't be. He deserves...something."

"Still. Shouldn't have given the detective that knife either."

"Eh. That might save us all from getting charged for obstruction. I think it's clear enough Lily had no idea what she was doing when she brought the knife here. She didn't mean to threaten me. I think in a roundabout way, she was trying to confess. She *wanted* us to hand over the evidence. Who knows if I was actually doing her any favors."

Tony wraps his arms tighter around Daniel, squeezing him. Then, he takes a deep breath, letting it go. He presses another kiss to the Daniel's cheek and pulls away reluctantly. "At least now, she has medical help. She wouldn't have if she'd gotten arrested."

Daniel hums in assent.

"We're okay?" Tony asks.

"We are."

"Good."

Worf takes the opportunity to squawk loudly at their feet.

"Don't let him lie to you." Tony glares down but rubs across Worf's tailbone all the same. "He got all his regular meals and then some."

"Filthy opportunist," Daniel coos, letting Worf rub his cheek against Daniel's fingers. "Cute, filthy opportunist."

"Any news?"

Daniel shrugs. "My phone is still somewhere in the bushes by the road to Germantown, remember?"

"Shit. We'll have to go to Best Buy or something."

"I can order something online. It's cheaper, anyway."

Tony remembers the state of the office and winces. "Right. We'll need to set up your whole desk system again."

Daniel cocks his head, brow furrowed. "What happened there?"

"My parents and our friends and your sister showed up as soon as they knew you'd gone missing, and my ma insisted on cooking for everyone. Wasn't enough space to sit and eat."

Slowly, Daniel nods. "Explains why the fridge is so full."

"You should have seen it before she cooked."

Daniel laughs. "Is it weird that I'm glad we have so many people who care?"

"No." Tony kisses him, soft and sweet. "Not at all."

He finds his phone on the coffee table not too long after. "Sweetheart?" he calls. "Looks like we have many people who want to continue caring."

"What do you mean?" Daniel emerges from the office, where he's been setting his computer to rights.

"Ma wants to see you, make sure you're okay. And Charlie and Blake G are both pissed no one told them what's going on. And Lisa wants to check in."

"Huh." Daniel runs a hand through his hair. It's frizzy from sleeping on it; putting his hands in it only makes it worse.

Tony wants to put his hands in Daniel's hair.

"Colette and Meredith will want to see us sometime today, too," Daniel points out.

"That's so many people."

"Mm." Daniel considers. "How about the Indian place in Red Hook? Don't they do a buffet?"

Anything to avoid having the apartment overrun again. Now Daniel's back where he belongs, Tony finds himself unwilling to have their space completely taken over.

"Good idea," he says.

"I'll call and ask if they have space." Daniel pats down his pockets and then remembers he still doesn't have a phone. Tony holds his out wordlessly.

While Daniel makes the call, Tony sets about finding his goddamn hair ties. He checks under the bed and under the couch and, finally, when he can't think of anywhere else they might be, in Worf's little cubbyhole in the cat tree.

He finds the little bastard, curled up and purring, with his paw on top of three hair ties.

"What am I gonna do with you, huh?" Tony sighs, scratching Worf's head behind the ears. "What is wrong with you? Why must you steal?"

He tries to pull a hair tie out, but Worf curls a claw around it and purrs harder.

"That's mine, kitten. Get your own."

Still, Worf refuses to give it up.

"Why are you like this?"

"You know, I have a theory about that." Daniel comes up behind him and works the hair tie out of Worf's claw.

"Oh?" Tony raises an eyebrow as best as he can while putting his hair up.

"Mm." A secretive half-smile spreads across Daniel's face. "You know when you put your hair up? It's when you're about to leave for the day."

Tony looks at Worf again, the cat purring away. He's rolled onto his back, paws curled up by his chest, expecting belly rubs. "Uh-huh. So?"

"So," Daniel says, hooking his chin over Tony's shoulder, "I think he doesn't want you to go."

Blood rushes in Tony's ears, excitement pooling in his stomach. "Really."

"Yeah. We have a lot in common."

"Huh." Tony tries to hide his smile, reaching out to rub at Worf's soft stomach. He squawks but accepts the tummy rubs. "Is he now."

"Mm-hm. I think he'd feel better if you...lived here."

"Very sneaky way of showing it." Tony fingers the two hair ties still in Worf's lair. Worf refuses to give them up. "What do you think we should do about this...problem of Worf's?"

Daniel sighs. "Hey. Look at me?"

Tony turns in Daniel's arms, so they're nose to nose. Daniel clasps his hands together behind Tony's neck; Tony's hands migrate to Daniel's hips.

"I don't want to rush you into anything. I get it if you want to stay with your family. It's not like we never see each other. And I would also get it if you wanted to live alone before jumping right into living with someone. I just think I—and Worf—would be happier if you were here all the time. So maybe it's something to think about?"

Tony tightens his grip on Daniel's hips. "I don't need to think about it."

"No?"

Tony shakes his head. He leans forward to kiss Daniel, slow and luscious and soft.

Daniel looks a little hazy when they pull apart. "Okay, that's not an answer."

"Daniel, sweetheart. I think I already live here."

A rueful smile spreads across Daniel's face. "I thought maybe you hadn't noticed."

"I was pretending. Badly. But if it will make Worf happy, I can move in properly."

"It will make Worf *so* happy."

"Anything for the cat."

They're both smiling too hard to kiss properly. They give it their best go anyway.

Tony wants to bask in it properly afterwards, but they lack the time. Daniel has to order a new phone off the internet and see about getting his cell phone contract switched to a new number, which involves several emails and a very long phone call with customer service. When Daniel's not using his phone, Tony texts various people, assuring them Daniel's okay and they can meet up for Indian in a few hours. Then, Meredith turns up, and she and Daniel abscond to the kitchen to call their parents and fill them in on a heavily edited version of events. In the meantime, Colette and Tony pore over the email from the college president announcing the police have secured a credible lead concerning Amelia Lawrence's murder, and campus has been declared safe, so classes are continuing as normal.

No further details are given, of course, but given Lily's room has been searched, and the police are trying to find her boyfriend as an accomplice, it won't be long before everyone knows. Neither of them says it out loud. Daniel might have gotten some sleep and some perspective, but he'll still be blaming himself.

"A credible lead," Tony repeats. "I'm impressed the detective thought highly enough of us to put it like that."

"It must have killed her to say it." Colette shakes her head. "When this gets out,

the college will really have to work on its image."

"I hope no one in the film department makes a movie about it." Tony shudders. Beyond his Mario-based prejudice against film professors, student films are truly terrible. Sean's description of his artistic ambitions only confirmed that.

Colette makes a face. "What an awful thought. I suppose we all know where they would screen it."

"Oh, I am never going there again." Daniel peers over Colette's shoulder at the email.

Colette scoffs. "You go back to Wordstone Mansion all the time, and Stacy shot you there. How is that different?"

"Wordstone is a nice place with a good view," Daniel argues. "The Continuum is a blight on humanity, *and* someone pointed a gun at me there. No, thank you."

From her position on the comfy chair, watching them, Meredith wrinkles her nose. "I'm running a tally of all the things you apparently say on a regular basis that would give our mother a heart attack."

"You should try a bingo," Colette suggests. "Winner gets a bottle of wine."

Meredith snaps her fingers. "Sold."

They drive to campus in Tony's car, which is running smoothly for a change. It's like it heard him threaten to get a newer model. He doesn't trust it. Colette, Meredith, and Daniel switch to Daniel's car when they get there, and Tony follows them to Red Hook. It leads them past the worst intersection north of Brooklyn, but Tony finds he doesn't mind it so much now. They have time to wait out three light switches before they can get across.

Their group ends up occupying a private room in the restaurant, which is slightly ridiculous. It's not a big restaurant, an impression only aided by the cluttered walls, low ceilings, and dim lighting Indian restaurants favor. Still, taking up a whole private room is not something Tony was planning on today.

"We're leaving a big tip, right?" Tony mutters to Daniel as everyone starts to filter in, talking over one another.

Daniel nods wordlessly.

Almost immediately, Tony is drawn into explaining to Charlie and Blake G what happened. He's helped by Blake W and, when she gets there, Lisa with Emilio in tow.

"What was I supposed to do, forget about him?" Lisa hisses to Tony.

"He works from home, he doesn't have any friends in the area, and his family lives in Jersey."

"It's fine by me. But remember, several of us suspected him of killing his wife, and he knows it. *And* we've been trying to help her actual killer. He has no reason to like us."

Lisa winces and glances over at Emilio. He's relating his involvement to Charlie in detail, and the way he narrates it, he has no hard feelings about Colette and Tony staking out his house.

"Well," Tony says. "That works, I guess."

It takes a while to get through the full story for everyone who wasn't there for all of it. It's not all pleasant. Rehashing what Lily did throws a pall over all of them. There's Emilio's anger, Daniel's guilt, Gianna's concern, and the collective knowledge that no matter what happens, no matter what they tried to achieve, Lily's life will be forever changed in the worst way. In Tony's opinion, the consequences are justified. Emilio's life has also been destroyed, not to mention his daughter's. But Tony knows Daniel won't magically stop wishing he could have prevented it even if he understands what an awful mess Lily's actions have created. Tony's still working out how he feels about it.

He's trying not to think about how it makes him feel—Daniel missing and possibly hurt, or worse, Lily causing it all, no matter how messed up she is. This is neither the place nor the time for working through it. Instead, Tony goes for seconds from the buffet, and most everyone follows suit.

Tony's ma, who has never had Indian food in her life, works on some lamb saag with a thoughtful expression on her face.

"Do you think they'd give me a recipe?" she asks.

Gianna rolls her eyes. "Have you heard of Google, Ma?"

Through a series of comments, which Tony misses half of, Daniel and Emilio end up discussing several different methods of storing recipes online, something Emilio apparently does for his own parents and Daniel used to do when he was a grad student who could only cook three things.

Tony leans into Daniel's space, bumping their shoulders together.

"You say that like you can cook more things now, sweetheart."

Daniel flicks his nose. "I wasn't starving before I met you."

"It's true," Colette says. "I used to think Daniel was a decent cook before you started feeding us."

Resting his arm on the back of Tony's chair, Tony examines her critically. "The Swedish Chef is a decent cook compared to you, Colette."

In the circle of Tony's arm, Daniel shakes with repressed laughter.

"When have you ever tried anything I've cooked?" Colette asks with supreme dignity.

"Never," Tony tells her. "Because you don't."

Under the table, Daniel pats Tony's knee. "Come on now. Don't make her too mad."

Tony kisses his cheek. "Fine. For you." He wonders if Daniel and Colette have worked out their fight yesterday, or if they're ignoring it.

When most everyone, including Daniel, has gone to examine the dessert selections, Tony catches his pa watching him.

"What's up?" Tony asks.

"Nothing."

That's definitely a "something" voice.

"Pa."

Pa shrugs. "He didn't need to get kidnapped for you to treat him like your boyfriend in front of us."

"Joseph," Ma hisses. "We agreed—"

Pa holds up his hands. "I know, I know."

"What did you agree?" Tony looks between them. Ma looks like she's been caught red-handed. By comparison, Pa looks a little disgruntled, the way he does when he's been asked to come to dinner right after his favorite show started.

"We agreed we weren't going to push you to talk about anything," Pa says matter-of-factly. "We didn't want to drive you away."

Tony clears his throat, heat suffusing the back of his neck. "That's, uh, why I didn't talk about it. In case it drove *you* away."

"Tony," Ma chastises. "You don't think we'd—"

"No, no," Tony says hastily. "Just—your church friends. Our clients at the shop. Didn't want to rock the boat."

"If *that* rocks the boat, they don't deserve to be on it." Ma tucks her napkin more firmly onto her lap as she says it, mouth drawn tight.

Wordlessly, Tony gets up and rounds the table to give her a hug.

If he squeezes a bit too tight and holds on a bit too long, well, no one says anything.

Gianna does take a picture, dessert in one hand and flash bright in Tony's face.

"Come on," she demands afterward. "Family photo. No, Daniel, you're in it, too, come on." She beckons him over, and he sets two bowls of rice pudding down at his and Tony's places before he obeys.

Blake W takes the pictures, forcing them to make all sorts of dumb faces. They pass Lia around between them until there's a picture of every one of them holding her, even Daniel, who still looks like he's holding a ticking time bomb every time he ends up with her in his arms. Pa even sticks his tongue out for one.

"I'm putting that one on the shop Instagram," Gianna says immediately, thumbs flying on her phone screen. "It's a business strategy. People dig the whole family-run thing."

Colette agrees despite having not entered an auto shop for the entire time she's been living in the US. "It helps them identify with the product. There are some excellent anthropology papers about that."

"Huh," Pa says. Beyond putting a sign on the shop roof, he hasn't ever demonstrated an interest in advertising.

Gianna, ever the academically minded d'Angelo, is far keener on anthropology. "You mind sending me those papers? We could definitely use some more marketing strategy if we want to beat out the new shop over on Ulster Avenue."

"We're not trying to beat anyone out," Pa says, not for the first time. "Staying in business is enough for me."

"With that attitude—" Gianna starts.

"Hey," Tony says.

They don't hear him at first, still occupied with their age-old discussion, so he tries again.

"Hey." He glances over at Daniel and smiles involuntarily. "Uh, you should probably know I'm gonna move out."

"Oh, we're doing this now?" Daniel murmurs, soft enough only Tony hears it. "Okay."

"Could have sworn you moved out in, like, June." Gianna's teasing, but she's also smiling. Approving.

"Gianna." Ma's tone is warning. "Tony, are you telling us you and Daniel are moving in together?"

At his nod, a whole other event begins other than a joint post-kidnapping dinner. Suddenly, he and Daniel are surrounded by congratulations and offers to help, although what with, Tony isn't sure on. Daniel's apartment doesn't need any more furniture except that dining table, and Tony doesn't have enough essentials left at his parents' house for more than one car trip. Everyone ends up ordering another round of drinks, and somehow, they still haven't left by nine.

Tony's not sure how long this restaurant usually stays open, but so far, no one tries to hurry them, and it's nice to be surrounded by friends and family wishing them well.

One of the massive stainless steel serving dishes at the buffet table clatters to the floor with a loud crash, pulling them out of the warm haze that has settled over the group.

Everyone quiets down, even Blake W, who was busy exaggerating his own involvement in Lily's recuperation for Blake G's benefit.

"Professor Rosenbaum," a voice calls from the restaurant's main room. "I know you're in here. Saw you playing happy families on the 'gram."

It's a voice and, more importantly, a series of utterly college-student words Tony would recognize anywhere.

"Sean," he mutters.

"Sean?" Colette gets to her feet. "Is that you? The police have been looking for you—"

"Yeah, I know they fuckin' have," he yells, still from the other room. "What the fuck did she tell you?"

"What did who tell me?"

"My lying, nutso girlfriend, that's who. She's been telling lies about me, trying to frame me, hasn't she— Hey, get the fuck down." He must be talking to the waitstaff.

A gunshot in a cramped restaurant with fabric on all the walls sounds muffled, but it's unmistakable. At least, it is if you've heard a gunshot before.

"Quick," Lisa says, the only one of them to have regular experience with active shooter drills. "Everyone under the tables. Hide."

The last thing Tony hears is Colette muttering "Only in this godforsaken country" before everything is chaos.

Lia is first under the table, Blake and Gianna following quickly after to crouch on either side of her carrier. Others follow, but there's not enough time to get everyone hidden.

The barrel of Sean's gun twitches aside the curtain separating the room they're in from the rest of the restaurant.

A whimper escapes from Ma, and Tony's on his feet before he can reconsider.

"Sean," he tries. "Sean, why don't you put the gun down."

Sean enters the room through the curtain, sneering at him. His eyes are bloodshot red. He looks exhausted, strung out and high. "I'm not looking for you, dude."

"Let's talk about this," Colette says, using what Tony's distantly aware of as her phone call voice. She walks around the table slowly, edging closer to where Tony's standing, his body between Sean's rifle and the rest of the room.

"There's nothing to talk about. You all took my girlfriend and hid her somewhere, and I need her back before she gets me all wrapped up in this."

"No one took Lily," Daniel says as he edges around Sean's side, the one opposite from Colette, effectively blocking Sean's exit from, the room. "She needed medical care."

"She doesn't need shit." Sean spits the words out, saliva catching in his mustache. "She needed to fucking confess it's all *her* fault, and then this would all go away."

"Sean," Daniel says, softly and calmly, as if he's talking to a four-year-old who has misbehaved and not a grown man holding a gun pointed at him. "The police already know she—"

"She's lying!" Sean waves the rifle emphatically, and Tony jerks out of the way, narrowly avoiding getting hit in the head with it. "She's the one who did it. I swear she did!"

He keeps going, and the longer he does, the more doubt starts to seed in Tony's mind about the version of events they've come to believe. Out of the corner of his eye, he spots the side door to the kitchen opening fractionally.

"So it was Lily who killed Professor Lawrence?" Tony asks, injecting as much sincerity as he knows how. He angles himself carefully, trying to block Sean's line of sight to the kitchen.

"Yes!" Sean says. "Man, she wanted Prof Lawrence *gone*. Kept telling me how she didn't deserve to teach. It was fucking annoying!"

"That sounds rough for you," Tony says.

Blake makes it through the kitchen door with Lia held closely to his chest. Tony can't spot who's next, not with his back to most of the table. He hopes the others are following close behind.

"Oh my god, you have no idea." Sean groans. The barrel of the rifle dips dramatically toward the floor.

Catching on to what Tony's doing, Daniel chimes in. "She's been really out of it, huh?"

"She's fucking crazy, man." Sean laughs, high and tight and out of control. "Don't know why she thinks anyone would buy that I did it."

"Why don't you tell us what happened?" It's too innocent, the way Colette says it.

Sean isn't thinking straight enough to be suspicious. He launches into a tirade about Lily, how she begged him to accompany her to Amelia Lawrence's office to help convince the professor to give her a chance to make up the missing final, how she wouldn't stop crying. It doesn't exactly inspire sympathy in Tony. Not for Sean, at least.

He keeps his eye on the gun instead. Sean's grip is loosening. He keeps shifting the gun, letting it slip lower and lower as though it's too heavy for him to hold up.

Daniel catches Tony's eye and shakes his head.

Tony looks back helplessly. What else are they supposed to do?

He inches forward.

Sean resettles his grip again.

Seeing his chance, Tony darts out to take the rifle from him or at least knock it out of his hands.

He's too slow.

Sean catches on, and suddenly, Tony's pressed up to the wall with one of Sean's hands crushing against his collarbone. The other holds the gun pressed to Tony's belly.

"Sean," Colette says, her voice shaking. "Sean, you don't want to do this. You don't—"

"Don't tell me what the fuck I want to do," Sean snarls. "You're trying to confuse me. Where is she? Where's Lily?"

Neither of them answers.

Sean pulls the safety.

Desperately, Tony looks to Daniel. "Daniel, I—"

"Don't," Daniel says. "Not like—"

"Put down your weapon," Detective Taylor calls. "Sean McAllister, we have you surrounded. Put down your weapon before someone gets hurt."

Sean's rifle clatters to the floor.

It's snapshots in Tony's memory, afterward, Sean being pulled away by the police, Daniel gathering Tony up in his arms, holding him close and kissing every square inch of his face. Giving the police his statement with his hands still shaking, allowing an EMT to check him for nonexistent injuries.

Letting his ma yell at him for being an idiot and playing hero.

Letting Gianna kiss his cheek for the same thing.

Catching Emilio before he leaves to thank him for being the one to call the police. Again.

"No one even had to tell me to do it this time." Emilio says with a half-smile. "You were right though."

"Huh?"

"Seeing him didn't help. He's just a messed-up kid. So's she, probably. It was never about Amy or our family."

Tony claps him on the shoulder before he gets into his car and drives home to his empty house.

They offer to help clean up the restaurant, but in the end, besides the bullet hole in the drywall behind a decorative tapestry, it's only one or two spilled dishes. Too little mess for how shaken Tony feels. They leave the biggest tip they can scrounge together between all twelve of them. Colette contributes a hundred dollar bill, poorly hiding how badly she's shaking with her arms crossed tightly over her stomach.

Detective Taylor waits for them as they leave the restaurant.

A sinking feeling spreads through Tony's stomach. He wishes it were from too much Indian food.

"I took Lily Peterson's statement this morning. She confessed. We're supposed to charge her with the murder tomorrow morning." Taylor is, as always, clear and to the point.

Tony wishes he didn't feel like it was his business. He wants to lie down, preferably somewhere no one can see or talk to him except Daniel and Worf.

"I'd rather not do that with loose ends," Taylor continues. "To be honest, besides her confession, we don't have much evidence. Her prints aren't on the murder weapon, and Mr. Lawrence was kind enough to tell me about a website you were researching, but the threatening posts about Professor Lawrence couldn't be traced to a single IP address."

Tony looks over to Daniel, at his mouth set in a firm line. Though still exhausted and shaken, Daniel won't back down on this. He committed to being responsible for Lily at the start, and if there is any chance he can do something to help her, he will.

"What do you need?" Tony asks.

"Ideally, I want to find out what actually happened."

"This was my fault," Colette says immediately, absolutely sure and absolutely wrong.

"No, it wasn't," Tony snaps.

- 282 -   S.B. Barnes

"It was. Sean is my advisee. I tried to get in touch with him to let him know about Lily and that he ought to come forward and—and tell you about his involvement. I thought it would help."

Daniel makes a move as if he's about to interrupt, but Colette holds up her hand to stop him.

"I thought he was more reasonable and adult. Once again, I severely misjudged."

"What exactly did you tell him?" Taylor asks.

"To get in touch with me or with you directly, in order to help himself now Lily has been caught."

"Well." Detective Taylor sighs. "As usual, I'd have preferred it if you had let me know. But in this case, Professor, it sounds like you offered a student reasonable advice. It's not your fault. You didn't know he would do this."

"That's the problem," Colette mutters. "I never seem to know."

"So what now?" Daniel asks.

"I need to talk to Lily. Preferably with someone she trusts. Someone like you, Professor Rosenbaum. Or your partner's sister and Mr. Walia."

"Gianna's gone home," Tony says.

Last time Tony saw her, she was in the back seat of Blake's tiny car, one hand curled protectively around Lia's car seat. They already asked so much of her that he can't stomach the thought of calling her away from her daughter again. Not after tonight.

Detective Taylor nods decisively. "Then it's you two."

Meredith, who's been waiting and watching the whole scene quietly, offers to drive Tony's poor little car to Rhinebeck so he doesn't have to get behind the wheel quite yet. He suspects it isn't only to do him and Daniel a favor. Colette's still shaking, though she's turned down every offer of a hot drink and a warm blanket so far. Maybe the comfort of a near stranger in the privacy of her own apartment will be easier to accept.

Daniel and Tony follow the police cruiser to Kingston and the hospital in Daniel's car.

They don't talk much on the way. Tony gives directions, and Daniel follows them.

In the parking lot, Daniel asks, "Are you sure you're okay to do this?"

"Me?" Tony wants to ask Daniel the same thing. "I'm fine."

"Tony. You can wait in the car. I know you're still angry."

He is, of course he is. But sitting alone in the car in the dark, waiting for Daniel to finish up inside—letting Daniel out of his sight *again*—

"No, I want to come in."

"Okay."

The fluorescent lighting in the hospital is jarring, too bright and somehow loud in Tony's skull. It's loud the normal way, too, even at night on a... Christ, he doesn't know what day it is. People in scrubs keep pushing past them, a phone rings, everyone's talking. There are too many things to process all at once.

"Right, so, Lily's in the psych ward?" Daniel doesn't know, how would he? But he walks toward the elevator with confidence, and Tony and Detective Taylor follow.

The nurse at the reception desk tells them it's past visiting hours six times before Detective Taylor gets impatient and flashes her badge. Then, the nurse insists on calling the attending doctor before letting them through, and there's some talk of informing Lily's next of kin. The whole thing takes so long, and Tony is so useless during it he starts to feel like he's floating somewhere over his own body, barely a part of this experience.

When they finally get there, accompanied by a doctor who seems to be running on the same level of exhaustion as the rest of them, Lily is asleep.

It isn't restful.

Against the white hospital sheets her skin appears pale, the dye in her hair washed-out and bland. She must be dreaming because she twitches, making soft little sounds.

The doctor wakes Lily gently. It doesn't help. She still shakes under the thin sheets, pulse speeding on the monitor.

When she sees Daniel, standing awkwardly behind the doctor, all the blood drains from her already pallid face, leaving her ashen and gray and seeming younger than she is.

"Oh no." She looks away, swallowing convulsively. Tony wonders abstractly if she's going to throw up. "Professor Rosenbaum, I—I'm so sorry. I—"

"It's okay, Lily."

Abruptly, Tony wants to scream. It's not okay. She kidnapped Daniel. She kept him in a freezing abandoned building, she threatened him with a gun, and then her terrible boyfriend nearly shot Tony.

Nothing about that is okay.

He curls his hands into fists, nails biting tight into his palms. He clenches his jaw tight as the doctor calms her down and helps her get settled.

"Miss Peterson," Detective Taylor says firmly but quietly when Lily is as ready as she's going to be. "I'm very sorry to come here so late, but this may be your last chance to revise your previous statement."

Lily looks out the window. Her lower lip juts out. "I don't... Why would I change anything?"

Daniel pulls the chair by her bedside up and sits directly next to her. His keeps his voice soft. "Lily, your boyfriend came to find us tonight. He was...uh..."

Trust Daniel to try finding the sensitive way to put it, even now.

"He had his rifle," Tony says, and on the bed, Lily stiffens. Tony keeps going anyway. "He wanted to know what you had told us, and he nearly—he tried to—"

"Is there anything, anything at all, you want to tell us about him?" Detective Taylor has her notebook out as she says it, eyes sharp and unwavering on Lily.

"Uh." Lily looks between them. She can't focus on any one of them, eyes skittering like the deer she never hit the day she lost control of the car. "He. I. Um."

Daniel leans forward. "Lily, why don't you tell us what happened that day when you found Professor Lawrence?"

She looks down at the sheets, picking at a fold. Her fingernails are bitten bloody. "I was having a bad day. Sean was mad at me 'cause I didn't want to get high and fool around, and he kept telling me I was a head case. I made an appointment with Professor Lawrence to talk about a makeup exam or something, and Sean helped me practice what to say. But he didn't think I'd actually do it, so he said he'd come with me."

"And did he?" Detective Taylor pauses in her notetaking, looking at Lily expectantly.

"Yeah."

"The knife was his, wasn't it?"

"Um, yeah, Sean...he carries that kind of stuff around sometimes when he's been dealing. He says it can get dangerous, meeting people at night to hook them up with coke or whatever."

Tony barely restrains himself from scoffing. There's a simple way to avoid dangers associated with dealing: Not dealing.

"Did he ever use it in front of you?" Taylor asks.

Lily stays silent.

From her jacket, Taylor pulls out the knife in an evidence bag, the blade pointed at the top, flat on the sides. Lily flinches at the sight of it.

"It would take a lot of force to stab someone with this," Taylor says conversationally. "Especially four times in a row, going through her clothing as well as layers and layers of tissue and muscle to hit organs."

She's talking about force someone Lily's size might be able to work up in a life-threatening situation, but over a grade? Tony studies the knife again. It's a weird shape for a blade, one he recognizes.

"He's in custody," Daniel reminds Lily. "He can't hurt you here."

Lily looks up from her lap, hesitant.

"Did he ever use it in front of you?" Taylor repeats.

Lily opens her mouth and then closes it again.

"How did you get the flat tire?"

Everyone in the room turns to Tony.

"When you came into the shop after your accident, Sean said he swerved to avoid a deer and banged up his fender. But that wouldn't cause a flat tire. It was—"

Taylor elbows him hard. "How did the flat happen?" she asks before he can continue.

"Sean got mad," Lily says quietly. "After the accident, he was so angry he stabbed the tire. It scared me, but I thought people did stuff like that when they're high, so I tried to forget about it."

"By 'it,' you mean..." Taylor pushes.

"That he carried it around with him. And used it when he was angry. I swear I didn't know he had it on him when he went to Professor Lawrence's office with me. I didn't know he would hurt—kill Professor Lawrence. I kind of...I lost it. I didn't know what to do, and I was scared. I didn't know who would listen to me, and I was scared he would hurt anyone who I talked to, so I left that letter for Professor Rosenbaum."

"And the knife?" Tony prompts.

"I found it under my bed afterward. I knew I hadn't touched it, so I thought maybe if someone else handed it in to the police Sean wouldn't think I...I don't know. I was high most of the time. It wasn't really a plan. I just hoped Professor Rosenbaum would try to help me. I didn't mean for him to get hurt too." Her eyes track over to Daniel for an instant, but she looks away immediately, ashamed.

She should be.

"Tell us what happened on Thursday." Taylor studies Lily, expression impassive. "Why did you bring the gun to Professor Rosenbaum's office?"

"I, um, I didn't get why nothing happened after I gave him the knife and why our rooms were being searched. I was scared about the drugs getting found, and Sean was getting angry he couldn't find the knife anywhere. He put all his weapons in my room, and I thought he might... I was scared. Of him, I guess. So, I brought the gun as, like, proof. But then..."

"He followed you to my office, didn't he?" Daniel smiles at her. How he isn't nervous or angry to be around her, now she's clear of mind and knows what she did, is a mystery to Tony.

"Yeah." Lily looks up at him again and then over to the detective. "He was—he was standing outside the door. I could see him. When Professor Rosenbaum asked if I knew who'd done it... Sean was right there, and I thought if I said anything, he would hurt me or the professor. I thought it was too late to call the police, with Sean watching. So I made Professor Rosenbaum come with me, and Sean did the rest."

"The rest..." Taylor says.

"He picked the Continuum," Daniel remembers. "He drove us there and got rid of my phone. My guess is he didn't have any long-term plan beyond keeping us there."

The detective writes something down on her pad and then turns back to Lily expectantly.

Lily examines the bedsheets again.

"Lily," Daniel tries again. "Why would you go along with everything he said? After Professor Lawrence? Why not call the police yourself?"

She shakes her head.

"You said you were scared. Was he threatening you with something? Was he going to hurt you?"

Caught, Lily glances between him and the detective. "I...no." She taps out a quick rhythm on the sheet with her finger now, anxious and offbeat.

"You're lying." Tony can't put his finger on how he knows, but he does. Her confusion made sense in the dingy bathroom of the movie theater when she was high and crying and confused. Now, though? Now, he doesn't buy it.

Lily doesn't have any problem meeting his eyes. That's all right; she probably doesn't understand what she did to him when she kidnapped Daniel.

"It's not a hard question," Tony insists. "What was he threatening you with?"

"I was scared—"

"Not what I asked."

"Tony." Daniel's voice is sharp.

Tony ignores him. "Don't protect him. Remember what Gianna said. Mario wasn't worth ruining your life over. Neither is Sean."

"But he—when I—the car— I *owe* him."

There it is. "A car crash is not the same thing as a murder."

"He said—the insurance— There's no way I can pay for it, and my parents can't either, not after all my hospital bills and tuition. Sean's going to tell everyone I was the one who killed her anyway, and who would believe me? I was too high to drive for, like, two weeks. I can't even remember everything that happened. Who knows what I could have done?"

Tony remembers Lily sitting in the reception area of the garage, shooting videos of her dumb boyfriend about the crash, miserable and pretending she wasn't for his benefit. Tony takes a breath and lets the anger go. "I'm not saying you made good decisions, but you're not a murderer, and we believe you. We can clear it up with the insurance. I can help you."

"I *crashed*. I shouldn't have been driving. I—"

"It's his car and his insurance. If you're not covered, he shouldn't have let you drive."

"But he was so *high*."

"So, none of you should have been driving." Tony gets it out through gritted teeth. "Still not your fault. And definitely not a reason to take the fall for him about Professor Lawrence."

"You really think so?"

Tony wants to laugh. All this over goddamn car insurance. If she'd told Gianna, there never would have been a reason to kidnap Daniel in the first place. Gianna might not have been at the garage much lately, but she knows her insurance loopholes. "Yeah, Lily. You did the right thing, getting us the knife. We believe you, and I think detective Taylor here believes you, too, no matter what Sean says."

Daniel looks between them, bemused. "How did you know about that?"

"Because Sean is a miserable shitstain, and he told me it was her who crashed."

Lily sobs once, and Tony feels a little bad, but not bad enough to stop talking.

"His idea of taking the fall for someone is pretty one-sided."

Detective Taylor has them walk through the entire car crash

incident, first Tony and then Lily. Lily tells them there was no deer, that she hadn't been able to concentrate, that she got too far to the middle of the road, swerved away, and hit the guardrail. After his angry outburst resulting in a slaughtered front tire, Sean came up with the lie while they waited for the tow truck, and Lily was so relieved she went with it.

With the car off her conscience, she explains fully what happened with Amelia Lawrence.

"He said no one would believe me." Her hands clench when she says it. "He said everyone knew I was nuts and unstable, and he could use the crash to convince them. He came with me to Professor Lawrence's office, said he would support me or whatever. Only, he took a bunch of pills before, and when I started crying, he got so *angry* at me. Professor Lawrence tried to—well, she got in his face, and then he—you know."

Lily looks up at Daniel. "I don't remember most of it. I wasn't lying. The molly made everything feel weird. And I...I couldn't watch, and I couldn't stop him. Professor Rosenbaum, I'm *so sorry*. You were the one person I could think of who I could trust. When nothing happened after I gave you the knife, I had to see you...and then Sean followed me to you, too, and I didn't know what to *do*—"

She breaks off, tears running down her cheeks.

Daniel pats her hand awkwardly. "I don't blame you. I want you to get healthy, okay?"

There are plenty of things she could have done differently. She could have not brought a gun to Daniel's office. She could have explained about the knife instead of taping it to the door like a serial killer. She could have decided not to threaten Daniel. She could have told him Sean was waiting outside the office door. She could have told her therapist about the drug use; she could have reported Sean's dealing to the police.

None of them can turn back time and undo what she did. At least this way, Daniel did everything for her he could. Even if Tony thinks it was the wrong call; even if he thinks Lily is to blame for at least some of it, Daniel will be relieved.

Taylor assures them all that Sean is in custody, and he'll be charged at the very least for illegal possession of weapons and drugs and for what happened in the restaurant. So long as Daniel doesn't press charges against her for abetting the kidnapping, Lily will be free to recuperate until she's needed as a witness. Later, after they leave Lily's room, Taylor adds that it probably won't be difficult to charge Sean for Amelia Lawrence's murder, forensically, as the stab wounds don't match Lily's height or weight.

Part of Tony can't believe it's over as they walk out of the hospital into the blanket of cold night air. Not after he thought everything was done once and turned out to be wrong. He sucks in awful, deep breaths, too done with everything to say anything about what they've just learned.

Daniel pulls him tight in a hug. "Thank you for being here. Thank you for... I know how rough this has been on you. I'm so glad you're with me."

Tony buries his nose in Daniel's neck and clings to him.

And then, Tony lets Daniel take him home.

They knock on Colette's door on the way up.

Meredith answers, shooting a wary look back into the room where Colette is sitting on the couch, crumpled up and small. "Is everything all right?"

"Definite all right."

"Daniel."

Daniel sighs. "It was probably Sean who did it. The murder, I mean. We'll find out in the next couple of days. He was trying to make Lily confess to cover it up."

Meredith nods sharply.

"Is she..." Tony tries, glancing at Colette.

"I can hear everything you're saying," Colette answers, sharp and clear.

"Are you okay?"

"No."

"Do you want—"

"Daniel, you're my best friend, but right now, I'm trying to process that I was once again wrong about who was trustworthy and who was not. You being here and being right about what it means to be an advisor or being responsible for our students...it's not helping."

"For what it's worth, I don't think I was right."

Tony almost whoops with relief.

"I don't think either of us could have stopped this by giving more," Daniel adds.

Colette tries to smile. "That's good to hear. I still don't feel okay about anything that has happened these last few days."

"Yeah. I understand. I'm upstairs if you need anything."

"I know."

Meredith looks between them shrewdly. "Hey," she says to Daniel. "I think I'll stay down here tonight, yeah? All my stuff is still here."

He nods and doesn't say thank you, to spare Colette's feelings, but Tony can tell he's thinking it before Meredith closes the door, and they head upstairs.

Neither of them is tired anymore, jittery and hopped up on adrenaline, not to mention they slept all day. They crowd into the shower together instead, unwilling to part for more than a minute.

Tony lets Daniel pull out his hair tie and leans against Daniel's shoulder as Daniel lathers shampoo into his hair.

"Feels good," Tony mutters. It's an understatement. He feels as if he's been carrying half the world on his back for the last few days, aching and worn through in body and mind. Daniel's hands in his hair draw the tension out one strand at a time.

Daniel presses soft kisses to Tony's shoulders and the side of his neck before tilting his head under the spray and carefully carding his hands through Tony's hair to rinse it out.

He repeats the process with the conditioner and then moves on to bodywash, choosing Tony's, and Tony misses the generic, store-brand scent of Daniel's. But he has Daniel right here in front of him, caressing down Tony's arms and across his chest with soapy hands.

Daniel kneels in front of Tony, the water darkening his hair and plastering it to his forehead, and caresses along one leg and then the other before reaching between Tony's legs and stroking his cock and balls, covering them in suds.

"Turn around?" Daniel asks, voice quiet against the thunder of the water.

Tony does it immediately.

Daniel's hands are just as soft on his ass, massaging the cheeks and then reaching between them to spread soap across the crack, across Tony's hole.

With a strange, punched-out ache, Tony becomes aware that he's letting Daniel service him, and it leaves him feeling cherished and guilty all at once. "You don't have to—"

Wet lips press against his left ass cheek. "Trust me. This is not a hardship."

"Okay."

Tony lets himself be moved under the spray again, lets Daniel follow the path of the water as if his hands are as important in ridding Tony's body of the last traces of soap as the shower is. Daniel continues to stroke across Tony's ass and cock, long past the point where any soap might still be on his skin.

"Can I take care of you tonight?" Daniel asks, low and right into Tony's ear, making him shudder.

"You were kidnapped," he protests weakly. "I should—"

"I was fine. You were here, alone, and you came to get me out. You almost—he almost shot you. Please, Tony, I need to feel you under my hands and make you feel good, okay?"

"Okay." If he's being honest, Tony couldn't return the favor tonight anyway, loose and hazy as he is on an adrenaline crash that's been two days in the making. Two weeks in the making. All year in the making. "I love you."

Daniel's mouth on his neck is warmer than the water, and Tony shivers under his touch. "I love you too."

He wants to protest Daniel toweling him off. He's not helpless or a child. But it feels so good to stand there and let Daniel do what he wants, let Daniel make the decisions. Tony can worry about it in the morning. Get Daniel back by fucking him over the arm of the couch or up against the kitchen counter.

Right now, Daniel leads him into the bedroom and lays him down on freshly made sheets. He sets a towel next to them and rummages in the nightstand.

He pulls out the cuffs, the fake leather ones that release as easily as the ones Daniel was wearing when Tony found him—Christ, was it only this morning? Last night?—but feel sumptuous and indulgent by contrast.

"Can I?" Daniel asks.

Tony nods.

"I'm gonna need words, honey."

"You can tie me up, Daniel." Tony stares up at him. "You can do whatever you want to me. Pretty sure I'd let you ruin me."

Daniel drops the cuffs on the pillow beside Tony's head and kisses him savagely as if he's trying to crawl inside Tony's skin. He grasps Tony's wrists in one hand and presses them into the pillow above his head. Their bodies slide together, damp and solid and real. Tony arches up into Daniel's touch, cock hardening against Daniel's hip.

"Keep them up there, just like that," Daniel says, his fingers light on Tony's wrists, a contrast to the heavy cuffs when he gets them situated. Their weight around Tony's hands keeps him grounded to the bed beneath him. "Sometime, I'm gonna tie you to the headboard with these, make you scream."

"Not tonight?" Tony asks, coasting pleasantly on the idea that Daniel wants to do this so badly he's already thinking about next time.

"Tonight, I'm gonna spoil you." Daniel kisses Tony again, first on the lips and then on each cheek, followed by the line of his jaw through the scratch of Tony's beard. He moves to the sensitive parts of his neck, usually hidden by the beard, and the thin skin at his collarbones.

Tony squirms under him, always so sensitive to Daniel's mouth there. He wonders, for a moment, how it would be if Daniel didn't shave, if he still had a little rasp of stubble on his cheeks, and shudders at the thought.

Daniel's teeth press into his shoulder once, briefly, and then his hands join in, stroking Tony's sides and across his pecs.

"You're so beautiful, you know that?" Daniel says, hushed and reverent.

Tony flushes and looks away.

"I know it's not the word you'd choose, but you are. I'm so glad you let me have you like this."

"You're the only one who gets to have me like this," Tony tells him, as close as he can get to articulating the complicated knot of feelings he has about loving Daniel, being in love with Daniel. There will be time in the morning.

Daniel kisses his breastbone, right on the center. "I'm the luckiest man alive, then."

Daniel's lucky for many reasons, not least of which have to do with escaping two murderers unscathed. But Tony thinks he'd give Daniel a run for his money on luck when Daniel sinks further to settle between Tony's legs.

He keeps the pressure of his mouth soft, licking up and down Tony's cock with little flicks of his tongue, rolling Tony's balls in his palm as he does it. He runs his tongue around the tip in slow, filthy circles until Tony throbs against it.

When Tony can't seem to keep his hips still on the bed anymore, Daniel takes the whole head into his mouth. Tony watches from above as his jaw stretches obscenely wide around it. Daniel's eyes, when they meet Tony's, are dark and wanting.

Tony would give him anything he asked for.

Daniel's hands spread Tony's thighs wide, fingertips running across his inner thighs, the space behind his balls, his hole. Tony wonders idly if Daniel will fuck him tonight, if that's where this is going, when Daniel suddenly swallows around him, half of Tony's shaft in Daniel's mouth.

A breathless cry makes its way out of Tony's throat. He's sweating against the urge to move his hips and fuck up into the warm heat of Daniel's mouth.

"You feel so good," he says, slurred with pleasure.

Daniel pulls off his cock. "Thanks." His voice is rough and used.

He goes back to kissing and licking the head and nothing more, and Tony whines.

He's leaking, thick drops of precome catching in his pubic hair, by the time Daniel takes his cock into his mouth again. Daniel doesn't seem to mind, moaning at the taste.

Still, he doesn't speed up. It feels indulgent, how slow Daniel goes, pulling off to run his lips and tongue across the shaft whenever Tony gets too into it, too desperate. With his hands tied above his head, Tony can do nothing but accept the glacial pace, his cock thick and heavy with blood, and his brain sluggish with pleasure.

He could use the quick release on the cuffs, grab Daniel by the shoulders, and pull him up so they can rut together until they both come. Instead, he lets himself float, lets himself beg for more.

"Please," he says between gasping, heaving breaths each time Daniel pulls off. "Please, more, please. I need it."

"I know what you need," Daniel murmurs, soft and almost condescending if it weren't so fond. He kisses Tony's hipbone and props himself up on his forearms. "Turn onto your side for me."

Tony obeys thoughtlessly.

Daniel reaches for the nightstand again. "Shit. Stay right there, honey, I'll be back."

As if Tony could move right now. His cock pulses against his belly, wet with cooling spit and his own precome. His toes curl against the comforter.

It only takes a minute, and then Daniel returns, holding up the pump bottle of lube. "Told you we were gonna regret keeping this in the living room." He kisses Tony's neck as he slots in behind him on the bed. "Lift your hips up."

Tony does as he's told, and the towel Daniel brought along is shoved under him.

"Spread your legs," Daniel whispers, and when Tony does, his cool, wet fingers reach between Tony's legs to cover the space there with lube.

Daniel's cock, fully hard for all it's been ignored so far, slots between Tony's thighs, and Tony clenches around it on instinct.

Behind him, Daniel groans. "That's so good."

Pride bursts hot in Tony's gut, a stupid, senseless reaction, but there it is.

Daniel moves his hips, slow and easy. The head of his cock bumps into the base of Tony's, and Tony whimpers a little.

"You want it?" Daniel's breath, hot on the juncture of Tony's neck and shoulder, sends goosebumps across his skin.

"Yeah," Tony gasps, "please."

Daniel's lube-slick hand snakes down to grasp Tony's aching cock and strokes it in time to the movements of his hips. Tony groans, head thrown back on Daniel's shoulder. He's wrapped up tight in Daniel's arms, their bodies pressed so close there's no space between them. Daniel's cock lies thick between his thighs, Daniel's hand firm around his cock.

Pleasure slides through Tony like a knife, cutting him apart before he knows it will happen. He gasps when it starts and moans low in his throat as it ends, thick ropes of come shooting across Daniel's hand and his own stomach. His thighs clench around Daniel's cock involuntarily.

"Fuck. Fuck, fuck, Tony—" The words end on a strangled gasp as more wet heat spreads between Tony's legs, Daniel's come filling the scant space between them.

After, the crash Tony half expected as soon as they returned home hits him full force. Daniel wipes him off with the towel before pulling the comforter over both of them.

Tony rolls toward him so he can wrap Daniel in his arms, utterly convinced he won't sleep unless he knows Daniel is safe in his grasp. Daniel lets himself be hugged close and tight, arranging them until it's comfortable enough to sleep.

"I'll see you in the morning, honey," Daniel says with a quick kiss.

"Mm," Tony mumbles. "'Cause I live here now."

He drifts off to the sound of Daniel's soft, pleased laugh.

Epilogue

I t takes another two weeks for Tony to officially move in.

He doesn't spend a single night in Kingston in the interim, but he won't feel properly moved in until he fixes the bookshelf in Daniel's—their—living room and cleans out his room at his parents' house.

There's too much to do before a proper move. First, they have to deal with the fallout of Sean's attack on the Indian restaurant in Red Hook. In light of Lily's changed statement, every other witness statement needs rehashing as well. Tony loses a full day at the police station, lucky as always that his employer is so lenient.

The college runs Daniel ragged between managing interviews with the local news, damage control with concerned students and their parents, and getting the place back into something approaching a functional environment for education. Tony works long hours at the shop, making up for the days he missed and babysitting Lia in equal measure, while Gianna visits Lily at Kingston Hospital.

Tony debates going to see her, but he's learning to be okay with not being okay with everything. Instead, he listens to Gianna and Daniel's updates on how Lily's doing and what charges she'll end up facing. He offers a little advice about how to deal with Sean's car insurance, but he lets someone else convey it to her.

The Sunday after, they all attend Amelia Lawrence's funeral. Even Charlie and Blake G, who have only met Emilio once, tag along to pay their respects. Wearing a properly fitting suit and a clean shirt, Emilio makes it through the entire service admirably. He carries Francie on his hip for most of it, letting her hide her face in his neck when she needs to. Though he doesn't look any less haunted, he seems to have started getting some sleep.

Emilio still makes time to thank them all personally for coming.

Tony caught Ma cooking extra, which convinced him she's been taking casseroles to Germantown all week.

Maybe that's why Emilio shows up to help the day Tony officially moves in. Tony's not sure who told him, but his money's on Lisa, who can't resist a stray. It could also have been Colette, who seems to have reached some sort of detente with Emilio on the whole "suspicion of murder" incident.

"Don't look so shocked," Daniel mutters to Tony as he watches the two of them chat next to the coffee maker he insisted on buying as part of the moving in process. "Suspecting you of murder is practically how we met."

"Ouch." In revenge for that particular comment, Tony makes Daniel come to the hardware store with him.

Tony still isn't sure why everyone felt the need to be here. All he did was text the group chat that he wasn't free today because he was moving in properly. Mostly, it's clothes, a few books of his own, and some photo albums Ma sneaked on top of the pile. He spent the last week dismantling his bedroom since he's not about to let them be the kind of parents who keep a shrine to him when they could use the space for something worthwhile. He could have used some help taking all the furniture apart, but he knew better than to ask his friends for that. Giving Blake a screwdriver counts as a danger to the public.

Instead, he asked someone actually helpful. Kyle raised his eyebrows practically to the top of his forehead when Tony asked to borrow his pickup to take his old bed and dresser to the used furniture store.

It was practically an out-of-body experience for Tony to tell him, "I'm moving in with my boyfriend."

Kyle waited a minute to respond while the pieces fell into place. "Ah. The sandwich-maker from Rhinebeck."

"Again," Tony told him. "I am fully capable of making my own sandwiches. But, yes."

Kyle shrugged, said, "Mazel tov," and handed over the keys to his truck.

Tony assured the Toyota multiple times that it was for reasons of space and transport, not because he was looking to trade up. If he keeps a lookout for reasonable used cars he could buy, well, he keeps quiet about it around his current car in case it refuses to start out of jealousy.

So Tony isn't taking Daniel to the hardware store for much. Some background lighting for that bookshelf, and some wood stain to match a two-by-four or two to the proper color so he can finally make sure the shelf doesn't collapse on them. If he can swing it, they'll stop by Target for a bigger frying pan as well. He still wants a table in the living room for when it's more than the two of them and Colette at dinner, but Daniel's been resistant about Tony building one himself, and Tony's holding out for him to agree to that.

What his friends intend on moving into the apartment while they're at the store is a mystery to Tony.

It takes them an hour and a half. As he suspected, when they get back, all five of Tony's boxes are still in his car, and his friends all sit around the living room eating pizza and drinking the case of beer Blake G brought along.

"It wouldn't be a move without pizza and beer," Blake W points out.

"I don't see any of you doing any moving," Tony tells him.

"Your boyfriend has it handled." Charlie gestures easily toward the door, where Daniel and Meredith are, in fact, handling two of the five boxes, Colette close behind them with a third.

Much like her stalemate with Emilio, Colette hasn't said a thing about whether or not Meredith's continued presence in her guest room is welcome or not. Nor has Meredith mentioned how her husband and children feel about her not heading home after two weeks in the Hudson Valley. Daniel tried asking and was stonewalled so efficiently he's decided to give up. Knowing Daniel, what this means is that he won't be asking directly again, but he will be snooping.

Daniel and Colette have been treading delicately around each other since Sean's arrest. She hasn't said much more about Sean and how betrayed she must feel; after all, he lied to her and threatened her. Daniel also hasn't mentioned his own struggle with feeling responsible for everything, and neither of them have talked about how tied up with Mario it all is. Instead, Colette's been talking about taking an extended trip to France this winter. It hasn't made Daniel any less tense, but it's not something he can solve, and he seems to have accepted that.

Tony has a list of therapists in the Hudson Valley area bookmarked on his phone. He hasn't gotten around to calling any offices yet, but he'll find the time eventually, and when he does, maybe he'll forward the link to both of them.

It only takes one more trip to get everything moved in. The remaining home improvement plans Tony wants to spring on Daniel can wait for tomorrow.

With a sigh, Tony settles on the floor with his back against the couch. From under the couch, Worf rubs his wet nose on the hand Tony's using for balance.

Lisa hands Tony a pizza box. Blake G hands him a beer. Daniel ruffles his hair from above him on the couch.

"If it makes you feel better," Daniel offers, "we can call this a housewarming rather than a move."

Colette boos. "Absolutely not. You get gifts for a housewarming. Don't shortchange yourselves."

"She makes a good point," Emilio says.

Lively discussion breaks out on whether this constitutes a move-in party, which Blake W argues vehemently against, given he paid for the pizza. Pretty much everyone else agrees it should be a housewarming to save money on a gift. Gianna and Colette are the only other holdouts,

Gianna because she enjoys making Tony uncomfortable and possibly because she feels bad for Blake W, and Colette because she wants to profit from the gifts.

It's a senseless debate; they should all know by now neither Tony nor Daniel is especially interested in throwing a whole party to celebrate the fact that they've been living together for what amounts to several months at this point. They just want Tony to cook for them some more.

Still, warmth suffuses Tony. They're surrounded by friends and family who love them enough to heckle them mercilessly. After it's all been said and done, they can look at him in the apartment he shares with his boyfriend, a man he's kissed and held close and been stupidly in love with right where they can all witness, and nothing much about what they think of him has changed. It feels like a new lease, a second chance at learning how to be himself out loud.

Tony leans his head back against Daniel's knee, craning up to look at him.

Daniel smiles down at him. "I'm glad you're here," he says.

"I'm glad I'm here, too," Tony tells him.

Acknowledgements

To Laurel and Allison: Thank you for reading the very first version of this I wouldn't want anyone else to see.

To Anina: Thank you for loving the first one so much.

To Claire: Thank you for not telling our parents about my books and for not reading them (and if you did, for not mentioning that I put you in the acknowledgements).

To Fabi: Thank you for taking the baby to the hardware store twelve million times to give me writing time.

Thank you to NineStar Press for sticking with this story.

Special thanks to Elizabetta for asking insightful questions and giving great feedback.

About the Author

S. B. Barnes attended college in the Hudson Valley, studying English Language and Literature and Anthropology (although unlike her characters, her time there was not interrupted by crime-solving). She grew up split between the USA and Germany, attending university in both countries before eventually settling in Germany. Today, she works as a teacher and lives with her husband, son, and two cats. Fiction has always been one of her greatest loves, as a reader, as a teacher, and as a writer, and she hopes you enjoy reading her work as much as she enjoys creating it.

Email
sbbarnesauthor@gmail.com
Twitter
@S_B_Barnes
Instagram
www.instagram.com/s.b.barnes
Tumblr
www.tumblr.com/sbbarnes
Website
http://sbbarnesauthor.wixsite.com/home

OTHER NINESTAR BOOKS BY THIS AUTHOR

A Hudson Valley Murder Mystery Series
Heart First

Coming Soon from S.B. Barnes

Two for Holding

Minor Penalties, Book One

It was four in the morning, and Tom was awake.

His hip was twinging again. It wouldn't stop doing that no matter how many stretches he did and arnica compresses he used. He had a fool's hope that rotating it the right way for long enough would make everything click into place the way it was supposed to, which was why he hadn't brought the issue up with the trainers yet. As he lay awake in bed examining the play of shadows across the ceiling as lone cars passed through Edmonton's otherwise dead nightlife, Tom had to admit to himself that he was, in fact, a fool, and the hope was probably for nothing.

With a groan, he leveraged himself out of the too-soft hotel bed and down the hall to the ice machine. He probably wouldn't get back to sleep anytime soon, but he might as well do something productive about the hip. He'd be spending hours cramped in an airplane seat to San Francisco soon enough.

He was limping back up the corridor when he heard it: the telltale sound of a door clicking open and the whoosh of someone leaving their room.

Tom was made captain ten years ago when he was all of twenty-two years old and touted as one of the most promising players the NHL had seen in years. He'd had three ninety-point-plus seasons behind him, no history of significant injury, and everyone had thought he'd be the one to take the Bay Area's brand-new expansion team all the way when he was drafted. It was a lot of pressure for a guy who was glad his helmet acne had cleared up, and he could actually grow a playoff beard.

One of the first lessons Tom learned as captain was to keep his nose firmly out of his teammates' business when it came to hooking up on the road. He did not need to know who was cheating on their wife and who had a penchant for waifish, potentially underage prostitutes. When the inevitable press conference about the divorce or the lawsuit came, he wanted to be able to say, as honestly as possible, that he'd had no idea and was as shocked as everyone else.

What compelled him to turn and look this time was anyone's guess.

In a series of events not unlike bearing witness to a particularly heinous traffic accident, Tom noticed three things in quick succession.

First, the room number. He'd handed the keycard for 2247 to Jaxon Grant some twelve hours prior.

Second, the person exiting. A dark-haired, dark-eyed man in his mid-to-late twenties in gray sweatpants and a rumpled #16 Grant jersey (not even a navy-and-sage San Francisco Sea Lions jersey, but one of the old, hideously orange Philadelphia ones) slipped through the door. He wore the shirt knotted at the waist the way Tom had seen some guys' girlfriends wear them.

Third, Jaxon Grant. He stood in the doorway, shirtless, his blond hair tousled, with his hand on the other man's bare hip.

Tom turned tail and explicitly did not run back to his hotel room. He did walk fast enough to make his hip twinge more than it already did.

He didn't think about what he'd seen while he lay in bed with ice slowly melting on his hip through a fluffy white hotel towel, concentrating instead on going over last night's penalty kill. Maybe they could experiment with switching out Phil Easton for Chris Calabrese. Calabrese was younger and less experienced, sure, but Phil was struggling with his knees this season.

Tom didn't think about it while he did a half hour of stretching on the scratchy carpet to the dulcet sound of CNN. He had a policy of not watching any sports broadcasting before 6:00 a.m. to establish some sort of work-life balance.

He definitely didn't think about it when he read the text from his mom.

Mom: *Good game last night, sweetheart! I hope you keep winning!*

It was a little too close for comfort, he typed out in response, and then deleted it. She wouldn't care that Edmonton had almost had them when they equalized in the third, and only Jax Grant on a breakaway had saved them from overtime. It was no wonder Jax had gone out to celebrate, leading to— But no, Tom wasn't thinking about it.

We can't win every game, he tried next. On consideration, it seemed a little unnecessarily defeatist since the season was just beginning.

Finally, he settled on *Thanks, Mom.*

Tom kept up his streak of not thinking about it during breakfast. He was the first of the team downstairs at seven sharp because he'd been one of the only ones who hadn't gone out last night. Briefly, Tom debated sitting with the coaching staff, but he wasn't *that* old yet. Not that the new head coach this year, Coach Morris, was old. He had barely ten years on Tom, but he had an air of exhaustion about him that spoke of having been around the block. And he brought his own homemade salads to work like a real adult. Tom still lived in the high-rise apartment right by the practice rink he'd bought with his first big contract, and while he was technically capable of cooking, he was in no way organized enough to do meal prep. He had no idea what he'd talk to Morris about over breakfast and doubted the man would appreciate his thoughts on the penalty kill before having his morning coffee.

Instead, Tom loitered around the buffet, pretending to decide between turkey sausage and turkey bacon for a good five minutes before Phil showed up.

"Up at dawn again, old man?" Phil asked jovially, reaching for the sausages and drowning them in maple syrup.

"You're one to talk." Tom loaded up on bacon and reconstituted egg scramble. It was both soggy and crumbly and tasted of wet cardboard, but it was protein-laden cardboard.

They both stopped by the cereal station for bowls piled high with Greek yogurt, oats, and raisins before finding a table close, but not too close, to the coaches.

"Have fun with the rookies last night?" Tom asked.

Phil groaned. "I was in bed by ten. Left them out there to experience the bright lights of Edmonton all by themselves."

"Phil."

"I know, I know."

"The *A* is for alt—"

"Fuck's sake, Tom." Phil thrust out his stupidly expensive watch. "It is 7:08 a.m. Do not tell me about the responsibility of being an alternate captain. So the rookies might have gotten a little wasted. We're in fucking Alberta. What's the worst they could do here?"

"I don't know, crystal meth?"

Phil gave him an unimpressed look. "Breezy seem like the kind of guy who could get himself a dealer at the drop of a hat?"

Chris Calabrese, a twenty-one-year-old defenseman, absolutely didn't seem like that kind of guy, and the younger guys on the team tended to follow his lead.

"You know they always let loose in Canada," Tom said. "They're all legal to drink here."

"Jax was there. It's fine."

"Jax was there," Tom repeated to himself darkly. As if his presence was at all helpful.

Sure, Jax had an *A* as well, but it was more of a PR move than a statement about his role in the team dynamics. Kayleigh Williams from the media team practically salivated the minute the call came in from the general manager about Jax joining the team. Having a personable, friendly guy would be a blessing for post-game media segments, even if he was a little too open with reporters if you asked Tom (which no one had).

Tom was awful at media.

Kayleigh, the bubbly, friendly sort of person who actually enjoyed making phone calls and using social media, was much too nice to tell him so. Though the longer she worked with them, the less well she hid her beleaguered sighs every time Tom clammed up when someone pointed a camera in his direction.

But PR gold or not, Jax had only been on the team for about five minutes. He wasn't a responsible senior member of the leadership group, and based on his media personality and the way he always seemed to be wearing the most expensive designer clothes he could get his hands on, Tom doubted he ever would be. Breezy might worship the ground Jax walked on, but who knew what Jax might talk the rookies into? Rumor had it Philly had dropped him like a hot potato because of all his extracurricular activities. No one needed the rookies to get in on those, whatever they were.

Unbidden, the image of Jax standing in the doorway of his hotel room, with his sweats slung low on his hips and his hair a mess, paraded across the forefront of Tom's mind.

Phil flicked at Tom's forehead, drawing him back to the here and now. "You've got to get over your problem with him."

Tom coughed up half his orange juice. "I don't have a problem with him."

"Uh-huh. That why you never talk to him outside of practice and you only hang out with the other guys when he won't be there? Not super captain-y of you, man."

Wincing internally, Tom admitted, "I didn't think anyone noticed."

"He definitely did."

Great. Now Tom not only had to start spending time with Jax, he had to make it seem as if he'd never seen what he'd seen last night. What a nightmare.

www.ninestarpress.com

www.facebook.com/ninestarpress

www.twitter.com/ninestarpress

www.instagram.com/ninestarpress

bsky.app/profile/ninestarpress.bsky.social

www.threads.net/@ninestarpress

www.ingramcontent.com/pod-product-compliance
Lightning Source LLC
Chambersburg PA
CBHW060236100726
47907CB00003B/659